NICHOLE VAN

Fiorenza Publishing

Published by Fiorenza Publishing
Print Edition v1.2

ISBN: 978-0991639113

Intertwine is a work of fiction. Names, characters, places and incidents are the products of the author's imagination or are used fictitiously. Any resemblance to actual events, locales or persons, living or dead, is entirely coincidental.

To Erin,
because it all began with you,
my dearest and oldest friend.

And to Dave,
throughout all *eternity*,
heart of my soul.
Love ya, babe.

Prologue

The obsession began on June 12, 2008 around 11:23 a.m.

Though secretly Emme Wilde considered it more of a 'spiritual connection' than an actual full-blown neurosis.

Of course, her brother, Marc, her mother and a series of therapists all begged to disagree.

Thankfully her best friend, Jasmine, regularly validated the connection and considered herself to be Emme's guide through this divinely mystical union of predestined souls (her words, not Emme's). Marc asserted that Jasmine was not so much a guide as an incense-addled enabler (again, his words, not Emme's). Emme was just grateful that anyone considered the whole affair normal—even if it was only Jasmine's loose sense of 'normal.'

Jasmine always insisted Emme come with her to estate sales, and this one outside Portland, Oregon proved no exception. Though Jasmine contended *this* particular estate sale would be significant for Emme, rambling on about circles colliding in the vast cosmic ocean creating necessary links between lives—blah, blah. All typical Jasmine-speak.

Emme brushed it off, assuming that Jasmine really just wanted someone to organize the trip: plan the best route to avoid traffic, find a quirky restaurant for lunch, entertain her on the long drive from Seattle.

At the estate sale, Emme roamed through the stifling tents, touching the cool wood of old furniture, the air heavy with that mix of dust, moth balls and disuse that marks aged things. Jasmine predictably disappeared into a corner piled with antique quilts, hunting yet again for that elusive log cabin design with black centers instead of the traditional red.

But Emme drifted deeper, something pulling her farther and farther into the debris of lives past and spent. To the trace of human passing, like fingerprints left in the paint of a pioneer cupboard door. Stark and clear.

Usually Emme would have stopped to listen to the stories around her, the history grad student in her analyzing each detail. Yet that day she didn't. She just wandered, looking for something. Something specific.

If only she could remember what.

Skirting around a low settee in a back corner, Emme first saw the antique trunk. A typical mid-nineteenth century traveling chest, solid with mellow aged wood. It did not call attention to itself. But it stood apart somehow, almost as if the air were a little lighter around it.

She first opened the lid out of curiosity, expecting the trunk to be empty. Instead, she found it full. Carefully shifting old books and papers, Emme found nothing of real interest.

Until she reached the bottom right corner.

There she found a small object tucked inside a brittle cotton handkerchief. Gently unwrapping the aged fabric, she pulled out an oval locket. Untouched and expectant.

Filigree covered the front, its gilt frame still bright and untarnished, as if nearly new.

Emme turned the locket over, feeling its heft in her hand, the metal cool against her palm. It hummed with an almost electric pulse. How long had the locket lain wrapped in the trunk?

Transparent crystal partially covered the back. Under the crystal, two locks of hair were woven into an intricate pattern—one bright and fair, the other a dark chocolate brown. Gilded on top of the crystal, two initials nestled together into a stylized gold symbol.

She touched the initials, trying to make them out. One was clearly an F. But she puzzled over the other for a moment, tracing the design with her eyes. And then she saw it. Emme sucked in a sharp breath. An E. The other initial was an E.

She opened the locket, hearing the small pop of the catch.

A gasp.

Her hands tingled.

A sizzling shock started at the back of her neck and then spread.

Him.

There are moments in life that sear into the soul. Brief glimpses of some larger force. When so many threads collapse into one. Coalesce into a single truth.

Seeing *him* for the first time was one of those moments.

He gazed intently out from within the right side of the locket: blond, blue-eyed, chiseled with a mouth hinting at shared laughter. Emme's historian mind quickly dated his blue-green, high collared jacket and crisp, white shirt and neckcloth to the mid-Regency era, probably around 1812, give or take a year.

Emme continued to look at the man—well, stare actually. His golden hair finger-combed and deliciously disheveled. Broad shoulders angled slightly toward the viewer. Perhaps his face a shade too long and his nose a little too sharp for true beauty. But striking. Handsome even.

Looking expectant, as if he had been waiting for her.

Emme would forever remember the jolt of it.

Surprise and recognition.

She knew him. Had known him.

Somehow, somewhere, in some place.

He felt agonizingly familiar. That phantom part of her she had never realized was lost.

The sensation wasn't quite deja vu.

More like memory.

Like suddenly finding that vital thing you didn't realize had been misplaced. Like coming up, gasping for air, after nearly drowning and seeing the world bright and sparkling and new.

She stood mesmerized by *him* until Jasmine joined her.

"Oooh, you found him." The hushed respect in her voice was remarkable. This was Jasmine after all.

Emme nodded mutely.

"Your circles are so closely intertwined. Amazing."

Jasmine turned the locket in Emme's hand.

"What does this inscription say?" she asked.

Emme hadn't noticed the engraved words on the inside left of the locket case. But now she read them. Her sudden sharp inhalation seared, painfully clenching.

Oh. *Oh!*

The words reverberated through her soul, shattering and profound.

Emme didn't recall much more of that day—Jasmine purchasing the locket or even the little restaurant where they ate lunch. Instead, she only remembered the endless blur of passing trees on the drive home, the inscription echoing over and over:

To E
throughout all time
heart of my soul
your F

Chapter 1

Emry Wilde was a disaster magnet.

She admitted it freely.

It was like she wore a t-shirt with the words "I attract acts of God" and a red bullseye. Basically, if the media coyly ended a disaster with *-mageddon*, Emme would find herself in the middle of it.

She planned. She prepared. Emme tried to anticipate every travel contingency. She hated the unexpected. But somehow the unexpected always found her. The universe took perverse pleasure in finding the most arbitrary calamity and thrusting her into it, front and center.

It wasn't as if she were normal-adverse. More like adventure-prone. Highly, unanticipated adventure-prone.

All of which explained her current situation.

Powerful winds lashed her rented English cottage as rain pounded the roof. Emme gave a resigned sigh, grimacing at the water streaming down the windows. Thunder rattled the doors, shaking the ground. Outside, an oak tree creaked in the garden, branches groaning in protest. She had experienced horrific storms often enough to know that this one portended no good. It was an angry beast, growling to be let in.

It was all a terrible disappointment.

Freddie was supposed to help prevent travel disasters.

Mmmmm, no, not Freddie. Emme did a mental hunt. Who should F be today? *Felix? . . . Francis? . . . No.* She thought further. *Finn.* Yes, definitely still Finn, just like he'd been all week.

She sat in front of a roaring fire, curled up in blankets on a comfy velvet sofa, nursing a hot cup of tea in her hands, her feet warm in pink satin ballet-like slippers with wide ribbon ties and cushy soles. She wriggled her snug toes. Seriously, best packing choice ever.

After days of lovely English sun, the weather had turned, unleashing an impressively ferocious summer storm, which was a pity. She had been looking forward to seeing the Beltane fires and other festivities planned for the evening, hoping to use them as part of her sabbatical research. Jasmine called Beltane one of the most powerful spirit days on the Celtic calendar. Though, trust Jasmine to take something as innocuous as May Day and make it arcane and mystical.

Oh, and to insist on using its Celtic name, Beltane.

But the bonfires had been canceled, rescheduled until the weather improved. Emme snuggled deeper into the plush sofa as a loud boom of thunder emphasized her thoughts.

Things had been going so well. No ash-spewing volcanoes. No random-illness quarantines. Remarkable, really, considering what usually happened when she traveled.

Her travel issues had started as a teenager on the evening ferry from Cozumel to Cancun. She didn't remember much about that night—just angry shouting, the rat-a-tat-tat of automatic weapons and hiding underneath the bench with Marc. Waiting. Terrified that the gunfire would come closer.

Then, after so much noise, sudden pounding silence. No hum of the motor, no buzz of the overhead lights, just pitch blackness and the sobbing whispers of other frightened passengers. After hours bobbing adrift, they were pulled ashore by a tugboat. Frightened but unharmed. *Piratas.* Pirates, the police said. Bandits after the payroll bag the ferry was carrying.

Of course, Marc being Marc had found the whole event wildly exciting. Typical. The lame pirate jokes had gone on for months. (*Emme, you look sad. Is something the matt-arrrrh?*)

So even in this day and age, Emme had to add pirates to her list of "Things to Worry about When Traveling." Seriously? How does one plan for pirates? Were there brochures on the topic? *Danger on the High Seas: Ten Steps to Avoiding Pirates While in the Caribbean.*

After the pirate incident, the travel disasters had come relentlessly. There were the standard hassles: lost luggage and delayed flights, being stranded by a winter storm, that lady in the seat next to her giving birth over Atlanta. Emme rarely batted an eye at such pedestrian events.

It was the true random acts of God—the travel disruptions that were outside anyone's realm of normal—that got her full attention. Arrested and questioned for two days by the Peruvian TSA about possible nefarious terrorist activity. (Emry Wilde = Terrorist? Really?) Quarantined with the swine flu in Mexico. Trapped on a farm in rural Hungary for two weeks due to a volcanic ash cloud. Escaping a military coup in the Philippines.

Ironically, none of these events had stopped her from traveling. Emme loved to see new places, new people. Raised by a single mother who worked as a flight attendant, Emme was well-versed in travel. Most school vacations had involved flying with Marc to meet their mother somewhere. With a never-ending supply of buddy passes at her disposal, reaching some exotic locale had never been particularly expensive. Just time-consuming. And, at times, life threatening.

After she had been trapped for several weeks in the mountains of Guatemala (worst flooding in a century, they said) without her luggage (of course) or any way to contact family, Marc had stepped in. He had jokingly enrolled Emme in a month-long survivalist camp run by one of his martial art friends. But Marc hadn't fully appreciated Emme's almost obsessive love of planning. Her need to be prepared.

So she had happily made her lists and packed her bags and headed off to *Rod's Awesome Mind and Body Overhaul* camp. With classes like "Assess! Arrest! Assist!" (a.k.a. first aid) and "Perp Recon and Neutralization" (a.k.a. self-defense). Only after arriving did she realize that the camp acronym was RAMBO.

Marc really had a sick sense of humor sometimes. And, quite frankly, a questionable taste in friends. But she had come home able to light a fire in any condition, as well as flatten someone twice her size.

Of course, disasters never hit at home. Mt. Rainer remained docile; the long overdue Cascadian super earthquake didn't happen; tsunamis never materialized. Home was always safe and blessedly calamity-free.

Which had made the relative smoothness of this current trip somewhat unsettling, if she didn't count the rental car fiasco—which she didn't. The car had been insured, after all. Emme jumped as a particularly violent gust of wind shook the whole house, causing an errant draft to slam one of the bedroom doors upstairs. Loudly. The heavy beams above her creaked in protest.

Emme shook her head, took a sip of tea and tried to think positively. If the whole house came down, at least when rescuers pulled her from the rubble, her feet would look stylish in uber-cute, pink satin slippers.

Of course, Finn had always been a good luck charm. Disasters were never quite as awful when Finn was with her, as this trip had already proved.

Jasmine had analyzed this ad nauseum, ever since Emme had found *him*. Why did disaster avoid Emme when she had Finn along? Jasmine attributed it to 'the bond' that tied them. Insisting that Finn—as the destiny of Emme's soul—was home for her.

Emme wasn't quite sure she understood. The soul or the home part.

"You're tied to him," Jasmine would say. "Life forces intertwined. Your circles definitely overlap."

This was Jasmine's favorite theory.

Time is not linear like a river but instead is an enormous sea, with all events occurring at once.

All things are present, Jasmine would patiently explain. *No past and no future. There is only now. Time is merely a construct of our minds. Any current action impacts not only the present but also the past.*

To her, the lives of everyone who had ever lived existed simultaneously as rippling concentric circles on the surface of some vast cosmic ocean. And from time to time, the rings of a person's expanding circle would intertwine with those of someone else, and they would be linked. Cosmically tied to each other.

For Jasmine, it made no difference that this person might have lived a couple hundred years ago. In a different country. On a different continent.

Emme still didn't quite accept it all—Jasmine's sense of reality was loose at the best of times.

This current trip was a last-ditch effort to reclaim Emme's emotional life. A final expatiation, a way to purge her soul of this impossible sense of connection—no matter what Jasmine might say. Technically on a research sabbatical, Emme had deliberately structured her trip to take Finn's history as well. A wise faculty mentor had once suggested she choose her research interests based on where she wanted to travel. Good advice indeed.

Emme startled as the rain suddenly shifted, rapping sharply against the window, begging for entrance. A gust of wind whistled down the fireplace, causing the flames to flare erratically. Emme took another sip of tea.

She would conquer this obsession. Once and for all.

James Knight ached for adventure.

He admitted it freely.

He longed to brace his boots against the rolling deck of a ship, sails snapping, wind buffeting his body. He yearned to memorize the smell of an Eastern Orient market. Or the sound of a hot summer breeze rustling through sugar cane in the West Indies.

Poets wrote odes to those born under a wandering star. But James was quite sure he had been born under the most boring, most staid star in the entire heavens. If there were mayhem and adventure to be had, he would find himself a hundred miles away and riding in the wrong direction.

James planned. He plotted. But somehow, life always found a way to tether him to home, to responsibility. Not that he didn't love his home. Not that he shirked responsibility. But sometimes when he stared at the predictable rolling fields of Haldon Manor, the tired draft horses bringing in yet another harvest, he felt that he had been born for something more.

James had long pondered the problem. Perhaps not all of him wished for change. His head and most of his left hand did seem generally free of wander lust. Perhaps his elbow too. But both his feet and his heart—yes, most definitely his heart—itched for adventure. Ached to stride out the front door of Haldon Manor and keep walking to the ends of the earth.

It wasn't as if he were adventure-adverse. Just more normal-prone. The unexpected never found him.

All of which made his current situation somewhat ironic.

Wind clawed at the trees and howled around him. Rain lashed against his caped greatcoat, streaming over the brim of his wide hat. James reached up and tucked a sodden lock of blond hair out of his eyes. Lightning regularly flashed through the dark night, brilliantly illuminating the muddy road in front of his horse. Though the lightning itself was actually helpful. At least he could see the road every other minute or so, keeping his horse from wandering into the night.

James generally appreciated any change from his normal routine. But he belatedly realized that this particular night was one adventure he perhaps could have done without.

The sky had been threatening when he left his valet and carriage at the inn. He had just assumed that the storm would quickly pass, leaving him to a pleasant summer evening ride home. So he rode into the storm thinking nothing would happen.

Because nothing ever did.

But tonight, adventure had arrived in the form of a violent Beltane storm. And for once, James wasn't exactly thrilled about it.

He tried to recall exactly why he had been so determined to reach Haldon Manor this evening. Why had he ridden out into the gathering clouds?

Of course, he worried incessantly over Georgiana's health when he was away. He could never breathe easily until he saw his sister's smiling face upon his return.

And Arthur would probably have been affronted by some small village mishap that James would then have to smooth over. Taking offense was a skill Arthur studied quite seriously—his younger brother practiced it regularly and at great length.

And then there was James' persistent restlessness, that constant twitch of his muscles to be up and doing. Sitting still had never been his forte. James knew resting quietly in the inn while the storm raged outside would have been a particularly keen form of torture.

But still. As of this moment, none of his reasons seemed as compelling as they had three hours ago.

Wind gusted, buffeting his body with rain, causing his great coat to billow around him. Snatching at the sodden fabric, James wrapped it back around his body, trying to force away the persistent chill. Lightning cracked, providing a flickering glimpse of the sodden road. James sighed and thought longingly of a warm bed and dry clothing.

His trip to Liverpool to consult with a renowned expert about Georgiana's health had been generally pleasant, if uneventful (of course). Dr. Carson had been helpful but had not given James the hope he craved.

Though amiable, the good doctor's recommendations for Georgiana seemed alarmingly drastic. Her condition was not so far gone as to demand the risky experimental surgery he suggested. At least not yet.

A particularly brutal down draft pelted him, sending his horse skittering sideways, but James easily corrected him. Thankfully, Luther was as adventure-adverse as the rest of his life, holding steadily to the water-slopped road no matter how the storm raged.

Georgiana's ill health prevented him from attending the Season in London. Not that James felt that to be a problem. The Season—that time of year when all of England's aristocracy gathered—was a hassle he had never particularly enjoyed. Though his easy manner ensured that James was welcome everywhere, comfortable in any situation—a ballroom, a drawing room, a hunting party, the local pub, pitching hay with his tenants and their pigs. It was those latter activities that his mother had deplored. What he saw as an open, accepting nature, she had seen as something common and vulgar to be stamped out.

And she had partially succeeded. James never exceeded his income, never drank too much, never visited houses of ill-repute. His father's lessons on responsibility and his mother's militant insistence on propriety had ensured that much.

James sighed. Even his personal behavior was devoid of excitement. How could everything about him be so boring? Fate had given him a longing for adventure but not an ounce of rebellion.

Ironic that.

Lightning cracked again, skittering across the sky, causing the hairs on his arm to suddenly stand on end. The night vibrated with electricity. James could feel the energy eddying around him, woven into the howling wind, pulsing through the fury.

The storm was edgy and laden. Jittery. Unbidden, James shivered. More of a shudder actually. Though not a superstitious man, storms like this created legends. It was easy to hear a beast's growl in the thunder, to feel angry wraiths in the tugging wind.

Shaking such maudlin thoughts from his brain, James pulled his sodden collar tighter around his neck. Truly, nothing would happen to him. Nothing ever did. He just needed to focus on staying on the sloppy road. All would be well.

As he rode deeper into the inky night, James found himself unwittingly repeating the refrain, the screeching tempest swirling around him.

Nothing will happen. All will be well.

Chapter 2

On the tarmac at Heathrow Airport
One week before Beltane
April 22, 2012

S o are you heading immediately out of town?" Next to Emme, the man with a cultured British accent smiled, as the plane slowly taxied after landing.

Emme sighed inwardly. He was undeniably yummy with kind eyes and wonderfully mussed hair. And, heaven knew, she had *such* a weakness for disheveled hair—rumpled locks that suggested a certain devil-may-care attitude.

But despite chatting with him for hours over the Atlantic, she couldn't summon a glimmer of attraction. Not a single spark. Just the typical emptiness.

Why couldn't she ever feel that flare of something more? For about the millionth time, Emme wondered if something inside her was irreparably broken.

He took her silence for encouragement and continued, "Because if you're not, I'd love to show you around."

Emme debated. She could imagine how it would go. She and Mr. Yummy Hair would hang out. Chat. Get to know each other. She would like him in a generally brother-ish, non-sparky sort of way. He would like her in a decidedly non-brotherly, let's-get-sparking sort of way.

This would lead to The Talk where she would tell him about F and the locket. At which point, Mr. Yummy Hair would stare at her with crazy eyes.

As in *you-are-totally-crazy* eyes.

Then things would get uncomfortable. And probably awkward.

"Ah, thanks for the offer," said Emme, "but I'm good. As I mentioned, my dad is British and I spent summers with my grandma growing up. So London is as familiar as home. Besides, I'm going straight west to the town of Marfield, itching to get started on my sabbatical research. The effects of the Industrial Revolution on woman and children in agricultural Britain, remember? But seriously, thank you." Emme hoped that was letting him down kindly. Why delay the inevitable? She was never one to put off a problem.

"Oh, of course. I'd forgot you mentioned that."

Emme had tried to feel some attraction to him. Really she had. Somewhere between Greenland and Iceland, she had even asked him The Question. She had found it to be a good way to tell if there might be a spark. Or even a flicker. A glint of something more.

"So what have you done to prepare for the zombie apocalypse?" Emme had asked, keeping her face a still mask. She found you had to ask The Question without a trace of irony. Would Mr. Yummy Hair get it?

He stared at her for a moment. Blinked. "Uh . . . ," he started. Blinked again. "Can't say I've given it much thought. You don't seem like the type to be into things like that."

Utter fail.

He shifted in the seat next to her, leaning in slightly. "Can I tell you how much I love your eyes? I've never seen a color quite like them." He ran a hand through his hair, mussing it even more, as if deliberately taunting her.

"Most people just call them hazel."

"I guess, but I love how they're almost gold in the middle and then green around the outside. They're lovely." His gaze indicated that her eyes weren't the only thing he found lovely.

"Thank you," was all she managed in response. He really did seem nice, but she knew she would let him walk away, like she always did.

He tried a different tack. "Your locket is beautiful, by the way. It looks old. A family heirloom?" He gestured to where the oval locket rested on its long chain.

"Not exactly." Unconsciously, she grasped the locket in her hand, the filigreed metal cool to her touch. "It's just a vintage piece I picked up at an estate sale. I consider it my good luck charm when traveling." Emme gave him her most convincing you-seem-nice-but-this-isn't-going-to-happen smile.

Her cell phone rang, startling them both.

"Hey, you made it. Though of course, I knew you would." Jasmine's voice sounded chipper. Jasmine was always chipper.

"Yeah, just landed. No incidents, thank goodness. Finn worked his magic."

"Of course he did. Love his positive energy."

Emme gave her a moment to remember.

"Finn, did you say? He's Finn today? So are you off to Marfield yet?"

"As soon as I get my rental car. I'm excited to see Spunto's other paintings."

Over the past several years, Emme's extensive research had determined the miniature portrait in the locket to be the work of Giovanni Spunto, an itinerant painter working near the town of Marfield in Herefordshire between 1811 and 1813.

"Explain to me again why you think this Viscount Linwood is F?" Jasmine asked. "This Linwood guy feels important to me, but I'm not sure he's your F."

How many times had Jasmine said this?

"Not helping," Emme sighed. "Support, Jaz. I need support right now. Don't undermine this. I've told you, Spunto painted a similar miniature portrait of Linwood's sister, Marianne, in the summer of 1812, remember?"

"Oh, that's right, and Linwood has an F in his name."

"Had, Jaz, he *had* an F in his name." When would Jasmine stop referring to dead people as if they were still living? Emme shook her head. "Timothy *Frederick* Charles Linwood. He could have gone by his second name. It's not outside the realm of possibility, and he would have been the right age in 1812, about 30. I can't wait to see the paintings of the viscount, as well as Spunto's portrait of Marianne. I'm hoping that will solve the mystery of who our F was."

"Well, as I've said, I do feel that Linwood is significant but I'm still not sure he's your destiny. With Finn, your circles are linked."

"Jaz, I love you, but again, this trip is all about purging Finn. Purging. As in, gutting him from my life and moving on."

"Yes, yes, you keep saying that. But just because you want something to be a certain way, doesn't mean the universe will agree with you. How many ways do I have to say it? Your life is intertwined with his. Remember, your soul is eternal, stretching in both directions. Past and future. Have you learned nothing from me?"

There really was no good answer to that. Time to change the topic. "How is Cat'n Kirk? Still loving his new scratching post?"

Emme allowed Jasmine to rattle on as the plane stopped at the gate. She made non-committal gestures and waved goodbye as Mr. Yummy Hair collected his luggage and deplaned.

Promising to call Jasmine when she reached the cottage she had rented for the summer, Emme made her way to immigration. The interview passed smoothly with only one question about her dual citizenship (American and British) and a few follow-ups about her intentions in the U.K. (six-month research sabbatical, staying in Marfield . . . yes, that's in Herefordshire on the border with Wales). Her luggage miraculously arrived safely in customs, so no need to rely on the toiletries stashed in her purse. Bless Finn.

The woman behind the rental car counter was polite. Emme's car was ready, just as Marc had arranged. They chatted about the beautiful spring weather and the woman laughed at Emme's ability to switch between her American and British accent. A useful trick learned from summers with her proper English grandmother.

Nanna had been insistent that Emme and Marc be fluent in all things British. Like which fork to use when eating partridge—the important things in life. Or rather, what Nanna perceived as being important. Because, as she intoned, the Cavendish's (*we're third cousins of the Duke of Devonshire on my grandfather's side of the family, don't forget*) would roll in their graves to find they had uncouth American relatives. Emme had serious doubts about that. But regardless, every summer had been filled with elocution lessons, horse-back riding and tea religiously at 4:00 p.m.

Emme let her mind drift as the rental car attendant tapped away on her computer. A 24-hour news station chirped quietly from the TV in the corner, interrupting an interview about a rare coin collection going to auction at Sotheby's to report on unprecedented wildfires somewhere in Australia. Emme smiled with relief. She was nowhere near Australia. Bless Finn.

Honestly, when was the last time travel had been this, well, normal? Emme pondered the question as she wrangled her heavy luggage up the four twisting floors of the parking garage to her rental car. She hated when things went too well, events matching smoothly to the plans she had meticulously made. It was like waiting for an ax to fall.

A moment later, Emme arrived at the stall to collect her car. She paused, double-checked the rental agreement in her hand and then actually read it.

Sigh. She was going to have to deal with this. And Emme was never one to put off a problem. In this case, her brother.

"Seriously, Marc?" she said when he answered the phone. "Did you deliberately book me the smallest car in Britain?"

"You said you wanted something that gets good gas mileage." Marc gave his best I'm-your-annoying-big-brother laugh.

Emme grimaced as she stared at the minuscule car. Tiny and squat, its top barely reached above her waist. So short she could see her reflection in the roof. Her dark bobbed hair was extra curly in the English humidity.

"Marc, I can't drive this," Emme said, her voice peeved. "I'll look like

LeBron James on a carnival kiddie ride. My knees will be around my ears."

"I know, right?! You're totally going to have to send me a photo."

Silence.

"I hate you so much right now, Marc." She almost meant it too.

He chuckled.

"How am I supposed to get all my luggage into a two-seater without a trunk?" Emme opened the passenger side door and assessed the lack of space, trying to decide which of her bags would fit.

"Well," Marc answered, "maybe you shouldn't have packed those ridiculous pink slippers of yours."

"Is there anything you won't do to annoy me?" Emme grunted in exasperation.

A long pause. "No, not really." He sounded totally unrepentant. "But think of all the guys who will hit on you because they dig yo' sweet ride."

Rolling her eyes, Emme wondered for probably the thousandth time if she and Marc were actually related. They could be so different. Even as children, she had loved horses and ballroom dance, while he had been into martial arts. "Yeah, nice try. I don't think this car is exactly a stud magnet."

Trapping the phone between her head and shoulder, she hefted her largest bag onto the passenger seat, pushing and wedging it against the dash.

"Look, Ems, I'm just helping you get over ol' Fabio."

"He's Finn today. Mind your manners."

"Finn? Seriously? As in Huckleberry?"

"You're trying to taint his name. It's not going to work." Emme debated whether to buckle the luggage in. After a moment, she decided against it. Bad enough to be a giant in a clown car, no need to look OCD too.

"Ems, I'm just trying to help you lighten up." Marc's voice grew serious. "You know I care about you, but let's face it, you've been hiding behind Fabio-boy for too long. You need to live, Emme. Like really live."

Walking around to the back of the car, Emme opened the hatchback and assessed what she could cram behind the seats.

"Yes, well, that's easy for you to say. Harder for me to do." She hefted another bag and rested it against the back of the seats. "Don't you think I know that this Finn obsession is a problem? Don't you think I've been trying for years to move past it? Like I didn't just spend six hours over the Atlantic trying desperately to be attracted to the guy sitting next to me!"

Emme leaned her back against the bag, leveraging her feet against the ground. Behind her, the bag gave slightly. Encouraged, she pushed harder.

"You did? Really?"

"Really. Look, I know I need to move past this, Marc."

Ah, a little more give. Maybe she could fit all her luggage in after all. She cantilevered all her five foot seven, one hundred and twenty-eight pounds against the car. "I'm going to go to Marfield, find the real F and then move on and—"

With a shriek, Emme fell backward, hitting the ground. The car no longer supported her weight. Gasping for breath, she rolled sideways and looked up. The car was rolling directly toward the spiral, corkscrew ramp of the parking garage, picking up speed as it went. Her luggage scattered onto the pavement like desperate sailors abandoning ship.

Traveling disaster number one hundred and fourteen.

The drawing room
Haldon Manor
Six months before Beltane
October 11, 1811

"My condolences again upon your mother's death," James murmured politely.

Timothy, Viscount Linwood stood staring out the large mullioned window as the last of the fall leaves skittered to the ground, his back to James straight and unyielding. The black mourning band for the recently buried Lady Linwood neatly tied around his upper arm.

Linwood did not immediately acknowledge James' comment. Instead his back seemed to become even stiffer, the set of his dark head more severe. James wondered for probably the thousandth time how someone his own age could be so cold. So off-putting.

Silence hung in the room. The white-washed paneled walls and high coffered ceiling of the drawing room were gloomy in the afternoon light. James moved to sit in a gold brocade chair near the marble fireplace, stretching out his legs and crossing them at the ankles.

"Thank you," Linwood finally said. Not, as James suspected, because he truly appreciated the sentiment. But because it was what a gentleman should say in such a situation. And Linwood played the proper gentleman to perfection.

The viscount remained silent for another moment. James waited him out; he would not break the silence first. Linwood would have to explain the reason for his visit without any help.

He knew Timothy well. They had grown up together after all. Linwood's estate, Kinningsley, butted against Haldon Manor. But they had never been friends. Linwood had always taken himself far too seriously. And James never had—taken Timothy seriously that is.

"But I am not here to discuss my family's recent loss." Linwood turned from the window. "I am sure you know that Arthur has finally offered for Marianne."

James nodded. He was well aware of his brother's affection for Linwood's younger sister. Their childhood friendship had blossomed into something more substantial over the summer. Marianne was as kind and docile as her brother was cold and domineering.

Linwood continued, "As I told Arthur, I have no particular aversion to him as a brother-in-law. But he is hardly the match I would prefer for my only sister." Linwood fixed James with an icy stare, his gray eyes so colorless as to be nearly transparent.

"Indeed?" James cocked an eyebrow. "To my knowledge Arthur is still the great-grandson of both a duke and an earl, with a family name that extends practically to the time of Edward III. Pray tell me, how is that insufficient?" James kept his tone light, knowing that would be most annoying.

The viscount's mouth moved ever so slightly. His eyes tightened imperceptibly. For Linwood, it was nearly a full on grimace.

"I do not cast aspersions upon your family's illustrious name or history. But rather point out that, as a younger son, Arthur's less-than-glowing prospects leave something to be desired. He would not be able to keep Marianne in the style and comfort to which she has been raised."

"It is true that Whitcomb, the estate my mother left to Arthur, is not large. But it is modern and generates a reasonable income. I have not seen that Miss Linwood would object to life at Whitcomb."

Marianne loved Arthur and Arthur, most decidedly, loved Marianne. It was rather cloying to see them together, all surreptitious glances and wistful sighs. Marianne was born to play the star-crossed lover.

However, the ever so top-lofty Viscount Linwood had little affection for their longing stares and aching whispers. Granted, he held little affection for most everything. But James knew that Linwood found the doe-eyed looks his love-lorn sister and Arthur cast at each together particularly irritating.

An irritation James was petty enough to enjoy.

Many days James wished he had not been born the eldest son. Arthur was made to be lord of the manor. He so perfectly encapsulated their illustrious ducal ancestors with his aristocratic air and sense of propriety. Arthur always acted the perfect gentleman, right down to his overly developed sense of honor and status.

Unlike Arthur, James took after the not-so-illustrious branches of the family. Knight ancestors who had risen dramatically above humble beginnings and made their own way in the world. Those branches that his mother had diligently tried to pretend never existed. (Though she readily accepted their money, which had replenished the family coffers.) To James, these ancestors were the truly admirable ones. The ones who had fought through poverty and insecurity to shape a prosperous future with the strength of their own raw hands.

The blood of those ancestors echoed strongly in James. He longed to grasp his future and forge it for himself. He made no secret of the fact.

"My sister is all that is amiable and good," Linwood continued. "But as with all young women, she lacks the foresight to understand how marrying Arthur would impact not only her future but the future of her children."

Linwood paused for a moment, considering, and then said, "I am not come here today to argue over Arthur's merits, but instead to inquire if you have decided to improve his prospects?"

The question hung between them. Heavy and laden with baggage.

Trust Linwood to come right to the point. James sighed and said quietly, "No. . . . As much as I would like to, in speaking with my solicitors, the family entail would be nearly impossible to break. My late father saw to that."

James knew that Linwood had held out hope that somehow the family entail could be broken. That James could declare Arthur the heir to Haldon Manor and give it over to his brother's capable (if somewhat self-righteous) hands, freeing James to pursue his own life as he wished.

But as James knew, nothing could change the fact that he had been born first. James could not sign away his responsibilities. He could ignore them. But he could not renounce his inheritance, could not decline it. His father had renewed the entail in its strictest form, perhaps sensing that his eldest son would bolt if given the option. The land and property and, well, everything had been left to James' care. And to him alone. Until he died and passed it on to his own heirs.

The entire weight of Haldon Manor and its ten thousand acres, its tenants, its industry, all rested on his shoulders. His unwittingly steady I-will-be-responsible shoulders.

"That's a pity," Linwood said slowly. "My sister turns twenty-one in less than a month and will be of age to marry without my consent. Do you think that your brother will act dishonorably given my rejection of his suit?"

Cocking an eyebrow, James replied, "Are you asking if Arthur will convince Marianne to elope? That seems unlikely. Arthur's sense of propriety and family obligations agrees with your own. He understands that Marianne is not for him unless you wish it."

It was true. Based on some time-honored sense of gentlemanly morality, Arthur couldn't even disagree with Linwood's assessment of him. Of course, this didn't stop him from pining for Marianne, which left the couple in an endless limbo, not able to marry, refusing to elope but still unable to leave each other and move on. James found it ludicrous.

He could not imagine giving his heart to another and then not fighting to secure a future with her.

Linwood pondered for a moment. "I would have no objection to your brother's suit if he were to inherit Haldon Manor."

"Yes, well, he is my heir currently."

"Indeed." Linwood gave his ghostly hint of a smile. "Unfortunately, at this moment you look to be in good health."

James blinked slowly, refusing to rise to Linwood's bait.

Silence.

"How fares your sister, if I may ask?" Linwood asked, changing the subject. "I understand the nature of her illness is quite serious."

"She is ill. Her cough worsens, but it is early yet. She might make a swift recovery. And if not, I have already begun to search out the best treatments for her. I am determined she will not remain ill for long."

"Well, given our mother's recent passing, Marianne will not attend the London Season. She will observe the required full year of mourning, so she will remain at Kinningsley through mid-summer at least." Linwood paused, glanced out the window and then back to James, his face utterly impassive. "I would ask that your sister reduce her visits until the true nature of her illness is understood. Marianne's comfort and health are the world to me."

James narrowed his eyes. Georgiana and Marianne were good friends and Georgiana's health was not precarious yet. Linwood was being needlessly petty.

James waited to reply, allowing the smallness of Linwood's request to hang in the room, silently condemning.

"Georgiana will be sad to hear it," James finally said. "She enjoys your sister's company so. Though it is no matter. I am sure that Georgiana will be recovered and whole in no time."

"Of course," Linwood intoned. But his back remained stiff, his entire demeanor saying otherwise. "Naturally, we all wish Miss Knight a speedy recovery. With my mother's recent passing, there has already been enough death in the neighborhood."

James managed a faint smile. Nothing more.

Chapter 3

E mme startled as her cell phone rang, the sound chirping through the growling thunder.

"Well, how is it?" Marc's voice sounded eager in her ear.

Emme understood immediately. "Oh, you know, uh-mazing." She crawled back under her blanket. An errant draft of wind caused the fire to flicker.

Marc laughed, rich and low. "I still can't believe they upgraded you to a BMW for the entire summer."

"I know, right? The poor attendant who left the tiny car in neutral with no parking brake on got an earful from his supervisor. But seriously, you should have seen it spiraling down the parking garage ramp."

It really had been quite the sight. The car, scraping its way along the corkscrew exit like some drunken escapee from the circus, ending in a dizzy heap three stories below.

"Don't you usually make fun of people who drive flashy cars?" Marc chuckled. "Let's savor the irony of this moment, shall we?"

"Even all of my luggage survived." Emme shook her head at the wonder of it, watching rain hammer against the window. "My traveling disasters never turn out like this. Finn seriously saved me."

"Well, tell Fabio 'thank you' for me. I'll enjoy driving that BMW when I come visit you after filming this latest martial arts project in Hong Kong. By the way, how's the internet at your place?" asked Marc. "Football season will be in full swing in September, and I'm going to have to stream all the Broncos games from my DVR." Marc hadn't held onto much of their growing up years in Denver, except for the city's beloved football team.

"Ugh! You and your Broncos! And you think my Fabio/Finn thing is annoying."

"Whatever. At least my obsessions are socially acceptable."

The rain slanted against the back windows of the room, making a grating rat-a-tat sound.

"Fine," said Emme. "You can watch your Bronco games while you're here as long as you promise to still go to the Jane Austen Festival in Bath. It's been what? Five years since we've been? I brought your outfit, breeches and all."

"Oh, please," Marc said, his voice pained, "it's embarrassing how much you geek out on that. I'm not sure my manhood is up to dressing in fancy clothes and prancing around like Mr. Darcy. My self-respect does have boundaries."

Emme rolled her eyes. "I think Mr. Darcy would take serious offense over being told that he pranced."

"Any grown man who wears a satin vest thingy—"

"Waistcoat."

"—and wraps his neck in a long strip of fabric—"

"A neckcloth."

"—and drinks tea with his pinky elevated can most certainly be said to prance. I think it's actually something they used to teach, . . . prancing."

There was a smirk in his voice.

"For the record, you wouldn't have to be Mr. Darcy. He would bore me to tears in about five minutes. I mean, take away all his money and what are you left with? An uptight, socially awkward guy who can't relate to people."

"You know, somewhere a Jane Austen angel just lost her wings over you saying that." Marc's good-natured laugh was buttery warm. "I really think that people have been lynched for less."

"Now you're imagining an angry mob of bespectacled ladies brandishing pitchforks and battered copies of *Pride and Prejudice* chasing me through the streets of Bath."

"Perhaps," Marc chuckled. "And given your bad travel luck, I wouldn't rule it out. Though I could choreograph a crazy fight scene to protect you. It would definitely require some ninjas."

Emme laughed. "I think you've read *Pride and Prejudice and Zombies* one too many times."

"Hey, gotta stay up on all the classics."

Suddenly, a large bolt of lightning flashed. Thunder cracked loudly and then boomed, rattling the house. The low noise reverberated, pounding against Emme's sternum.

"What was that?" Marc exclaimed.

"A bad storm. And it's Beltane today—that's gotta be bad luck."

"Beltane?"

"It's like Halloween," explained Emme, "only on the opposite side of the calendar, in the spring instead of the fall. They're exactly six months apart, actually."

"Sounds like something Jasmine made up. Listen, I gotta go, but you need to promise me one thing—"

"What?"

"No catastrophes this summer." And then, whether because of the storm or Marc's underdeveloped attention span, the phone call dropped.

A crash outside reminded Emme she was in the middle of the closest thing she'd known to a tornado—not a comforting thought given her history. She pulled the blankets tighter around her.

Tonight the cottage seemed oppressive and breathless. Nothing like how it'd felt a week earlier when she'd seen it in person for the first time, with its golden stone and ivy growing up over the peaked front door and paned windows. To the right of the cottage an oak tree wrinkled and stooped with age drew it protectively under its branches. The words Duir Cottage were carved into a board to the left of the front door, *duir* meaning oak in ancient Celt. Indeed, honey-colored oak covered the house's interior, most walls boasting wood paneling.

The house epitomized the romanticized American notion of a quaint English cottage. It was beyond postcard perfect, like Emme could reach out and touch the paper it was printed on. From the first time she'd seen it on the internet, the place had seemed to be . . .

. . . waiting for her.

Lightning flashed again. Emme tried to ignore the clap of thunder that followed. But it was useless. The house was tense, air heavy and laden. She absorbed all the apprehension of the wind, the furor of the pounding rain. It hammered against her chest, jittery.

Trying for a distraction, Emme walked to the large stainless steel fridge. The unknown owners had recently renovated the house with an open kitchen/dining/sitting room at the back. An enormous stone fireplace dominated the space, flanked by high back chairs, flat screen TV and comfy sofa. A rough hewn antique dining table finished off the look. The whole house looked like it had been staged for a Restoration Hardware catalog photoshoot. Pulling out leftover Indian takeaway, Emme watched the rain pelt against the kitchen window as her food rotated in the microwave.

Sitting at the large table, she decided she needed company. Emme looped the oval locket off her neck and opened it gently, noting the familiar pop of the catch. She then propped the opened locket next to her plate of naan and tikka masala.

And looked at *him*.

As usual, she felt the familiar shock of recognition. That disorienting sense of deja vu. Over the years, it had never changed.

He still stared out at her in his blue-green jacket and neckcloth. Blond hair stylishly disheveled as was *a la mode* for any gentleman around 1812. Sun-bleached and tousled. Begging to run her fingers through it.

Emme stopped and then shook the thought out of her brain. Honestly.

The tiny portrait carefully rendered minute fine details, showing strands of hair and subtle laughter lines around his mouth. His blue eyes looked kind with a dash of devil-may-care, like he laughed at himself as much as he laughed at the world.

More than just eye-candy, he seemed larger than life, beckoning, his smile always just out of reach.

Even now as she gazed at Finn propped on the table—rain pounding the roof overhead—the inscription jarred her.

To E
throughout all time
heart of my soul
your F

As usual, the words rushed unbidden through her mind:
You. He means you. Emry.

Emme brutally repressed them. She was in Marfield to overcome this sense of connection, not wallow in it.

It didn't help that Jasmine relentlessly insisted the connection was real, not just imaginings in her head.

"Look, Jaz," Emme had said on one particularly exasperating occasion. "I know you think it's something significant, but it's impossible for my life to be connected with someone who died two hundred years ago."

"Well, you can believe that with all your heart," Jasmine replied. "But as I keep telling you, belief alone can't change the nature of reality. It is what it is and no amount of wishing reality were different will actually change it."

Emme shook her head. There was no arguing with Jasmine when she got like this.

"What do you think his name is?" Jasmine speculated. "Obviously, E stands for Emry. Don't look at me like that," she insisted. "E is you. Definitely. But who is F?"

Emme shrugged. "E is not me. And I'm sure that they had sensible names for the time period. Probably something simple like Elizabeth and

Frank. Or Eleanor and Freddie."

Jasmine pursed her lips and thought for a minute. "No, I'm voting more for Eversly and Faxxon. Total hipsters."

Emme rolled her eyes with a smile. "No, they were literary snobs: Emerson and Faulkner. Oh, or a Jane Austen character mash-up. Emma and Fitzwilliam."

"Elsbeth and Fergus. Star-crossed Scottish lovers." Jasmine grinned. "But seriously, Emme, E is you. Not letting you distract me. The real question is the mysterious Mr. F. What is his name?"

Emme couldn't decide. Neither could Jasmine.

And so they never settled on a permanent name for F, his name changing on a regular basis. One day he was Francis, the next he was Ford. Once he spent six months as Felix. But nothing ever stuck. Nothing ever felt exactly right.

Emme picked up the locket, turned it over to look at the plaited hair and brushed her fingers over the stylized combined initials. Why take the initials and turn them into a design on top of the crystal, almost like a modern logo, with the F looping and nestling into the curvy shaped E? Such a puzzle.

Wind again rattled the house, banging against the doors and windows, pounding for entrance. It's violence mimicking Emme's increasingly maudlin mood.

She had tried hard to keep her obsession over the locket to a low simmer. But that hadn't really worked. It was too easy to turn Finn into the perfect boyfriend. He was a fantastic listener and was always happy to see her. His welcoming smile on the edge of bursting into actual laughter. Sometimes she found herself straining to hear his voice, as if the connection she felt could will him into being.

Which really had been the problem. Particularly as she had watched relationship after relationship fizzle. She had struggled with dating before Finn. She often felt attracted to a guy. But that attraction just never seemed to move beyond a physical sense. There was never that deep, soul-nourishing emotional spark that books, movies and friends assured her did exist.

Since finding the mysterious Mr. F, her longest relationship had been with Carl. Web programmer by day, uber-Trekkie by night. At least, he had understood her obsession with the locket. The problem had come when she realized that he took his own obsession just a little too seriously. How could she *not* tease him when he tried to teach her Klingon? A person was born with only so much self-restraint. And he had gotten way too into her zombie apocalypse question. He had even drawn up multiple Star Fleet Command evasive maneuver charts in preparation. And hadn't once seen the humor in the whole exercise.

And then she had had the temerity to question his choice of forehead prosthetic for an upcoming Trekkie convention. Well, not really questioned. More like giggled. Which had led to a huge fight where he had insisted she give back his "Keep Calm and Klingon" coffee mug. And that had led to more giggling. Quirky, yes. Self-deprecating sense of humor, not so much.

Then there had been Steve. The accountant. Her mom had particularly liked him. And he did have wonderful hair. Emme and Steve had really clicked because she loved to create lists, and he was a whiz with spreadsheets. They had had many a planning session together.

Emme found his obsessive need for order rather endearing. Not annoying at all. At least, not at first. But when she'd had The Talk, he had gotten the crazy eyes. And zombies? That hadn't gone over well either.

This had led to Steve's polar opposite: Forrest. Forrest was a photographer. And a wannabe poet who adored knitting. He cried over beauty. And sappy love songs. And internet memes. He had wanted to discuss the metaphysics of zombies for hours on end. To the point that Emme was sorry she had brought it up.

And then there had been the locket. At first, Emme had been excited that Forrest didn't mind her obsession. In fact, he had gotten into it with her. It was one of their best bonding moments. But then he had started to refer to the guy in the locket as Forrest too. And she got jealous. Things became awkward, and so she broke up with him.

All of this left Emme alone with Finn and his enigmatic half smile—her perfect fantasy man. Dead men didn't really make for good boyfriend material. Why couldn't she connect with actual living, breathing human males? Sometimes she felt helplessly paralyzed. Unable to let go of Finn and the pull she felt to him, but equally unable to forge a bond with someone else. She feared something inside her had been broken long ago.

Emme had come to Marfield to find Finn. The real F. She would pull him from the realm of myth down to reality. Assign real names to the initials. Real people.

Screeeeeee! A branch scraped against the window opposite the dining table. Loud and shrill.

Emme jumped, her heart suddenly clawing its way up her throat.

Seriously. This storm would be the death of her—

No wait. Given her track record, that wasn't even funny to think about.

Chapter 4

IN THE VILLAGE OF MARFIELD
BELTANE
APRIL 30, 1812

By the time James reached Marfield, he considered taking shelter for the night. The wind still beat ferociously. Thunder boomed. But he was so close to home and his own bed. It seemed a shame to disturb anyone so late at night.

Every now and again, he thought he could hear the peal of church bells. Was someone ringing the parish bell or was the violent wind swinging the bell of its own accord? Local superstition held that church bells rung in a storm would keep thunder and lightning away.

Not that it seemed to be working.

At least James wasn't the only one absorbing the bewitching quality of this fierce storm. Though not terribly superstitious himself, the local inhabitants around Marfield were.

James had often noted the stonecrop growing on his tenants' roofs, supposedly to protect from lightning. And witches too. Some even took to placing a cross of whitethorn above their front door, also to ward off enchanters and their spells. The list went on and on. James shuddered to think what ill omen the villagers would make of this horrific Beltane weather. Bad weather on one of the most powerful spirit nights of the year would not ease superstitious minds. He would probably spend the next month seeing his tenants wear pouches of hazel leaves and twigs to ward off ill luck.

Nearly all of the local folklore and mystical beliefs came from one source. Auntie Gray with her gnarled hands and kind eyes was a fount of information, both historical and arcane. Though sensible and kind, Auntie Gray's stories and knowledge fed rather than allayed local superstitions. James suspected that in an earlier time she might have been burned for being a witch.

Fortunately, they lived in a more enlightened era.

Pulling his greatcoat more tightly around him, James let his mind wander to his plans for the week, assuming the storm broke soon. He hoped Ethan Fletcher would have time for one of their famous bouts with swords or sticks or both. He would let Ethan choose. An old childhood friend, Ethan had recently cashed out of the army to take over the running of the large family farm after his uncle's death.

Though a yeoman farmer, Ethan excelled at fencing and quarterstaff fighting, a legacy of his time as a soldier. Even if adventure never found James, he enjoyed being ready for it, knowing how to move his body in a fight. And James found he usually had a reserve of latent aggression to burn through. A drive to pulverize his overabundant energy into a limp mass.

Finally a flicker-flash of lightning illuminated the gates to Haldon Manor to the right of the road, comforting James with the promise of dry clothing and a warm bed. He turned down the familiar track, grateful as the sloppy mud of the main road turned into the more grass-laden lane.

Just a mile more and he would be home.

"Well, what does Dr. Carson say? What does he recommend for Georgiana?" Arthur asked impatiently from his position near the fireplace, watching James at his desk reading a letter.

When James didn't immediately respond, Arthur began to slowly pace the dark paneled room, irritation evident in the tightness of his shoulders.

Georgiana sat motionless in a chair opposite James' desk, wrapped in a shawl despite her long-sleeved morning dress and seat near the roaring fire. Sun poured through the window behind James, glinting off her golden hair. Her eyes vividly blue in the afternoon light, but restless. Almost feverish.

Finishing his reading, James set the letter down. "Dr. Carson makes some suggestions for herbal treatments, many of which we have tried already. But he recommends one involving birch bark that could be promising. Other than that, he suggests a consultation when I am next near Liverpool."

"Liverpool?" Arthur said, slight contempt lacing his tone. "Why would you ever just find yourself near Liverpool? The entire town is full of merchants and commerce. Hardly the place that a proper gentleman just *happens* to go." Arthur snorted as if he had made a very fine joke.

James gritted his teeth slightly. Really, his brother was rather absurd at times. Arthur had inherited more than just their mother's grey eyes and brown hair. He had also absorbed her love of propriety. By contrast, James and Georgiana heavily favored their golden-blond father, both in looks and easy-going nature. He knew that Arthur found James' careless appreciation of status and societal position to be a sore trial.

"Well, fortunately, you have never really thought me a truly proper gentleman, Arthur, so I shall be able to venture to Liverpool with equanimity."

James saw Georgiana give a small grin, her eyes dancing briefly. It was the barest hint of herself, of the woman she had been before this illness. Before fatigue and dullness had engulfed her.

James watched as she coughed, deep and harsh. The bones of her hands moved in sharp relief under her skin. Her weight loss had been slow but relentless. His heart clenched at the sight. Georgiana was his champion, the one person in the world he could always count on to see reality as he did. Though separated by nearly eight years, their ability to read each other's thoughts and moods was often uncanny.

Recovering from her cough, Georgiana said, "Don't Lord Preston and the lovely Miss Preston live near Liverpool?" Her tone was teasing, her grin sly. It filled James' heart to see her face with some animation.

"Indeed, he does." James gave wry smile. "But I cannot think that Miss Preston would appreciate my attentions. I believe she nearly fainted from fright the last time I tried to talk with her."

Though passably pretty, James could only think of Miss Anabelle Preston as colorless. This described more than just her nearly featureless white-pale hair, brows and lashes. She seemed washed of life. Empty. Bland.

Arthur snorted. "Miss Preston is merely reserved and well-mannered, brother."

"She trembled for a full five minutes the last time I endeavored to engage her in conversation, not once raising her voice above a whisper." James fixed Arthur with a stare. "Is it now fashionable for well-bred ladies to quiver like a leaf in a gentleman's presence?"

Arthur opened his mouth to deliver a blistering retort, but Georgiana intervened first. "Please, don't argue. Miss Preston does not warrant ill words."

Arthur and James eyed each other for a moment.

"Though James is right, Arthur," Georgiana continued with a glance at him. "Miss Preston is impeccably well-bred but terribly shy. She would hardly be a good match."

James knew he was that most sought after of species: An eligible bachelor. The first-born heir to a wealthy estate with impressive holdings in the five per cents and a revered family name, despite his lack of a title. Though, he was the great-grandson of both a duke and an earl.

All of which made him a enticing matrimonial fish to be landed. Wherever he went, conspiring mamas threw out their lures, casting their fresh-faced daughters in his path, trying to reel him in. As a rule, such girls were well-mannered and polite. Often they were pretty. Occasionally witty and passably clever.

But never thrilling or truly fascinating. Never compelling or with a promise of adventure. Nothing in them generated a spark of something more within him.

James had tried to find such women interesting. Truly he had. He had no particular aversion toward marriage.

There had been the lovely second daughter of a marquis, Lady Margaret. She had been everything his mother had ever wanted for him. Well-bred from an illustrious family. But when she had thrown herself at James in the family library, he had realized that she wasn't everything *he* had ever wanted. James had decidedly strong feelings about the importance of self-worth. Feelings Lady Margaret apparently did not share.

Of course, that hadn't been nearly as bad as Miss Mariah Croft. Well, Miss Croft herself was actually fine and amiable. Mrs. Croft had been the problem. Hinting not so subtly that if he were to marry her daughter, James could enjoy more than one marriage bed. As if he were that type of man.

It all had left a bad taste in his mouth.

"True, sister. I don't think I will bother Lord Preston with a visit. Instead, perhaps I will head north to Liverpool to consult with Dr. Carson and stop by Lyndenbrooke as well. I should ensure that your steward is managing the estate well."

"Lyndenbrooke," she sighed. "It would be lovely to see it again.

Perhaps in the spring. I miss it so." Lyndenbrooke was Georgiana's estate, left to her by their paternal grandmother. Though small in comparison to Haldon Manor, it provided an adequate living. James knew that Georgiana had had hopes of perhaps living there independently one day. A hope that James profoundly prayed she would realize.

"Heavens, Georgiana!" Arthur said, his voice too loud. "You are so ill. How can you even talk of visiting Lyndenbrooke? It is completely out of the question."

"Arthur, really, that is uncalled for—"

"—James, she needs rest not a holiday!"

"You have no right to assume—"

"Enough! Both of you." Georgiana's eyes snapped with anger. "Arguing with one another will not help me. I know you both would like me to live. But the reality is that very few survive the white death. It kills in degrees, but it kills nonetheless."

"Really, Georgie."

"Georgiana—"

"No, hear me out. I want to live. Trust me, I do. But I want to live fully. Death will claim all of us at some time. Neither of you can stop that. But until then, I want to live, . . . not die beforehand, slowly in inches."

Georgiana looked between them both. James could feel the strength in her. The determination.

Arthur stared and then turned away. James swallowed and slowly nodded, letting out a low, harsh breath, raking a hand through his hair.

She was right, but that didn't mean he had to like it.

For the thousandth time, he silently vowed that she would live. He would find a way. Somehow.

Georgiana had always been the brightest part of his life. The one thing that held him firmly to Haldon Manor.

As a youth, James had planned to leave, despite his responsibilities as heir. To find adventure. But then his father had died unexpectedly and he had found himself suddenly the head of the family. Everyone looking at him, requiring something of him, their mother distraught with grief, Arthur and Georgiana needing someone to guide them. Then their mother passed away too, leaving Georgiana to find her way to womanhood alone.

And now Georgiana herself was ill. He would not leave, not when his sister needed him so much. Not when he needed her so much.

"Well, Georgie, we will just have to get you well. I won't tolerate this illness of yours any longer," James said quietly. "Just promise me you will be careful while I am gone."

"Oh, James, you must stop pleading with me to be careful." Georgiana paused, looking sightlessly past James for a moment. Then she brought her eyes back to his. "Life will bring what it will. We cannot change that."

James grimaced and hoped that Georgiana didn't see the pain flicker in his eyes. There for a second and then gone, tucked back away.

She would live, he promised. He would find a way.

Chapter 5

The branch screeched along the window. Once, twice—a terrible nails-on-the-chalkboard sound. And then the wind gusted again, moving the branch away from the house. Rain continued to pour, pounding relentlessly against the roof.

Sighing, Emme finished the last few bites of food and then reached for her purse slung over the back of the chair next to her. Flipping it open, she grabbed out her tablet. She loved her leather purse with its clever hidden clasp and series of zippers. Well, really it looked more like a satchel than anything else. But it was the only purse she had found that met all her disaster traveling needs, fitting her tablet, some makeup and travel toiletries. And a first aid kit with a couple of MRE's, solar charger and a fierce looking multi-tool. Marc had gotten creative through the years.

Turning on her tablet, she reviewed what she had learned over the last several days in her hunt for Finn. Trying to ignore the fearsome weather outside, refusing to allow the howling wind to rattle her mood.

Between 1811 and 1813, there had been at least three families of consequence in the Marfield area. The preeminent family were the Viscounts Linwood, which she had already known.

Another family—the Knights—might also be good contenders. There were three living Knights during the time period: two brothers, James and Arthur, and a sister, Georgiana. Both of the brothers were about the right age to be Finn, but Emme could see no connection with the letters F or E within the family.

Unfortunately, the Knight's family home, Haldon Manor, had burned to the ground sometime around the end of the Napoleonic Wars, destroying all the estate records, family history, paintings and, well, everything. Haldon Manor had been rebuilt a few years later in the Gothic Revival style the Victorians so loved and had been converted into a hotel and spa in the 1950s.

Emme had visited Haldon Manor earlier in the week, as the estate was less than a mile from Duir Cottage. She had spent the afternoon chatting with the friendly staff and sipping tea in the dining room. Interestingly, she had learned that Duir Cottage had actually once been the dower house for the estate. Haldon Manor was known for its large enclosed garden, a riot of flowers and trees surrounded by an ancient wall—all that remained of its time as a medieval monastery. Emme had particularly loved the ruins of the gothic cloister, taking an embarrassing number of photos with her phone.

After the Knights, the Stylles were another family of prominence in the area. Sir Henry Stylles was the only member of the family listed for the time period, and the parish registry indicated that Sir Henry was older, in his mid-50s. Not a good candidate for Finn. However, Sir Henry had been a voracious collector and his former estate near Haldon Manor now functioned as a de facto museum for the entire area. In fact, the museum had Spunto's miniature portrait of Marianne Linwood in their collection.

Rain pattered loudly against the window. Wind clutched at the shutters outside, twining around and shaking them. Though latched against the house, Emme could hear them rattle in protest, shivering against the window casement.

Emme sighed and thought back to her visit to Sir Henry's estate just the day before, the home still owned by the same Stylles family who had inhabited it in the early 19th century. She had arranged a guided tour with the curator, Mr. Betton, to see the estate's impressive collection, particularly Spunto's portrait of Marianne Linwood.

Mr. Betton had been nice enough, but it was obvious that he had an academic's love of mind-numbing minutiae. He had gone on at length about the provenance of a large rare coin collection believed to have belonged to Sir Henry. Apparently, it was going to auction in a matter of days.

"Auction estimates put the value of the entire collection around £100 million," he intoned. "But the actual value could go even higher. Of course, the actual owner of the collection has chosen to remain anonymous. . . ." Emme vaguely remembered seeing something about it somewhere, maybe on her rss reader app. She finally interrupted his monologue to inquire about the museum's portraits from the Napoleonic era.

Leading her through a series of drawing rooms, Mr. Betton showed Emme a canvas of Timothy, the 4th Viscount Linwood and his sister, Marianne. The large portrait depicted a man with a younger woman wearing a soft pink, high-waisted dress covered with a gauzy overdress. The sparkling highlights of the fabric bounced out of the image. Her companion was dressed in the height of Regency gentlemanly fashion: dark coat, gold waistcoat, white shirt and neckcloth, tan breeches with polished Hessian boots. His gray-silver eyes stared challengingly at the viewer.

Emme's heart plummeted. This stern man was Timothy Frederick Charles Linwood, the man she had hoped was her F? She met the viscount's haughty stare. Lord Linwood seemed the kind of man who had found little in life amusing. She couldn't conceive of someone who was more Finn's opposite. Well, as she perceived Finn.

Mr. Betton also showed her Marianne's miniature portrait. As was typical for the time period, the tiny portrait had been painted in watercolor on a thin ivory panel. A jeweler had then mounted the miniature into a pretty gold case with a chased filigree edge, covering the front with clear crystal to protect the fragile painting. As was common, the miniature had been turned into a pendant. The recipient would wear the pendent around the neck on a chain or attached as a brooch to a garment, displaying the loved one for all the world to see.

It was rarer to turn a miniature into a locket like Finn, to hide the beloved one away. Usually the image was left exposed to the light like Marianne's portrait. The exposure to sunlight had faded the flesh tones of her skin to gray. However, Emme could see similarities in the way Spunto had painted her: the minuscule brush strokes, the hair thin lines that suggested gentle eyes and a shy smile.

Emme turned the pendant over. There was no locket of hair, no entwined initials, no inscription. Marianne's portrait had clearly been set by a different jeweler. Though painted by the same person, the similarities ended there. It seemed unlikely that Finn had been associated with the Linwoods.

In the end, Mr. Betton had suggested she visit the offices of Hartington, Chatham and Ware. They were a long-standing local solicitor firm that had been around at least since the 1790s, still owned by the same original families. Their old files would have more specific information, particularly as would relate to the gentry of the area.

Emme had been disappointed that F wasn't Lord Linwood. Well, she was choosing to label the emotion disappointment. She didn't want to consider that it was actually relief.

She wanted to find him. Right? She didn't think her life could get any more pathetic.

Emme just needed to know. She needed to know that Finn had sired ten children, had grown stout and lost his hair and then died of influenza. Or that he had been a terrible rake who squandered the family fortune and was killed in a duel for deflowering some innocent girl.

She touched her finger to the glass which protected his portrait. He looked too nice for that. He had probably been just a person. One who had been at times cheerful and irritable and sad and joyful—all the normal emotions of life. And he had loved E. She hoped that E had been worthy of this love, that they had had a good life together.

Throughout all time. Sometimes Emme hated the familiarity of him, the disorientation that sometimes came before being fully awake, when she almost felt him breathing next to her.

Jasmine still doggedly insisted that their lives were interconnected. Emme had long ago decided that Jasmine's well-meaning optimism was at least partially to blame for her own prolonged obsession. Without someone spouting fantasy and keeping these feelings of familiarity and connection alive, would Emme feel so drawn to him? Or was it just the pathetic fact that she couldn't emotionally connect with someone else that had her pining after a dead guy?

Seriously. She needed to get a grip. She was 29 years old and going nowhere with her love life. She was going to do her research, attach names and a story to E and F and purge him from her heart. She was going to move on, find some perfectly normal man who could actually speak with her. It was the not-knowing that made F so powerful, that gave him such a hold on her imagination.

A powerful gust of wind shook the house again, causing a loud crash and bringing Emme back to the present.

She jumped, looking around for the source of the noise and then realized it was the window, the one opposite the table.

Moving toward the window, she saw one of the external shutters had finally come loose and was now flapping with the wind, slamming with each gust. Emme debated just leaving the window as is. The storm was so fierce. But she knew given her luck, the shutter would tear free or worse, crack the window. Then she would have an even larger mess. And she had never been one to avoid a problem.

Gritting her teeth, Emme opened the window and gasped as the storm howled into the room, blasting her skin. Wincing against the pelting rain, she grabbed the errant shutter and, pitting her weight against the roaring wind, pulled it shut. Her drenched fingers slipped twice before she could latch it securely. She was thoroughly wet by the end.

Emme stood dripping in the kitchen, shaking the water off of her hands, red and stinging from the sharp rain. Sighing, she trudged upstairs to soak in a hot bath, change into dry clothing and cuddle into her warm bed.

Later, as she shivered under her covers, Emme had to wonder if she had just averted disaster or if this was merely a sign of things to come.

The dream came, soft and vivid. Emme found herself in a large meadow. The heat of summer sun slid along her back, broken occasionally by a fitful breeze twisting through the canopy of the surrounding forest.

A solitary towering oak spread over the entire meadow, straining to hold up gnarled and twisted branches. Limbs that only a thousand years of life could create.

It was a relic of ancients, of a time when man worshiped nature instead of forcing his will upon it. Emme continued forward into the cool shade of its beckoning arms. The air was suddenly fresher, lighter, purified by thousands of leaves. The tree seemed to sigh and rustle its branches in welcome.

It had been waiting for her.

"Emme! Emme wait!"

She stopped, surprised. Who had found her here?

Turning toward the voice, she saw him, half walking, half running out of the forest. Emme felt a jolt.

She had dreams about *him* from time to time, but he was usually a phantom presence, a shape known but not really seen, just a hazy suggestion of reality. More of a feeling. A longing.

But this was different. Here he was vivid and utterly clear. He walked quickly, anxiety on his face. Emme could see every detail with startling clarity: his golden hair, eyes a shocking blue subtly shifting color as he moved. His coat, not the blue-green in the locket, but instead a brown overcoat swinging down to his boots.

He was so alive, so vibrant. She drank him in. He stopped in front of her, and surprised, Emme realized he wasn't much taller than she.

"Please, Emme," his voice pleaded, gentle and smooth. He reached his hand out tentatively to her. "Please, my love, don't go. Don't leave me."

Emme could only stare, his face so familiar and yet not. He lifted his right hand and gently touched her cheek, his fingers warm and tender.

Emme's heart pounded in her ears.

"Please," he whispered, blue eyes pleading.

Anguish clutched her heart. She had to leave, had to go, but why? She couldn't remember.

He brought his left hand up to cup her face in his hands. His touch searing her skin.

"I don't think I can live without you. Please. Stay."

Emme still said nothing. Her voice choked, eyes blurred. She felt his thumbs brush the tears from her cheeks. He drew her near, sliding his arms down around her waist, pulling her close. Emme felt a gasp escape, heavy emotions crushing her. She wrapped her arms fiercely around his neck, twining her fingers into his hair, pulling his head tight against her own. She could feel his breath hot on her neck.

Was the trembling her? Him? He moaned in her ear, burrowing his lips into her hair.

Suddenly, the oak tree came alive, branches reaching, wrapping around her. Emme was wrenched backward, lifted, ripped from his embrace. Terrified, she tried to scream and reached out for him. She stared at his horrified face, his stricken eyes. His hand outstretched, just enough to brush her fingertips before they were utterly torn apart. He was yelling something she could not hear as more branches filled the growing space between them. She watched him frantically push against the woody vines, trying desperately to reach her. Emme twisted and turned, trying to free herself, but the snaking tendrils held her tighter. Over the sound of crunching, grinding wood, she heard him.

"No! No! NOOOO!"

His cry still echoed in her bedroom as Emme shot upright, bedclothes tangled and twisted around her legs.

Chapter 6

Emme's heart pounded with adrenaline as she wiped her damp cheeks. Thunder pounded through the room. What a terrible dream. She sat shaking in her bed, trying to understand. It had been so clear, so real. The anguished sense of loss lingered.

The storm still raged, somehow even more furious, rattling her bedroom window, battering the roof overhead.

Taking a deep breath, Emme realized the night was dark. Too dark. Swathed in inky-blackness dark. Emme blinked, straining to see some glimmer of light. The power was out.

A sudden crash of lightning illuminated the room. Emme caught a startled scream in her throat.

Really? The whole jumpy-jumpy thing was getting old.

Rain beat heavily on the roof above her head. Something outside repeatedly thumped in the wind.

Horrific storm, disturbing dreams and now no power. Perfect. She refused to think about how this disaster could get worse. No need to tempt fate.

Sighing, Emme rolled over and punched her pillow, trying to calm her mind. But not succeeding.

Her phone suddenly *bing*ed in the darkness of the room. Reaching for it, she pushed the home button and then blinked against the instant brightness.

Text message. Jasmine.

you up

> Yes, bad storm. No power. Terrible dreams.

on beltane that's such bad luck

> Not helping.
> Why am I so obsessed with a dead man?
> It's wrong.

your head is messed

> Exactly. It's beyond pathetic. Don't you think it's time to exorcise Finn?

no i've been telling you for years that he is part of you circles intertwined and all

> You know comments like that just don't help, right? Feeding my Finn addiction isn't in my best interest right now. You're supposed to be my friend. Not my enabler.

i'm not enabling you, you just haven't been listening, i'm telling you that Finn is your destiny

> Wait! Did you just use punctuation?! Wow. You must be serious.

more serious than i've ever been. period. you are linked and he will
find you. it's your fate

When would this obsession end? How had it gotten so out of control? Emme texted a few more lines and then said goodnight, turning off her phone screen.

She was now good and wide awake. And the power was still out. But when she twisted to look out the window, she could see lights punctuating the darkness here and there through the storm. Marfield wasn't dark. Just Duir Cottage. Which meant that it was most likely a popped fuse. She really should wait until morning. But then her laptop wouldn't be fully charged. And the baseboard heaters would be off all night. And it was cold.

And Emme was never one to put off a problem.

She threw off her warm covers, trying to ignore the rush of cold air against her skin. She loved her nightgown, old-fashioned and trailing to the floor, but its silk fabric wasn't much for retaining body heat. She picked up the matching robe and pulled it on, tying its little ribbons across her chest, stuffing her feet into her pink slippers. Grabbing her phone, she flipped on its flashlight.

Following the weak, ghostly light of her phone, she navigated the stairs as thunder rumbled. The house still felt alive, thrumming with energy. Emme took in a measured breath, trying to remember if she had seen a breaker box anywhere. Her memory pulled up nothing.

She reached the bottom of the stairs, puzzling through the options. The kitchen? No. Laundry room? No. Was it in the closet underneath the stairs? She hadn't done more than casually glance through closets, but it was a possibility. Lightning pulsed through the house instantly flooding every corner with light. A crackling crash of thunder immediately followed. The energy in the air tingled her skin. The booming sound trembled the floor beneath her feet. Emme's heart raced. This storm needed to be over.

She pulled open the little door to the hallway closet, shining her light to inspect it. She noted the vacuum cleaner and bucket of cleaning supplies, and then her light illuminated something shiny on the floor. Bending down, she realized it was a handle to a trap door. Ah, a cellar. That would be a likely place for the breaker box. She briefly imagined the whole house shining with light, banishing all the ghoulish shadows of the storm. Yes, electricity would be good.

It was simple to twist the handle and pull up the trap door, locking the hinge to hold the door open. To her chagrin, Emme couldn't help but remember all the movies where bad things happened to heroines—particularly those who wandered into dark unknown basements in the middle of thunderstorms. But she was hardly a heroine. And this was most definitely not a horror story. Spiders were the worst she would find, right?

Her phone light showed steep wooden stairs leading downward, dusty and darkened with age. Gathering the long skirt of her nightgown into her hands, she carefully descended the stairs, ducking her head as she went. At the bottom of the steps, her feet touched uneven ground, packed dirt. The room smelled musty and cool, of things long shuttered and ignored, the rumbling thunder muted. Swinging her phone around, she made out a space just larger than the span of her arms, lined with large cut stones. Her head nearly brushed the ceiling.

A shadow of something unexpected caught her eye on the wall opposite the stairs. The breaker box? Another sweep of her light and she saw that one stone was larger than the others, nearly two feet wide and traveling the height of the space, from floor to ceiling. Stepping closer to inspect, Emme leaned forward.

Impossible! Just impossible. She must be seeing things.

An emotion somewhere between panic and thrilled hysteria swept her. Swallowing hard, she forced herself to think, trying to comprehend what she might be seeing.

She needed a stronger light. And Finn.

Taking a deep fortifying breath, she raced back up the stairs, stumbling over her nightgown, dashing frantically into the kitchen. Where was her purse? Where had she left it?

Glancing around wildly, she cursed the weak light from her phone, unable to penetrate the blackness around her. Another burst of light flashed through the room, allowing her to see her purse lying on the kitchen table. Two steps and she had it in her hand.

She grabbed it and shoved her hand inside, looking for her more powerful flashlight. Finding it and turning it on, she dropped her now dark cell phone into the purse and then dug Finn out of a padded side pocket. Her tablet with all her research notes was in her purse too, so she closed the bag and slung it over her shoulder, wrapping Finn's chain around her palm, clutching him in her fist.

With the bright flashlight in one hand and Finn in the other, she headed back down the stairs.

Once her slippered feet hit the packed dirt, she took a deep breath to steady herself. Honestly, she was probably just seeing things. It had been an unsettling night. Another round of thunder vibrated through the house, as if to emphasize her mental point. The air was alive with charged particles. She shone the light forward, not sure what to expect.

It was still there, illuminated clearly in the center of her light, on the large stone that stretched from floor to ceiling.

She took a step, her breath loud and harsh in her ears. She swallowed and then lifted the locket in her other hand to compare.

It was the same. Exactly.

The curvy intertwined initials on the back of the locket were etched into the stone on the wall, mirror perfect.

Impossible.

The symbol was too unique to be coincidence. What connection could F possibly have to this house? Why carve initials here too? It was so fantastic. Too amazing.

She took another two steps forward, eyes still darting back and forth between the locket clutched in her outstretched hand and the symbol on the rock, comparing just to be sure.

Yes, it really was the same.

Close enough now, she quickly looped Finn around her neck to free her hand. Lightning pulsed long and sustained, bright enough to illuminate even the dark cellar. Emme felt the hair on her arms and neck raise, prickling with electricity. Thunder vibrated heavily through the air, causing the trapdoor behind her to slam shut.

She stretched out her hand to trace the symbol on the rock, wanting to confirm with touch what her eyes already knew. That it was real.

The bristling feeling of charged electricity became stronger, magnetic, almost pulling her arm forward of its own accord. Blinking in surprise at the sensation, Emme touched the stone.

And then true disaster struck.

Emme saw a blinding flash of light and felt the strong jolt course through her, matched by crashing that threatened to burst her ears. She was pulled forward and vertigo over swept her.

She was falling, falling, falling.

And then suddenly she was not. She could feel pelting rain against her face, wind tugging at her body. A flash of light illuminated black sky as she swayed gasping in the sudden biting cold.

What had happened? Where was she?

Branches whipped at her, tugging at her nightgown now soaked through. Wrapping her arms around her chest, Emme staggered forward trying to see through the gloom, but wooden arms kept grabbing at her. Trying to catch her. Stumbling, she desperately tried to see some sort of habitation in the inky blackness, but limbs tripped her as she lurched onward.

She didn't know how long she struggled to walk. The cold seeped deep into her bones and made dodging branches harder. A sudden pulse of lightning showed a slight clearing in the trees ahead. Maybe it would contain some sort of shelter.

She hurried forward, a buffeting gust pushing fiercely against her back. Suddenly, a loud crack sounded. Something heavy knocked her head.

And then blackness took her.

Chapter 7

James was almost home. He pulled his coat tightly around his shoulders, trying to ignore the damp that seeped into his bones. He conjured the image of a hot fire and warm bath waiting for him. Anything to pull his mind from the pelting rain.

Suddenly, lightning lit the sky bright as noon-day, causing Luther to jump and dance sideways. The bolt was more than just the usual flicker of light. It was a cascade that lingered, pulsed, illuminating the world bright as noon day for several long seconds. Casting forest and path into sharp relief. The lightning faded slowly, pulsing again and again. James could taste the metallic air, his hair prickling from the electricity. Long before the light faded, thunder cracked and then boomed, trembling the earth.

But within the loud rumble, James heard something else. A distinct crash to his left, the sound of something large shattering. The sound continued after the thunder faded, echoing through the dark night.

James paused, his mind racing to identify the noise. The lightning must have struck something. Something large. There was really only one possibility.

The ancient oak tree. That age-old relic of earlier times with its enormous branches over-stretching a meadow in the middle of his land.

Everyone well knew the propensity that oaks had to attract lightning. Though usually if the strike were not severe, the tree could survive. Granted, that bolt of lightning had been less of a glancing blow and more like a full-fledged battle. The ancient oak losing.

With sinking heart, James realized that such a powerful jolt could actually kill the tree. If true, this did not bode well. The villagers were already so superstitious about the gigantic oak, claiming that it held supernatural powers. What mayhem would they read into its destruction? Particularly on Beltane? James sighed inwardly. Perhaps he was wrong. The noise could have been something else. Perhaps.

James shook his head and urged Luther forward. Nothing could be done about it tonight regardless; he just wanted to be dry. He continued along the road, focusing on reaching his warm bed.

Lightning flashed yet again, leaving the impression of white trees and dark sky lingering in front of his eyes. Trees and briefly something else. A flicker of white lying off the side of the path, a bare arm clutched against a tree. Puzzled, James stopped again and waited for the next pulse to light the sky. When it came, it confirmed what he had seen: a figure dressed in white clinging to a tree trunk, dark hair wet and tangled.

What insanity would bring a person out into a night like this?

James urged Luther forward and then dismounted, waiting for another burst of light before plotting his path off of the lane. Light skittered across the sky, lighting a woman's slender body crouched low, her eyes closed, skin gray with cold.

Fearing the worst, James stumbled through knee-high brush lining the lane, sinking to her side. He used his teeth to strip off a glove and brushing rain from his eyes, tentatively felt for her neck in the pelting darkness. Her skin was slick and cold to his touch, short hair clinging to his hand. James exhaled in relief when he felt her pulse, strong and steady.

"Madam?" he asked, shaking her gently. No response.

Another flash of light showed that she was thinly dressed in what appeared to be a nightgown and wrapper, the drenched fabric plastered to her figure. She shivered and trembled with cold.

How had a woman thinly dressed come to be on his lane in this weather? She must be a tenant or some other young woman from the village, lost in the storm. Though it seemed odd. Terribly odd, as he thought about it.

Knowing she would likely die of exposure without his help, James slid his arms under her and gently carried her back to the waiting Luther. Somehow James managed to place her limp body before his saddle and then swing up behind her, clutching her close. Curious, he pulled her slightly away from his body, brushing hair from her cheeks

James waited.

When the lightning came, it lit her face. Oval, fine-boned, features delicate and regular.

A haunting face. An unfamiliar face.

And yet somehow not.

A jolt of recognition.

Not so much a memory. More a sense of knowing. As if his whole life had been coming to this moment. To her.

Which—given his current situation—seemed a little . . . unexpected.

James shook his head. He must be more exhausted than he thought. He never felt this way about women. Particularly strangers found clinging to trees along his lane. In the middle of the night. During a thunderstorm of epic proportions.

She shivered more violently and quietly moaned. Who was she?

Tucking her trembling body against his chest, James wrapped his greatcoat around her, hoping his body heat would help. Whoever this woman was, she was not from Marfield. This woman he would remember. How had she come to be here on a night such as this?

James had had quite enough adventure for one night. Cradling the unknown woman's body closer, he turned Luther for home.

Chapter 8

Hours later, James, finally dressed in dry clothing and wrapped in a warm banyan, silently entered the bedroom. He was ready to drop from fatigue. His restless body begged for stillness and sleepy oblivion. But courtesy—and curiosity, if he were honest—required that he check on his guest. And James Knight might legitimately be called many things, but discourteous was not one of them.

The mysterious woman lay under the counterpane, her breaths gently stirring the heavy blanket, short dark hair spread on the pillow. Though still pale, her color was much improved, her breathing more even.

Again, he felt that strange sense of familiarity. Like he knew her.

But he didn't. He was confident they had never met. Perhaps she reminded him of an acquaintance or the relative of a friend—just enough connection to give that sense of recognition. He found it puzzling.

James walked to the fireplace opposite the foot of the bed. Candles danced on the mantle and bedside table, reflecting off the dark paneled wainscoting and blue bed hangings. A fire crackled brightly in the hearth, lighting and giving the room a cozy warmth.

Georgiana sat in a chair next to the large bed, her face weary, fingers of one hand stroking her long golden braid. She was so thin, so fragile. Truthfully, she looked more in need of rest than the woman she watched over. Georgiana coughed—thankfully shallow for now—and looked up, seeing him.

She instantly stiffened, something tense and unreadable in her eyes.

"How is she?" he asked quietly.

"Resting," Georgiana replied, her tone shuttered. "She does not have a fever. Aside from some scratches, she seems to be in fine health. Just tired and recovering from the cold. She is an utter mystery to *me*." Georgiana oddly emphasized that last word, meeting his eyes challengingly. Expectantly.

James tilted his head, confusion apparent. Georgiana's agitation was a subtle thing, showing only in the rigid uprightness of her shoulders, in the clipped emphasis of her speech.

"Well, once the storm breaks, I will send for the doctor. Perhaps he will have more answers for us," James said, scrubbing a tired hand through his hair.

Whatever upset Georgiana could wait until morning. A good sleep often solved most arguments anyway. Georgiana looked exhausted. She needed rest more than any of them.

"Is there something you would like to tell me, James?"

Georgie did not want to wait, apparently.

She stood and walked toward him, her hand a fist at her side. She took in a breath as she stopped in front of him.

"I have always trusted you. As I hope that you will always trust me. With anything." Her face again expectant and now also slightly accusatory.

James sighed the sigh—that sound that men intuitively perfect from the cradle. That sigh that connotes equal parts weariness and resignation.

That can-you-just-tell-me-what-I-need-to-say-so-I-can-go-to-bed sigh.

"Georgie. . . ." He paused letting out a tired puff of air. "I'm tired. I've had a long day and an even longer night. I would really just like to find my bed." He waited, pushing all his fatigue and cluelessness into his face.

"I trust you," she said her low tone injured. "When anyone says a word against you, I defend you. When Arthur criticizes your behavior, I take your side. When Linwood or Marianne start in on your lack of propriety, I stand up for you. I have always championed you. Never played you false. Why would you not trust me in this? Do you think me too young to understand?"

She blinked rapidly, her chest heaving, and then she coughed, deep and harsh.

James blinked. He searched his memory, trying to think of something, anything he might have done. . . . Nothing. He had nothing. The silence between them lengthened, stretched. His night had only needed this.

He swallowed. "I know this will only make things worse, but I honestly have no idea what I have done. I have always tried to be honest with you, Georgie. You know I deeply value your loyalty. I would trust you with anything. Everything. You are truly the best and brightest part of my life. I don't know. . . . I mean . . ."

His voice trailed off. James shook his head, sighing that sigh again and running a hand again through his hair. "Georgie you really should be in bed. Your health . . ."

Georgiana clenched her jaw even tighter, naked hurt blazing in her eyes, making James feel like the worst sort of scoundrel. For what, he had no idea.

How did women do this, filling a man with unknown guilt? Was it something they cultivated or was it a god-given talent?

"Why, James? Why would you persist in denying this? To me of all people?" The aching emotion in her voice cut him.

"Georgie, please," James pleaded, fighting to keep exasperation out of his voice. "How have I not trusted you?"

"What is this then?" She quietly raised her fisted hand and slowly opened it, revealing a locket nestled in a golden chain. "It's something that obviously means so much to you. Why would you not tell me? Did you wish to keep it from me until . . . until . . . " Her voice trailed off. But James easily filled in what she left unsaid.

Until I am gone. Until I am dead.

She waited expectantly. As if this would suddenly change everything.

Giving Georgiana a quizzical look, James took the locket from her upturned palm. "Is this locket supposed to mean something to me?"

He laid it in his hand, its gold case catching the light, throwing filigree decoration into sharp relief.

Georgiana rolled her eyes at him. Actually rolled her eyes. She had probably been thirteen-years-old the last time she had done that.

"Truly, do you think me a complete idiot? That you could bring her here and none of us would be the wiser?" Georgiana gestured toward the still figure in the bed. "Who is she, James? Your mistress? A secret wife? How could you . . ." She paused, reconsidered. Coughed again, sharp and bleak.

Yes, James was definitely floundering. "What is going on? What would ever make you think that I know this woman? Honestly. I never laid eyes on her until this evening. Truly. My story is exactly as I told. I found her along side the road. Why would you not believe me?"

Georgiana sighed, reached for the locket in his hand and opened it. She turned it in her hand so the light illuminated the image on the inside right. Frowning, James took the locket from her again and stepped closer to the candelabra on the mantle, tilting the portrait into the dim light.

He gasped. And then swore, lowly and impressively.

His own face gazed back at him. Or what seemed like his own face. The resemblance was almost eery: blond hair styled just as he wore his, playful blue-eyes, strong jaw. Even more strange was the blue-green jacket the figure wore. He had ordered just such a jacket from his tailor.

Puzzled, James turned the locket over in his hands, noting the gilt showed some slight wear in places. It was obviously not new. An utter mystery. Where had such a thing come from?

"Where did you get this?" he questioned again, looking up at Georgiana and shaking his head in baffled wonder.

"She had it." Georgiana gestured toward the bed. "Around her neck."

Still shaking his head, James turned back to the locket. Uncanny. How could such a thing exist?

"The resemblance is remarkable," he said, lifting his eyes to Georgiana's. "But truthfully, this is not me. Sincerely. All appearances to the contrary, I am not the man in this portrait. Please, you must believe me." His eyes pleaded.

A coughing fit suddenly swept Georgiana. Instantly, James wrapped his arm around her and half carried her back to her chair, settling a blanket around her shoulders as she sank down.

"Really, Georgie. You should be in bed. This night will half kill you. Perhaps when our guest awakes in the morning, she will have a simple explanation. It is possible that there is another man in the world who resembles me. Besides," he turned to the locket again, "this locket has seen wear and must be several years old at least. And the man in the image is as I am as of this moment. Not a younger version of myself. So you see, it cannot possibly be . . . rather, it is *not* me." James turned the locket in his hand again, trying to better discern the sitter's identity.

"Oh, James," Georgiana whispered with a sigh. "I suppose I do believe you." She blinked, as if trying to convince herself.

"Truly, Georgiana, she is unknown to me." James pled for understanding with his eyes. "I would not lie to you about this. Why would I keep something like this from you?"

He turned the locket over in his hands again and caught a glimpse of lettering opposite the portrait. With a low exclamation, he tilted the locket into the light and then read the inscription.

"Ah-ha! You see, Georgie, here is proof!" He jabbed at the locket with his finger. "Proof that this is not me. Read this inscription."

Crinkling her forehead, Georgiana leaned forward and read:

To E
throughout all time
heart of my soul
your F

"Oh!" she breathed. "I hadn't noticed that!"

"My initials are neither E nor F, thank goodness," James chuckled in relief. "So you see, I speak truth. This isn't me. It is just an odd coincidence." James breathed a hefty sigh. He had started to doubt his own sanity as well. But truly, it was simply a twist of fate, nothing more.

"Please tell me you believe me now? Truthfully, I have always held your trust dear and have sought to be worthy of it. I would never abuse you in such a manner. Were I to take a wife—secret or no—you would be first to hear of it." James arched his eyebrows conspiratorially.

Georgiana managed a weak smile. "Perhaps, James. Though you have given me such a fright tonight. To wonder why you would not trust me," she swallowed. "It was horrid."

She paused suddenly and then noticeably brightened. "But who is this mystery woman then? How intriguing!"

James watched his sister's eyes light up. Georgie loved nothing so much as a good mystery. Some puzzle to unwind. She devoured gothic novels at an alarming pace, reading them again and again.

"Incredible! You find a strange woman lying by the side of our lane in the middle of a terrible storm. And then she just happens to have a locket of a man who looks astonishingly like you around her neck. Oooooh! How romantic! I cannot wait to hear her story!"

She was grinning from ear to ear now. For the briefest moment, her illness fell away, and James saw the young woman she had been a year ago. Vibrant, curious, bouncing with life. But then a cough intruded. Deeper, persistent.

"Georgie, you must go to bed," James urged, his voice all concern. He placed a hand under her elbow to help her rise. "Your patient is resting easily. And as you said, there is no fever as of yet. I will have Fanny look in on her once before morning. She can let us know if anything is amiss." Georgiana nodded in acceptance and rose to her feet.

The mysterious woman stirred in the bed beside them. She moaned and tossed her head back and forth, her lips moving soundlessly, eyelids fluttering. James released Georgiana's arm and, picking up a candle from the bedside table, leaned over their guest.

He swept her face with its light, surveying the smooth porcelain of her complexion. It was nearly unnatural, as if she had never known the mark of illness. She looked so young, younger than Georgiana. Almost absently, he noted the lack of a wedding band on her left hand.

"Madam?" James said, gently shaking her shoulder. "Madam, are you awake? Can you hear me?"

She moaned again and then slowly, blearily opened her eyes, blinking into the dim candlelight. She struggled to focus on James' face, drawing her head back into the pillow. Narrowing her eyes, she gazed at him. An emotion flickered within her. Not quite recognition but . . . something. As if seeing him were important somehow. Pursing her lips, she scrunched her forehead, shifted her gaze to Georgiana beyond his shoulder, blinked and then brought her eyes back to James.

"Welcome," James said. "I am Mr. James Knight and this is my sister, Miss Georgiana Knight. You are in our care at Haldon Manor. You seem to have had an eventful night. May I ask your name?"

Their guest looked puzzled and lowered her eyes slightly, darting them back and forth as if deeply pondering his question. Her lips moved in agitation, and then she lifted her gaze.

"I don't know," she whispered, eyes wild and terrified. "I don't know who I am."

Chapter 9

Emme couldn't breathe. Blood pounded in her ears and her lungs fought to fill with air. Anxiety overwhelmed her.

You're having a panic attack. A quiet part of her mind helpfully labeled the sensation for her. Taking deep breaths, she tried to calm her racing heart.

This was okay. Everything was going to be okay. Emme closed her eyes and mentally hunted again. This was absurd. Of course she knew who she was. But the harder she tried to capture the information, the more it skittered just out of reach.

Nothing. She remembered nothing.

She didn't know her name, her family, her history. She had no memory of anything before this moment. No sense of how she had ended up in this bed with strangers bending over her. As if a heavy fog had rolled in over her mind, smothering every effort to reach through it. Emme breathed in slowly and deeply, trying to contain the fluttering hysteria pressing in.

Opening her eyes, Emme grimaced at the pulsing pain against her skull. Dizziness assaulted her as the room tilted on a crazy axis. Wincing, she focused on the couple leaning over her in the dim light and, with effort, brought them into coherent shapes. Slowly their forms stopped moving for a moment, allowing Emme to see them clearly.

The woman was thin and frail-looking, though pretty with her heart-shaped face and wide-set large eyes. She had a fey, otherworldly quality.

But it was the man who demanded her attention. His blond hair and sculpted face seemed . . . familiar. Familiar and yet not at the same time.

For some reason, seeing him felt momentous. Important. Significant.

Her mind associated his cultured accent with rose perfume, blue hair and the clink of fine-boned china.

Emme drew in a shallow, stuttering breath, trying desperately to control her panic. "Do I know you?" she asked the man, low and wispy, instinctively matching the cadence of her voice to his.

She groaned as the throbbing pounding inside her head increased. Emme fought against the blackness skittering in, determined to claim her.

"I'm sorry, madam," the man said quietly, his voice farther away and tinny. "We have never met before tonight."

She closed her eyes and licked her lips, letting a gasp escape. Her back arched slightly. The pain and crushing anxiety dragging her under.

"Heavens, James!" The woman's voice sounded from far away. "What a mystery. But she is in such pain. I have some of my laudanum. That should help."

Dimly through the growing fog, gentle hands lifted Emme up. She swallowed the bitter liquid pressed against her lips.

And then allowed oblivion to claim her.

The weather had finally lifted. In the days since returning home, rain and wind had lashed Haldon Manor relentlessly. But this morning, a bleary sun gingerly peeked out from loose clouds.

James glanced appraisingly at the still dripping world as he descended to the breakfast room. His muscles twitched to be outside and doing something. Anything. He had been grateful that Ethan Fletcher had braved the storm, showing up in his study dripping water and a wicked grin, anxious for trouble. They had fenced until their muscles collapsed into a rubbery mass. But that restless energy was back again today. It never left him for too long.

James had just checked on their mystery guest. She lay asleep and motionless in the bed, her breaths deep and slow. She had drifted in and out of consciousness over the last two days, but each time she woke, her memory had not returned.

He had forced himself not to linger beside her quiet sleeping form. Forced himself not to think about the pull he felt toward her. Decidedly did not trace the graceful curve of her jaw with his eyes.

He most certainly was not going to ponder upon what drew him to her. They knew nothing about her. And there was the man in the locket who most likely had an emotional, if not legal, bond to her.

The doctor had come and gone earlier, finding a large bump on the back of the young lady's skull, and pronouncing that she most likely suffered a concussed head. This also explained her memory loss. The doctor could give them no assurances as to when or if her memory would return. Only time would tell. Other than the blow to her head, however, he had found nothing else wrong with her. She seemed strong and healthy with no sign of fever or other injury. But he recommended that she remain in bed for several more days.

What they were to do with her after that remained to be seen. The good doctor had volunteered to help them find her identity, her people, asking during the course of his visits if anyone knew of her. James was confident that, with the storm now passed, the word would spread quickly. Someone surely would come soon to claim her.

And until then, who knew? Perhaps this latest bit of gossip would finally eclipse the incident involving Miss Croft and the vicar's wandering heifer. James still recalled hearing the gunshot and running to see Miss Croft, righting her mobcap on her graying hair, as she glared angrily at the vicar, smoking gun in her hand. The poor vicar had stared at his dead cow, lying in the remains of Miss Croft's prized vegetable garden, which it had disturbed for the last time.

The incident still held first place with the local gossip mill, even four years later. Ample proof, yet again, that nothing exciting ever happened in Marfield.

James entered the breakfast room to find his brother and sister already there. Georgiana sat while Arthur filled a plate for her from the dishes along the sideboard. Her color was improved, though her soft blue morning dress hung loosely on her bony shoulders. He felt again the stab of pure anguish, that desolate confirmation that he would lose her. The disease would slowly eat her until only a shell was left. James exhaled slowly. He would find a way, something that would save her.

James nodded a greeting as Arthur turned toward the table, handing Georgiana her plate. Arthur sat and James strode over to the waiting chafing dishes.

"I thought Ethan would be over again this morning for another fencing bout," Arthur commented as James piled his plate with coddled eggs and crisp sausage. "Your boundless energy is ever a source of annoyance."

"True, brother," James agreed, glancing at the filtered light streaming through the north facing window, "though you must know by now I only live to be an irritation to you. Of course, all would be solved if you would agree to join me in a match or two. We could even use quarterstaffs." James finished filling his plate and sat himself at the head of the table.

"Ha! As if I would engage in something so decidedly common. Sticks have never been a nobleman's weapon." Arthur waived his hand dismissively, turning his brown head back to his food. "Swords are all a gentleman needs. "

James snorted and cocked an eyebrow at his brother. "Really? Is that truly the reason? Or are you just not in the mood for another of my humblings?"

As a general rule, Arthur did not engage in activities he could not win.

"I promise to let you win," James continued disingenuously. "Well, at least once . . . maybe." He threw a wink at Georgiana.

"Oh, James, don't bait poor Arthur." Georgiana smiled a tight little grin that said she loved him but did not quite approve.

Arthur grunted in agreement, not looking up.

James grinned, his wide mouth crinkling his cheeks. "Please, brother-baiting is a time honored tradition."

Georgiana shook her head, turning back to move her eggs around her plate.

Arthur cleared his throat and changed the topic, raising his gray eyes to James. "And how fares our guest this morning? I overheard the doctor as he left."

"She is well. Still unconscious, so we will just wait until she wakes. Fanny is with her and will alert us." James waited patiently, watching the cogs turn in Arthur's head. Understanding his brother as he did, James knew exactly where this conversation was heading. Arthur was nothing if not predictable.

Arthur paused, grimacing. Down went his knife and fork.

Ah, here it came.

"Truly James, this whole situation is most unusual. She really should not be allowed to remain here."

James raised an eyebrow. "Indeed, Arthur? I am not in the habit of tossing unconscious young women out of my house."

"You know that is not what I meant."

"Really? Then what do you mean?"

Arthur sighed and leaned back in his chair, crossing his arms across his chest. "This whole situation is dashed improper, particularly with Georgie in the house. I am sure the vicar and his wife would take her in until she is recovered enough to return from whence she came. Or until someone comes to fetch her. What will others say about this situation?"

James shrugged. He wasn't sure if he should be annoyed at Arthur's extreme sense of propriety or amused by his predictability.

Arthur neatly placed people into boxes clearly labeled with tags like *Esteemed Nobleman* or *Virtuous Lady* or *Lowly Relation*. And as their mystery lady did not yet fit into any known box, Arthur had preemptively put her into the box stamped *Dangerous Connection*.

"James, how can you have such little sense?" Arthur continued, pursing his mouth in annoyance. "What will happen when Linwood hears of this? I'm sure he will forbid Marianne from visiting. And . . . and what will Sir Henry think?"

James barely resisted the urge roll his eyes. "Please, Arthur. As you are well aware, I am not overly concerned about the opinions of our erstwhile neighbors. Linwood does not need the excuse of a stranger under my roof to forbid Miss Marianne from seeing you. He will deprive you of her company merely because the sky threatens rain. Or because he doesn't like the look of your cravat. Or because it's Thursday. He needs no real excuse."

Georgiana made a noise that sounded suspiciously like a choked snort.

"And as for Sir Henry," James continued, "I guarantee that he will be ecstatic to make our guest's acquaintance. She is a mystery and therefore somewhat exotic. And you know, there is nothing Sir Henry loves more than the exotic. In fact, I completely expect him to show his face here as soon as the gossip reaches Sutton Hall. Which most likely will be sometime this afternoon, I warrant. The good doctor's housekeeper is usually most diligent in spreading scandal which is not her own."

"Yes, well, it has been three days and no one has come for her yet." Ah, Arthur and his persistence.

"Please, Arthur. The storm broke only last night. How could anyone have been out searching for her in such weather? I am sure that the village gossips will ferret out her story in no time. Most likely, someone will be on our doorstep this afternoon to collect our guest."

Arthur merely huffed and shook his head at his older brother. "In the meantime, James, at least think of poor Georgiana's reputation. To have a woman like this in our household will be scandalous."

"Oh, heavens, Arthur," Georgiana interjected, her fork clattering to her plate. "Please. As if propriety concerns me at this point. It would be a glorious thing if all I had to worry about were my reputation." She punctuated this with a small coughing fit, drawing a shaking breath. "Besides, what about this woman has you so convinced that she would be a threat to my reputation?"

Arthur shrugged, trying to buy himself time to come up with an appropriate response.

James knew Arthur had no real argument. Just the sense that this woman did not immediately fit into his brother's neatly labeled world and therefore must be cast out of it. An opinion James did not share.

Arthur tried changing topics. "And what of her supposed memory loss," he asked. "Are you so sure that it is genuine?"

"Arthur! How could you think that? Really, you are just trying to be vexing!" Georgiana exclaimed, turning to James. "Is he just trying to be vexing?"

James smiled ruefully. "As you well know, dear sister, Arthur can generally be annoying without having to try." Georgiana laughed appreciatively.

Arthur heaved his most resigned you-are-both-a-trial-to-me sigh.

Still smiling, James held his hand in a placating gesture. "But it is actually a valid question. To answer you, Arthur, both Georgie and I were there when she woke for the first time. Her distress at not being able to remember her own name was, well, almost overwhelming to her. She would have to be better than any Drury Lane actress I have ever seen to pull off such a convincing performance. I do believe her memory loss to be genuine."

"You should be ashamed of yourself, Arthur, instantly thinking the worst of her." Georgiana gave Arthur a stern look. "Personally, I think it's utterly thrilling."

"Thrilling?" Arthur's voice was incredulous. "What is possibly thrilling about this ridiculous situation?"

Georgiana shook her head, clearly disappointed with his inability to see the obvious. "It's such a thrilling mystery. Who is she? How did she come here? I have been doing some detective work, you know," Georgiana said, her voice animated.

James loved seeing her blue eyes dance, looking so much like the woman she had been.

"Ugh, Georgiana, you have read one too many novels by that dreadful Radcliffe woman." Arthur gave a decidedly long suffering shake of his head.

"And what, dear sister, have you deduced?" James chuckled.

Georgiana wriggled in excitement. James couldn't remember the last time she had done so. It warmed his heart, her wriggling.

"Here are my thoughts. Our mysterious guest—let's call her E, as that is what it says on the lock—" She caught herself abruptly, looking questioningly at James and then glancing at Arthur.

"I haven't told him," James said, slanting his eyes toward his brother.

Arthur cocked an eyebrow. "Told me what?" His expression grew slightly alarmed as Georgiana and James continued to look at each other. "What have you discovered? You know our guest's name?"

"Not a name exactly . . . more like her initial." Turning his head to Georgiana, James asked, "Do you have it with you?"

"Yes, I do. I have kept it on my person. No one else has seen it."

Arthur continued to glance back and forth between his siblings. "Come now," he said. "What are you keeping from me?"

James shrugged his shoulders in acceptance. Georgiana gently reached into a hidden pocket in her morning dress and withdrew the filigreed locket. Wordlessly, she handed it across the table to Arthur. Puzzled, he slowly opened it.

His loud gasp echoed through the empty room.

"Dash it, James! What have you been keeping from us?!" he exclaimed, still staring at the portrait in the locket. "How could you?!"

James sighed and ran a hand through his hair, opening his mouth to reply.

Georgiana cut him off. "Look at the inscription, Arthur. It's not a portrait of James." Arthur read the etched words with pursed lips, a frown clouding his brow.

"It seems almost too much of a coincidence to be believed," Arthur said in a low voice, staring accusingly at his older brother.

"I agree," James sighed. "But I can only tell the truth. I do not know our mystery guest. Trust me, I would remember a face such as hers."

Georgiana's eyebrows rose at this admission.

"I honestly never laid eyes on her until two nights ago. The locket is truly a random act of fate."

Arthur snorted in disbelief.

"Why would I lie to either of you about this? What would I gain? If she were known to me, I would admit it freely. Both of you know me well enough to realize this. I have never been one to hide my deeds in the dark. I am as I seem. You know it was Mother's greatest despair. My inability to pretend something that I am not."

"Yes, that is true," Arthur nodded in agreement, handing the locket back to Georgiana. "You do generally own up to your improprieties. But even for you, this situation is highly unusual. No one else will believe it."

"Agreed," Georgiana said, tucking the locket back into her pocket, "which is why no one else has been—or will be—told about the locket's existence. There is no need to fuel gossip further by implying some untrue connection between this woman and James. The locket will remain our secret. Even from Marianne." She said the last bit looking most forbiddingly straight at Arthur.

"Not tell Marianne?"

"Yes, particularly not Marianne." Georgiana cut him off with a wave of her hand. "You know she cannot keep a secret from Linwood. And he is the last person who should know about this odd coincidence. Things are already awkward enough with him. Really, next time you decide to carry on a not-so-secret, we-are-not-precisely-engaged engagement, please choose someone who's brother is a little less high in the instep."

Arthur held her eyes for a moment and then looked tensely away.

James shrugged, trying to understand when his world had become all Shakespearean. A brother bound by honor on one side and desperate aching love on the other. A sister dying of consumption. A half-dead maiden discovered clinging to a tree along his lane. He only needed the ghost of his dead father to appear to round out the play. James wanted adventure. Not drama.

"Fine. I will refrain from telling Marianne . . . for the time being."

"Thank you, brother." James turned to Georgiana, "You were saying earlier, Georgie, that you had made some deductions about our mystery guest?"

"Oh, yes!" Georgie smiled, sitting up straighter. "It is amazing how much one can learn from so little! So here are my thoughts." She paused for dramatic effect. "To begin, I am convinced that our guest is a lady."

Arthur raised his eyebrows in disbelief.

"Before you say anything, hear my reasoning on this. First," Georgiana raised a hand and ticked off fingers as she spoke, "the portrait she carried is obviously the work of a competent master, not to mention the case which is gilded and beautifully designed. It has the mark of a master-jeweler.

"Second, her hands are softer than my own and perfectly manicured. Not a single callous. They are the hands of a high-born lady.

"Third, the few times she has spoken, she has the refined accent of a genteel education.

"Fourth, she has such a delightfully fashionable haircut. Truly. I have rarely seen its equal. Only the best French hairdresser could have cut it.

"And lastly, Fanny and I examined that nightgown and wrapper she was wearing when James found her. Can you believe that they are both made of the finest silk? Two utterly proper garments, but for some reason made of the most luxurious, expensive fabric. Oh, and her shoes! Pink satin slippers, so similar to the blue pair I have with the little yellow rosettes and ribbon ties. . . ."

Her voice trailed as she noticed the twin glazed looks from her brothers. "Well, that's not important," she continued. "What I am trying to say is only a person of significant means would indulge in such lavish extravagance."

Both James and Arthur blinked in surprise. Trust Georgiana to clearly see what neither of them had considered.

"That's remarkable, Georgie," James said. "How did you arrive at these deductions?"

"Oh, simple. I made a list!" She beamed and plucked a folded sheet of paper from her lap, waiving it at James.

Ah, of course. No one loved making lists quite as much as Georgiana. "You most certainly have convinced me. I agree that we should treat her with the deference given a lady until proved otherwise. Better to err on the side of courtesy, I say," James said.

He slanted a look at Arthur and waited patiently, anticipating the conclusion that Arthur would likely draw from Georgie's deductions.

He didn't have to wait long.

"You're being too kind, James!" Arthur snorted. "She does not actually have to *be* a lady in order to have all of the qualities that Georgie just listed. Particularly her short haircut. Some would call such a thing more daring than fashionable." Arthur glanced at Georgiana, obviously not wanting to speak plainly in front of her. "In fact, most everything about how she was found would point to another, more logical conclusion."

And one that fits more easily into your existing mental boxes, James thought.

Georgiana sat back in her chair and appraised her brother with a wry smile on her face, shaking her head slightly. "Really, Arthur. In case you have forgotten, I turned twenty-three two months ago. I'm hardly a babe. You mean to imply that our mysterious E is someone's cast off paramour? Some nobleman's mistress?"

Arthur scowled at her in dismay. "You should not know of such things, Georgie," he muttered.

Georgiana stared at him and made a less-than-polite noise, one that clearly indicated her feelings on what she was allowed to 'know.'

"Really, James, given all of this, you cannot allow this woman to remain at Haldon Manor. Or at least, we should send out discreet inquiries to find out her origins." Arthur gave his older brother a reproving look.

James shook his head. "I think it far too early to send out inquiries. No one has even had time to learn of her whereabouts. That being said, I do admit that there is a small possibility that our mystery lady's precedents may not be entirely proper for polite company—"

"Precisely!"

"—but there are also a good number of perfectly respectable explanations as well." James fixed Arthur with a hard stare. "I am confident that someone will be along shortly to claim her. And I would rather be known as one who is too kind and generous to a stranger than not kind enough. For now, we will treat her as we would appreciate others treating Georgie were she to find herself in a similar situation."

Arthur grimaced. He obviously believed his sister would never be so gauche as to find herself in such a predicament.

After a long pause, Arthur stiffly nodded his head in agreement. "But the second we find out differently, she must be removed from this house. You do run a risk in housing her, James. A risk to us all."

Chapter 10

Emme placed her finger-tips against the cool window pane and leaned forward, noting the blond gentleman—Mr. James Knight, she supposed—swing onto his horse, his large overcoat brushing his boots. He nodded and spoke as another man rode into her view. This man was darker than Mr. Knight but dressed in the same tight buckskins, top hat and long overcoat. His brother, Arthur, perhaps? Their clothing felt odd somehow. Like it wasn't quite right. Old-fashioned, perhaps?

Emme watched as the men briefly spoke, her gaze following as they turned their mounts down the drive. Mr. Knight felt so familiar and yet not somehow. Another memory flitting just outside her consciousness. It was maddening.

You're losing it, supplied a dry voice in her head.

Perhaps.

She wasn't quite sure she liked the tone of that dry voice. It seemed a little . . .

Emme searched for the right word.

Snarky? the voice helpfully supplied.

Emme sniffed and, shaking her head, turned away from the window.

She had awakened this afternoon with her mind much clearer, the dizziness gone. Her terrible headache had also receded to a dull thrum, a little bothersome but not the blinding pain of before. But even though the mental fuzziness had dissipated, her memory had not returned.

It had been nearly three days since she arrived at Haldon Manor. Or at least so said the little maid who had been attending her bedside. She had only three days of hazy memories. The familiar-ish golden haired man talking softly to the equally blond slim woman. The kindly doctor who had gently examined her head, finding the tender bump. The bedroom with its dark paneled wood and beamed ceiling, soft blue bed hangings and large mullioned window that overlooked a gravel drive, an expanse of lawn extending to a forest and rolling hills in the distance.

And the young maid sitting quietly at her side every time Emme opened her eyes. Fanny was her name.

Fanny. Isn't that name somewhat unfortunate? asked the dry voice. *Did her parents consider child-naming an exercise in character building? Or was it more of a drunken dare?*

The voice was odd. Like a less censored version of herself.

An Alter Self.

Just what she needed. No memory and now she was hearing voices. It was like a catastrophe with a bonus tacked on.

Two for one, Alter Emme said. She sounded smug.

Emme shook her head, trying to clear her mind. Fanny had been there this afternoon when she awoke, more alert and desperately hungry. The maid had brought her some beef broth and a crusty roll which Emme had eaten, listening to Fanny tell how Mr. Knight had found her stranded in the middle of a terrible storm and carried her on his horse to Haldon Manor.

Mmmm, why couldn't you at least have a memory of that? Alter Emme had asked.

After eating, Emme realized she hadn't noticed a connecting door that might lead to a bathroom..

"I find that I need to . . . ," Emme had waived her hand, looking for the right euphemism, "relieve myself," she had finished lamely. "Is there a water closet perhaps down the hall?"

Poor Fanny had looked a little embarrassed and wrung her hands. Both actions caused Emme some confusion. What about a bathroom would cause embarrassment and hand wringing?

"Oh, I'm so sorry, miss," Fanny had said in her delightful country accent. "The master hasn't seen fit to install a water closet in Haldon Manor yet. Though I hear tell that Lord Linwood installed four water closets and two bath rooms at Kinningsley earlier this year. My cousin is a kitchen maid there and says they are the most wondrous things she ever saw." Still with the embarrassment, Fanny had continued, "We just use a night commode here at Haldon Manor." She gestured toward a wooden chair in the corner with a rather large hole in the middle of its seat, a porcelain bowl peeping out from underneath.

"Ah," Emme had said, finally understanding. Though still confused by the whole exchange. Night commode. She had committed the word to memory. It was obviously a term that she should have known. What other basic things had she forgotten?

After using the night commode, Emme had asked about perhaps bathing as well. This had resulted in two footman carrying in a round tub which Fanny had called a hip bath. They had placed this in front of the fire and circled it with a screen, presumably for warmth and privacy. Then Emme had watched as bucket after bucket of hot water was brought into the room, filling the bath.

Though time consuming, Emme had thanked them all and sunk her form as far as possible into the warm, soothing water. The soap had been small and round but pleasant, smelling of lavender. Fanny had even provided a toothbrush and a chalky dust she called "tooth powder."

But the entire experience had felt odd. Everything just a little off, but Emme was at a loss to explain exactly how. Again memories skittered frustratingly just out of reach.

She had been somewhat comforted by the cream silken night gown and matching robe with pink satin slippers. Fanny had stated that these were the clothes she had been wearing when Mr. Knight had found her. These items at least didn't feel odd. Just good and right against her skin.

Hugging her arms around herself, Emme tried yet again to remember her own name, her family, a friend. A detail that had the taste of memory. Anything. But the harder she concentrated, the more everything danced out of reach. Nothing. She could remember nothing. Emme fought against the now familiar anxiety that threatened to overwhelm her.

Another panic attack, Alter Emme murmured.

Taking deep measured breaths, she walked over and studied her reflection in the mirror above the fireplace. Dark hair curling into loose ringlets. Oddly colored eyes with pale amber around her pupil drifting to light green farther out. Dramatic arching eyebrows, making her pale skin seem even more colorless. She traced her lips with her fingertips, the touch convincing her that the reflection was truly herself. A face that was achingly familiar and yet not. Emme started at a gentle knock on the door.

"Come in," she called and then smiled as Georgiana Knight cautiously peered around the door.

"Oh," Georgiana said brightly, "how wonderful to see that you are awake and up!"

Georgiana shut the door and moved into the room. Though too thin and shockingly pale, Georgiana's eyes bounced with excitement. Her dress was a light blue with a high waist and flowy material that swirled around her as she walked. Her golden hair was piled on top of her head with curls escaping to frame her face. Georgiana's generous mouth spread in a welcoming smile.

"Yes, thank you," Emme agreed. "Fanny has been most attentive and helpful."

"How are you feeling?" Georgiana asked.

"Better," Emme replied. "Though nothing of my memory has returned, I'm so sorry to say." Emme found herself instinctively matching her speech and accent to Georgiana's. It seemed fitting but not entirely normal. Again, just one more thing that was a little off.

"I thank you and your brother for your kind hospitality," Emme continued. "I shudder to think what would have become of me had Mr. Knight not come to my rescue."

"Oh, think nothing of it. In fact, James insists that you are to stay as long as you would like. Most definitely until your memory returns or someone comes to claim you. Or both. I know I am delighted to have your company."

Georgiana cocked her head in surprise at Emme and moved to stand much closer to her, eying her up and down. And then turned so she and Emme stood side-by-side, their shoulders the same height and nearly touching. As if appraising her, taking her measure. The entire time, Georgiana's smile had grown larger and more pronounced, her full lips stretching wide.

"Has anyone come looking for me?" Emme asked, raising her eyebrows at Georgiana's odd maneuvering.

"Remarkable," Georgiana murmured from her position next to Emme's shoulder, still looking her up and down.

"Pardon?" Emme blinked her eyes in surprise.

"You match my height so perfectly. How delightful!"

Emme gave a low chuckle. "Do you always instantly measure a stranger's height against your own?"

"Oh, dear," Georgiana sighed, blushing slightly and taking a step backward. "I am terribly sorry if I seemed forward. I act and speak without thinking far too often. Please forgive me."

Oh, I do so love people with poor filters, Alter Emme whispered.

Ignoring the voice in her head, Emme smiled what she hoped was a comforting smile. "Please don't worry on my account. You are speaking to someone who has no memory. It is more likely that I will be the one to say or do something that isn't exactly proper. Not you."

Unexpectedly, Georgiana bent over, giving several short, harsh coughs. Instantly concerned, Emme reached out a hand to her, only to have Georgiana recover quickly and lift her head with a broad smile.

Acting as if nothing had transpired, Georgiana said, "At least we shall be improper together! And please don't worry. It will be fun to help you remember everything." She reached out and took one of Emme's cold hands in her own. "I know that I am such a trial for Arthur. He is forever shaking his head and correcting me. Well, James and I both. We are both hopeless. Life is far too short to be wasted on worrying about what is strictly proper."

Emme smiled. Oh yes, she and Georgiana were going to be fast friends. How wonderful to have a little bit of sunshine in the midst of so much uncertainty.

"And I must own that I find this entire situation far too diverting," Georgiana continued. "It is such a wonderful mystery! I do hope that we can become dear friends. Oh, but your hand is so cold. Please, come lay down. You mustn't overexert yourself." Emme delighted in Georgiana's rushed speech, how she flitted from topic to topic.

Emme allowed herself to be led to the bed, propped up with a mountain of pillows, the heavy bedspread tucked firmly around her. She found the entire situation somewhat ironic, as Georgiana looked like she could use a good rest herself.

Though pretty, Georgiana's eyes were sunken with dark circles underneath, her skin stretched across the bones of her face. She didn't look well. And that cough. Not the simple throat-clearing of a healthy person. But a deep, rasping hack that shuddered the whole body and spoke of weak lungs and fragile health.

"Thank you," Emme said once she was settled. "So as I asked, has anyone come looking for me? Certainly I have been missed?" She felt anxious, desperate for any news of herself.

Georgiana settled herself into the chair next to the bed, scooting a little closer to Emme. "Well, not yet," she began hesitantly. "But the storm broke only late last night, so there hasn't been time for the news of your arrival to spread. We all expect that someone will arrive any moment to offer an explanation. And if not, my brothers have promised to send out inquiries. But until then, you are our guest. I am wonderfully excited to have another lady in the house."

"I wish there were some way to know more about me. I have endless questions about myself. How old am I? Do I have a family? A husband? Heavens, do I have children?" The last thought struck Emme with terror. Panic rushed in again.

Just relax, Alter Emme said helpfully. *Deep breaths. In and out.*

"Yes," Georgiana agreed eagerly, "I have thought through all those same questions myself. It is such a marvelous puzzle. I think that I can put your mind to rest on a couple of counts."

"Oh, please!" Letting out a slow stuttering stream of air, Emme forced the anxiety away, tamping it down firmly.

"First of all, you were not wearing a wedding band when found," Georgiana said. Emme glanced down at her unadorned fingers. "Which isn't to say you are not married, as a ring could have been lost or just not worn. But I think we can say with surety that you haven't any children of your own."

Emme blinked in surprise. "How could you know such a thing?" she asked.

"Well, Mrs. Clark, our housekeeper, helped Fanny and I tend to you when you first arrived." Here Georgiana leaned in and lowered her voice, as if telling a secret. "And she said that bearing a child usually leaves marks upon a woman's body, lines where the skin stretches to accommodate the growth of a child, and your body does not bear any of those marks."

Emme nodded with some relief. That rang true somehow. At least there wasn't a small child somewhere sobbing for her lost mother. She most definitely couldn't fathom being a parent.

Amen, sista, Alter Emme agreed.

"We have deduced quite a bit about you from your clothing, to be honest," Georgiana admitted, giving a faintly proud smile.

"Truly?" Emme asked. "What have you learned?"

Georgiana leaned forward and recounted everything she had told her brothers over breakfast, though she omitted the worst of Arthur's suspicions. Emme added it all to her mental list. She was probably a lady, someone with money and a place in society. Somewhere out there, someone had to care about her. They would come. Knowing that eased her anxiety. Well, somewhat. She might be a genteel lady, but she had no memory of how to act like one.

"Thank you," Emme said sincerely. "Though it seems like so little, each small piece of information helps."

A firm rap sounded at the door, causing her to jump slightly.

"Come," Georgiana called.

Emme looked up as Mr. James Knight walked into the room.

Chapter 11

The air whooshed out of Emme's lungs at the sight of him, all wind-blown hair and lively blue eyes.

Again, his presence felt important. Significant.

As if her life had been focused down to this one, singular moment.

She had that odd sense of recognition—that she should know him somehow.

He was dressed in a form-fitting dark blue coat, a white cravat loosely tied around his neck. Tan buckskins disappeared into the top of knee high boots.

He looked . . . looked . . .

Yummy, Alter Emme noted with satisfaction.

Emme took a steadying breath, the room suddenly too warm.

"I was informed that our guest has awakened," he said with a broad grin. "I can see that was correct."

He had a crinkly smile. The kind of smile that took over the entire face, broad creases and wrinkled eyes. Emme immediately liked his smile. She found herself echoing it back.

Yep. Definitely yummy, Alter Emme approved.

Yes, indeed.

"Welcome, James," Georgiana said. Then turning to Emme, "This is my eldest brother, Mr. James Knight. Though you most likely remember him a little."

"Indeed. I believe I most likely owe you my life, Mr. Knight. Thank you."

His smile deepened as he made her a small bow. "It was my pleasure, madam."

Emme instantly liked his voice, low and rumbly.

"Please sit with us, brother. I was just telling our mysterious guest everything we have deduced about her."

"Excellent," James said, coming forward. He casually picked up a chair from the fireplace and swung it around to rest next to his sister's. He sank into it, stretching out his legs and crossing them at the ankles, clasping his hands behind his head.

Emme noted his restless energy. How it bounced off the walls in the small room. Some part of him always in motion. A foot bouncing. A hand twitching.

"So what have you already told our guest?" he asked Georgiana. "What does she make of the locket?"

"Locket?" Emme asked, senses instantly on alert. "What locket?"

"James," Georgiana scolded. "We have not reached that part of the conversation yet."

"Does this locket belong to me?"

"I'm so sorry. I really should have shown you this first thing." Georgiana reached into a hidden pocket in her skirt and pulled out a golden locket. "We found it around your neck."

"It's most extraordinary, to be sure," James said with an enigmatic smile.

"Extraordinary?" Emme asked. She took the locket from Georgiana's outstretched hand and studied it.

"Is it familiar to you?" he asked.

A memory stirred, brief and fluttering. Her hand reaching into brittle cloth, the smell of moth balls. And then nothing else. Chasing the elusive thoughts through her brain, Emme tried to hold them, but the memories refused to be caught. Nothing more came.

"It seems somewhat familiar," she said tentatively. Holding the locket, she examined it closely, noting the interwoven hair and gilded initials on the back. The initials felt significant. She briefly saw them, as if looking down a dark tunnel, larger and etched into something.

But as soon as the image came, it flitted away, dancing just out of reach. Shaking her head, Emme opened the locket and then stared in puzzlement.

Mr. Knight's kind face stared back at her.

Blinking, she raised her head to the flesh and blood Mr. Knight. And then back to the portrait in the locket. Their expressions were mirror images of each other.

"Is this some kind of joke?" she asked, raising her eyes back to his, cocking an eyebrow in confusion. "I thought Georgiana said we had never met. Is there an explanation for this? Do I know you after all?"

"No, we had never met before this week," Mr. Knight replied with a slight sigh, shifting his weight forward and resting his elbows on his knees. "Though it appears you know someone who greatly resembles me."

"Truly? This locket is just a tremendous coincidence then?" Emme tried to keep the disbelief from her voice but didn't completely succeed.

Mr. Knight shrugged and scrubbed a hand through his golden hair, turning it from tastefully disheveled to deliciously mussed.

"I know it seems terribly suspicious. I've had a devil of a time convincing Georgiana and Arthur that this portrait is not of me. It does seem an almost impossible occurrence, but I assure you we have never met before."

"Are you certain? Perhaps we have met and you have merely forgotten."

Mr. Knight laughed, an enigmatic expression on his face. He gave her a long, measured look. "I assure you, madam, I would most certainly remember if we had met before."

Emme blinked.

Indeed.

She swallowed. "What a remarkable coincidence. I guess that explains the sense of recognition. You do seem vaguely familiar to me. But not exactly like a memory." She paused trying to catch onto the feeling, but it darted away.

"Does the inscription mean anything to you?" Georgiana asked, gesturing toward the locket case.

Inscription? Emme paused and, with a quizzical glance, looked down and quietly read the engraved words.

To E

throughout all time
heart of my soul
your F

A visceral reaction robbed her of breath. This was familiar, painfully and achingly so. Was this her? Was she E? And who was F? Did he love her as the locket implied? She searched her mind, trying to find something, anything that might offer an explanation. But again, nothing. Her confusion and surprise must have shown on her face.

"Are you well?" Mr. Knight asked. "The inscription means something to you?"

"Yes . . . ," Emme replied, and then instantly following, "no. . . . I mean it feels so familiar, but I have no concrete memories of it. I don't know who E or F are. What do you think the inscription means? Aside from the obvious, of course."

"It would imply that you have someone who cares deeply for you," Georgiana said. "Someone who is probably not a brother or father, as the gentleman in the portrait is too young to be your father and most likely too fair-headed to be your brother."

"Besides," Mr. Knight interjected, raising his eyebrows, "that inscription is hardly fraternal in tone."

"Indeed not, Mr. Knight," Emme agreed, matching his smile with one of her own.

Oh yes, she definitely loved how he welcomed smiles and laughter easily. Like they were old friends.

Their eyes met and held for a moment.

And then another.

Emme found it slightly harder to breath.

Are you sparking on him? Alter Emme asked. *Cause I'm definitely feeling a spark right now.*

Emme ignored her. A spark was the last thing she needed right now. Mr. Knight was clearly the wrong man, despite his laughing eyes and delectable mussed hair.

She looked back down at the inscription and the portrait of F. Was he the right man? With a slight shake of her head, Emme hunted for some scrap of memory, anything that would bring her to herself.

James watched emotions skitter across their guest's face as she looked at the locket in her hand. He hadn't lied when he said he would most definitely remember a face such as hers. Truly. All pale skin contrasting with dark chocolate hair, short and curling around her face. A smile making her eyes dance.

And those eyes. Large and expressive. He had imagined them to be dark like her hair. But instead, he found himself at a loss to describe their surprising color. Green and gold all at once. Startlingly unexpected.

James wondered if there might even be a little bit of whimsy deviltry behind that smile. Beauty and good-natured wit?

Ah, that would be delightful.

Of course, Georgiana immediately brought his thoughts back to reality.

"It must be a comfort to realize that whoever gave you this locket must love you," she said. "Do you suppose he is your betrothed?"

The locket. Of course. There was that small fact. Their lovely guest most likely was attached to someone else, emotionally if not legally. He needed to keep that thought front and center.

Their guest sighed and gazed at the portrait for a moment. "I don't know," she finally said. "I feel a tug of recognition when I look at it. But then I felt the same sense of familiarity when Mr. Knight walked in the room. And as you both insist that we have never met, then everything just becomes cloudy and confusing."

Georgiana looked at James, exchanging a meaningful look. "We feel that it might be best to avoid mentioning or showing the locket to others," she said turning back to their guest. "We know that James is not the man in the portrait, but others might not be so understanding. And gossip can be malicious."

"Of course," their guest said, nodding her head in agreement. "I completely understand."

Georgiana pursed her mouth. "Do you think that your name starts with an E?" she asked. Georgiana was drifting into detective mode, James realized. No mystery would remain unsolved on her watch.

"I couldn't say. Is that likely?"

"It is a definite possibility," James replied.

"My thoughts exactly, brother," Georgiana agreed, her voice business-like. "To that end, I made a list of possible ladies' names that start with the letter E. I figured it would give us a place to start."

James chuckled, "Ah, Georgie, you and your endless lists."

"There is nothing wrong with the making of a good list, brother dear," Georgiana said primly as she reached into her pocket and pulled out a folded piece of paper, smoothing it open.

"Indeed there is not," James agreed. "Though you must admit your penchant for list-making borders on the absurd at times. Remember when you listed—and named, I might add—all your freckles?"

"Oh, James! Don't be horrid." Georgiana exclaimed, swatting him good-naturedly on the shoulder and then said, turning to their guest. "You must understand, I was only nine-years-old at the time. Obviously, a novice at list making."

James merely laughed again, ignoring the mock-scowl Georgiana gave him.

"List making is not to be taken lightly," agreed their guest. "Had I pen and paper, I think I should like to make a few lists of my own." Her face showed not an ounce of irony. Just honest sincerity.

Perhaps he had been mistaken about the trace of wit.

"Truly?" Georgiana asked, looking up from her paper, happily eyeing the woman in the bed. "Oh, I knew that we should be friends from the moment I first saw you! How delightful!"

Their guest smiled warmly. She had the straightest, whitest teeth he had ever seen. Nearly unnaturally so.

"Truly. List making is probably the first thing today that has felt absolutely right," she laughed.

Again, no irony.

"List-making?" James asked with an arched eyebrow. "Am I really sitting here watching you two bosom-friending over lists? Shouldn't you be bonding over bonnets or embroidery circles?"

"Ignore him," Georgiana instructed, adding a note of prim righteousness to her voice. "He's impossible about things like this. He does not respect the power of the list."

Their guest sighed mournfully, nodding her head in sad agreement.

"Few men do," she said. Maybe less sincerely. "Much to their detriment. I firmly believe that I could conquer the world, if only I could make the right list." Her eyes glinted with mischief now, catching his with a slight smile.

James chuckled, "Indeed, madam? No memory and yet you harbor dreams of global dominance, it would seem. Impressive. Most gentlewomen of my acquaintance usually satisfy themselves with the mere running of a large household. But now I am curious, what would you do as Empress of the World?"

She matched his smile, her eyes lively. "You pose a most interesting question, Mr. Knight." Their guest pondered for a moment and then gave a mock-weary sigh. "To be honest, I find myself much too lazy to rule the world directly. A puppet regime would be more my style."

James blinked in surprise. "A puppet regime?" he asked.

"Exactly," she said emphatically, seeming to misread his confusion. "I would leave an underling to deal with the tedious day-to-day bureaucracy. Really, who has time for such a headache? Instead, I would just rest in my luxurious palace and pull strings from a distance. Though I do believe that my first decree as Empress of the World would be to ban all morning people and insist on chocolate with every meal."

"Chocolate? Interesting," James chuckled appreciatively. "Well, madam, you should start on that list as I think you would make a delightful Empress of the World. And I would be honored to assist you in finding a qualified underling to act as your puppet." He gave her an abbreviated bow from his chair. She smiled and exchanged a sly glance with Georgiana.

"Indeed? Are you volunteering?" Her eyes sparkled as she snuggled back against the downy pillows.

James laughed. Ah, lovely, witty and intelligent. A deadly combination.

He had hoped his sense of connection with her would fade as he got to know her. That she would do or be something that disillusioned him. Or at least that the inexplicable attraction he felt would abate.

But that was decidedly not happening.

Georgiana laughed too, smoothing out her paper with her hand. "Perhaps we should go through the names on my list and see if one feels right. It would be nice to be able to call you something other than "our mystery guest" or "Lady E." Would that be all right?"

"Of course. Please, list away!" said their guest with a flick of her hand. She seemed to be enjoying herself.

James groaned and shook his head. He wondered how much mischief the two of them would get into. The last thing Georgiana needed was a partner in crime when it came to lists and mysteries.

"Wonderful," Georgiana smiled, lighting her entire face. "Let me start reading names, and please stop me when I get to one that feels familiar."

Their guest nodded.

"Elizabeth," Georgiana started, looking hopeful.

The woman in the bed puzzled for a moment and then shook her head.

"No? Eliza or Ella perhaps?" Georgiana continued. "Elizabeth is by far the most common woman's name that begins with an E, so I thought to start there."

"No, that doesn't feel familiar," their guest said.

"Let's move on then."

Ellen, Eleanor, Esther, Edith, Elena, Eva. The list continued. Each one met with a quick shake of the head.

"Well, the last name on my list is Emily," Georgiana said in resignation.

"Emily? That seems closer than all the others, to be honest. Though I don't think it is quite right."

"What about Emma?" James suggested. "It's about the only E name that Georgiana didn't list."

"Emma," she said, pondering. "Yes, that feels a lot closer. Perhaps not perfect, but definitely better than all the others. . . . Yes, it feels good. Not right, but close somehow."

James smiled broadly. "Emma it is. Or I should say Miss Emma, as that will be more proper. It will most definitely do for now."

Emma. He tried out the name, liking how it slid against his mind. It suited her.

"I like it," Georgiana agreed. "Well Miss Emma, seeing how we have finally been properly introduced, you must please call me Georgiana."

"Georgiana," Emma smiled. "And please just call me Emma. It is nice to have something to call myself. And truly, thank you both again. I can't tell you how much it helps to feel your kindness and care."

"It is most definitely our pleasure," Georgiana said, leaning forward to grasp one of Emma's hands. "You have brought more excitement to Haldon Manor than . . . well, than I can ever remember. It is good to have something different to look forward to."

Georgiana smiled wistfully, with a look of yearning sadness James knew too well. The familiar stabbing agony of impending loss. How long could he bear this? Months, perhaps years of knowing that he would lose her, watching her slowly fade before him? The reminder of it always intruding, a thief stealing life's joy.

"Indeed, Georgie is right," James said fondly, keeping all his painful emotions from his face. "I think every person in Marfield must know of our mystery guest by now. In fact, Sir Henry is beside himself to meet our fascinating Emma." He continued with a laugh, "He has sent two notes already today—"

"Three," Georgiana corrected

"Three? Well, Sir Henry definitely wishes to meet you. 'Tis a pity that Sir Henry's patience is not as strong as his persistence." James chuckled, deliberately trying to erase the sadness from Georgiana's face. She laughed with him. "In fact, he has been so persistent that he . . ."

His words trailed off as Georgiana's laugh quickly turned into a hacking cough. James laid a concerned hand on her shoulder and dug a handkerchief out of his breast pocket. Georgiana doubled over, her cough sounding deep and wretched, tearing at her too thin shoulders.

James lifted his eyes to Emma's, holding them. Pale gold-speckled pools, willing him to fall deeper into them. He ignored the sudden speeding of his heart. He could sense her concern as well, the innate kindness within her.

He broke off the gaze first, turning back to Georgiana. She pulled a shaking hand from her mouth, his handkerchief tinged with blood. James hated the helplessness of moments like this, where all he could do was watch and wonder what would happen next.

Chapter 12

Emme watched Mr. Knight tenderly wrap his arm around his sister, supporting her as the coughing wracked her body uncontrollably. After a moment, he rose and poured a glass of water from the pitcher sitting on Emme's nightstand.

"Is she well, Mr. Knight?" Emme asked, concerned as he sat back down and handed the water to Georgiana. "Truly, Georgiana, you should get some rest. You have worn yourself out looking after me. Your cough sounds dreadful."

Her coughing settling down, Georgiana straightened slightly and gratefully took the water from her brother.

"Dear Emma, we are only a few minutes into our new friendship, and I have already arranged a trial for it," she said with a sad smile. And then, sipped the water and took a fortifying breath, "There is nothing to be done about my illness, you see. I am consumptive. The illness will kill me, little by little, until I fade entirely away."

Emme stared at her in shock. This pale, ethereal creature was dying?

"Consumption is a terrible sickness," Mr. Knight agreed, holding his sister's hand. All his carefree easiness gone, concerned intensity in its place. "It slowly eats at one's health, killing by degrees."

This is wrong, Alter Emme whispered, stunned. *People don't die of consumption.*

Emme found herself looking back and forth between them. It did feel wrong. Very, very wrong. Someone so young should be not be dying of a bad cough. Again, something tickled at the edges of her consciousness. Something that should be done.

"I am so sorry," Emme found herself saying. "I don't even know what to say. It seems so dreadful. Are you sure?"

"As long as I am still breathing, there is always hope, but so few receive a miracle. Not many survive consumption."

Her brave smile tore at Emme.

"I am not a fair weather friend to be chased off by the first sign of rain," Emme said, matching Georgiana's little smile with one of her own. "We shall care for each other in our trials." She reached out and took Georgiana's hand, giving it a reassuring squeeze.

You'd better remember to wash that hand, Alter Emme said.

"Thank you, Miss Emma," Mr. Knight said, his eyes meeting hers warmly. "I know that Georgiana often pines for company. We are isolated here in the country and not many care to associate with a consumptive."

"I am here and delighted to make Miss Georgiana's acquaintance. I do feel that we will be great friends." Emme smiled what she hoped was her warmest smile.

"I feel the same," Georgiana said, clutching Emme's hand. "And now, as James knows I do not like discussing my impending doom, I am going to officially change the topic. What were you saying about Sir Henry earlier, James?"

"You had best prepare yourself, Miss Emma," he said, turning to Emme. "Sir Henry has invited us all to dinner later this week. And I fully expect that he will join forces with Georgiana to uncover all of your secrets!"

"Damn," James muttered. "This is bad."

Somehow from the moment James had heard that terrible noise several nights ago, he had known.

"Very bad." Arthur nodded in agreement, twisting in his saddle to survey the damage.

"Very, very bad," James repeated slowly, reaching down to pat Luther's neck.

The ancient oak lay fragmented. Huge limbs shattered and jumbled across the meadow.

Its enormous girth had been neatly cleaved in two—sheered to the ground. As if carved into a steep canyon by a giant's ax. The two halves of the trunk yawned apart.

With a sighing shake of his head, James dismounted and tethered Luther to a low tree branch, Arthur following suit. Picking their way through the wooden carnage, they walked slowly out into the meadow.

It was obvious they weren't the first ones to have visited. Votive offerings dotted the meadow: a bottle of wine here, a beaded necklace there, several handkerchiefs and a shawl tied to branches. Gifts from the villagers, his own tenant farmers, all the hardworking folk from the county roundabout hoping to placate the witches who must have caused this dreadful mischief. The myths tied to the ancient oak were still strongly felt. Indeed, the legends were potent enough even the not-so-superstitious gave them heed.

Arthur sighed next to him, surveying the scattered offerings. "We are going to have to do something about this. The tenants take these ridiculous superstitions much too seriously."

James grunted and wandered away from his brother, climbing over and under piles of tangled limbs. He stopped short of the trunk, his hands on his hips. There was nothing to be done. The tree was dead, though its still green leaves belied this reality, bobbing in the breeze as they lay sideways on the ground. They would wither soon enough.

James took a few steps closer to the sheered trunk, wondering at the power of lightning that could have so neatly severed the tree in two. Charred cindery streaks contrasted sharply with the stark brightness of raw wood. Though sharply cut apart, the massive trunk towered over James, dwarfing him. He stopped just outside the large crevice.

Though the day was cool, the air suddenly turned heavy. Peering inside the deepest depths of the oak, he saw white and charred wood give way to darkness. The very base of the tree was somehow hollow. James stepped closer, trying to see into its depths. As he did, the air around him began to tingle, reminiscent of the electricity he had felt along the road.

He sensed a bit of a tug, some unseen force drawing him forward. Startled, James retreated several steps backward, his heart suddenly beating rapidly.

That was extremely weird. Odd. Almost uncomfortable.

He shook his head. Even he wasn't immune to all the superstition around this ancient relic.

Hearing Arthur come up behind him, James turned, surveying the meadow. "The villagers are obviously concerned. Perhaps we should chat with Auntie Gray. She might be able to help put this into some sort of perspective for everyone."

Arthur snorted. "You do realize she is the reason so many firmly believe in the old legends. Without her stories and knowledge of the ancient ways, most of this nonsense would just die out."

"True," James said, pulling off his hat to run a hand through his hair. "But she understands better than anyone the ramifications of this. And despite her understanding of ancient ways, she is a sensible, rational woman." Arthur nodded slowly and then turned with a grimace back toward their horses.

Following his brother, James caught a gleam from underneath the tangled branches to the left of the trunk. Squinting into the brush, he crouched down to get a better look. Something was in there, nestled in a little hollow on the ground, sheltered from the elements. It was too hidden to be an offering. It looked to be a satchel or bag of some sort. A poachers pouch, perhaps? James braced his hand against a nearby branch and reached in until he felt the smooth leather against his palm. Grasping the bag, he pulled it out.

The bag was different from any he had ever seen. Rectangular and made of a reddish, soft leather, it had a strange clasp on one side. Or at least what James assumed was the clasp. It was all intricate metal work and interlaced straps. Perhaps some gypsy-made piece accidentally left here.

"What do you have?" Arthur asked.

"I have no idea," James answered, handing him the bag. Arthur turned it over in his hands, puzzling at the odd clasp. "Probably belongs to someone who brought an offering."

"Or a poacher trespassing on our land," Arthur grumbled.

James cocked an eyebrow in acknowledgment. "I'll give it to Howard. He might know who the owner is." Howard, the gamekeeper at Haldon Manor, knew just about everyone and everything. Arthur grunted and handed the bag back to him, turning away.

Retrieving their horses, James wrapped the purse around his saddle as he mounted.

"Have you given more thought about what to do with Emma?" Arthur asked as they nudged their horses back toward the house.

"You mean in the hour since you last asked the question?" James countered, trying to tamp down his irritation.

Arthur clenched his jaw slightly.

"It has been a week and no one has missed her or inquired after her. Does that not strike you as odd?"

"As I promised, I have sent out a few local inquiries."

"Which have yielded nothing."

"What precisely are you saying, Arthur?"

"That I still feel there is only one good explanation for her presence upon our lane late at night in a blinding storm. Someone driving through Marfield must have cast her out."

James snorted. "That is hardly the only possible reason."

"Then what else, James? What respectable explanation do you propose?"

"She could have been part of a traveling party set upon by highwaymen. She could have wandered from an estate in the neighboring county. There could have been a carriage accident, and we just haven't found the wreckage yet. There are any number of plausible explanations. It is absurd to assume because we don't know how she arrived here, she must therefore be a woman of loose morals. It is logic of the most ridiculous kind—"

"Come now, James!"

"—if one could even call such *reasoning* logic!"

Arthur rode for a few moments in stony silence, obviously trying to reign in his temper.

James loved his brother but knew Arthur would be relentless. He would pick and pester until he got his wish, relying on James' good nature to give way. But for once, James felt almost inexplicably obstinate. Emma was harming no one, and she was quickly becoming a much needed friend for Georgiana.

"Why?" Arthur finally asked. "Why do you persist in defending her?"

James sighed inwardly. Part of him wondered the same thing. He was at a loss to explain the relentless pull he felt toward her.

Arthur misunderstood his silence.

"Or is there something more about her you would like to tell me?" Arthur asked, his voice taut.

"Again with your sordid implications. Truly, Arthur—"

"That locket of hers is too much of a coincidence to be—"

"Enough!" James interrupted, giving his brother his most icy stare. "To suggest I would keep such information from you, from Georgiana, from Emma herself. . . . It is . . . revolting. Painfully wrong. Why would I lie? Truthfully, I am heartily tired of defending myself against that damning locket."

"Even you must admit that—"

"Leave it be, Arthur! I am not the man in that locket. I will not repeat myself again."

They rode in silence for a few moments. A silence that James knew wouldn't last.

"We should turn her over to the vicar or even the poor house until someone comes to claim her."

James let out an exasperated sigh. Why couldn't Arthur let this go?

"Arthur, I am done with this conversation. Really and truly done."

Arthur apparently was not.

"You do not understand how her presence is affecting us all. Linwood is horrified that you have allowed her to stay here for so long."

"Linwood?!" James exclaimed and then paused, controlling his temper. "I honestly don't know what appalls me more. The fact that you discuss these matters with Linwood or that Timothy feels compelled to insert himself into them. He has no business offering an opinion about whom I allow to reside under my own roof."

"Timothy cares because there is the potential for an alliance between our families."

"An alliance he has so far rejected, might I point out."

Arthur wisely ignored the jab. "We cannot sit here and do nothing about this situation. We should at least send out more inquiries, perhaps even involve some of our contacts in Bristol and London. If she truly is respectable, as you assert, then someone somewhere will have missed her."

James nodded grudgingly. Arthur did have a point there. "If I agree to send out further inquiries, will you stop your incessant pestering?"

James captured and held Arthur's eye until his brother curtly nodded.

"I believe Ethan knows people, men that he fought with in France who worked with intelligence gathering. I will ask him about it. And perhaps Sir Henry will have suggestions as well. I believe we are to dine there tomorrow evening. Will that satisfy you?"

Arthur grunted in assent.

Arriving back at Haldon Manor, James tossed Luther's reins to a groom who came striding out from the stable to greet them. He grabbed the odd bag off the saddle and headed toward the house.

Glancing to his left, he caught a glimpse of dark curly hair and the flutter of a skirt disappearing into the old walled garden. He decided not to analyze why his heart instantly beat faster at the sight, why his mood suddenly lightened. He immediately walked toward the garden, determined to follow Miss Emma.

Realizing he still held the lost bag in his hand, James quickly diverted to the house, taking the wide steps of the back terrace two at a time. Stepping through french doors into the drawing room, James gestured to a passing footman and handed him the purse.

"Put this into the left side drawer of my private desk, please."

"Yes sir." The footman bobbed his head in acknowledgment, holding the bag firmly.

Turning, James walked briskly back out the doors and took the steps in three large leaps down, half jogging to intercept their lovely guest. The purse already forgotten.

Chapter 13

Emme breathed in the fresh spring air, reveling in the warm sun against her face. How wonderful it was to be out of her small room. The walled garden had beckoned her along its gravel paths, riotous clumps of blooms and greenery drawing her in.

She had awakened that morning to Fanny bringing in dress after dress, hanging them in her armoire. Georgiana trailed behind, explaining she had far too many dresses from her three Seasons in London and insisted on lending some to Emme.

"Besides," Georgiana laughed, bouncing slightly as she sat on Emme's bed. "You are so thin. The dresses fit you without any alteration. I often find my too slim figure somewhat embarrassing. Do you feel the same?"

Again with the no filters, Alter Emme murmured. *I don't think you can ask another woman that.*

"I honestly don't know. Should I be embarrassed?"

Georgiana shrugged. "No, I suppose not. But I wonder if you haven't been ill too."

"Well, I feel fine and have recovered quite quickly—"

"Perhaps," Georgiana interrupted, "you were so ill with fever that you went out of your mind and wandered into the night. And there you were, at death's door, soaked through and clinging to the tree. And then James found you."

Emme sighed. Georgiana kept coming up with possible explanations for her past. Of course, each scenario ended with how romantic it had been for James to find her along their lane. Which was really not helping Emme's peace of mind. She had no intention of thinking of Mr. Knight as anything other than her kind host. It was too dangerous to her fragile emotional stability.

"Again, that seems somewhat unlikely given that I had no fever after Mr. Knight found me." Emme kept trying to gently rein Georgiana in without much success.

"True," Georgiana said, tapping her lips, lost in thought. And then she gasped, something occurring to her. "Do you suppose you were living with a wicked uncle?"

Emme merely laughed, shaking her head.

Fanny dressed Emme in a pale pink, muslin gown that Georgiana called a morning dress, its empire waist tight around her ribcage, her bobbed hair pulled back with a wide ribbon, a few curls left forward to gently frame her face. Georgiana sent her outside with a shawl wrapped around her shoulders, just in case a "cool breeze disturbed the warm spring air." It all seemed perfectly normal and yet not. The dress was lovely but its long skirts felt odd against her legs. Everything seemed slightly off. Even the sky seemed too blue, like it was the bluest sky she had ever seen.

Walking through the enclosed garden, Emme took a deep breath, loving the mingled scent of wildflowers and herbs. Moss and grass grew out of its walled crevices. Lush and well-cared for, the garden welcomed her. Against the far wall, she could see aged gothic arches overgrown with ivy. And again, she felt that vague sense of knowing. Like she had been here before and yet not.

It was utterly maddening.

Emme continued along the path, focusing on the sound of gravel crunching beneath her feet.

"Miss Emma!" A voice called.

Startled, Emme turned to see Mr. Knight striding toward her, a welcoming smile on his lips.

Again, the disorientation hit her, everything feeling agonizingly familiar. That she knew him. That he was right.

He was dressed in what she recognized as riding clothes: tan buckskins disappearing into knee high boots, green wool coat with a loosely tied cravat, all covered by a large gray-brown overcoat that hugged his shoulders and then fell straight practically to his ankles, moving loosely as he walked, his stride lanky. The walk of a man comfortable with his body. With himself.

She suppressed, yet again, that little flip of her heart.

Such eye-candy, Alter Emme swooned. *Delicious eye-candy.*

Emme ignored that. Seriously. Her alter voice was not helping.

He tipped his hat and bowed his head slightly in greeting as he stopped in front of her.

"Miss Emma." His wide crinkly smile did funny things to Emme's breathing. "How delighted I am to see you out and about! How are you feeling today?"

"Well, thank you," Emme answered, fighting to keep her own smile more politely serene and less school-girl infatuated silly.

She also refused to make any mental comparisons between his intense blue eyes and an ice blue winter sky. Refused to notice how broad his shoulders looked in his overcoat. Refused to think about the glimpses she had seen of a clever wit and accepting open nature.

No. She was determined not to notice such things.

Emme had given herself a stern talking to regarding Mr. Knight the previous evening. Yes, he was charming and kind and funny.

Don't forget all that divinely mussed hair, Alter Emme had not-so-helpfully chimed in.

He had rescued her, given her shelter and, even more, extended his kindness, for which she was eternally grateful.

But there was the small matter of the mysterious F in her locket. She had studied the miniature portrait for hours. Memorized the man, the tilt of his head, the hint of his smile. The man who most likely held her heart.

It was just an unfortunate coincidence that Mr. Knight and F looked so much alike. Her affection for F was the source of this undeniable attraction to Mr. Knight.

James, Alter Emme whispered. *You can at least think of him as James. What will that hurt?*

Emme sighed and agreed. *James.* She mentally curled inward, cradling his name against her mind. And then instantly repressed that thought too.

"I can see that Georgiana arranged some clothing for you. It suits you well. Are you enjoying your walk?"

Was he always so courteous? And did his voice have to sound so mellow smooth?

And why was she noticing such things anyway?

"Oh yes. The sun feels wonderful. I was just admiring the beautiful wisteria." She gestured back toward the red brick house and the enormous ancient wisteria vine twining across the mullioned windows, limbs drooping with fragrant purple flowers. Her mind labeled the old house as Tudor. "The house is lovely. I would enjoy learning more of its history."

Did that sound as lame as she thought it did? Was she trying too hard?

"With pleasure." James smiled that broad smile of his and extended an elbow toward her. Emme paused at the gesture and then understood, sliding her hand around to rest in the crook of his arm.

Trying to ignore the flex of hard muscle in his forearm.

She listened as they strolled through the garden. He recounted the history of the house: its beginnings as a medieval monastery, mostly destroyed by Henry VIII in the 1530's, the current house being built during the reign of Queen Elizabeth and subsequently added on to over the years, though still retaining its mostly Tudor character. The facade undulated with bay windows and abbreviated towers, a multitude of mullioned windows crosshatched across the front, scores of chimneys rising to the sky. The whole effect a jumbled mess and somehow harmonious at the same time.

She appreciated how James' face lit as he talked of his home and enjoyed the pride in his voice as they wound along the gravel path.

No. Wait. She had decided not to notice such things. She had the man in the locket. And James was not that man. Emme took a deep breath and let it out slowly, trying to will away the intense pull toward him.

"And this garden?" Emme asked when James paused. "It's lovely and the walls surrounding it look so old."

"The garden is all that remains of the ancient monastery. If we stroll along this path, you can see the remains of the gothic cloister. As a child, I used to play amid the ruins, imagining life here when it was ruled by monks and knights." James' expression was somewhat rueful. "Though Georgiana was generally too young and Arthur always felt being anything other than lord of the manor was beneath him. So I was often left to make up the stories myself."

Emme suppressed an image of a tow-headed little James mock fighting a dragon, face fierce with emotion.

"How charming," she said. "I imagine you must have rescued many a distressed damsel."

James laughed good-naturedly. "Of course. This is most definitely where I honed my distressed damsel rescuing skills." He gestured expansively toward the cloister, covered in roses and climbing vines.

"Thank goodness, you did," she answered with a wry smile, "because I have most certainly benefited from your expertise."

Emme caught his eye as she spoke, seeing a flicker of something warm that made her go all melty inside.

James stopped and looked at her intently, drawing her arm closer to his body. "Well, I have been charmed to be of service," he said gently, bowing his head. The air rushed from her at his sudden nearness.

Mmmmm, I really like him, Alter Emme sighed, trying to breathe him in.

"But it is I who must thank you," James continued, gesturing for them to continue walking along the path.

Emme gave a startled laugh as they started to walk forward again. "Whatever for?"

"Because your presence has provided me with a much needed adventure. I'm not often provided with opportunities to play the hero." James looked at her somewhat conspiratorially.

Still smiling, Emme shook her head slightly. "Adventure? Heroes?" she asked in a little confusion.

James chuckled somewhat ruefully. "Well, I longed for adventure as a child, something different from the sameness of rural life. I hoped my longings would change as I got older. But I find nothing has changed. Not really."

"Truly? You still long for adventure?"

James shrugged, as if trying to move something uncomfortable off his back. "Yes, I suppose I do. Seems immature, doesn't it?" His grin was part shame, part humor. "I mean, I have everything most anyone would want, and yet I long for more."

He paused and then continued, "No, not more . . . just different. Though I'm the oldest son, the heir, I never really took to it. I struggle to sit still, struggle to focus and just be content with the sameness of this life. Obviously, I love Haldon Manor. I love my family and my people. I feel my obligations to them keenly. And yet, I can't shake the sense that this isn't the life I was meant to have.

"As a boy, I often dreamed of jumping a ship to somewhere exotic. I even made definite plans once, when I was about twenty. Secretly, I purchased passage on a ship to India. I was going to leave a note and sneak away in the dead of night. Shameful, but I was desperate. For anything. For a change. But then life happened."

James stopped and shook his head. "It's probably a foolish hope anyway. I long ago realized my romantic notions of faraway places probably don't match the reality."

Emme blinked as he spoke, fleeting things beckoning against her mind. Skimming with the wind along glass-clear blue water, while a hot, tropical breeze buffeted her face. Looking around a colorful exotic market, its over-loud sounds grating on her ears.

She grabbed at the images, trying to force them to remain, but they skittered frustratingly out of reach.

And then another thought darted through her mind.

James noticed her slight grimace. "Mocking my immature notions? Should I just grow up and accept my adult responsibilities?"

"Not exactly." Emme allowed a slight smile to touch her lips. "I just wished that my life could be a little less adventuresome. I fear my life has always been prone to disasters." As soon as the words left her mouth, she knew they were true.

"No return of your memory, I take it?"

"Nothing. Just the locket that remains maddeningly familiar. I do have fleeting images here and there. As you were just speaking, I felt a brief flash of the heat of tropical sun—the blue water and hot sand of a lush beach. Have I been to such places?" Emme shook her head. "It's impossible to know what is real and what isn't. Things that should be familiar are not. And yet when you talk about faraway places that I am unlikely to have ever seen, I have this sense of recognition."

"How frustrating," James agreed with a wry hint in his voice. "Though I admit to being somewhat jealous that you might have visited such places. I shall be most interested to learn your history once your memory returns."

"*If* it returns," she said, wistfully.

Oh dear. That was the wrong thing to say.

The panic that had been at bay throughout their entire conversation instantly roared to life. Emme stopped suddenly, clutching a hand to her chest, attempting to stop the anxiety from claiming her. Her other hand dug tightly into his arm.

Gulping, she tried to slow her breathing. To pretend as if nothing were wrong.

Apparently, she was not convincing enough.

James abruptly turned and gently wrapped his hands around her upper arms. "Close your eyes. Just breathe. In . . . out . . . in . . . out . . ."

Emme concentrated on his voice, focusing on it like a pinprick of light in a dark room. She used his strength to calm her racing heart. To again swallow back the panic. Slowly, she relaxed. Letting out a final long breath, she opened her eyes, giving him a tight smile to indicate that she was better.

He was standing close. Too close. Radiating concern and safety. His hands still held her arms, loose and comforting.

"It will be all right," he murmured, his blue eyes sincerely staring into hers.

Emme forced herself not to drown in those eyes. To not focus on the warmth of his hands, his attentive gaze. It was too much. She lowered her eyes to stare at his cravat.

"You are safe here with me—" He stopped suddenly, catching himself. "I mean, with us. You are safe with us."

Drawing in a stuttering breath, she whispered almost to herself, "Why has no one come for me?"

James shook his head and took a step back, releasing her arms. As if acknowledging something only to himself. He raked a hand through his hair, a nervous habit.

"I don't know," he said quietly. "I don't know why no one has come. I find it impossible to believe that someone somewhere isn't frantic with worry about you." He paused, as if considering something. And then he nodded his head. "I realized today it is time to send out more probing inquiries to London and Bristol. We will find your people, Miss Emma. Or at least exhaust ourselves trying."

Emme took in a deep breath, surprised she was suddenly holding back tears. "Thank you. It seems inadequate to say, after all that you have done."

James smiled. "No, it is you who I must thank. Georgiana has been so isolated with her illness. So alone. Your presence here . . ." Again he paused and looked off sightlessly at something above her head, swallowed as if fighting some emotion. "Well, it has helped my sister almost more than anything else. It feels like she has come alive again." James brought his eyes back to hers. "So bless you for that. Whoever you are. You are welcome here for as long as you would care to stay. You will always have a place with us."

A tightness in Emme's chest took hold again, only this time it wasn't panic. She blinked and then dashed a tear away.

"Thank you," she whispered again, looking to the garden to hide her emotions. A handkerchief suddenly slipped into her hand. Surprised, she turned.

"Please, don't tell Georgiana I made you cry," his voice teased. "She will have my head." His crinkly smile appeared again.

Emme managed a watery grin in return.

Really, what person could be this perfect?

Oh, oh, I know! I know! Alter Emme eagerly waved her hand.

"Now come, let us not talk about worrisome things like lost memories or missing adventures." James tucked her hand back onto his forearm and gently tugged her toward an arched doorway. Passing through the archway, a large lawn opened before them, sloping down to a glistening lake lined with trees and reeds.

With an expansive sweep of his hand, James continued, "Fine days like this do not occur so often in England that we can spoil one with gloomy thoughts about things that cannot be changed."

Emme sighed. Was this just her luck in life? To find a perfectly wonderful man, but without her memories, be unable to do anything about it? It was bad enough to be stranded. To have lost her memory and not remember the man in the locket. Did fate really have to add this sharp attraction to James Knight as well?

It seemed decidedly unfair.

Seriously! The universe has a sick sense of humor. Alter Emme sounded frustrated as well.

"Come, ask me something outrageous." His tone light and bantering. "I am in a mood to hear you laugh again. And sincerely this time. Not a drop of melancholy in it."

Of course, Emme laughed at that, shaking her head, feeling her anxiety recede to a more manageable level. He needed to stop being so . . . so . . . well . . .

Dreamy? Alter Emme supplied.

No. Not helping.

"Something outrageous?" she asked, liking the teasing edge in her voice.

"Indeed," he replied, wagging his eyebrows mockingly. "Do you feel up to the challenge?"

Emme nodded and then said the first thing that came to mind.

Utterly without thinking.

"What preparations have you made for a possible zombie apocalypse?"

Now why had she said that?

Oh yes, The Question! Perfect! Alter Emme said happily.

James blinked. Paused. As if hunting for meaning within the sentence.

"Zombie? I don't believe I'm familiar with that word."

As if that were the only problem he could find.

"The living dead," Emme deadpanned.

She watched from the corner of her eye as a delighted smile spread across his face.

"The living dead?" he repeated. "Ah well, in that case, preparations are going well. One can never be too careful when dealing with the living dead." Grinning widely now. "They could rise at any time and threaten the well-being of the entire county. I mean, they have an insatiable appetite for . . ." He paused searching for what to say next.

"Brains," Emme helpfully supplied. "They feed on brains, preferably human ones."

A low chuckle. "Yes, yes, brains. And of course they can only be dispatched through superb skill with a sword. In fact, I have had the local militia conducting specific zombie defense training drills. My field marshal says their fighting abilities have improved remarkably in recent months."

"Excellent!" Her voice filled with sincere approval. "You should consider investing in some ninjas to aid in your defenses. I hear they are most useful against the living dead."

"Ninjas?"

"Uhmmm. . . ." She hunted for the answer. "They're like secret Japanese assassins. They wear all black and creep along in the dead of night. Deadly and silent with super sharp knives and sabers."

"Intriguing. I would dearly love to get my hands on a squadron of them. Strictly for defense purposes, of course." His mock-serious face was convincing. Only his dancing eyes betrayed him.

"Of course." For some reason, the entire exchange warmed her through. As if she had been waiting a long time for this exact conversation.

"One can never be too careful with the living dead." He seemed to be enjoying himself. "Are they intelligent?"

"Oh no," Emme said quickly. "Their own brains have turned to mush, thankfully. They are like persistent slugs, slow, shuffling but uncaring and difficult to stop."

But then she had to stop, because she had an image in her head of a rotting corpse, animated, shuffling forward with its arms outstretched. Which of course was an impossibility, right?

Would all of this ever make sense?

She sighed and decided the sun was too lovely and James' honey-smooth voice too tempting to wallow in 'what ifs.'

Instead, she laughed as he came up with zombie counter-attack maneuvers, and she followed outlining the finer points of ninjas for him.

Chapter 14

Sutton Hall
The drawing room
Two days later
May 9, 1812

"Welcome!" Sir Henry boomed as they walked into the room, Emme on James' arm. Georgiana and Arthur trailed behind. Emme stared as a portly man with permanently flushed cheeks hurried across the room to them, his impressive salt and pepper mustache vibrating as he spoke. Though 'impressive' was perhaps too light a term to capture his facial hair. 'Work of art' was a more apt description. The mustache stretched thick and expansive with slightly upturned ends completely hiding his mouth.

"Welcome," Sir Henry repeated, stopping in front of them. "James . . . Arthur . . . Miss Knight." He nodded his head toward each in turn. Then turning to Emme, "And this must be your lovely mystery guest."

At her side, Emme felt James grin. "Sir Henry, please allow me to introduce Miss Emma," he said pulling away, gesturing toward her.

Sir Henry made her a slight bow, his wide mid-section jiggling.

"Pleased to meet you, madam," he said in loud clipped accents with a smile.

Or at least Emme thought he smiled. His eyes crinkled as if smiling and his mustache inched upward.

"Miss Emma, may I present our neighbor, Sir Henry Stylles?" James continued, gesturing toward their host.

Emme took a deep breath and without thinking did the first natural thing. She took three steps forward and held out her hand, preparing to shake his.

"It is a pleasure to meet you, Sir Henry," she said giving what she hoped was a pleasant smile.

Her hand still extended, she paused as everyone in the room went instantly quiet.

Wait. . . . Everyone?

Emme looked past Sir Henry into a sea of faces, all staring back at her with startled eyes. The space seemed full of dark evening coats and shimmering silk dresses, topped with waving feathers, amongst the gilded furniture of Sir Henry's large drawing room.

Her eyes instantly rested on a tall, dark-haired man who looked at her with disdainful gray-silver eyes. A petite woman hung on his arm wearing a gauzy lavender dress, her stare surprised. They both seemed vaguely familiar.

Wow. So awkward. Alter Emme whispered.

Emme quickly pulled her hand back to her side, darting a glance back and forth between Sir Henry and Georgiana.

"I . . ." she began and then sighed. "Obviously, I did something wrong." She gave what she hoped was a contrite smile and looked with wide eyes at Georgiana, pleading for help.

"A lady does not shake hands with a gentleman," Georgiana murmured quietly in her ear. "And I should have anticipated that Sir Henry would have invited half the county."

Emme groaned inwardly. Only three minutes in and she had already blundered. It promised to be a long evening.

Emme watched as Fanny finished pinning a curl. She had spent the last hour tucking and twirling Emme's hair into an elaborate coiffure with a ribbon running throughout, soft curls framing her face. The overall effect was . . . good. Lovely. With a pleased expression, Emme rose and turned to Georgiana sitting in a chair behind her.

"Well? Do I look like a lady?"

Georgiana smiled and rose gracefully. "Indeed! You look every inch the proper lady. Do you feel more yourself now that you are rightly dressed?"

Emme wasn't sure how to answer that question. She turned and looked in the mirror.

She stood clad in a sage green silk evening dress, the empire waist gathered high around her rib cage, sleeves puffing slightly our from her upper arms, the low-cut bodice edged with delicate lace. The dress itself was beautiful.

Emme turned sideways, noting how the heavy fabric draped to the floor. She could feel the pressure of the boning in her tight corset or *stays,* as Georgiana had called them. The stays kept her posture perfectly upright, her back almost unnaturally straight. But it felt odd to have her chest and waist squeezed so tightly while the rest of her body was so free.

Isn't it a little risque to not wear underwear? Alter Emme murmured.

Emme frowned at that. She had only a knee length garment Mary called a chemise underneath the corset and dress. She felt quite under-dressed. And yet somehow not.

Again, the now familiar panic threatened. Emme took several calming breaths and willed it back. They were becoming old friends, she and anxiety.

Georgiana must have noted her slight frown as she looked at her reflection.

"You don't like it?" she asked. "I thought that the green would be most becoming with your darker hair and pale skin. And it brings out the green hints in your eyes as well."

Emme turned to her with a smile, determined to put on a brave face.

"Thank you, Georgiana. The dress is truly beautiful and I love it." She did. "I was just feeling some concern over my faulty memory. I hope that I don't embarrass you this evening."

Georgiana laughed. "Oh please, don't fret, Emma! This evening should be a small affair with only you, James, Arthur and myself in attendance. Sir Henry rarely gives large dinner parties at Sutton Hall. There is no one you need fear. Now come, let us show the gentlemen how well you look!"

Emme nodded and looped a shawl over her arms, following Georgiana down the stairs. Georgiana's color had seemed better the last several days, her coughing less harsh. She was more lit from within, more cheerful. They paused after entering the drawing room door, allowing the two men within to rise to their feet. Arthur gave a stiff bow.

James looked absurdly distinguished in a dark navy coat with an ivory and gold striped waistcoat, snowy neckcloth expertly tied. Tan breeches hugged his legs, his hair carelessly styled, as usual. James' eyes lit up as they locked with hers, an appreciative grin tugging his lips.

I want to drown in that crinkly smile of his, Alter Emme swooned.

Really, couldn't that dry voice make itself more useful?

This is *being more useful. Trust me.* Now she just sounded smug.

Emme mentally rolled her eyes.

She reminded herself (again!) that she had a mystery man in a locket upstairs who obviously meant something to her. Thinking of James as anything other than her host and the brother of her friend would be wrong. It was the buried memory of another man that caused her insides to go all boneless when James smiled at her.

It wasn't James himself. No. Definitely not.

Besides, she had her first post-memory-loss dinner party to navigate this evening.

Emme swallowed, trying to force the butterflies back into her stomach as they stepped outside to the waiting carriage and the short ride to Sutton Hall.

Emme stood frozen, unsure how to proceed.

Like a deer in headlights, Alter Emme unhelpfully suggested.

So if shaking hands was taboo, how did one greet another human being?

Really, when had things become so needlessly complicated?

"I am so sorry . . . ," Emme hesitantly began.

"Think nothing of it, m'dear," Sir Henry boomed. "We all understand you are having to relearn so many things right now. Must be dashed difficult not having one's memory."

Emme managed a wan smile. He had no idea.

"Indeed," James' amused voice sounded near her ear. Perhaps too amused.

Emme flicked an annoyed glance at him. She was not ready to see the humor in this situation.

"When greeting a new acquaintance, a lady generally curtsies and nods her head in acknowledgment," Georgiana said quietly. "Watch."

Georgiana did just this, elegantly bowing her head and murmuring, "Tis a pleasure to make your acquaintance, Sir Henry."

Sir Henry bowed properly again, his mustache wafting slightly. As if it too were bowing.

Georgiana surreptitiously gestured for Emme to try.

With a weak smile, Emme placed the ball of one foot behind the other and bent her knees slightly, lowering her head at the same time, hoping to mimic Georgiana.

The action did not feel familiar in the slightest. It was like her brain was determined to make everything as confusing as possible.

Hey, be nice, Alter Emme warned.

"The trick is to keep the movement constant and fluid, graceful from start to finish," Georgiana encouraged in her ear.

Fortunately, the next fifteen minutes provided Emme with ample practice. Sir Henry insisted Emme take his arm as he led her around the room, introducing the vicar and his wife, two elderly spinster sisters, an aged gentleman and his portly son, an eager matron with three unmarried daughters who squirmed uncomfortably as their mother described how 'eligible' they were. The list went on. She greeted each one with the same smooth bend of her knees and dip of her head.

One introduction stood out.

"Lord Linwood, Miss Linwood, may I present Miss Emma?"

This was said to the icy-eyed man with the pretty petite woman at his side. Emme was struck again by a sense of familiarity. Did she know them?

Lord Linwood oozed money and power; a man to whom the world never said no. Miss Linwood smiled kindly at Georgiana in greeting, her dark hair curling around her face, thick lashes framing her dark eyes.

So this was Miss Marianne Linwood then, Arthur Knight's we-are-not-betrothed betrothed. Small and dainty, she had a helpless look that would make men fall over themselves to care for her. She dipped a small curtsy in return to Emme's, quietly murmuring, "Miss Emma."

Her brother, on the other hand, . . . well, his response bordered on incivility. Which, Emme realized, really was his point. His gaze remained fixed on a mark about a foot above her head, a nod of greeting scarcely perceptible. His murmur of "Miss Emma" low and barely heard. Utterly dismissive but still adhering to proper form.

Oooh, he's good, Alter Emme clinically noted. *Man, it must take generations of inbreeding to get that just right.*

Emme sighed. Her evening had only needed this.

Miss Linwood glanced past Emme's shoulder and suddenly blushed.

"Mr. Knight and Mr. Arthur Knight, how pleasant to see you this evening." Turning, Emme saw the Knight brothers coming to a stop beside Sir Henry.

"Lord Linwood. Miss Linwood." James' nodded his head in greeting, though his polite smile seemed faintly annoyed.

Annoyance. It was an emotion she had yet to associate with James. In fact, this was the first time she had seen him wear it.

Lord Linwood turned his head and actually made eye contact as he nodded his head in greeting to the brothers. Though Emme noticed his eye twitch slightly as Arthur exchanged strained, love-lorn looks with his sister.

It was comical to watch. Marianne kept trying not to stare at Arthur, but it was a losing battle. He would catch her eye and she would stare at him longingly. And then one of them would realize what they were doing, and they would break contact, each looking away, Marianne blushing.

Please tell me they aren't always like this? It's a little nauseating, Alter Emme buzzed.

Emme silently agreed.

Searching for something to break the awkward silence, Emme asked, "Miss Linwood, please forgive my presumption, but are you sure we have never met? You seem somewhat familiar." Emme noted James' look of surprise from the corner of her eye.

Lord Linwood also reacted to the question, briefly fixing steel-gray eyes on her. His gaze flicked over her face, a gleam of something briefly flaring and then instantly veiled.

"Indeed?" Sir Henry beamed. "How fascinating! Do you suppose you have met in London?"

"I . . . I couldn't say, Sir Henry," Emme stammered.

Miss Marianne pursed her pretty mouth for a moment and then shook her head, "I am afraid I cannot recollect ever having been introduced, Miss Emma. But I must be honest, our acquaintance is so large it is hard to remember everyone I have met." Her eyes shown with sincerity. How could such a haughty man be related to her? "My dear brother is forever scolding me to be more diligent in remembering faces and names." She smiled wanly, looking expectantly at Lord Linwood.

He merely gave a hint of smile. "Indeed, sister. It would be an impossibility to remember all who come within our acquaintance, particularly those who are . . . unremarkable."

Emme felt herself stiffen at his slight. Really, he was a fairly horrid man. Again, his gaze skimmed over Emme, still dismissive but somehow speculative.

"Yes, of course, Miss Linwood," Arthur enthused, taking the opportunity to move closer to her, ignoring the tension. "It can be hard to remember everyone."

"Memory can be a tricky thing," Sir Henry agreed, his mustache wiggling as he spoke. It was truly impressive, wide and bushy below his nose. Like some furry animal had taken up residence on his face. Emme assumed Sir Henry had a mouth underneath somewhere. Not that she could see it.

"Thank you all for your patience," Emme said, determined to not be cowed. "I am sorry to be such a trial. Sometimes the first idea that comes into my head is correct and other times it obviously is not."

Linwood expelled air from his lungs, clearly indicating his wish for the conversation to end. James tensed at Emme's side.

"Never fear, Miss Emma!" Sir Henry boomed. "I am most eager to help you recover your missing memory, m'dear. I knew a fellow once in Antigua who had been hit on the head by a yardarm. Poor fellow lost his memory and most of his power of speech. He could barely walk for three months afterward. . . ."

Sir Henry continued his story until the butler announced dinner.

An hour later, Emme wondered when simply eating dinner had become so difficult. As the guest of honor, she found herself seated next to Sir Henry at the head of the large table, heavy with crystal and silver.

This would have been fine but Lord Linwood—as the highest ranking peer in attendance—had been placed opposite her. He managed to communicate his disdain of her continued presence without so much as lifting an eyebrow. Fortunately, James had been seated on her other side.

Sitting down, she had recognized the array of silverware and glasses next to her plate. She knew generally which item to use and when.

The food had been less so. Some things she recognized (the roast beef that Sir Henry carved) but other dishes not so much (a gelatinous mass with what looked suspiciously like a hog's foot suspended inside). There had been a chicken curry dish with fluffy rice that she had particularly enjoyed. It was the most familiar tasting entree of the entire evening, and Emme said as much.

"Fascinating, madam," Sir Henry nodded. "You find the taste of curry familiar then?"

"I do. Though I think the curries I have eaten in the past have been a little spicier than this. But it is still delightful." The last part said with an apologetic smile. Lord Linwood flicked his eyes sideways as she spoke, the look somehow conveying absolute annoyance and boredom in one single glance.

"Fascinating," Sir Henry said again, mustache twitching, indifferent to Linwood's haughty behavior. "Perhaps you have spent time in India, Miss Emma?"

Sir Henry continued to treat Emme as if she were some sort of archaeological dig. That if he managed to explore the right spot, he would reveal all her secrets. So far he had uncovered that Emme spoke a little French, an astonishing amount of Spanish, had a decent knowledge of Homer and a startling understanding of the current conflict with Napoleon.

He brought another bite of food to his mouth. Emme had to force herself to stop watching him eat. Sir Henry somehow navigated food around his mustache without leaving any behind. Impressive. They both were. The mustache and the eating.

Emme considered his question and then shrugged her shoulders. "I could not say. You have traveled much then, Sir Henry?"

"Sir Henry is famous in these parts for his exploits as a young man. I understand he cut quite a figure with the ladies in his day." James murmured the last part from behind his hand, deliberately pitching his voice to carry.

"You are being too kind, James m'boy." Sir Henry wagged his eyebrows in a way that Emme supposed to be expressive. However, as his eyebrows were only slightly less bushy than his mustache, they looked more like arching caterpillars. "I was always the despair of my father, never able to stay put for too long. Had too much wanderlust. I have visited a great many places, though I never made it to India or the East

Orient. My family had holdings in the West Indies, and so I spent much of my youth in the Bahamas."

"The Bahamas . . . ," Emme repeated softly, pausing. The word instantly conjured a distinct image of white sand, lapping ocean and palm trees waving in the breeze. She could practically taste the salt sea air.

"It is a cluster of islands off the coast of the Americas." Linwood misunderstood her silence, his tone clearly conveying his opinion of her intelligence. Emme blinked in surprise at his speaking at all.

"Yes," she replied, trying to capture the fleeting image. "It's a tropical place with miles of white sandy beaches and palm trees full of coconuts. Isn't Nassau the capital?"

Now it was Linwood's turn to blink in surprise. She managed to force him to meet her eyes for a fraction of a second before he dismissed her gaze again. It felt like a victory.

Sir Henry's face brightened. Or rather his mustache quivered in approval. "Indeed! Not everyone would know such a thing. Fascinating!"

Linwood's fork clattered to his plate as he dabbed at his mouth with his napkin, his mouth set in a firm line.

Emme nodded silently and turned her head back to the stuffed little bird she was currently eating. Or rather pushing around her plate to make it appear as if she were eating. It had eyeballs. And a beak.

It was unnerving.

But, really, that described her entire evening.

Linwood was being an ass.

James recognized this was nothing new. Linwood had long been a connoisseur of boorish behavior.

But he was quite sure that Linwood had hit a new low (or was it a high?) with his performance this evening.

And when faced with such churlish behavior, James only knew one way to respond.

"Sir Henry is a great collector of the exotic, particularly rare plants," James said to Emma and then paused, deliberately catching the viscount's eye opposite him. "Do you not agree, Linwood?"

Linwood blinked at him, slow and deliberate, conveying a wealth of disdain in the simple gesture. James gave the tiniest ghost of smile. Emma and Sir Henry glanced at them both as the pause lengthened.

Finally, Linwood said, "We all know that Sir Henry has a great love for the unusual. His taste is generally acceptable, unlike . . . others . . . with whom I am acquainted."

James nodded. It was a decent hit by Linwood's standards. But far too predictable.

He waited for Sir Henry's reply, grabbing and holding Linwood's gaze as their host spoke.

"Thank you, m'dear boy." Sir Henry beamed at Linwood. "You have always been such a capital fellow!" He reached over and gave Linwood a hearty slap on the shoulder and then turned back to eating the quail on his plate.

James held Linwood's eye throughout, smiling slightly. Linwood had walked easily into the set up. There was little that annoyed Linwood more than being called *boy* and *fellow*. Not to mention the unauthorized touching of his person.

James considered it a win.

Linwood's lips twitched, conceding the score.

"Thank you, Sir Henry," the viscount said, leaning back into his chair, "though I understand that Knight might finally be interested in selling you his father's coin collection." He gestured toward James, raising an eyebrow fractionally.

James blinked, acknowledging the parry.

"Indeed! Indeed!" Sir Henry turned with excitement to James. "How wonderful! Your father's coins would be the pinnacle of all my collections. Is this true, Knight?"

James allowed a grin to slide across his face. Was that the best Linwood could do?

"Alas, Lord Linwood must be ill-informed." James paused long enough to lend the word a wealth of meaning. "But as I have always said, should I decide to sell, I will contact you first, Sir Henry."

James lifted his wine glass in a subtle salute to Linwood, indicating the viscount needed to try harder. Linwood responded with a faint clenching of his jaw.

Emma stirred at James' side. Almost unconsciously, Linwood's gaze flicked to her.

In that fleeting glance, James saw in the viscount's eyes something he did not like. Linwood surveyed her with a look of . . . interest. There was no other word for it. As if Linwood were shopping for a new mare and liked what he saw.

Something bristly and ugly reared within James. It was a new emotion. One he had no memory of ever feeling before.

Linwood brought his gaze back, noting James' narrowed eyes, the sudden tensing of his shoulders. Linwood's mouth curved up ever so slightly. Though unintentional, the viscount realized he had scored a direct hit.

"What are your favorite things to collect, Sir Henry?" Emma said, drawing their host's attention back to herself.

Emma turned and shot a loaded glance back at James. She was trying to deflect the tension. Bless her.

Sir Henry beamed. "Such an excellent question, Miss Emma. Exotic plants are the prize of my greenhouses. In fact, there was one plant I discovered while traveling in the back country of Virginia. . . ." Sir Henry continued at length.

Of course, asking Sir Henry about his collections was also another excellent way to annoy Linwood, who turned to glare icy daggers at his food.

James shifted his gaze back to Emma, noting the small wry smile that hovered on her lips. She flicked her eyes to Linwood and then rolled them slightly into her head, indicating her opinion of the viscount. James' own answering grin tightened.

Ah yes, she was a delight.

She turned back to their host, giving him her attention. But James found himself looking at her as Sir Henry rattled on.

The dusky green of her gown lent her skin a gentle glow in the candlelight and caught the mossy highlights in her eyes. The clever mind and good humor behind her wide smile drawing him in. James took a deep breath and ignored that kicked-through-the-gut feeling that was becoming all too familiar when around her. It was a serious nuisance. Making his thinking crowded.

He still smiled over their walk yesterday. Zombies? Ninjas? How did she come up with such delightfully absurd things? He loved watching emotions skitter across her face. How she seemed to be constantly exploring the world around her, finding everything different and new. Her eyes radiant and so alive.

James groaned inwardly. He was doing it again. After he had sworn not to. He had given himself a stern talking to while dressing for dinner. No matter how charming and delightful their guest appeared, the simple fact remained she knew nothing of herself. She could be betrothed or even married, making him a cad for looking at her as anything other than his guest.

A guest who would regain her memory, return to Mr. F and leave James' life as abruptly as she had entered it. As she should. As was right.

He needed to resist.

Resist her droll wit. Resist her melting hazel eyes. Resist the pull that whispered she was meant for him.

To call her intriguing was an understatement. Captivating. Bewitching, perhaps. Enough to make a man forget himself.

As long as he was the only man to do so. Linwood could take his perusing looks and go—

"Sir Henry! Sir Henry!!" Emma suddenly exclaimed, interrupting James' thoughts.

James jerked his head back to see Sir Henry staggering to his feet, his hands around his throat, his face slowly turning purple.

James swore and instantly jumped up, toppling his chair with a crash. One of the ladies behind him screamed. Dashing around Emma, he pounded upon Sir Henry's back, trying to dislodge whatever was choking him.

"Sir Henry!" he cried frantically. "Help! Can someone help?!"

Chapter 15

Emme stood in confusion. Time moved in slow motion. Later she would wonder why she hadn't panicked too. Why she had felt such calm.

But at the moment, she experienced no fear. Just puzzlement. Choking seemed a simple thing to solve. But James wasn't doing what needed to be done. In fact, he seemed desperate.

Darting her eyes around the room, Emme realized Sir Henry would die unless someone helped him. But no one moved. No one seemed to know what to do.

With a shake of her head, Emme rushed forward and pushed James aside. Standing behind Sir Henry, she wrapped her hands around his girth, placing one fist into his solar plexus, her other hand on top on it and then jerked upward hard and swift.

Once. Twice. Three times. The movement was difficult in her tight corset. Emme's ribs strained against the whalebone stays. But on the third jerk, a large piece of quail launched from Sir Henry's mouth and shot down the table, landing with a splash in the vicar's glass of claret.

Sir Henry collapsed, drawing in a ragged deep breath of air and sank to the floor, coughing violently. Emme sighed in relief and lifted her head.

Everyone in the room stared at her. James. Linwood. Arthur. Marianne. Georgiana. The vicar and his wife. The portly son frozen with fork halfway to his mouth. The horrified matron shielding her daughters from the excitement. Even the white-haired spinsters peered cautiously from behind.

All with the crazy eyes.

Not knowing what to say, Emme shifted her gaze to James, who stared at her with a look somewhere between awe and dismay. That startled I-have-no-clue-what-to-say look.

"I . . . I believe Sir Henry will be okay," she said. Even to her ears it seemed lame. "So . . . nothing more to see here. Keep calm and . . . uh . . . carry on."

That sounded even worse.

Not knowing what else to do, Emme bent over and slid a hand under Sir Henry's elbow to help him back into his chair. He continued to cough, and Emme pressed a glass of water into his hand. He took it with shaking hand and drank deeply.

"Thank you, m'dear. This indeed does take all," Sir Henry murmured to Emme when he could talk, his voice hoarse. "You saved my life. I thought you to be remarkable, but now I know you to be so."

James met her eyes over Sir Henry's head, his expression clearly stating he felt the same.

"Are you ready to try this?" James asked, gesturing toward the placid mare being led by a groom.

"Of course," Emma replied with a confident nod of her head.

James noted that she seemed well-rested despite all the excitement of the night before. Sir Henry had a sore throat but was otherwise fine from his near-death experience. He had thanked Emma over and over until his voice ran out entirely. All of the other guests had treated her with a mixture of awed respect and wary suspicion. Linwood had merely looked bored, acting as if the entire incident had not occurred.

This morning, Emma wore Georgiana's red velvet riding habit and a jaunty little hat. James suppressed a pang at seeing her in it. How long had it been since Georgiana had felt well enough to ride? Any strain made breathing difficult. Another reminder of how his sister's illness had limited her choices. Though Georgiana's health had improved with Emma's presence, she was far from cured.

Emma, however, glowed with vitality and warmth, the deep red of the gown catching highlights in her dark hair. He mentally sighed against the feeling of familiarity whenever she was near. Like she was the other half that completed him—a piece of his life that he hadn't realized had been lost. Like a telescope where initially all is blurry and confused, but then with a few adjustments, everything becomes sharply distinct.

What had started as a simple, good-natured attempt to put their guest at ease was rapidly turning into something more. A something more that could never be. James realized he needed a good bout with Ethan. That usually settled his thinking.

However, he ruefully acknowledged seeing Emma again would immediately unsettle his thinking. The way things were going, he would need a good fight about every four hours or so to work out his tangled emotions. James shook his head. When had he become so maudlin?

Emma approached the mare, making calming noises and gently

scratching the horse between the eyes. The sedate mare would give her no trouble.

"Are you ready?" he asked again.

"Yes. Though it seems you chose a decidedly calm mount for my first excursion. Perhaps a little too docile for my taste." She gave him a wry grin.

Moving comfortably around to the mare's side, she inspected the side-saddle.

"But this saddle. . . ." He watched as she paused and studied it with a puzzled look. "So I place my right knee over this pommel and wedge my left knee under this one, correct?" She gestured toward the forked pommel of the saddle.

James nodded. "Would you like help up?"

"Please."

James stepped close to her and cupped his gloved hands together, making a pocket for her left foot. He watched her breathe in and tried to ignore the subtle scent of lavender that clung to her. Tried to ignore the searing touch of her gloved hand as she placed it on his right shoulder for balance. He lifted his head and found himself staring into her hazel eyes, green and gold in the morning light. Pools of liquid summer.

Her eyes widened slightly, as if his nearness affected her too.

The moment lingered just a little too long.

James felt his chest constrict sharply. And in that moment he realized.

He was falling. Fast and hard.

With a swallow, Emma broke their gaze and placed her booted foot into his hands, springing up. She twisted herself into the side saddle, hooking her right knee over the top pommel and settling her balance, back straight and facing forward.

"Here is your riding cane," James said, handing up a long quirt to her, trying to bring his heart rate down.

She took it with a somewhat puzzled look.

James smiled. "It's your opposite leg, for cuing the horse as you ride."

Emma nodded her head in understanding, though seemed to be thoughtfully considering something too. "This all makes perfect sense.

But may I be shockingly honest for a moment?"

James chuckled. "Please. Complete candor is always a delight."

"I do believe I am used to riding a horse astride, not side saddle."

James felt a small jolt of surprise. *That* was a mental image he had not needed this morning. Riding astride was not common for a woman, though not unheard of either.

"Side saddle may take some getting used to," Emma conceded.

Taking a deep breath and forcing his unruly emotions aside, James swung up onto Luther's back. "Let's get started, shall we?"

They rode at a sedate pace, James keeping an eye on Emma to ensure she stayed in her saddle. Though slightly wobbly at first, she seemed to have settled in, controlling her horse easily. Of course, the gentle mare was not one to cause trouble.

"This is lovely. Thank you for suggesting a ride," Emma murmured after a while, patting the mare's neck. "Though next time, I might request a more spirited mount, Mr. Knight."

"James," he corrected her without thinking.

Now why had he done that? He was supposed to be putting distance between them. Not encouraging more intimacy.

But for some reason, his mouth was acting separately from his brain.

So, of course, he continued, "You call Georgiana by her first name. You should extend the courtesy to me as well."

Her eyebrows rose fractionally. "Wouldn't it be considered a little fast for me to call you James?"

"Probably."

He watched her consider it for a moment and then shrug her shoulders. "I suppose it shan't hurt. I admitted earlier to riding astride, and I seem to know a great many unusual things, like how to prevent gentleman from choking."

"Which proved miraculously useful, as Sir Henry would assure you," James chuckled.

"And we mustn't forget I was quite thoroughly snubbed by a viscount, so calling you James shouldn't detract too much from my already doubtful reputation." She finished with a teasing smile.

James snorted. "Linwood can be a complete ass at times."

"Only at times?" she quipped. "From the little I have seen and heard about him, it seems to be more a permanent state for the erstwhile viscount."

He laughed in surprise. "That is true too. We played together growing up. Arthur and I were the only children in the area that the old viscount considered worthy of associating with his heir. But Timothy was always so serious, too serious for me as a playmate. And Arthur practically hero-worshipped him, always following Timothy about like a lost puppy."

"Arthur didn't worship you? Isn't that what younger brothers are supposed to do?"

James snorted. "I am hardly worship-worthy material. My mother made it clear from an early age that my behavior was something of a disgrace. Arthur was quick to absorb her lessons."

"Truly? What do you do that is so disgraceful?"

"For starters, I try but usually fail to care about propriety as much as I should."

"Indeed?"

"For example, I just realized I should have included a groom on our little excursion here." James glanced around them with a slight grimace. "So now you find yourself alone with me without a chaperone. A classic example of my thoughtlessness, as Arthur would say."

James shook his head. He would never learn. Thoughts struggled to stay in his head at times. And unless something was important to him, he usually completely forgot about it.

"Are we not to be alone together?" Emma's brow creased, as if trying to recall something but failing.

"Propriety would say so."

"Oh dear, how could you!" Her hazel eyes held his, teasing. "And if I call you James, doesn't it also follow that you should call me Emma?"

"Probably." James slanted a sideways glance at her. She had a small smile on her lips.

"Perfect," she said, locking and holding his gaze. "James, do you think that this sweet mare might be able to stretch her legs a bit? I would love to go for more of a real ride."

James merely winked at her and kicked Luther into a gallop, grinning as she gasped and encouraged her mare to follow.

"Cheater!" Her voice called after him.

They rode their horses into a lather and then turned back toward Haldon Manor, the path taking them through the north end of Marfield. James tipped his hat to each tenant he encountered. People who had either raised him or he had grown up with or he now provided for. Sometimes all three at once. It never ceased to surprise him how intertwined rural country lives were. They stopped to chat with Mr. Peters and asked about his goats (who had escaped yet again). And when the youngest Griffith boy darted by, James inquired after the health of his prize sheepdog (who had just been delivered of a record twelve puppies). They had set their mounts toward home again when commotion erupted from the row of houses down a side street.

A large woman was unceremoniously tossing things out her front door and into the road. Her bright red hair escaped from her matron's cap, and a stream of obscenities flowed from her mouth. A bumbling man staggered in the street, trying to alternately catch and dodge items as they flew at him.

It appeared Mrs. Baker had had enough. Again

Mr. Baker was something of a philanderer and a lot of a drunk. Neither of which set well with Mrs. Baker, even on a good day. Every couple of months, he would do something truly outrageous, and Mrs. Baker would toss him—along with random possessions—out of the house. Mr. Baker would gather them up and go sleep at the blacksmith's until his wife invited him back. It always created quite the ruckus, giving Mrs. Baker some much needed attention and sympathy from her neighbors. It also afforded Mr. Baker a much needed reprieve from his wife.

James paused. He should probably shepherd Emma away from Mrs. Baker's somewhat expansive use of the English language. But turning, he caught Emma's eye, saw the delighted mischief in them. Watched her lips twitch with repressed laughter. Their gazes locked and held.

Current hummed between them.

Emme found herself staring as the woman tossed things out of her house, streaming vulgarities.

It was quite the performance.

The woman would stand in the doorway and scream, gesturing wildly, and then she would stride back into the house, muffling her language, and then appear at an upper window, still mid-sentence, flinging shirts and breeches and shoes one item at a time dramatically out the window. All the while turning the air blue, her face red as her hair from the exertion. Her half-drunk husband staggered below to catch the items as they fell. Trying to look bashful or ashamed but failing at both. And throughout it all, little dogs squealed and ran.

No. Emme took that back.

Not dogs. Piglets. Those were piglets.

Three of them, squeeing and oinking and generally adding to the mayhem. They would first hide behind Mrs. Baker. When she moved back into the house to drag something else out, the piglets ran into the street and danced around Mr. Baker, only to dodge whatever Mrs. Baker decided to throw. The piglets would then squeal and surround Mr. Baker, trying to jump up with their too short little legs.

It was totally awesome.

Or so thought Alter Emme.

Even better, that dry voice in her head kept inserting a beeping noise every time Mrs. Baker swore.

"How dare you show your *beeping beep* face here after what Mrs. Jenkins told me you were up to last night with that *beep beeeeeping* trollop! *Beep, beep BEEEPPP*!! How could you make me a laughing stock yet again?!" She punctuated each profanity by jabbing a hand into the air.

Alter Emme was of the opinion that Mrs. Baker was doing a fine job of humiliating herself sans her husband's assistance. The squealing piglets seemed to agree.

Emme chanced a sideways glance at James, catching his eye. She held his gaze for a moment, noting his suppressed mirth. She loved that they both saw humor in the absurd. Something deep within her whispered that this kind of connection was rare. But Emme wasn't prepared to analyze such feelings.

So instead, she said, "If I had to choose a winner, I do believe I would place my money on the piglets."

James smiled, wide and crinkly as usual. "Indeed. They do look small but fierce."

"You are going to interrupt my fun, aren't you?" She flitted a glance back to the emotional carnage. It truly was a spectacular site.

"Probably."

"And say that my tender ears shouldn't be listening to such profane language. Am I right?"

James chuckled, "Why, yes, indeed. Mrs. Baker has expanded our linguistic horizons quite enough for one day. Come. I want to check on something on the way home."

He turned his mount and continued on down the road. Reluctantly, with a longing backward glance at the ongoing circus, Emme nudged her mare to follow.

Outside Marfield, they turned down the road to Haldon Manor but soon left the lane. Wending their way through the rustling forest, Emme blinked as they emerged from the shade of the trees and rode into a wide clearing. The large meadow felt familiar though somehow not.

Enormous branches were strewn across the space, tumbled with leaves turning brown. Here and there were signs of people having visited. Jugs of ale, bowls with grain, bundles of tied herbs dangling from branches.

James stopped and dismounted, tethering his mount to a convenient branch.

"Give me a moment," James said, turning to her. "I am just curious to see what offerings the villagers are leaving. It will just take a moment." Emme watched as he walked through the branches, bending to examine different objects.

And then she saw it. The enormous trunk, cleaved sharply into two gaping halves.

It stood apart in the middle of the meadow. Beckoning.

Without thinking, Emme slid off her horse. James had moved to the other side of the clearing, sifting through the downed limbs, smelling one of the jugs with a grimace.

Emme walked toward the split trunk, carefully picking her way over the debris. The old tree drew her forward. She lifted her skirts high, surely showing too much leg to be thought proper, but not wanting to snag Georgiana's beautiful habit.

At the edge of the trunk, she paused. The air felt heavy around her, even though a chill still clung to the damp morning. Peering into the tree, she found the trunk oddly hollow at the bottom, dark and yawning. The air around her crackled, as if charged with electricity. Something seemed to tug her forward, pulling her into the oak. She jumped backward, startled, stumbling.

That had felt odd. Very odd.

A little spooked, Emme turned to leave, only to find the back of her habit snagged on something.

Sighing, she tried to twist to untangle herself, only to get her hair and hat caught too. Lifting her hand to untangle her hair resulted in getting her sleeve stuck. Before long, each slight movement ended in the sound of fabric stretching and tearing. The ancient oak had a thousand little hands all determined to keep her in place.

Like a Christmas goose trussed for the fire, she was hopelessly caught. One hand behind her back, the other stretched over her head. It seemed impossible to get free without destroying her clothing in the process.

It was a ridiculous mess.

And then she heard James.

"Emma? Emma, where did you go?"

"Here!" she called, feeling a mixture of relief and embarrassed dread. "Here and quite thoroughly stuck." She tried for a game little laugh. James was not one to let her live this down.

She saw him out of the corner of her eye, coming toward her, picking his way through the downed limbs, his brown overcoat swinging around his calves. Concern in his eyes.

"Trying to get away, were you?" he said with a slight smile as he came closer and saw her predicament.

Emme felt an almost overwhelming feeling of deja vu. As if this scene had somehow played out before. In this very meadow. His worried look. Her feeling of distress and relief at seeing him.

Again, so odd.

James paused in front of her, frowning at her convoluted position and the tangled mass of branches.

"You did all this yourself? Are you sure you don't have a knack for trouble?"

At her simple nod, James gave a low chuckle. He stepped close and began to break and pull sticks, gently freeing her.

"It is truly impressive." James leaned in, his chest lightly brushing her shoulder, reaching around to untangle the back of her habit. "Utterly remarkable."

His warm breath tickled her ear, as she absorbed his double entendre. Her heart suddenly galloped.

He was so close, closer than he had ever been, smelling of leather and sandalwood and clean soap. Emme could see the pulse jumping in his throat. Feel the heat of his body. See the smooth skin of his neck and freshly shaved cheek.

It took all of her restraint not to lean into his warmth. To bury her nose in that hollow between his jaw and ear and breathe him in. It would feel so natural. So right.

Alter Emme melted in delight. *He is so delish.*

Emme sighed. He was.

For his part, James seemed to move slowly. Taking his time in freeing her. His hands lingered in her hair, on her arms, around her waist.

As he untangled the last branches, she finally dared to lift her gaze to his face. Only to find him staring intently at her, his blue eyes fathomless. All smiles gone, gaze focused and serious. His eyes flitted down to her mouth. Emme knew with a certainty if she leaned even slightly toward him, he would kiss her.

And even worse, she realized that she wanted it. She wanted his kiss. Wanted to feel his warm lips on hers. Ached to drown herself in his arms.

Oh yes! Alter Emme whispered.

Almost unbidden, Emme felt herself start to lean in, closing those last few inches. James' gaze remained fixed on her lips, his eyes closing as he drifted closer.

But then a thought flitted through Emme's head.

The locket. You have another man.

With a jerk of her head, Emme swallowed and took a small step backwards.

Argh! Alter Emme groaned in frustration.

"Thank you for not teasing me," she managed to whisper, trying to break the tension. "These scrapes are ridiculously embarrassing."

She watched as James blinked and pulled his eyes from her mouth. His heavy breathing matched her own.

"I am glad I was here to help." His gaze stayed for a moment on her face, and then he turned away, his expression shuttered, though Emme heard him mutter quietly, "Teasing was not *my* intention."

She knew he hadn't meant for her to hear, but the truth of his words seared her. She felt herself blush, hot and uncomfortable.

Blushing? Seriously? When was the last time you blushed? Alter Emme sounded amazed.

Emme agreed, silently hoping to avoid any other blush-worthy situations.

Particularly those that involved one Mr. James Knight.

Chapter 16

Again, Miss Emma, you must accept my profound thanks for saving my life," Sir Henry exclaimed for the sixteenth time.

Or was it seventeen? Emme had lost count.

"And again, Sir Henry, you are welcome," she replied. "I am glad I had some lingering memory which helped me know what to do."

Emme was seated on a sofa in the drawing room with Georgiana perched beside her, passing out cups of tea and slices of lemon pound cake. Sir Henry sat in a chair opposite, mustache twitching with gratitude.

His voice was still raspy and hoarse, but otherwise Sir Henry seemed in good health despite his ordeal. He had arrived in grand style, accompanied by a footman bearing a large draped basket that now sat on a side table. When Emme had asked what was in it, Sir Henry had merely chuckled—or rather his mustache had bounced—and said she would see in due time. He insisted on waiting for James before unveiling the contents of his mysterious basket.

Emme pushed aside thoughts of that moment earlier near the old oak. It had been a momentary lapse and would not happen again. Fortunately, James had let the moment pass without further comment and had even matched her easy banter on the ride home. She hoped he understood. With no memory and no understanding of her past, she was hardly in a position to embrace a new future—either literally or figuratively. She just needed to not think about James Knight.

Determined to do so, Emme murmured thanks as Georgiana handed her a plate of cake. Georgiana's cough had been better the last couple days, but her breath wheezed from time to time—a deep rasping from her chest that strained to bring in enough air. James mentioned he had been seeking out doctors who specialized in consumption, though he had found little that would give them hope. But today Georgiana seemed better. Her skin less gray, her eyes bright and full of life.

"James, there you are!" Georgiana exclaimed rising to her feet, looking past Emme.

Emme stood as well, turning to see James stride through the door, his crinkly smile in full view.

Really, did the air have to whoosh out of her lungs *every* time she saw him?

His restless energy filled the room, drawing every eye to him. Emme paused, hunting for the word. . . .

Charisma, Alter Emme supplied. *The word you are looking for is charisma.*

Yes, that was it.

Lucky her.

"Sir Henry. Georgiana." James nodded his head in greeting. "Miss Emma," he said as he stopped in front of her. His smile became slightly teasing as he gave a short bow, extending his hand to her. Clearly she had been forgiven for whatever had not transpired in the meadow earlier.

Emme hesitated, locking eyes with his, and then remembered. Smoothly dipping her head to James, she laid her hand in his, palm facing down, murmuring "Good afternoon, Mr. Knight."

"Well done, Miss Emma," said Sir Henry from behind her. "Your memory must be improving. Perfect greeting, m'dear."

"Yes, indeed, very pretty," James said approvingly, bowing over her knuckles, leaving Emme to wonder what exactly he found 'pretty.' His touch scalded her fingers, while his mischievous eyes danced, letting her know the vague meaning had been intentional.

"Thank you." Did her voice sound a little breathless? She gently removed her hand from his, wistfully letting her fingertips slide along the length of his warm hand. How was she supposed to fight this?

Oh, you are so geeking out on him, Alter Emme grinned.

James accepted an offered plate of cake from his sister, moving to stand in front of the fireplace. Emme bit her cheek, forcing her heart rate down. Her mind full of a thousand "what ifs."

What if the man in the locket didn't exist? What if her memory never came back? What if she decided to just lose herself in a pair of melting blue eyes?

Exactly! Forget locket-boy. I want to drool over Mr. Swoony Smile.

Emme swallowed and sat back down on the settee, drawing a deep, steadying breath.

Her dry voice was not helping. Again.

Oh, I'm sorry. I meant Mr. Uber-Delicious, Alter Emme taunted.

Okay, she needed to stop.

Mr. Hot Hotty McHotterson?

Really? That was just bratty.

Yes. Yes it was. Alter Emme was totally unrepentant.

Emme shook her head slightly. Maybe more than her memory had been addled.

Hey, who's being bratty now? And you do realize that Mr. Charisma is more than just a melting smile, right?

Yes, indeed. That was precisely the problem.

Emme mentally shook her head and brought her attention back to the room.

"I am glad to see you are up and about, Sir Henry," James was saying.

"Thank you, m'boy. I was just telling Miss Emma how thankful I am she was my guardian angel last evening." Sir Henry beamed at her.

Eighteen, Emme mentally tallied. She couldn't help it.

"Oh, did Miss Emma mention that we caught Mr. and Mrs. Baker in the middle of a fight this morning?" James said turning to Georgiana.

"I have always heard about their terrible rows. How lucky you were to actually witness one!" Georgiana said with a thrilled grin. "I wonder what Mr. Baker did this time?"

"Why do I feel you will ferret it out, dear sister?" James chuckled.

Georgiana tried to give James a disapproving look, but he merely raised an eyebrow at her and held her gaze until she broke off with a laugh.

"I could deny it, brother, but it is too true." She tapped her lips, lost in thought for a moment. "I bet Fanny would know what happened."

"You are shameless," James said, though his wide smile belied his words.

"Indeed I am, brother dear. Though you of all people should know that by now," Georgiana laughed in return, her eyes mischievous.

Emme found endless delight in watching James tease his sister and Georgiana give it back to him in full measure. It felt familiar somehow. Emme sighed. Not that she could remember.

Yeah, so over the whole no-memory thing, Alter Emme agreed. *It's so last week.*

Georgiana smiled and changed the topic. "Sir Henry, when will we get to taste some of your prized gooseberries?" she asked as she passed him a cup of tea, glancing slyly at James.

"My gooseberries?" Sir Henry suddenly came to attention as he grasped the cup. His mustache positively quivering in delight.

James gave his sister a warning look and a slight shake of his head. Georgiana just smirked in reply, biting her bottom lip to stifle a smile. The entire exchange puzzled Emme.

Fifteen minutes later, she thoroughly understood.

When it came to gooseberries, Sir Henry could not be diverted. He rhapsodized at length on the virtues of green versus red gooseberries, on the quirks of size, on the nuance of flavor, sometimes leaning toward that of an apple and other times that of a grape. Emme tried to picture a gooseberry but came up with nothing.

As Sir Henry talked, Georgiana and James kept exchanging loaded glances. Georgiana helping Sir Henry along whenever necessary. James giving long-suffering looks.

I knew I liked her, Alter Emme whispered.

"Sir Henry's gooseberry club is the most famous of all," Georgiana murmured when the man in question took a breath. James glared warningly at Georgiana again.

"Indeed?" Emme saw no reason not to encourage Sir Henry, as he was clearly enjoying himself. "I would love to hear more, Sir Henry."

Emme shot her own pointed look at James. He shook his head at her in mock annoyance, eyes narrowing slightly.

She tried and failed to keep the teasing grin from her face. James stared at her in return and retreated to the chair next to Sir Henry. There he sat, crossing his arms. His entire body saying oh-you-will-pay-for-this.

Sir Henry was happy to oblige, the twinkle in his eye clearly indicating he knew what was going on but didn't care, which resulted in another ten minute discourse about the vagaries of being president of the Greater Herefordshire Old Gooseberry Society. Apparently the position required exceptional tact and expertise, balancing the overblown egos of other gooseberry enthusiasts with a thorough understanding of their craft.

Fascinating, Alter Emme muttered.

Emme ignored the sarcasm in that remark, preferring instead to watch James slowly glower mock-daggers at Georgiana. She returned his glares with innocent, fake-batting of her eyelashes.

They were both clearly enjoying themselves.

Sir Henry was still going on about his precious gooseberries, James realized. Everyone in Marfield—

No, scratch that—

Everyone in Herefordshire knew better than to ask Sir Henry about his gooseberries. Unless you had a couple hours to drown in a painful, fruit-filled monologue.

He took a deep breath and stared at his traitorous sister, who returned his stare with a decidedly mischievous twinkle. What had Georgiana been thinking to bait Sir Henry so? The wretch!

But then he caught himself. How long had it been since Georgie had been like this? That laughter-loving girl he so adored?

He instantly knew the answer. Emma drew Georgiana out. Out of that gray world of half-living. Out of waiting for death to claim her. His sister's laugh filled him with an aching joy. An intense longing. And he silently thanked Emma for bringing even a little sunshine to Georgiana's life.

Emma's name on Sir Henry's lips brought his attention back.

"You do realize there is the occasional trace of an American accent in your speech, do you not, Miss Emma?" Sir Henry was saying.

James blinked. American? Again, something unexpected.

"American?" Emma's voice echoed his surprise.

"Indeed! There is a hint of it in your short vowels from time to time. Subtle, but most definitely there."

James watched emotions flicker across Emma's face. "America," she almost whispered, shaking her head as if trying to hold on to something.

"That is fascinating, Sir Henry. I wish I could remember more for you." Her face wore that befuddled look that James was coming to adore: brow furrowed, eyes pensive and inwardly searching.

"Oh, I nearly forgot," Sir Henry suddenly exclaimed. "James, m'boy, would you be so kind as to bring that basket over here." He gestured to the chair next to him. "I brought a few things for Miss Emma as a thank you."

James stood and brought the basket over. Sir Henry uncovered it with a flourish.

"Oh goodness, Sir Henry!" Georgiana exclaimed. "How delightful!"

"Indeed!" Emma echoed.

James stared at what could only be called an astounding assortment of exotic fruits. All the pride of Sir Henry's extensive greenhouses.

Emma smiled broadly and stood to examine the basket more closely. James watched her exclaim in excitement over small bananas and something he thought was an alligator pear but which she called an avocado.

"And this, Miss Emma, have you ever seen anything so delightful?" Sir Henry almost reverently pulled out a brown oval fruit about the size of an egg, covered in what looked like woolly fuzz. "I have it on good authority that I possess one of the only Chinese gooseberry bushes in all of Europe. It is the rarest of all gooseberries. Is it not marvelous?"

"Gracious," Georgiana said, looking at it with wide eyes. "I have never seen anything like it." James nodded in agreement. Even he had never beheld this oddity.

James watched as Emma's eyes lit with delight. She carefully took the fruit from Sir Henry and gently squeezed it.

"Oh, how wonderful, Sir Henry. It feels perfectly ripe. Chinese gooseberry, you say?" She frowned, giving that same little puzzled look. "I would have called this a kiwi. It is sweet and bright green inside, right? With small black seeds?"

Sir Henry blinked in surprise, nearly too stunned to speak. "Heavens, child! How could you know such a thing? This fruit is not seen outside China. How very exceptional." Sir Henry seemed almost in awe.

"What else do you recognize, Emma?" James asked, gesturing back toward the basket.

"Well, let me see." Emma peered into the basket and then started to name items. "We have pineapple, of course. One of my favorites. And then there is passion fruit, mango, star fruit and, oh look, peanuts!" She eagerly picked up several of the small wrinkled pods. "Are they roasted, Sir Henry?" And then without waiting for a reply, she cracked the shell with her fingers and released a small reddish nut into her hand.

"No. Are they better roasted?"

"Oh yes. And best of all with chocolate. We should melt some chocolate and dip them." And then she paused, as if puzzling something out. "Do we have any solid chocolate? I think I have only seen it in drinking form."

James frowned. "I am not sure. Perhaps Mrs. Clark knows. I believe there was a traveling merchant here last month with some of that new solid chocolate from Italy. Do you remember, Georgiana?"

He turned to his sister who most certainly looked as surprised as himself. What life had Emma led before finding herself along his lane? Instead of finding answers, time seemed to be creating more questions.

Indeed, in the end, the only item Emma could *not* identify from Sir Henry's basket was the common English gooseberry.

Chapter 17

Is Auntie Gray expecting us?" Georgiana quietly murmured as she took James' offered hand and stepped down from the carriage.

"Probably. You know as well as I that very little remains a secret in Marfield," James ruefully replied.

He turned back to hand down Emma, looking lovely in a ribbon trimmed straw bonnet and rich blue pelisse over her white muslin walking dress. He caught and held her gaze as she slid her gloved hand into his, her hazel eyes wide underneath the brim of her hat, looking far too lovely for his peace of mind.

From the corner of his eye, he noted Arthur dismount and offer Georgiana his arm. Relishing the fine weather, James and his brother had ridden, while the ladies had come in the carriage intending to call on Marianne Linwood at Kinningsley afterward. James had business with Mr. Chatham, his solicitor.

James politely knocked and heard the answering "Come in" from inside. He stooped to enter the cottage, grateful that his head cleared the low beamed ceiling. The house smelled of wholesome things: fresh cut herbs, warm hay and earthy woodsmoke. James caught a glimpse of one of Auntie's granddaughters in the back kitchen, kneading bread.

Auntie sat by a popping fire, wrapped in blankets despite the warm May air, hunched slightly with age, seeming as ancient as the great oak itself. Stooped and bent but still sparkling with life. She looked up as they entered, light engulfing her face.

"Laddies! 'Tis good to see you!" she said warmly.

"Auntie," James replied respectfully, removing his hat and bowing. He loved that no matter how old he grew, Auntie could always be relied upon to make him feel like a five-year-old boy. He silently enjoyed watching Arthur's lips twitch at being called 'laddie.' The merry twinkle in Auntie Gray's eyes clearly indicated the term had not been unintentional.

"Auntie," Georgiana said warmly, moving to take the chair at her side, favoring the woman's worn cheek with a fond kiss. "It is so good to see you!"

"How fare you child?" Auntie's voice cracked with the weight of age, threaded with a slight reediness. She patted Georgiana's hand affectionately with her own arthritic one and gestured for them all to sit at chairs arranged around the fire.

"Well enough, Auntie."

James watched Georgiana swallow a cough, trying valiantly not to appear as weak and tired as she must feel. "Some days are better than others. I make the best use of the time God has seen fit to still allow me." She ceded and coughed slightly.

"Oh, you mustn't worry, m'dear. I have always said God has a bright future in store for you! You just need to have the faith to believe upon it."

"Of course, Auntie," she said weakly, though not quite agreeing with the words. "You are always such a comfort." Georgiana coughed again. James quietly handed her his handkerchief, forcing his face to reflect nothing of the pain of watching her struggle to take a breath.

"I see you have brought your mysterious house guest for me to meet. How charming!"

"Yes, Auntie, please allow me to introduce Miss Emma." James smiled as Emma nodded her head in greeting.

"It's a pleasure to meet you, ma'am."

Auntie smiled, broad and wrinkly. "Indeed, child, the pleasure is all mine. You have given us all much to talk about. I greatly appreciate you providing me with some much needed entertainment. Life here can be quite dull at times."

Emma's face broke into a hesitant smile. "Well, as confusing as I find my current circumstances, if they have lifted your spirits, then perhaps there has been some good in it all. Though I think I shall be most grateful when my memory returns."

"Yes . . . perhaps." Auntie looked thoughtful for a moment. Then her voice soft and faded, nearly whispering the words, "My heart tells me you are a long way from home, child. Perhaps a good deal farther than you think. A wandering soul in search of its place. . . . A voyager of sorts."

Emma's mouth pursed into a little 'o' of surprise. Like Auntie's words had struck something deep within her. "Thank you." And then again, gently nodding her head. "Thank you."

"Have faith, child. All will makes sense in time. It always does."

"Auntie, I'm sure you know why we are here." James shifted and leaned forward in his chair. "The ancient oak tree . . . it seems that offerings are still being left. Though I know that the old superstitions are fading, it seems there is still apprehension over the oak's destruction. Some worry about the supposed secret the oak guards."

"Well, m'boy, first of all, there is nothing 'supposed' about the great oak's secret. It has guarded its burden well. But it is obvious that the burden still exists." This last bit was said with an odd slanting glance at Emma. "And as the ancient oak is on your land, it will be up to you, lad, to protect it going forward."

"Indeed," Arthur said, caustically. "And what precisely is this terrible secret that needs protecting? You have never been particularly forthcoming with that piece of information."

Despite his acerbic tone, James had to agree with Arthur. Auntie had never explained what exactly the oak was guarding.

"The oak's secret remains the same as it ever was." Auntie's gleaming eyes danced slightly. She seemed to be enjoying herself.

"And that is. . . ." Arthur waved his hand, indicating for her to elaborate.

"The ancient oaks have always been portals into the netherworld."

"Right," Arthur said with a disbelieving huff. "And how precisely is this gateway such a danger?"

"Because you never know who might fall into it or who might come out."

Arthur gave a heavy, long-suffering sigh.

"And is really that such a danger? Netherworld people coming and going?" Arthur seemed to have found an outlet for his frustration. "Have you truly ever known anyone to use this netherworld portal?"

"Of course not. . . . Well, not until now. The great oak was indeed truly ancient. The Romans ruled this area when it was planted and it has guarded its secret ever since. But, of course, now that it is no longer, this gateway to the netherworld could become a problem unless it is secured somehow."

"Indeed." Again, Arthur's tone oozed condescension. "Honestly, if we have to address every superstition—"

"How do you propose we do this?" James interrupted. Really, Arthur could be such a nuisance.

"That is for you to decide, I am sure," Auntie replied. "Personally, I would suggest building something over the oak's location, something that can enclose and safeguard its secrets. Haldon Manor has never had a dower house, has it?"

James considered for a moment, glancing around the room. Arthur's face hung with disbelief, while Georgiana and Emma looked on more calmly.

Slowly nodding his head, James said, "That is not a bad idea, Auntie. A dower house could provide a home for pensioned off servants until it is needed as a dower house proper. Do you feel that would allay worry?"

"I do," Auntie answered, eyes approving, "and protect the gateway."

James smiled in reply, noting Georgiana's approving grin.

As they made their goodbyes, James noted a few children loitering in the yard, obviously hoping for some tidbit to fuel the village gossip mill.

One of the braver boys approached Emma and bowing awkwardly, asked nervously, "Is it true, miss, you saved Sir Henry's life?"

"Cor!" Another boy breathed in excitement. "My sister, Annie, works as a maid at the big house, and she heard from the second footman that you made the food shoot out of his mouth, like this." The boy grabbed a loose rock and pantomimed the motion.

"And are you truly from the West Indies?" This question was from a pigtailed girl standing next to the first boy. "All of Sir Henry's servants say that . . . well . . . that Sir Henry says you are most likely from there. Is that true?"

Emma laughed good-naturedly. "Sir Henry most certainly is quite the investigator."

"Do you have memories of the West Indies?" the girl asked breathlessly. "Sir Henry says it is hot, and my cousin Betsy's neighbor's son served on a merchant ship that sailed to there, and she said that he said that the water there is as blue as a robin's eggshell. And always summer with no winter at all. Can you imagine?" This last bit was asked to the younger boy at her side.

"I really don't know," Emma replied. "I seem to have vague images of palm trees and warm, sandy beaches, so maybe I have been there." Her face appeared wistful. That same puzzled lost look.

"It is no matter," James said, trying to deflect more questions. "I am sure all will be made clear in time."

The drawing room
Kinningsely, seat of the viscounts Linwood
An hour later
May 12, 1812

"My dear friend, Miss Knight! How delighted I am to see you. And Miss Emma too." Miss Marianne Linwood walked across the room toward them, smiling broadly and welcoming, her gray half-mourning dress rustling. Reaching them, she stopped suddenly and instantly blushed, looking past to the door.

"Arthur," she breathed, her entire heart in her eyes. Quickly masking her tone of familiarity, she continued, "I mean, Mr. Knight. How delighted I am you should all call."

She gestured for them to follow her into the room and be seated. Emme and Georgiana sat in a pair of matching chairs, while Marianne and Arthur situated themselves together on a settee opposite, carefully ensuring their bodies were an appropriate distance apart. But Emme noticed Marianne let her hand rest on the cushioned seat in such a way that Arthur could casually rest his own against it. They sat staring intently at each other, exchanging emotionally laden glances. No one said anything for a handful of moments.

Emme sighed. Why had Georgiana capitulated and allowed Arthur to accompany them instead of going with James to visit their solicitor?

"I trust you are well this morning, Miss Linwood?" Georgiana asked politely, trying to draw her friend's eye away from her brother.

"Oh yes, very well indeed, now that you have come." That last bit said while letting her eyes draw sideways to Arthur. He was no better, gazing at Marianne with unabashed longing. Marianne shifted, managing to move herself a little closer to her beloved.

Wait, did she just curl her pinky finger around his? Alter Emme asked.

Indeed, she had.

Good for her, Alter Emme said approvingly.

They continued with small talk for a few minutes, Georgiana answering inquiries after her health (much improved) and the weather (beautiful since that terrible storm on Beltane).

"Oh, I have such news," Marianne said suddenly. "My brother has commissioned Mr. Spunto to paint my portrait. You know, the Italian miniaturist? He has been in the area since last year, but Lady Jenkins—not the elder, but the younger Lady Jenkins with twelve children who lives near Worcester—has kept poor Mr. Spunto quite busy this year. But now he is coming to Marfield, and Timothy says I shall have my portrait done. I thought to mention it to you, my dear Miss Knight, as perhaps yourself and your brothers would like to have your portraits done as well."

Marianne blushed rosily and then gave Arthur a decidedly pointed look.

"That is an excellent idea, Miss Linwood," Arthur breathed, his eyes drinking in her face. "I am sure James will agree. I shall have our man of business contact Mr. Spunto. It has been several years since we have had our portraits taken. I appreciate your suggestion."

"How delightful!" Marianne exclaimed.

"I could not agree more," Arthur murmured, never once taking his gaze off of Marianne, who again blushed prettily and moved her hand more fully into his, gently squeezing his fingers.

Suddenly, someone loudly cleared his throat from behind Emme and Georgiana. Startled, Emme watched Arthur instantly release Marianne's hand and jump to his feet, staring anxiously at whomever was behind them.

There really was only one option.

Emme and Georgiana also rose, though more slowly, turning to see Lord Linwood standing in all his glory. Or at least, that was how Alter Emme snarkily described him. Linwood stood looking urbane in a black coat, silver-threaded waistcoat and elaborately tied neckcloth. If nothing else, the man did have an excellent tailor. He nodded his head in greeting.

Linwood's eyes flitted to Emme, lingering for just a moment. Again, she saw something unexpected there. Something that assessed her. Something that looked suspiciously like interest.

Dude! Did he just check you out? Alter Emme sounded aghast.

Ignoring her inner alter voice, Emme followed Georgiana's lead and curtsied to the viscount who stared them down with his haughty gaze.

Chapter 18

"Lord Linwood, what a pleasure," Georgiana murmured.

"Timothy, how lovely for you to join us," Marianne said with a faint smile, ignoring the tension that had followed her brother into the room. "Mr. Knight was just stating he and Miss Knight will engage the services of Mr. Spunto to paint their portraits as well. Isn't that delightful?" She forced her smile wider as they all sat back down, Arthur putting as much distance as possible between himself and his not-betrothed. Marianne gave Arthur a pained look, obviously not happy about the sudden space between them.

"Indeed. Delightful," Lord Linwood intoned dryly, communicating the exact opposite of his words.

He moved to take a seat in front of the fireplace, facing them all. His body language stated he intended to protect his sister from any unwanted influences. Silence hung in the room.

Drawing in a deep breath, Marianne turned back to Emme and Georgiana with a shuttered expression. Emme felt momentarily puzzled. Was Marianne annoyed?

"Do you read much, Miss Emma?" she asked politely, trying to put her guests at ease despite her brother's chilling presence and her own frustration.

"Oh yes, Miss Linwood, I enjoy reading very much." Emme watched Marianne squirm under her brother's watchful eye, trying to curtail her longing looks toward Arthur.

With only marginal success.

She kept her head toward Emme, but every other word was punctuated by a sidelong glance at Arthur. "Have you read the latest book [glance] by the author of *Sense and Sensibility*? [long look] I believe it is called [pining stare] *Pride and Prejudice*. I just finished it and found it a delightful read."

"Yes," Georgiana agreed, studiously ignoring Marianne's longing glances, "it was a lovely read."

Emme felt relief. Here was a question she could answer. "How wonderful you both have read it. I so love *Pride and Prejudice*. It is my favorite of Austen's works."

For some reason, Emme's attempt at small talk brought the room to attention.

"Austen?" Georgiana questioned.

"Indeed, who is this Austen?" Marianne looked confused.

"Jane Austen . . . the author of *Sense and Sensibility* and *Pride and Prejudice*."

Everyone stared at her, even Lord Linwood, his eyes again looking her up and down, unsettling.

"I'm sorry, am I yet again missing something?" Emme asked, noting the resigned tone of her voice.

"How remarkable!"

This came from Marianne. She had managed to drag her gaze from Arthur and now regarded Emme with wide eyes.

"I was unaware the identity of the author of *Pride and Prejudice* had been made public. Both books have been published anonymously, merely being attributed to being written 'by a lady.' You actually know the lady's identity?" Georgiana asked.

"I cannot say." Emme frowned in confusion. The information had just sprung free from her brain. She searched her mind trying to place a face with the name Jane Austen but came up with nothing. As usual. "I cannot say if I know her or not. It's just the name that came to mind when you mentioned the books. But I do clearly remember *Pride and Prejudice*. It seems I find Mr. Darcy somewhat lacking as a romantic hero."

"What?!" Miss Marianne looked outraged.

"Lacking? Mr. Darcy? But he is so amiable." Georgiana was clearly scandalized.

"With all due respect, I must disagree. Lizzy is bright and utterly charming, but aside from his great wealth, Mr. Darcy has little else to recommend him. All the advantage in the match is on her side. He merely sits stiffly, says little and, quite frankly, I find him utterly boring." Emme only barely managed to avoid giving Lord Linwood a pointed look. However, she did see him stiffen slightly out of the corner of her eye, so perhaps her meaning had not been entirely lost on him.

Nice.

"Have you been talking to James, Emma?" Georgiana pursed her mouth. "Because he says the same thing, but I had thought he just wished to vex me!"

"Really?" Emme raised an eyebrow.

Miss Marianne's eyes opened even wider. "Mr. James Knight has read the book then? How extraordinary."

"Yes, indeed he has, Miss Linwood. I am afraid I insisted, and James is usually kind enough to humor my whims. Though I must deal with his opinions after the fact." Georgiana smiled somewhat ruefully.

"Good heavens!" Lord Linwood interjected with an ungentlemanly snort. "I cannot believe Knight would actually read such sentimental drivel."

"Yes, well, Lord Linwood, we cannot all live to your fastidious standards," Georgiana said quietly.

The room went instantly still.

Lord Linwood turned his head with deliberate exactness and fixed

Georgiana with a chilly stare. She blushed a deep pink but didn't break under his scrutiny.

I knew I liked her, Alter Emme said approvingly.

"Indeed, Miss Knight. When it comes to your eldest brother, that is quite obvious." Lord Linwood kept his tone austerely cool and distant. Georgiana blushed even deeper but did not lower her eyes.

Lord Linwood blinked as if considering a multitude of comments but deciding against them. Emme felt a small sense of surprise at his restraint.

Instead, he merely sat back stiffly.

Finally, after a decidedly awkward silence, he said, "Perhaps we have kept you too long. I fear you being knocked up if you remain too long, Miss Knight."

Uhmmm, say what? Alter Emme choked.

Emme blinked. That couldn't mean what she thought it did.

Alter Emme started to giggle.

"Do you think, Timothy?" Marianne asked, looking with concern at Georgiana. "I had thought Miss Knight's color to be greatly improved today. Do you feel tired, Miss Knight?"

"I am feeling better of late, Miss Linwood, thank you. Not nearly as fatigued."

"Yes, Georgiana has been much improved," Arthur agreed. "Though, she was quite knocked up after visiting the vicar last week."

Alter Emme went from giggle to full on rollicking laughter. *Oh, . . . he's making it worse,* she snorted.

Emme's lips twitched. She viciously tried to swallow back her amusement.

"Indeed, it would not do for her to be knocked up today, as well," Lord Linwood continued.

He's got to stop. . . . I swear I'm going to pee my pants. . . . Wait, you're not wearing any!

Emme felt a chuckle escape her.

Really, how could she help it?

Lord Linwood turned to her, cocking a decidedly not-amused eyebrow.

Emme forcefully pinched her lips together.

"Are you laughing, Miss Emma?" Lord Linwood's voice dripped with disdain. "I fail to see the humor in Miss Knight's being knocked up."

Which really was just the wrong thing to say.

Emme collapsed into full blown laughter.

Oh, oh, oh . . . can't . . . breathe . . . , Alter Emme chortled.

"I'm . . . so . . . sorry," Emme managed to gasp, trying desperately to stop. But the harder she tried to stifle her laughter, the more forcefully it came.

"Are you quite all right?" Georgiana asked, touching Emme's arm with a concerned hand.

Emme folded over in her seat, hand covering her mouth, heroically trying to stuff her mirth back inside.

Without much success.

"Perhaps she got a touch of sun," Arthur suggested. "Though riding in a carriage is usually not enough to knock one up so."

Please . . . make . . . them . . . stop! Alter Emme choked.

Doubled over in her chair, Emme laughed until her sides ached. She dug for her handkerchief, trying to wipe the tears from her face.

"Perhaps we should take our leave," Georgiana said, a small smile hovering on her lips as she helped Emme to her feet and curtsied politely.

Emme walked with her out the door, laughing the whole way.

On the road between
Kinningsley and Haldon Manor
Fifteen minutes later
May 12, 1812

"Oh heavens! What a disaster that was. Do you think that Marianne will ever forgive me?" Emme asked Georgiana, still wiping tears from her cheeks, her stomach muscles sore.

After helping them into the carriage, Arthur had merely shaken his head and nobly—with a healthy dose of long suffering—said he would stay for another moment to smooth things over with the viscount, obviously hoping to spend more time with Marianne.

Georgiana grinned fondly. "Most likely. Miss Linwood is not nearly as high in the instep as her brother. Though I daresay Lord Linwood may never speak to you again."

"Considering he has barely uttered two sentences to me up to this point, that shall hardly be any loss."

"Are you ever going to tell me what you found so humorous? You know I am often tired, so I'm not sure why my being knocked up would be funny."

Oh no.

"Please, Georgiana," Emme choked, "I would like to go a few minutes without laughing." Emme took a deep steadying breath. Really, she needed to get a handle on herself. "Tell me, have you been feeling better?"

"Indeed, I have. And I must be honest, my dearest friend, you are very much the reason for it." Georgiana nodded in amusement. "Everything about you is so diverting. Have you given any more thought to your history? How marvelous that you might be American with connections to the West Indies! I admit I stayed up half the night considering the possibilities. It is such a delightful mystery."

Emme smiled. Georgiana had been relentless in exploring every potential explanation for her appearance. Most of them cast Emme as the unwitting victim of evil relatives. Her favorite so far had Emme escaping a cousin's dank castle by crawling down a cliff and running for her life. Never mind the fact that Herefordshire, as a whole, generally lacked dismal dungeons, high cliffs and nefarious guardians.

"Of course, I made a list of all plausible ideas. Would you like to hear my personal favorite?"

Georgiana did not wait for a reply but instead instantly leaned forward, as if imparting something secret and thrilling.

"You are the daughter of a great nobleman but your beloved father remarried a horrid woman. And she demanded he cast you out, sending you to live with a kindly uncle in the Bahamas. After your uncle's untimely death—eaten by sharks when his ship sank off Jamaica—you returned here to England, only to find your father dead and your stepmother refusing you entrance to the family estate. Grief-stricken and distraught, you wandered the countryside and would have perished but for James finding you."

Georgiana gave her an eager expectant look, blue eyes wide, waiting to see if anything struck a chord with Emme.

Emme chuckled and shook her head. "Really, Georgiana, your imagination is unmatched. Though I sincerely hope that none of my relatives have been eaten by sharks."

"True," her friend agreed. "But it is fun to think of the possibilities."

Georgiana leaned back into her seat and paused for a moment, staring out the window, and then shook her blond head.

"Emma, though I know you wish desperately for your memory to return, I hope it never does."

Emme blinked in stunned surprise. Georgiana instantly blushed and then gave a resigned sigh.

"Oh dear," she said with droop of her shoulders. "I did it again. Arthur is right. I really must learn to reflect more before I speak. Here, let me think for a moment and try to phrase that better."

Emme watched as Georgiana pursed her mouth and tapped her fingers. The carriage swayed gently, trees slowly passing outside the window as they moved through the hills surrounding Haldon Manor. Emme enjoyed the smell of leather and polished wood that emanated from the carriage interior, the scent familiar somehow. After a moment, Georgiana brighten noticeably, as if coming to some conclusion.

"What I ought to have said, dearest Emma," she began, "is that I greatly enjoy your company. Your presence improves my spirits. When you are around, I do not feel the weight of my illness as much. Because of this, I dread the thought that your memory will return and you will then leave us. Of course, for your sake, I hope your memory does return and you can be reunited with your loved ones. But please forgive me for being somewhat selfish in wanting to keep you here as long as I can. I have so valued having you as a friend."

Touched, Emme reach out and took Georgiana's hand. "Oh, you are too kind, Georgiana. For the time being, I am not going anywhere, particularly as no one has yet come for me. And if someone does come to claim me, that doesn't mean that you and I cannot continue to be BFF's."

Now it was Georgiana's turn to blink in surprise. "B . . . F . . . F's?" she asked in confusion.

"Oh dear, is that an unfamiliar term?" Emme sighed. "Well, I believe it stands for Best Friends Forever. No matter what happens, you and I can still be dear friends."

Georgiana gave a light-hearted laugh. "Oh, that is delightful! The odd phrases you come up with. I should love to be your B. F. F." She pronounced the initials distinctly, obviously finding it humorous to abbreviate the words. They both laughed.

Suddenly, from the forest to their right, a tremendous crash sounded. Loud and booming, like the explosion of gunpowder. Crunching and grinding as it came closer.

The carriage abruptly lurched sideways, throwing Georgiana against Emme, both of them shrieking in terror. After a series of jolts, they came to rest slanted on the brink of the road. Georgiana and Emme stared in surprise, realizing that they were shaken but unharmed. Climbing awkwardly from the carriage, they stood in the rutted road, surveying an enormous boulder that now blocked their path.

In hindsight, Emme felt she should have seen the huge rock coming.

Not that she considered herself to have some sort of boulder sixth sense. But upon reflection, it just didn't seem like that odd of an occurrence. As if nearly being killed by a rock the size of a house were something entirely normal for her.

They were still dusting off their clothing when James found them.

He rode up on Luther and stared in wonder. At the house-size boulder blocking the road. At his sister and Emme straightening each other's bonnets. At the carriage resting at an angle off the track. At the coachman and footman struggling to unhitch the still spooked horses.

"Well," James said when he had recovered. "No one can say life is boring with you around, Emma. The unexpected always manages to find you, doesn't it?"

Chapter 19

Emme was drowning in a sea of conflicting emotions.

She had been at Haldon Manor for nearly three weeks. Three amazing and yet equally difficult weeks. Every day was full of laughter (and James) and riding (and James) and visiting with Georgiana (and James) and . . . well . . . mostly just being with James.

Every night, she pulled the locket out of its hiding place in her vanity drawer and studied the man in it. Long ago, she had memorized each familiar detail, but she hoped maybe this would be the night her memory returned. This would be the moment when everything would slip into place—that she would remember the man who held her heart.

But she found studying the locket didn't help. The more she looked at the small portrait, the more she saw James staring back—his wavy blond hair, his wry blue eyes assessing her. Her head knew that the man in the locket was not him. But her heart kept refusing to believe it.

James.

She let his name wrap around her mind. Let it drip into her soul.

She felt like a moth drawn to her own destruction. He burned too brightly. Scorching. She ached for him when they were apart and yet fought her attraction to him when together. Keeping her wayward heart in check was proving impossible.

Unable to force her heart back into her chest, back to the man in the locket where logic dictated it belonged, she followed James around like a love-sick fool.

She was an idiot.

She reminded herself—yet again—that the locket was her only tie to her identity. That she needed to let go of this obsession over James. That she only liked him because he looked like the guy in the locket.

End of story.

But what if? Alter Emme whispered treacherously.

What if . . .

What if the mysterious F of the locket is dead and that's why you kept it in the first place? What if you don't love F? Or even worse, . . . what if you don't love him enough? What if you love James more?

Love.

Emme shied from that. She didn't love James. She barely knew him. And how could she truly understand her heart without knowing her whole self? But what if there were no Mr. F? What if her memory returned and she found herself free to give her heart to James?

What then?

Would James feel the same way about her? Would she feel the same way about him?

And then there was the worst thought of all.

What if she regained her memory only to be bound to a life that was unhappy? Had she been running away from something on that stormy night?

By this point, all the 'what if-ing' threatened to give her a headache. It was too confusing to sort through.

And so Emme didn't.

She deliberately chose not to dwell on the similarity between the sitter in the portrait and James. It just tangled her emotions. Made her thinking crowded.

And then there were the "incidents." Had she always been so accident prone?

After the boulder, there had been other minor scrapes: a small fire while visiting a tenant, a runaway cart that nearly ran her down, a stone which tumbled off the parsonage roof, narrowly missing her. None of which James had been present to witness, thank goodness. He was always blessedly absent when disaster struck, though he often showed up to help her afterward. And James being James, his 'help' usually involved as much teasing as actual aid.

Emme had faith this afternoon would be blessedly incident free. The day shone bright, hinting at full-blown summer. James was locked in his study with his steward and Georgiana rested. It seemed far too fine a day to waste indoors. And the little lake beckoned, the trees surrounding it rustling slightly in the heat, lush and inviting.

Upon reaching the water, Emme decided to take a small skiff from the boathouse. The sun warmed her back as she pulled the oars of the boat. She peeled off her heavy walking halfboots and gartered stockings, relishing in the feel of bare feet against the smooth bottom of the boat.

Well, until the skiff started leaking, cold water pouring in around her. Emme gasped as the freezing water lapped over her bare feet and then started to climb higher.

She immediately turned back toward the distant shore, trying desperately to reach it before the skiff foundered altogether. She panicked, momentarily, belatedly wondering if she knew how to swim. Emme made it about halfway to shore before the boat completely swamped, leaving her to swim slowly towards the edge of the lake.

The good news was she could indeed swim.

Unfortunately, her water-logged skirts dragged her down, making the going arduous and exhausting.

She managed to reach the more shallow waters where she could touch bottom, her bare feet squishing in the chilly mud when she heard a shout. Looking up, she saw James running toward the lake, struggling out of his coat as he came. He paused briefly at the water's edge to cast off his boots, toss his coat, waistcoat and cravat on top of them, reaching to help her out of the water.

"Good heavens, Emma!" he exclaimed, his eyes wide with worry. He took her cold hand in his warm one, steadying her. "What ever happened?"

The entire event suddenly caught up with her. Emme's teeth chattered with a combination of cold and shock as she wrapped her arms around her chest. She muttered about the boat leaking. He guided her away from the water's edge.

She staggered, dripping onto the sun-heated grass, and sank down gratefully. James picked up his coat and gently wrapped it around her shoulders. Assured that she was fine—just chilled—James sat beside her as she warmed up, propping one arm on a bent knee. Emme buried her head slightly into his coat, breathing in the smell of it, all wool and sandalwood and James.

"You look like a drowned kitten," he stated in his best matter-of-fact voice.

"Indeed?" she laughed. "You do know how to make a woman feel pretty."

"It's part of my legendary charm, you know."

"Legendary? Truly?"

He merely waggled his eyebrows at her.

"Is your humility also legendary?" she asked, her tone wry.

"But, of course. Anyone in Marfield can attest to it. I'm the most humble man in at least three, . . . no, make that four counties." His voice was heavily-laced with mock self-assurance.

"That is humble indeed," Emme agreed with feigned severity. "You know if you continue with these dramatic rescues, I will have to start calling you my 'knight' in shining armor."

It was Emme's turn to wiggle her eyebrows. For some reason she felt the urge to put air-quotes around the word knight. She added it to her list of odd-things-that-I-want-to-do.

James groaned at the pun.

"I believe you can give me a better nickname than that. It is a somewhat pathetic effort. Try again."

She arched an eyebrow at him.

"Go on," he gestured, leaning back on the grass, clasping his hands behind his head. "I can wait."

Emme pretended to think for a moment.

"Nothing?"

She could hear the teasing in his tone as she turned her head to look at him.

"No worries," he continued, grandiosely. "It's understandable you would struggle to think of something dashingly brave enough to describe me."

"Dashingly brave?" Emme asked, cocking her head toward him. "Oh please."

"Absurdly handsome, then? Devastatingly debonair?" James supplied helpfully. "Any of them will do. Go on. Say it."

Emme laughed, shaking her head. "You, sir, are impossible!"

"Impossibly irresistible? Or just impossibly wonderful?"

Uhmmm, both? Alter Emme sighed.

"Impossibly incorrigible," Emme said, swatting his leg with her hand.

James gave a weary mock-sigh. "Yes, I do regularly have that effect on unsuspecting young women. Particularly beautiful ones." He murmured the last part, his eyes growing warm as he slowly sat up.

Emme was suddenly intensely aware of him, of the way muscles rippled and moved underneath his shirt. The way a light breeze ruffled his golden hair. Of the breadth of his shoulders and the bit of tanned chest she could see where his shirt fell open at the collar. He was almost too much. The ache in her heart nearly too crushing to bear.

The air between them crackled, alive and thrumming. They stared for a long moment. He reached for her, tucking a wet curl behind her ear. His fingers lingering on her cheek, scalding. Emme drank him in, forcing herself not to lean in for more.

Alter Emme groaned in frustration. *Lean,* she urged. *You have got to leeeeeeeean.*

Emme swallowed. Hesitant and undecided.

James took a deep breath. He dropped his hand and looked away, staring at the lake. The moment passed.

"I guess I'm going to have to strip off my shirt and go after the poor sunken skiff, aren't I?" he said with a grimace.

Oh yes, please, Alter Emme replied, breathless and chirpy.

Emme wisely chose to ignore that.

"Is that the gentlemanly thing to do?"

"No, not in the slightest." He gave a quick unapologetic laugh.

"I'm sure you could get one of the gardeners to do it," Emme offered helpfully.

"What? And let them have all the fun? Oh no. I've spent most of the day locked up with Arthur and my steward. Trust me, I have considerable restlessness to burn off." He pushed to his feet. "Besides, if you're going to sit here and watch someone show off, it might as well be me," he finished archly, winking at her.

Emme laughed in surprise. Then she stared as he tugged his shirt out of his breeches and pulled it over his head in a swift motion, tendons flexing. All the air rushed from her lungs at the sight of his muscled, bare chest.

Oh my, Alter Emme sighed dreamily.

Her day had only needed this.

James cautiously approached the water's edge. "So, how is the water?" he asked.

"Balmly," she lied.

"Really?" He tentatively dipped a toe in and then turned to her with a disbelieving look. "My toe informs me the water feels decidedly frigid."

"Is your toe to be trusted?" Emme deadpanned. "Either your toe is a liar or you're a wuss."

He let out a short bark of laughter. "A wuss?"

"A wimp? Fraidy cat?" Emme thought further. "Lily livered?" she offered.

"Lily livered. Ouch. That one I know. I may legitimately be called many things, but lily livered shall not be one of them. Balmy, eh?"

"Like a warm bath," Emme answered, her voice laced with humor.

"Right, then." With another wink, James strode into the cold water, though he did let out a high-pitched gasp when the cold water hit his chest.

Emme considered politely averting her eyes. It seemed the best way to punish his arrogance. Besides seeing James without his shirt and clad in skin tight, wet breeches was not helping her situation.

But as she started to move her gaze elsewhere, Alter Emme insistently muttered, *Don't you dare look away! We are going to sit here and enjoy the show.*

James did not disappoint. She called out directions to where the skiff had sunk, watching his strong arms cut through the water as he swam effortlessly. He flexed his muscles whenever possible and lazily flipped from his stomach to his back, spouting a great fountain of water from his mouth.

He was utterly shameless.

You mean utterly magnificent, right? Alter Emme sighed.

Emme forced herself not to agree.

Chapter 20

Two weeks later, James was quite sure of one single fact—the tension between Emma and himself had grown to epic proportions.

Their days had settled into a pleasant routine. James had secured a slightly more spirited horse for her, and now they devoted each early morning to chasing over fences and fields. After breakfast, he would attend to estate business with his steward, but afternoons were usually spent with her—playing chess, discussing some book one of them had read, laughing over nothing at all.

Georgiana joined them when she felt well enough, her health variable. Some days she seemed almost normal and others her cough nearly tore her frail body apart. But throughout it, Emma was a comfort, her presence giving Georgiana much needed company and support.

Of course, there was Emma's astonishingly bad luck. How could one person so consistently end up in completely unexpected scrapes? No wonder she had turned up abandoned on his lane in the middle of a storm. After having experienced the last several weeks with her, he realized it was exactly the kind of situation that Emma would find herself in. Predictable, really.

Not that he minded.

She was adventure and spirit and, well, everything he had never known but had always wanted. Clever, witty and decorous without being entirely proper.

She sparkled. Incandescent.

She filled holes in him he had never even realized existed.

He adored everything about her. Adored her throaty laugh. Adored that little curl that always seemed to escape. Adored the slanting look she would often give him through her thick eyelashes. Emma constantly intruded on his thoughts, and James found himself in a losing battle with his better self.

James knew a gentlemen should not become involved with a lady who had no memory of her past. Not that he had read up on the topic in an etiquette book. But he was quite sure—were he to find a chapter entitled 'On the Courting of Ladies with Missing Memories'—that would be the general recommendation,

He also logically recognized they could not go on as they were indefinitely. At some point, something would intrude to force a change. Emma would regain her memory. Or the mysterious Mr. F would appear to claim her as his own.

His head rationally pointed out that Emma would most likely leave his life as suddenly as she had entered it.

His heart, however, was a different matter. His heart insisted Emma was a part of him, something vital that could never be replaced.

That if she left, he would never be whole again.

To his heart, she was something to cherish. Something to fight for. His heart could not face the emotional carnage of a life without her.

And so he couldn't help thinking *what if.*

What if . . .

What if the mysterious Mr. F never came to claim her? What if Mr. F had cast her off? Or what if he were dead, which was why Emma had kept the locket?

And if he did come, would Mr. F love her as much as James did?

Love.

James shied away from the thought. Emma was beautiful and charming and wonderful in every possible way. But did he love her?

He examined his heart. No. Not yet. But it would be so easy, so simple to fall in love.

He recognized Emma could be a different person entirely if and when her memory returned. And in the meantime, how long could they carry on in this bubble? Longing and wanting but avoiding further emotional entanglement because of her unknown past. A past that would most likely take her from him.

His rational mind told him to keep his distance, to keep his heart safe.

And so following sound logical advice, James borrowed a tactic from his brother and created a mental box labeled *Not Mine*. And every time Emma popped unwanted into his thoughts, his rational mind would pick her up and place her back into the box.

Not mine.

Again and again.

While reading the newspaper. While discussing drainage and crop rotations with his land steward. While watching her laugh with Georgiana, heads bent together.

Pick her up and put her back. Over and over. *Not mine. Not mine.* The chant almost hypnotic at times.

But his aching soul stubbornly refused to be thrust aside in favor of his logical, responsible mind. It rebelled.

So, as James would mentally reach for Emma to place her back into that *Not Mine* box, his heart would slide around her, treacherously slipping a hand into her silky short hair and pulling her close.

Close enough he would be able to feel her breath against his cheek, her heart pounding. As he had in the meadow. Only this time, he wouldn't allow her to pull back. He would dip his head down, would feel that slight exchange of air back and forth before touching her soft lips. . . .

Not mine! Not mine! He would pull his thoughts back and try to find that mental box again, to shut her away.

His heart was utterly traitorous. Betraying him. Tearing him apart. His emotions constantly fighting with each other.

Not knowing which path to follow.

It didn't help that Arthur continued to resent Emma's presence at Haldon Manor. Her memory showed no signs of coming back, and Arthur constantly grumbled about how improper it was to have her under their roof, regularly cornering James about it.

Arthur was nothing if not persistent.

"Really, James, something must be done about her," Arthur said in exasperation from his chair opposite James' desk. They were seated in the study going over tenant accounts, rain tapping against the window and casting the room in blue-tinged gloom.

James stifled a groan.

Not again.

"We are not having this conversation, Arthur. We have said all that there is to say," James replied, refusing to look up from the accounts book.

"James, it has been over a month. A month! We have sent out runners and made inquiries and come up with almost nothing."

James shook his head, not looking up, scratching down a note with his quill.

"Still not having this conversation, Arthur."

"I know you had hopes over that small lead Ethan's man found near Bristol," Arthur continued, relentless.

"It's a pity the weather turned so dreary today. Don't you agree?" Head still down. "Let's talk about the weather."

"But it now appears that the missing Miss Willis had actually just eloped with a footman."

"Or gooseberries. We could talk about gooseberries."

"In any case, you cannot continue to give Emma shelter."

"What about ninjas? I understand they are fascinating."

Arthur paused. Wisely, he ignored the comment. "James, even you must admit that she knows far too much about the world."

"Or zombies. We could talk about zombies."

Arthur blinked.

"I hear they like to eat brains." James permitted himself a small smile as he continued to stare at his accounts book.

Arthur let out an annoyed grunt. "Zombies? Ninjas? What on earth are you talking about? I swear, James, sometimes you are addled in the head."

"Yes, well, that is most likely true."

Arthur sighed his most long-suffering sigh. "James, she cannot continue to remain. The only logical explanation is, well, . . . you know."

James exhaled, still not raising his head. He made a note in the ledger, letting the silence stretch.

"Again, Arthur, that is not the only explanation," he finally said. "And I *cannot* express how tired I am of saying that sentence. Once we know the truth, everything will make perfect sense. We just have to be patient until then."

"But, James—"

"No, Arthur." James pushed the account book away and returned the quill to its stand.

Raising his head, he looked his brother in the eye.

"We are done with this conversation. Done."

James rarely became upset. His even-temper was the one positive trait that all his acquaintances agreed upon. He was the easy-going one. The gentleman who would step in to create harmony when tempers flared. He indulged in exasperation at times. Irritation on occasion. But true blood-boiling anger? That was almost a complete stranger.

Only Arthur had the incessant persistence necessary to goad him into losing his temper.

"James—" Arthur started again.

"Are you accusing the lady of improper behavior?" James asked, trying but failing to keep anger out of his rising voice. "Besmirching her name? Has she been anything other than a proper lady while here in my home?"

"You know exactly what I am saying, James. Dash it, do not try to twist this into me accusing her. You ride with her everywhere. Unchaperoned—"

"Which is my own fault, Arthur!" James interrupted. "I am the one who keeps forgetting to take a groom along, not Emma."

"You haven't heard the talk around town. I don't need to say anything. I just let the facts speak for—"

"What facts? I don't like the tone of this conversation." James tried again, without success, to keep his own tone level.

"She knows things that are quite improper. That maneuver with Sir Henry, for example."

"She saved the man's life! Good grief, Arthur. Would you have had her watch him die?"

"No, of course not. But she recognized all of those odd fruits including the Chinese gooseberry and—"

"Oh, heaven protect us from ladies armed with a knowledge of exotic fruit!"

"—even you must admit that any normal young lady would not have such knowledge, much less the impertinence to act on it. Can you imagine Marianne doing such a thing? Her excellent sense of propriety would never allow for it!"

"Oh please, Arthur," James said with a grimace. "Marianne hasn't enough backbone to say 'boo' to a stray dog, much less insert herself into a crisis. Propriety has nothing to do with it."

Arthur gasped. "How dare you impugn Miss Linwood's honor!"

James rolled his eyes, trying to figure out how their conversation had arrived at this place.

"Arthur, now you are being ridiculous. Stating that Miss Linwood has no pluck is hardly attacking her honor. It's just declaring the obvious."

Arthur flushed dangerously. "Marianne represents all that is lovely and virtuous."

"Agreed. And if she had even an ounce of courage, she would have renounced her brother and run off with you months ago. You know I would do everything in my power to ensure your future happiness. You would never want for anything."

"Marianne is bound by honor and propriety, just as I am. Unlike others I know." Arthur's narrowed eyes made his meaning obvious. "This conversation isn't about Miss Linwood and her exemplary behavior. We are discussing Emma's continued residence under this roof. Or rather her removal."

James took a deep breath and forced his anger down. "I have made my feelings on this matter abundantly clear, Arthur. Miss Emma will stay until she decides to leave. This conversation is finished."

James stood and turned away and walked over to the window, staring unseeingly at the lush dripping landscape, his hands clasped behind his back. He heard Arthur stand behind him and shuffle his feet, as if undecided about something.

"James, I know you better than you might think." Arthur's voice had lost its edge. He sounded almost weary. "It is obvious to me you have developed an attachment to this woman. But you must see nothing can come of it. Even if she truly is a lady of genteel birth, the man in the locket is most likely her husband or at least her betrothed."

James said nothing. He let the truth of Arthur's words wrap around him, tried to force his traitorous heart to believe them.

Unclenching his jaw, James took a deep, stuttering breath, gazing out the window, tracing the rain as it snaked down the glass.

"Do you have any idea how much I would give to actually *be* the man in that locket?" he asked after a moment. "To have that kind of claim on her? I would rejoice in finding her free."

"And what if you find that she is free but not entirely respectable, as I strongly suspect?" Arthur asked quietly. "Would you still pursue her?"

"You have known me your entire life, Arthur, and yet you still understand me so little." James turned back to his brother. "I have always cared more about who a person is than what society tells me about that person."

"Even you would not take her as your mistress, James. Under your own roof with Georgiana in residence."

"You are quite correct, brother. I would not take her as my mistress. I have significantly more respect for Emma than that. I would marry her."

James ignored Arthur's dismayed gasp.

Really, Arthur had insisted on this conversation. Now what right did he have to be shocked by it?

"Marry?! You would marry a courtesan?"

James snorted wryly. "It's been known to happen, Arthur, in case you have forgotten recent history."

The shocking scandal of the current London Season had been the marriage of Thomas Hill, Baron Berwick, to Sophia Dubochet, a Swiss clock maker's daughter and popular, well-known courtesan amongst the *ton*. Everyone had scratched their heads in surprise, as there was no apparent reason for Lord Berwick—who was not much older than James himself—to have married the girl. But James, being acquainted with Berwick, knew of his love of art and general disregard for the opinions of high society. He had a suspicion that Berwick and Miss Dubochet had fallen in love and Berwick respected her enough to honorably commit his life to her.

Arthur snorted. "Yes, well, Berwick's family is currently suffering the result of his poor choices."

"Truly, Arthur? How? His sisters are all long married and his brothers could care less. The only thing he suffers is the loss of acquaintances such as yourself. Which, begging your pardon, I don't think he considers much of a loss at all."

Arthur clenched his jaw at the insult.

"I would like to think, James, that you wouldn't do that to Georgiana and myself. We are both as yet unmarried and a stain upon our family honor could be devastating. So why keep her here, if any future involvement is moot? You are just putting off an inevitable separation."

Again, James said nothing. Arthur did make a valid point.

But James refused to give up on the idea so quickly. Georgiana was dying and would not be with them for much longer, much as it pained James to face the fact. Marriage seemed an impossible prospect for her. And as a man, Arthur would hardly be irreparably tainted by any decision James made.

"Arthur, you are making assumptions that simply may not be true. We will not know anything about her past until Emma's memory returns or until someone comes to claim her. In the meantime, Emma's presence has lifted Georgiana's spirits and improved her health. You condemn her based on supposition, not facts."

Every instinct cried that Emma was meant for him. That their lives were intertwined together. If they were indeed fated to be separated,

James would not be the one to precipitously cause the break. He would wait out their drama to the bitter end.

Arthur scoffed.

"James, be reasonable—"

"This is my house and my decision to make." James cut him off. "Emma stays. If you have a problem with it, you are more than welcome to leave tomorrow for Whitcomb. No one is forcing you to remain here."

Arthur ground his teeth, obviously perturbed. "You would like that, brother. But Linwood has relented and will allow Marianne to attend the assembly ball this week, despite her still being in half-mourning. I will hardly absent myself from her side."

"Then you will have to deal politely with our house guest, as I most certainly will not turn her away."

Chapter 21

The warm night beckoned Emme outside. Everyone had said their goodnights and trudged upstairs, but Emme wasn't tired.

Instead she felt confused and lost.

Gathering a shawl around her shoulders, she slipped down the stairs, across the back terrace and out into the walled garden. The scent of green growing things enveloped her. Wildflowers and wisteria and the season's first roses, all wrapped in cricket song and the far off hoot of an owl.

The moon was a pale sliver, leaving the night in darkness. Nearly unnaturally dark and yet . . . somehow not.

Though the actual sky was inky black—darker than seemed normal to her—the heavens glistened with stars. Millions, . . no, billions of them.

The entire sky pulsing with pinpricks of light—the Milky Way a clear, glittering ribbon cutting through it all.

Had there always been so many stars? Though the moon shone faint and thin, the starlight was still bright enough to cast shadows.

Odd that.

Looking up, Emme felt as if she were falling into the heavens. Vast and unnerving.

She drew in a deep, shuddering breath, closing her eyes to blot out the blinking stars, fighting back the panic. She had gone almost a week without an attack. Funny that the night sky should bring one on.

Emme heard a rustle of sound behind her and jumped with a slight cry of alarm as a strong hand grasped her arm.

"It's fine. It's just me." His voice was low, warming her. She sighed in relief.

"You startled me." Her own voice sounded husky. Sultry even.

She could make him out even in the starlight, catching the gleam of his bright hair, the white of a cravat against his dark jacket. He shifted and slid his hand to the small of her back, directing her toward a bench she could see, glinting in the light of the stars.

"Come. Sit with me," James murmured, his lips close to her ear.

Emme sank into the bench, drawing her shawl more tightly around her shoulders. James sat next to her, his leg pressing against hers.

"You seemed sad tonight. Want to talk about it?" His voice ached with caring. Or was that just her own heart? Emme gulped, her throat suddenly tight.

"Oh, James," she whispered into the night. "What are we ever to do?"

He found her hand and curled it into his grasp. Rough and slightly calloused. A man's hand. Strong and solid and encircling.

She clasped it tightly, twining her fingers with his. He sighed and ran his free hand through his hair.

Her own hand ached to follow it. Longed to touch him.

"Yes. This situation is ridiculously difficult."

"I don't know . . . ," she began and then choked.

Inhaling slowly, she started again. "I don't know what to do. Who is that man in the locket to me? And how long do I hold on to him?"

"I understand."

"Do you?"

She heard him exhale slowly. "I understand your hesitation."

"It's been weeks and no one has come for me. What does that mean?"

"It means that someone somewhere is probably looking frantically for you. Or if they aren't, then they are fools and don't deserve you, dearest Emma."

"You know my name most likely isn't Emma, right?"

"Probably. But it suits you for now."

They sat in silence for a minute. Just being. His hand warm and comforting in hers.

"I worry . . . ," she paused, staring sightlessly out into the dark night. ". . . my feelings for you."

"Ah." He stirred next to her, shifting closer. "I am suddenly liking the direction of this conversation." Teasing in his voice.

Emme smiled. Trust James to make her laugh, to chase away her sadness.

He's perfect, you know. It's like he's your destiny or something, Alter Emme whispered.

Now why did that sound familiar?

Emme nudged him with her shoulder.

"Be serious," she said, still smiling.

"Oh, I am, I assure you."

"I often wonder, do I like you for yourself?"

James let out a low chortle and leaned into her.

"You just admitted you like me," he whispered, his warm breath tickling her ear.

Oh handsome, you have no *idea,* Alter Emme muttered.

Emme smiled wider and shook her head. Again, she nudged him.

"As I was saying, do I like you for you? Or is it just that you remind me of your doppelganger in a locket in my vanity drawer?"

"Doppelganger?" James gave a burst of startled laughter.

"Uh . . . ," Emme hunted her brain for the meaning of the term. "I think it's German. It means your double. This idea that there is someone else in the world who is your exact twin."

"My twin? That is interesting. Is this twin possibly evil?"

Emme laughed. "Possibly. Though it's more likely you are the evil twin."

"True," James chuckled in reply. "Mr. F does look a little too saintly to be the evil one."

"Indeed, he does."

"But if I am the devilish one, does that mean I get to steal you away?"

The question hung between them.

The agony of longing and loss suddenly clenched her chest. Emme felt balanced on a precipice, where one slight move one way or the other would make all the difference.

And she had no idea which move to make.

They sat in silence again for a few moments.

"I keep going over all the what ifs," he finally said.

"Me too. I even made a list of them."

"Really?"

"Really. You shouldn't be surprised. You know I enjoy making lists."

"That is true. I love your lists." But his warm voice and the caress of his hand made it obvious he loved something else too.

Something more.

Do you really think locket-boy could be any better than this? Alter Emme asked.

The question caused Emme to shiver slightly. James misunderstood the motion.

"You're cold," he said quietly.

Emme anticipated him offering her his coat, as he usually did. She sat expectantly.

But instead James released her hand and slid his arm around her shoulders, pulling her gently against his heated chest.

Emme tensed for just a moment and then she gave in, melting into him with a sigh. She nestled her nose into his neckcloth and breathed him in.

He smelled of crisp linen and something else she recognized as being entirely James. She rested her hand on his chest, sliding it slightly under his jacket and waistcoat to rest on his shirt. She could feel his muscles, firm under her hand, his hammering heart mimicking her own. His arm encircled her waist, resting warm and secure on her hip, his thumb tracing unconscious circles.

James sighed with contentment, like having her body tucked against his side made the whole universe feel aligned.

It felt impossibly right.

As if they could face down any obstacle, as long as his hand was in hers. As if together, they were more than just the sum of two.

He gathered her even closer and buried his face in her hair. She felt a soft kiss brush her curls.

"You are far too captivating a creature. I fear if you leave me, you will take something vital and necessary with you." He exhaled into her hair.

"Oh, James," she murmured.

"I will fight to keep you. Consider yourself warned."

She felt of his strength. His commitment. Unlike Mr. F. Where had he been the last three weeks?

Yeah, really, Alter Emme agreed.

Emme knew instinctively that James would be there for her no matter what came. He would hunt her to the ends of the earth, on hands and knees if he had to. And suddenly that mattered a lot.

More than some unknown man in a locket in her vanity drawer.

Emme sighed again and allowed herself to melt into him a little more.

James shifted and sent his nose wandering down to her ear. And then continued down her throat, pressing his face into the crook of her neck.

His lips remained still. He didn't kiss her.

He just breathed her in, silent and longing.

His free hand came around and cupped her cheek, sliding into her short hair. He raised his head slightly, cradling her cheek against his.

Holding her with aching tenderness. As if she were too precious to ever let go.

Later that evening, Emme sat at her vanity, slowly slid open the drawer and pulled out the locket. She opened it and stared at his familiar face.

Him.

Trying one last time to remember anything, something.

But nothing came.

All she saw was James. The set of his jaw. The wave of his hair. That knowing twinkle in his eyes. Perfectly reflected in the locket. She read the inscription one more time.

Throughout all time. Heart of my soul.

The words still had the power to sear her. But was it enough? She blinked against the tightness in her throat.

Gently she closed the locket. Held it cupped in her hands for a long moment. And then, with a shake of her head, brought it to her lips, kissing it softly.

"I'm sorry," Emme whispered. "Whoever you are."

She held the locket for another moment and then quietly tucked it back into the vanity drawer.

Crawling into bed, she dreamed of a living, breathing man with a teasing smile that promised the whole world.

And then some.

Chapter 22

THE ASSEMBLY ROOMS
MARFIELD
THREE DAYS LATER
JUNE 12, 1812

The room was suffocatingly hot; the assembly rooms tightly packed with bodies.

Public balls were popular in Marfield, making this one quite a crush. Worse, it had been a warm June day and the arrival of evening had not brought much relief.

Emme fanned herself, moving slowly along the edge of the crowd toward an open window, hoping to catch a cool breeze. James was trapped in conversation with Sir Henry on the other side of the room. She caught a glimpse of Georgiana dancing with Arthur, a stately minuet that would not hamper her breathing. She looked radiant and happy, thrilled to feel well enough to attend.

Marianne had arrived on the arm of her brother; Arthur had been eager to see her. Lord Linwood had not danced—Emme assumed he found it beneath his dignity—and had instead spent most of the evening staring either at his sister or at Emme, which she had found odd and unsettling.

As for herself, Emme had already apologetically declined several requests to dance, as she didn't remember the complicated steps—something that they had realized only that morning.

Georgiana had mentioned something about dancing over breakfast which had led to Emme asking questions. Which led to Georgiana fetching James and playing the piano for them as he tried to teach her various country dances. As she moved gracefully through the steps, it became quickly obvious Emme was an experienced dancer. But she could not remember the figures. It all proved too complex for her to memorize in so short a period of time.

"Why can I not remember the simplest things sometimes?" Emme moaned to James

"Come, come, Emma," James tried to cheer her. "Let us try a waltz." The twinkle in his eye indicated a certain amount of mischief.

"A waltz." Emme looked at him thoughtfully, slowly nodding her head. James stepped forward, his arms outstretched, intending to show her the proper form for a closed dance position.

But Emme noted his surprise as she instantly matched her arm position to his and stepped readily into his arms, gently placing one hand on his upper arm, resting the other in his hand, arching her back slightly and elongating her neck.

She sighed in relief. It felt incredibly right. As if dancing the waltz were the most normal, natural thing to her.

With a nod, Georgiana began playing a lilting tune in three-four time. With slight pressure from his hand in the small of her back, James led her into the familiar down-up-up rhythm, Emme effortlessly following.

Emme breathed in delight. Though she may have forgotten everything else about dancing, remembering how to waltz had been a lovely gift. A much needed boon.

Of course, it didn't hurt that James was an excellent partner. Floating her easily around the room. Providing just the right amount of pressure on her back as they twirled, subtly guiding her with shifts of his hand. His extremely warm hand.

Emme smiled at the memory.

Of course, he had claimed her waltz this evening too. The only one during the entire evening, mores the pity. She would not have minded an entire evening of waltzes with James.

At the moment, however, she just wanted out of the stifling heat. Reaching the open window, she stepped in front of it, breathing in the cooler air with relief. She looked down and noted the window was actually a door opening onto a small balcony. She could see a staircase leading down into the back garden—a garden that looked cool and beckoning.

It was too much temptation to resist.

Emme carefully lifted the skirts of her cream silk ball gown and slipped out onto the balcony, quietly descending the steps into the garden. Enclosed by a wall, Emme could just make out a gate in the back. The space seemed overrun by roses and flickered with candlelight from the bright assembly room above and several torches set along the path. It felt lovely and fresh. Emme breathed in the cleansing night air as she wandered toward the back gate.

"Madam!" A cool voice accosted her from behind. Startled, Emme turned to see Lord Linwood's tall form coming toward her, his features dancing in the torchlight.

"My lord?" she said in surprise, instinctively bobbing him a stiff curtsy as he stopped in front of her.

Staring. And saying nothing.

"To what do I owe the courtesy of this conversation?" Emme liked the frosty tone of her voice.

She heard him exhale loudly.

"Do not pretend to misunderstand my purpose here, madam," his voice low in the torchlight.

He took a step closer to her and seemed undecided for a moment. As if hesitating over what to do.

Was he trying to use his height to intimidate her? To force her to back away? Well, she could play that game. Emme stood her ground.

Linwood studied at her for a long moment and then broke, moving around her to stare out into the garden, his back stiff and proud.

Emme cocked an eyebrow as her gaze turned to follow him. She rapidly searched her brain, trying to remember anything that would make sense of his presence.

I got nothing. You got anything? Alter Emme asked.

Emme mentally shook her head.

"I know who and what you are," he said, menacingly.

Emme sucked in her breath. Did Linwood know something about her past? Was he the key to understanding how she had come to be along the lane that night?

He turned back to her, moving to block her way.

She shook her head, bewildered. "If that is the case, my lord, then you know more than I myself. Perhaps you would care to share what you know with me?"

Linwood snorted. "Let us not play these silly games. As I said, I know what you are. Did Knight think that his little secret would remain hidden? That I would not find out?" Emme could see a small amused grin dance on his lips.

Truly puzzled, Emme stared at him in confusion. At a loss to say anything. His words made no sense to her.

"I don't understand . . . ," she hesitantly began.

"Do not play innocent," he cut her off. "It is hardly convincing."

"Again, my lord, I really have no idea of what you speak. Truly. If you know something about me, about my past, please share it."

"Are you still pretending to have lost your memory then?"

"It is no pretense, sir! How dare you imply that I am deliberately lying to everyone!" Emme could feel her temper rising.

Really, the arrogant man was impossible.

We're just going to take a second and imagine him riding a pig through Marfield, Alter Emme said. *And maybe only the pig will have clothing on.*

He looked at her, contempt evident in his stance, his stare.

"You forget, madam, that Arthur is incapable of keeping a secret from Marianne. And Marianne, in her turn, is incapable of keeping a secret from me."

Emme cocked her head at the statement. It made sense but still didn't illuminate her understanding.

"I'm still not following what this has to do with me. What dastardly thing does Arthur know?"

"Are you really this obtuse or just pretending stupidity to annoy me?"

Oh, is this annoying him? Alter Emme muttered. *Cause I can get behind that.*

Emme stiffened her neck, refusing to rise to his insult. "Pretend that I really am this obtuse. What, my lord, are you accusing me of?"

Linwood continued to stare at her. "I know about your locket. I know everything."

Emme blinked.

Uhmmm, okay, so he knows about the locket. And that's bad why? Alter Emme was equally befuddled.

"My lord, I do have a locket. It has been kept a secret because of the odd resemblance between the sitter and Jam—I mean, Mr. Knight—but I fail to understand why this simple fact is so significant."

"Ah, so you claim the sitter is not James Knight?" "Of course. It would simplify everything if it were Mr. Knight, but the inscription within the locket itself makes it clear that the sitter is not him. And then there is Mr. Knight's word."

Linwood snorted and shrugged his shoulders. "We know what Knight's word is worth, what honor means to him."

Emme bristled at the derision in his tone. "I will not stand here, sir, and allow you to speak ill of Mr. Knight. He has been all that is good and kind to me. He is a man of honor and—"

"Honor! Please, Knight cares little for honor. But I do believe that he has been kind to you." Linwood stepped closer to her. Too close. "Has he been all that you would wish? Generous? Are you happy with your current arrangement? Or would you perhaps be interested in a change?"

Emme gasped. "What are you implying?"

"My implication should be obvious, madam."

Emme frowned as Linwood looked her up and down. Assessing. Contemplating a new purchase.

"I am a wealthy man. You would be wise to consider coming under my protection. I will happily double whatever Knight currently offers you."

Emme stood still with shock.

Uh, honey, does Mr. Arrogant mean what I think he means? Alter Emme gasped.

She shook her head in disbelief. "I find this conversation offensive, my lord. I am done with it."

Emme turned on her heel and prepared to leave, shaking in anger. How dare he! How dare he suggest what she thought he was suggesting! As if!

She had taken only one step when a strong hand on her forearm stopped her, holding her tightly. Forcing her back to him.

"You would be a fool to walk away from me," Linwood said lowly in her ear. "I am always fair. Lavish even. You would have everything you could wish for. An establishment of your own, clothes, a carriage, jewels. Is Knight currently offering you that? Or do you just subsist on his sister's cast-offs?"

Emme found she was actually too stunned to reply. She just stared at him, at his hold on her arm.

Wow! Could he be any more offensive? Alter Emme whispered in shock.

Linwood raised his opposite hand and stroked her shoulder. Slowly, almost possessively.

Why, yes. Yes, he could.

Emme suppressed a shudder. She took a step back, pulling on the arm he still held.

"You will release my arm and stop touching me. Now." Emme could feel her temper rising. "You clearly have mistaken my relationship with Mr. Knight, not to mention the kind of person that I am."

Linwood snorted in disbelief. "Please, spare me your protestations of virtue and innocence. As if anyone would believe such a thing after your behavior here over these last weeks. "

Emme gasped. "How dare you! Release me!" Emme kept her voice low and firm. "Release me or I will be compelled to release myself."

"Release yourself?" Linwood gave her a thoroughly amused look and strengthened his hold on her arm, his eyes taunting. "You are merely a woman. What could you possibly do?"

Emme had had enough. He had insulted her in every possible way. Linwood was not a small man and his grip on her arm was tight and hard. Vice-like. But she suddenly understood with lightning clarity what she could and would do.

"You were warned."

Hardly thinking, Emme stepped slightly sideways and swung the arm he held in a tight circle, breaking his grip. At the same time, she grabbed his forearm with her free hand and used the leverage to thrust her knee squarely into his groin while simultaneously driving an elbow into his jaw. Hard.

The moves felt fluid. Practiced. Instinctual. Like she had done them hundreds of times in the past.

Linwood went down with a whimpering moan, collapsing on the pavement.

Emme didn't wait for him to rise. She turned and half ran down the path, eyes intent on the back garden door and escape.

Suddenly, another hand snaked out to grab her. She stifled a scream and nearly lashed out again, but stopped herself in time as James' voice washed over her.

"Hush! It's all right."

Chapter 23

James had noticed Emma slip out through the door onto the small balcony, Linwood following shortly after. Concerned, he had worked his way through the crowd and slipped out after them. Hurrying down the stairs, he heard Linwood's low voice rumble and Emma's tense reply, seeming to defend him, James. Coming around the corner, he noted with alarm that Linwood held Emma's arm and stood over her threateningly.

But his shout of "Release her!" stopped in his throat. James watched in wide-eyed astonishment as Emma moved sharply, breaking Linwood's hold on her arm and, with a well-placed knee and elbow, dropped the viscount to the ground like a stone.

It was the most amazing thing he had ever seen. Smooth and clean. The movements of a fighter but unlike any he had ever witnessed.

James fell completely and utterly in love with her at that moment.

Whoever and whatever she proved to be.

He was hers.

Grinning, he stepped back into the shadows and snared her hand as she rushed past.

As she turned on him, he realized a little late that grabbing her probably hadn't been the best decision.

Instantly releasing her, he whispered, "Hush! It's all right."

She gave a little sob of relief and partially collapsed against him. Grasping her hand, he led her away from Linwood, still groaning on the ground, drawing her through the garden and out the side door, emerging into an alleyway that opened onto the village green.

James could feel her shaking as her altercation with Linwood sank in. He drew her next to him as they walked down the alleyway, wrapping an arm around her bare shoulders. And then, as she continued to shake, he stopped and shrugged out of his coat and tucked it around her. He watched as she snuggled into its warmth.

"Come," he whispered and led her into the trees of the village green, settling her onto a bench that looked toward the parish church and cuddled her into his side.

"Are you all right? Would you like to talk about it?" he murmured in her ear.

Emma stared ahead, her face expressionless. Then she sighed and looked down.

"Linwood knows about the locket. He thinks my memory loss is a sham and that you . . . that we are . . . ," her voice faded off.

"Lovers?" James supplied.

"Yes. And he also implied that I am . . . well . . . that you are not . . ."

"Your only lover?"

"Yes. That I am a professional."

James stared angrily ahead, unseeing.

"That wasn't the worst of it though."

"Truly?"

"Linwood . . . well . . . he suggested I might like a change of, uh, scenery, if you will."

James felt as if he had been clubbed in the chest. The breath hissed out of him.

"Linwood is an absolute ass."

"Yes."

"How hard did you hit him?"

"Hard."

James nodded in satisfaction.

"That's a good start. Would you like me to call him out for you?" he asked.

Emma turned slightly to look up at him. "You would do that for me? I thought you didn't hold much to silly old-fashioned notions of besmirched honor?"

"I don't," he said, carefully tucking that one stray curl behind her ear. "But I will always defend you."

Emma silently considered him for a moment, blinked and then turned her face away.

"What if he is right?" she whispered. "What if that is the reason I was on your lane that night? What if someone had cast me off? What if I am no better than someone's unwanted mistress?"

James shrugged. "That is a possibility. But I decided long ago it makes no difference to me."

"But it matters to me." Her voice hung quietly between them. "I would like to think that I am more than that. More than a person who would sell herself for profit."

James sat silently, contemplating her lovely profile, wishing he had answers for her.

"I want to be more for you." She turned to him. Her hazel eyes dark in the dim moonlight. "I want better for you than some . . . someone's cast-off mistress."

James captured her chin between his fingers before she could turn away. "You are a lady to me and that is all that matters."

Her eyes swelled with unshed tears. At that moment, James gave up resisting.

She belonged with him. Not *to* him. But *with* him.

She was part and parcel of his soul.

And he was done denying it.

"No matter what anyone says of you. No matter what you might have been in your past, I will always treat you with respect."

His voice was emphatic. Impassioned.

"I want you by my side. Honorably. Not as a purchased possession. I may not care too much for society's rules, but I care very much about personal dignity. Particularly in those I love."

She gasped at his words, blinking as tears slipped down her cheeks. James leaned in and brushed them away with his lips, tasting their bitter saltiness.

He slid his fingers off her chin to cup her cheek, rubbing her petal soft skin with his thumb. Slowly, he turned his head toward her mouth, giving her ample opportunity to pull away. To say no to his kiss.

But he willed her to stay. Willed her to accept him.

And she did. In fact, she leaned in, moving her mouth fractionally closer to his.

They exchanged breaths for a moment, each testing the other, waiting for one of them to draw back. Neither did.

And then James moved that final inch.

Her lips were as soft as he had dreamed. Warm and full and sweet. Yielding and lush. She tasted of honey and exotic shores he had never visited.

James kept the kiss light and gentle. Letting her lead. Taking what she will.

She tentatively lifted a hand to his hair. Raked her fingers against his scalp. Possessive. She then moaned softly and melted into him. He sensed something shift within her. Felt her hand tightened against his head. Her lips parted and the kiss suddenly stopped being sweet and gentle.

And turned into something much, much more.

His kiss devastated her. Tore through to her very soul. Crumbling every defense.

Emme tried to keep it light. Soft.

But then she buried her fingers in his thick hair and something exploded within her.

Something that she had needed for far too long.

Something her heart understood. That her mind had forgotten.

Something she yearned to keep forever.

Emme had no idea how long they stayed locked together.

Long enough for her to memorize the taste of him. Long enough for her to never want to leave.

And also long enough for them both to silently realize Emme's kissing skills were somewhat advanced for a proper young lady.

Finally, Emme drew back and rested her forehead against his, her fingers still laced around his neck.

"I meant what I said," James whispered, his breath a puff of air against her lips. "You are a lady to me and that is all that matters."

"Thank you," she murmured in reply. "Though given everything that you have done, a simple 'thank you' seems terribly inadequate."

She felt more than saw his answering smile. He brushed his lips over her nose and pulled back slightly.

"I have watched Arthur torture himself for years over Marianne. I have seen Georgiana lose all hope of love as her illness claims her body. Love happens so rarely, it seems. It is a shame to let it slip away because of fear."

Emme sighed and nestled her nose against his neck, cuddling her body closer to his. James wrapped his arms around her.

"We will sort it out," he murmured against her hair. "You will see."

THE STUDY
HALDON MANOR
THE FOLLOWING MORNING
JUNE 13, 1812

James awoke the next morning feeling optimism and hope. He had kissed Emma and they were going be together.

Period.

He would find a way, with or without her memory.

Emma was alone in the breakfast room when he arrived, not even a footman in sight. Grasping the opportunity, he snatched her around the waist, pulling her to him. Kissed her achingly in greeting, Emma every bit as soft and warm as she had been the night before. James decided then and there that he wanted each morning to begin with Emma's kiss.

After a laughing breakfast, they had adjourned to his study to discuss things. Their things. Their future.

"We will make this work," James said, staring at her intently, leaning back to half sit on the front of his desk, arms crossed on his chest. "I haven't come this far to lose you now."

"But, James, without my memory . . . ," her voice trailed off. Emma sat in a chair opposite his desk, looking particularly lovely in teal muslin, short dark hair curling about her face. Her hazel eyes pale in the morning window light, full of concern.

"If it returns, we will deal with it. But in the meantime, we plan our future. It seems that I have waited my entire life for you. I have no intention of ever letting you out of my sight again."

Emma smiled faintly. "You must realize there might be a lot of truth in what Lord Linwood implied. With everything that we do know about me up to this point, it's becoming harder and harder to believe I fit neatly into some respectable box. You want us to be together, but I fear the price for you might be too high."

"As I said last night, I have spent my life watching those around me cast off what they want most because of convention, because they fear the unknown. I will not follow in their footsteps."

"But I feel like you are giving up everything for me. I have read enough novels to wonder if love is enough. So, James—"

"No, Emma, hear me. If we find your past is such that we cannot stay here, then we will leave. I am not afraid of starting over. We will go to America or the West Indies. It matters not to me, as long as we're together. I have money and can leave Haldon Manor in the care of my steward with Arthur to advise him. You know Georgiana's health is the only reason I have stayed as long as I have." His face suddenly brightened. "Perhaps we can even take Georgiana with us. A warmer clime might improve her lungs."

"But without my memory, . . . I don't know if I can embark on a new life without knowing what my old one was." Emma let out a heavy sigh. "We are at such an impasse."

"Darling, you will not dissuade me. I will find a way. You must trust me." James unfolded his arms and moved around the desk.

This would work. He would make it work. She had become too vital to him. Too necessary.

"Sir Henry has some contacts within the East India Company that he is forever pestering me about. He gave me the man's direction again just last week. Now, where did I place it?"

James scanned the top of his desk. Not seeing the scrap of paper from Sir Henry, he started opening drawers, ending with the left side drawer of his desk. He shuffled through the drawer, pulling out that odd purse he kept forgetting to hand over to his gamekeeper. He placed the purse on his desktop and continued to look through the drawer, raking a hand through his hair.

"Truly, it was just here," he muttered in frustration.

He heard voices and then a knock sounded on his study door.

"Come," he called.

His butler entered, a hint of concern showing on his usually mask-like face. "Sir, Lord Linwood is here and has insisted upon having a word with you. I placed him in the drawing room."

James sighed. He had expected a visit from Linwood. Just not quite this soon.

"I'm sorry, Emma dear," he murmured. "Linwood must be dealt with. I will return shortly."

He turned to leave and then noted her suddenly startled eyes. "Don't worry. There is nothing Linwood can do to harm us. It will all be all right." James smiled tightly, following his butler out of the room.

Too distracted by the upcoming confrontation with Linwood, James forgot to analyze why Emma's eyes had looked shocked. He did not notice her panicked breathing as he left the room. Did not see her stand—shaking—and reach for the purse he had left on his desk. Did not watch her trembling fingers fumble with the complex clasp, opening it.

But when he returned over an hour later, James did notice one thing.

His study was empty.

Chapter 24

Emme stared at the purse in her hands. Its smooth leather so impossibly familiar. Besides the locket, it was the most familiar thing she had yet seen.

Tentatively, she lifted it up, surprised at its heavy weight. The clasp was unlike anything she remembered seeing, but her fingers undid it with practiced ease. Under the clasp, there was a zipper.

Zipper. She hadn't seen one since arriving at Haldon Manor, but her mind remembered the word.

Shaking, she unzipped the bag, sinking back into her chair. With quaking hand, she pulled the purse open and looked inside. There she saw wondrous things. Achingly familiar things. Items she hadn't seen at Haldon Manor.

Her hand reached in and pulled out a thin rectangular object made seemingly of glass. It was about the size of a book and felt heavy and cool.

Tablet. Her mind labeled the object for her.

Emme's breath quickened. The trembling in her hands became even more pronounced. Images skittered against her mind. Memories. Real ones. Of things before Haldon Manor. Sitting in a vehicle with a wheel in front of her. Glancing at her reflection in the mirrored surface of a car.

Car.

That's right. There should be cars. Why were there no cars here?

She placed the tablet into her lap and reached into the purse again, her hand closing around another thin object. Smooth and glass and heavy like the last. Only smaller.

Phone.

She stared at the glossy surface of the phone, seeing her reflection in its dark surface.

Hiccupped. Shoved her hand violently over her mouth to stop the sobs that escaped. She reached into the bag and pulled out one more item.

Passport.

Hands shaking violently, she opened it. Her own face stared back.

Emry Wilde.

And then it came.

Her memory.

All of her.

She remembered. Everything. Thoughts and memories crowding her mind so quickly she felt overrun.

Dual citizenship. US and Great Britain. Her mother American, her father British. Born in 1983. She had an older brother. Marc.

Overwhelmingly, her past life crowded into her mind, pushing all other thoughts aside. She let the memories wash over her in waves, nearly drowning in everything that she had ever been.

Her childhood in Colorado, Jasmine, graduate school, her travels to places tropical and not, her little apartment in Seattle, her research, her recent trip. It all fell into place, clicking as if the memories had never left.

Whoa! The locket!

Wow!

That memory was particularly unexpected. There was no Mr. F. She was free. But her sense of relief was incredibly short-lived.

What the hell was going on?!!

Emme sat shocked for a moment. Still. What had happened?

She had been in the cottage in Marfield. There had been a thunderstorm, and she had gotten up to turn the lights back on. She had gone down to the basement, and there on the stone had been the carved initials. So like the locket.

But that was as far as she remembered. Nothing followed. Her next memory was waking to James and Georgiana.

James!

She experienced a moment of intense relief. She had no attachments. They could be together. But before happiness could flood her, she felt a sudden sinking, her stomach plummeting.

Who was James really?

What was going on? What was real? Where was she?

Getting her memory back was supposed to provide answers. Not create more questions.

She grabbed her phone and tried to power it on. Dead. Of course.

Digging through her purse, Emme pulled out the solar recharger she always carried. It was still fully charged. She plugged in her phone and then sat back, waiting.

Hearing voices in the hall, she realized she absolutely did not want to talk with anyone. Not until she had more concrete answers. Not until she had sorted through all the questions in her head.

Stuffing everything back into her purse, she crept to the door, peeked out until the coast was clear, and then silently made her way up to her bedroom, locking the door behind her.

Emme dumped out her purse, spreading its contents across her bed.

Tablet and phone, currently plugged into her military-grade solar charger. Wallet and passport. Makeup and travel toiletries. The first aid kit Marc had given her two years ago for Christmas. Three MRE's (beef stew, chili macaroni and bbq chicken) and an MRE warmer. Her intense multi-tool. Notepad and three pens. Her favorite pink ear buds. Sunscreen and sunglasses. Two Cadbury chocolate bars and cinnamon gum.

Gum. She smiled and popped a piece in her mouth, relishing the strong punch of flavor, and then dabbed on some lip gloss. Just for good measure.

She was feeling more herself already.

Now to sort through her current situation. The more she thought about it, there really were only two options.

Option One. She was on a weird reality TV show, something like Jane Austen meets *Jersey Shore.* And if so, how did it work? What about the the legal ramifications of abducting someone, giving them amnesia and then airing it all on prime time television? It seemed problematic. And why choose her? Emme paused, not sure whether to be flattered or appalled.

Then there was *Option Two.*

She really was in 1812, somehow having been transported two hundred years into the past.

Both options were utterly ridiculous.

Emme sighed, realizing there probably was an *Option Three.*

She could be stark raving mad. But she had never heard voices before. And she had a strong personal and family history of sound mental stability. So it seemed unlikely.

Perhaps.

Emme figured her cell phone would be a good place to start. If she had area or a GPS signal, she was still in 2012. And if she were in 2012, well, then she would call Marc.

Followed by the police and a good lawyer.

Foot tapping, Emme waited for her phone to have enough juice to power on. The entire time, she diligently tried not to think about James.

About his scrumptious wide smile and delicious soft lips. His infectious laughter and kind eyes. The way he looked at her as if she were the beginning and end of his world.

Was he just an actor? Had everything been a complete lie? An act?

If so, he was good. Very good. Oscar worthy.

Emme didn't know what to believe; she would go crazy thinking about it. Had they all been laughing at her all along? Was there a green room somewhere where everyone gathered and snickered about her?

It was a humiliating thought.

Restless, Emme crawled off the bed and began a more careful inspection of her room, looking along the walls and baseboards for any sign of outlets or electricity.

Nothing. It all was perfectly 1812 period.

She walked over to the window and opened it. Leaning out, she tried to see any contrails in the blue sky. Tried to hear something beyond the chirping of birds and the distant bleating of sheep, the gardeners' murmuring voices.

Nothing. No sound of cars or a motorway. No rumble of a tractor.

A quiet *bing* intruded on her thoughts and Emme jumped. At last!

Turning back to her bed, she grabbed her phone and walked over to the window, staring as it hunted for cell reception.

Searching. . . . Searching. . . . And then, . . . *No Service.*

With a deep breath, she switched to maps and GPS. Masking satellite reception would be harder. After a few minutes, she got a satellite interference message: *Uh-oh. Sorry, there is no GPS reception in this location. Make sure you are outdoors.*

Emme nodded. Fine. She could do that.

Gathering everything into her purse, she slipped on her halfboots and a pelisse. She paused while tying on a straw bonnet, shaking her head over the ludicrousness of it all.

As soon as she got this sorted out, Emme vowed to wear jeans and a t-shirt for a month straight. Oh, and underwear. Definitely underwear. Not to mention soaking in a hot, steamy shower.

Clutching her purse, she slipped out of her room and furtively made her way down the front stairs. She had no desire to see anyone.

She heard the rumble of James and Linwood in the drawing room as she walked quietly along the main hallway. Unbidden their words reached her.

"I swear to you Knight, I will have her brought up on assault."

"Damn you, Linwood, I saw the whole exchange. Again, how dare you offer *carte blanche* to a respectable lady who is a guest in my house! It's so utterly despicable, I can scarcely get my head around—"

"Respectable? Might I point out again, she attacked me."

"Attacked you? I swear sometimes you are dicked in the nob, Timothy.

It was self-defense! You forget, I saw you grab her—"

"Bah! Really, Knight, now you are just—"

"—and if you continue to press this point, I will have no problem whatsoever in describing the scene—in exquisite detail I might add—to the entire county!"

James actually sounded angry. Was he still acting out a part? And Linwood too? And if so, they were good.

Slipping out the front door, she saw a stable boy walking Linwood's horse in circles on the front drive. If this were a reality TV show, they certainly were thorough.

Refusing eye contact with anyone, Emme headed onto the terrace and then into the walled garden. Once on a secluded bench, she dug her phone out and tried again.

No service. No GPS reception.

That was odd. She stood up and looked at the house she had just left, standing beyond the garden wall. Its red brick Tudor walls covered in wisteria, mullioned windows reflecting the blue sky.

She realized she had been here before. In this garden. But it had been different.

Turning back to her phone, she dug into her photos, finding what she was looking for. Images she had taken the day she visited Haldon Manor. She stopped on one in particular. A view from the garden back toward the house.

Lifting her phone, she compared her current view with that of the photo. The photo showed the same medieval wall, but rising beyond it was a different building. Not the Tudor one she currently saw, but a newer one, built in a later Victorian Gothic style.

Emme swallowed convulsively. Tried to catch her breath. She remembered that day, visiting this place, chatting with the staff, drinking tea leisurely in the dining room, exploring this garden and the gothic cloister. The old house had burned down, they had said. Sometime in the 1820s? She couldn't remember exactly, but it had been after 1812.

Shivering despite the heated summer air, Emme needed to think. To see more. Tucking everything away again, she made her way out of the garden, across the lawn, past the lake. All the while, not finding cell phone signal, no sound or sign of modern civilization. No matter how far she walked, no hum of a car. No distant rumble of machinery. Just peaceful quiet.

She thought of Marfield. The town looked similar and yet different. Cobbled streets instead of pavement. Some buildings the same. Others gone. She walked for hours. Trying to locate the motorway that should be here, just outside town, but finding only fields. Finally, Emme was so hopelessly turned around, she didn't know what to think anymore.

Being summer, the day stretched long and bright. She stopped at one point to put on some sunscreen, as she didn't trust the brim of her bonnet to keep her face from burning.

It was impossible to comprehend how, but perhaps, just perhaps, she really was in 1812.

She could find no sign of modern Britain.

And then she remembered the night sky. So impossibly black and dotted with more stars than she could ever remember seeing. In modern Britain, light pollution was ever present, even in Herefordshire.

But here, the night sky was different. The heavens inky-black from horizon to horizon, while the stars shown clearly, glittering and eternal. A dense forest of twinkling lights.

Only a pre-modern sky could be so dark and yet so bright.

An 1812 sky.

But if she was in 1812, how had she gotten here?

Looking around, she realized her steps had unthinkingly turned toward the meadow and the ancient oak. Stopping at the edge of the meadow, she noted the lowering sun. Work on the new house had wrapped up for the day.

The remains of the enormous tree were nearly entirely gone, the votive offerings with them. Only the large trunk remained. It appeared they were taking it apart in pieces, preparing to build the new dower house.

A dower house for Haldon Manor. Emme gasped as she remembered.

Duir Cottage.

The ancient tree's secret—a gateway. The oak must be the key.

Quickly she crossed the meadow, walking toward the huge split trunk. As she neared it, she again felt the same heaviness in the air, the tingly hum of electricity. She paused at the cleft and peered down into the hollow trunk. Into the black, yawning cavern. She could feel it pull her. Willing her to jump in.

Blinking, she pulled back. Was this the portal home? How did it work? And was she ready to leave?

Swallowing in the slanting light, Emme sank against the trunk, tucking her knees into her chest. She wasn't one to put off a problem, but there were no travel pamphlets on what to do when you discover yourself to be in a different country. On a different continent.

In a different century.

This traveling disaster was truly spectacular. Eclipsing all others.

Amnesia plus time travel? That had to be some sort of disaster magnet record. If anyone kept track of such things.

Thoughts kept crowding in. The locket. That crazy, enigmatic locket. It probably was James in the portrait. She nodded her head in amazement. The coincidence was too much. It had to be him. The entire thing created for her after all.

She let the wonder of it envelop her, hugging the pleasure of James' love tight against her heart.

Throughout all time. Heart of my soul.

The words echoed in her heart. Deep and profound.

Then she paused, frowning. Why the F? She puzzled for a moment over it and then shook her head.

Knowing James, it probably stood for something absurd, like 'your Fantasy.' Emme snorted. That seemed a likely possibility. The man was utterly shameless.

She pulled out her phone, happy to see it almost fully charged, and then switched it to airplane mode to preserve her battery life.

Emme noticed an unread email. Something from the night she had left. Opening up her email client, she found a message from Marc.

She brushed away the tears as she read:

Hey! Been thinking about our talk on the phone earlier and decided
that maybe it was time for one of my heartfelt (and in no way girly)
pep talks. You know I hate watching you struggle over this whole

Fabio thing. But I also understand that you need to chase your dream. Find him, Ems, and then move on. Know that you'll always have an awesome big brother to back you up. Whew! Enough said.

And no disasters with the BMW. I want a chance to drive that car before you send it off the white cliffs of Dover. Cause if it would happen to anyone, it would happen to you. Love ya, sis!

Emme choked, covering her mouth to stifle her sobs, feeling the powerful pain of his loss.

Phone in one hand and purse in the other, she wrapped her arms around herself, like a talisman. Getting her memory back was supposed to make everything simpler. Easier. Instead everything felt infinitely more complicated.

She couldn't remain here, in 1812. Emme didn't think she could live in a world where women were still viewed as property. Where a woman's only options were marriage or prostitution, as she had already seen firsthand. She couldn't bring a child into a world where the threat of disease constantly loomed.

Not to mention living in a time without iTunes, indoor plumbing and Xanax. She shuddered at the thought.

But could she live in a world without James?

Exhausted, Emme crept back into her bedroom, the last rays of sun kissing the horizon. She was too tired to see anyone—to smile and pretend nothing had changed.

She felt utterly drained. Nearly lifeless and void. Tomorrow she would think things through. Make a list and a plan.

Perhaps she would even consider telling James. But would he believe her?

James was ready to accept her as a courtesan—which really was incredible for a man of his time—but would he be willing to accept a 21st century American woman who had been raised to be bold and strong? A woman who would see him as a partner and not a protector?

It seemed too much of a stretch, perhaps even for James. Assuming he didn't just commit her to an asylum.

Fanny was waiting, asking where she had been, stating everyone had been a little worried about her. Emme murmured a few noncommittal replies and pled a headache, asking for a dinner tray to be sent up.

As Fanny helped her undress, Emme had a thought. She asked if Fanny could get her some breeches, a shirt, coat and riding boots, preferably by tomorrow morning. Fanny's eyes widened in shock, but then she bobbed a curtsy saying she would look for some of Mr. Knight's cast off clothing up in the attic. Emme nodded her thanks and then sank gratefully back into her bed, cuddling under the covers.

She fell asleep with a hand wrapped around her phone, her thoughts buried with friends and family many lifetimes away.

Chapter 25

Morning did not bring much clarity to Emme's thinking. She had finally found her mysterious F but to have him meant giving up everything she had ever known. And to have everything she had ever known, she would have to give up James.

It was a ridiculous catch-22.

A large part of her was terrified to see him.

James would realize something was different. He would know she had changed. Besides she couldn't—no—she wouldn't lie to him. Not about something as important as this.

But would he believe her?

And even if he did, Emme was afraid. Afraid that if she looked into his blue eyes, she would give everything up. Would turn away from the only life she had ever known.

She didn't feel strong enough to see him yet.

And so she had decided to ride instead. Riding had always calmed her. It had been her escape after her father had left them. The pounding oneness with a horse driving away fear and pain. She awoke to find Fanny had unearthed some male clothing, all neatly folded on the bench at the foot of her bed.

Emme dressed quickly, pulling on her short stays, which fit sort of like a sports bra. Well, if a sports bra were made of linen with boning in it instead of spandex. How many years before spandex would be invented anyway?

She shook her head. Thoughts like that were not going to help her sort things out.

Clad in shirt, breeches, coat and riding boots, she felt more herself. More the modern woman. She placed the solar charger on the window sill to recharge, hoping to power her tablet next, and then stuffed her phone into her stays along with her hot pink earbuds and slipped out of her room.

The stables were thankfully empty. With a nod of appreciation, she walked to the tack room and grabbed a saddle—a real one, not a side saddle. She contemplated saddling the mare she usually rode, but she wanted more out of her mount today. So instead, she headed straight for Luther's stall. He pranced slightly as she saddled him.

Leading him out into the yard, Emme shoved her earbuds in and plugged into her phone. Scrolling through her music until she found something suitably loud and angry to match her confused emotions, she pushed her phone back into her stays and swung onto Luther's back. He danced sideways slightly but quickly recognized her skilled hands on the reins.

With a kick, they went flying out of the stables and into the fields beyond. Music and blood pounding in her ears. Drowning out the conflicting wants of her heart.

James had experienced a puzzling twenty-four hours. Things had started well. He had enjoyed chatting with Emma in his study, but then Linwood had come and provided James with an infuriating hour-long conversation. As if that hadn't been bad enough, when he emerged from the drawing room, he discovered that Emma had run off somewhere to be alone. And then, after causing him several hours worry about her whereabouts, she had turned up in her room, pleading a headache.

He had replayed their discussion over and over, trying to recall if he had said anything amiss. Had she had been upset over something? He thought everything had been going well.

It made no sense whatsoever.

And so this morning, dressed casually in a shirt, breeches and long overcoat, he was determined to have a bruising ride, burn off all his excess energy and then chat with Emma.

But as he walked toward the stables, he saw a lad go tearing out of the yard on Luther, riding hard toward the nearest fence, something pink wrapped around his neck.

What the hell? Who was riding his horse?

Shocked, James shouted and ran toward the stable, only to realize, it wasn't some strange boy riding Luther, but Emma herself. Blinking in surprise, he watched her take the first fence with practiced grace and ease. She really had spent time riding astride.

Swearing, he turned toward the stables and rushed to saddle Arthur's horse.

Emma had some explaining to do.

Ten minutes later, James wondered if he was going to be able to catch her. Luther was tireless in general and Emma weighed less than James. But eventually he caught sight of her, slowing as she wound through a field. He shouted her name, clearly loud enough for her to hear, but Emma pretended not to heed him, continuing on her way without a backward glance.

What the devil was she up to? And why was she suddenly ignoring him?

Urging his mount faster, he raced toward her. Finally after another five minutes of chasing, he managed to pull up beside her, shouting at her to stop. She still refused to acknowledge him, looking straight ahead.

Frustrated, James lightly tapped her knee with his riding crop, forcing her to turn to him. Gasping in surprise, she instantly pulled up, slowing Luther to a stop, her eyes wide above the coat and shirt she wore.

Without thinking, James spun his horse around and dismounted, scowling as he stalked toward Emma and Luther. Eyes still surprised, Emma dismounted too, meeting him halfway to stand panting in front of him.

In his anger, he refused to notice how absurdly darling she looked in one of his old coats and breeches, the sleeves just a little too long, dark curly hair tousled from her galloping ride.

With a flick of her hands, she popped something pink out of both her ears to rest around her neck.

"What is going on? Why are you ignoring me?" James realized he was yelling. How had they come to this?

She merely blinked at him. Looking so lost and forlorn. Her eyes drinking him in.

As if seeing him for the first time. As if he were everything she had ever wanted. As if she had finally found that one vital thing that had been lost for so very long.

"Sorry," she said between breaths without breaking his gaze. "I didn't hear you."

"Didn't hear me? How is that possible? I'm pretty sure that they heard me two counties over! What's wrong?"

Emma blinked again. And then, with a shake of her head, she did the last thing he expected her to do in that moment.

She took the remaining two steps to him, grasped his coat lapels with both hands, pulled him to her.

And kissed him.

A kiss that was hot and hungry and needing. A kiss that said she had been thirsty for far too long.

A kiss unlike any he had ever experienced.

Her hands slid up his coat and into his hair and she held him tight, demanding that he return everything she gave.

Moaning, James wrapped his arms around her waist and pulled her close. Reveling in the shocking sweetness of her. In the rightness of her in his arms.

Their kiss went on endlessly, aching, longing, until James pulled back slightly, gasping her name.

"Emma!"

Breathing heavily, she held his head firm, refusing to let him move his lips more than a few inches from hers.

James found himself liking this newfound side of her.

"Emry," she whispered.

And then she kissed him again. The same starved need coursing through her. Through him.

"What?!" James exclaimed, realizing what she had said, pushing her away slightly. "What did you just say?"

She seemed to be struggling to focus on anything other than his mouth. Grabbing her chin, he forced her eyes up to his.

"What did you just say?" he repeated quietly.

She swallowed, her eyes suddenly wary.

"Emry," she whispered again, moving a hand from his hair to softly caress his cheek. Her eyes devouring him, still full of stunned awe.

"My name isn't Emma. It's Emry. Emry Wilde."

They both froze and James felt the shock of her words sink in. Words said in the most American of accents.

"Emry," he whispered, trying her name.

With amazement, he moved his finger from her chin to stroke her cheek.

Swallowed.

"Well, Emry Wilde, it is a pleasure to make your acquaintance."

James dipped his head closer to hers. "At last."

He closed the distance, claiming her mouth in another kiss. This one sweet and yearning.

"My family and friends call me Emme," she murmured against his mouth with a soft sigh.

"Emme," he breathed, leaning to brush her cheek with his lips. He moved his mouth toward her ear, nibbling along the way.

"Am I to understand from the fact that you are kissing me that there is no Mr. Wilde?" James felt her tense slightly.

"Well," she began, "there is a Mr. Wilde, . . ."

His blood chilled. He instantly stilled but then realized there was laughter in her voice.

". . . a Mr. Marc Wilde, my older brother. But there is no one else. No other man in my life. No one with a claim on my heart." She pulled back to drink him in. "Other than you."

James was sure his confusion showed on his face, because she laughed suddenly and hugged him fiercely.

"I don't understand. If you are not angry, then why were you ignoring me? While riding?"

He thought he understood Emma. But this new Emme, with the American accent and extra-assertive personality, was a bit of a stranger.

She laughed against his ear, as if his question were particularly funny. James struggled to see the humor.

"I honestly couldn't hear you, my love," she said, pulling back to look into his eyes. "It's a long tale. Or at least, a rather unbelievable one. Do you have a morning to listen to my story?"

Chapter 26

Yes, Emme realized, she probably should have waited longer before seeing James.

Maybe a couple years without seeing him would have tempered the kicked-through-the-gut jolt that swept her as he dismounted and came striding angrily forward. His hair windblown and sunkissed. Overcoat snapping in the wind. His shirt slightly open at the collar. Blue-eyes bright and alive.

He had looked insanely delectable. Like a scene from every woman's fantasy.

Well, . . . hers at least.

This was James.

James!

The man from her locket. The person she had spent years wondering over and obsessing over and trying to get over.

And now he was really here. Standing in front of her.

And then holding her and kissing her. Emme buried her face in his neck, hugging him fiercely. With a sigh, she pulled away, taking his hand.

"So, do you have a morning to listen to my story?" she repeated.

"Of course." A wide smile split his face, delighted and amazed.

James gathered the reins of both their horses and led Emme to sit under a large tree, where he tethered the horses. Emme sat crosslegged on the ground, leaning against the tree trunk. James settled next to her, reaching out to twine his fingers through hers.

"Come. I want to hear everything about you. Slowly and from the beginning. Every possible detail." He practically glowed as he looked at her. Emme found herself staring back, still thrumming from the wonder of him.

Smiling, she squeezed his hand, moving her fingers along his. "Where to begin?" She paused. "First of all, let me say I am nothing that Linwood assumed. Not even remotely close."

James released a quick hiss. "Well, for your sake, I'm glad then. Though as I have said, it would have made no difference to me."

"You might want to save statements like that until *after* I've told the rest of my story." Emme gave a little knowing laugh.

James answered with a decidedly wicked grin. "That good, eh?"

"You have no idea. Trust me." Emme shook her head. "And surprisingly, everything makes sense."

His grin even wider, James leaned back into the tree, rubbing his thumb in absent circles across the back of her hand. "I can't wait. You are American then? I hear it in your voice."

"Yes. Well, I'm both actually. My mother is American, my father British. I spent time with my British grandmother growing up. She insisted that I learn how to be a proper lady, because we are Cavendishes on my great-grandfather's side of the family, third cousins of the Duke of Devonshire, you know." She said that last bit in her best upper-crust, old-lady voice.

"Impressive. I always knew you were respectable."

Emme laughed, settling her palm further into his, loving how his larger hand engulfed her smaller one.

"And no husband? No betrothed either?"

"No, no one. You seem concerned about it."

"Well, it has caused me much worry over the past weeks." He reached over to her with his opposite hand and wrapped a stray curl behind her ear. He seemed excessively fond of that curl. "I don't want there to be any impediments to our being together."

"Impediments. . . ." Emme let out a puff of air and glanced away from him. "In some ways, a husband or fiance would be easier than the actual truth. Our reality is much more complicated, I fear."

"Really? Are there obstacles then?"

Staring out over the lush Herefordshire countryside, Emme said quietly, "No, not precisely. Just pain, I guess. Compromise."

"Compromise," James said thoughtfully. Slowly. "I can accept that. So, who is the mysterious Mr. F?"

"Oh, goodness." Emme gave a small laugh. "The locket . . . the locket is part of this whole odd tale." She exhaled. "I'm not sure you will believe me."

"Not believe you? Why wouldn't I believe you?" James looked puzzled, a slight smile playing around his lips.

"It's quite the fantastic story. If I didn't have the memories in my head and some other items to prove it, I don't think I would believe it either."

"Does it involve these?" He released her hand and plucked at the pink earbuds still dangling around her shoulders. "Because I'm not sure they will become all the rage. Though the color is certainly . . . eye catching."

With a wry face, Emme unwrapped the headphones from her neck, staring at them for a moment. Hot pink and shockingly anachronistic.

"Yes, actually it does."

She paused, absently pulling the pink cord through her fingers. How do you tell someone you come from the future?

"Are you from the West Indies after all then?"

"Not exactly. Though I have visited there. Jamaica. The Mexican Riviera. I actually attended a cousin's wedding in the Bahamas."

James merely looked at her, one eyebrow cocked, encouraging her to continue.

When she didn't, he said, "It sounds exotic and wonderful. Come now. Why do you hesitate? It's not that bad, is it?"

"No, it's not," she agreed. "Nothing at all like we feared. Just shocking. Surprising."

"Well? You are teasing me with the agony of this suspense. It's hardly kind of you."

Emme wrapped the earphones around her hand, studying them. There was no easy way to do this.

"I was born in the United States," she said, raising her eyes to meet his. "In Colorado. In a town just outside Denver."

James stilled, a quizzical look on his face. He tilted his head. "I don't think I have ever heard of a place called Colorado. Where is it exactly?"

Emme grimaced. "That's the problem, actually. Currently, it's at the edge of what Americans call the Louisiana Purchase. There is probably not a single person in all of Britain who has been there."

"I always thought you were a taste of adventure."

"More than you ever anticipated, I think," Emme smiled faintly.

She just needed to get it over with. Untangling the earbuds from her fingers, Emme reached into her stays and pulled out her phone. James gazed questioningly at it in her hand.

Shaking her head, Emme looked into his eyes. "Things have felt off to me from the beginning. I would know things that seemed impossibly contradictory. And the simplest things would feel foreign while other things would be familiar. . . . The problem, it turns out, is not where I'm from, . . . but *when*. . . ."

She allowed her last word to sink in. James instantly stilled. Emme caught and held his blue eyes with her own.

"James, I was born in 1983," she continued, staring intently. "I left Britain in the year 2012. It seems the old oak tree really is a portal after all, just not to the netherworld." She paused. "It's a portal through time."

Emme could feel his shock. Palpable. A gut-punched widening of his eyes, a hissing inhalation through his teeth.

James swallowed. Ran a suddenly shaking hand through his hair. Looked out over the fields and then after a moment turned his gaze back to her.

"You are serious, aren't you," he murmured, stretching out his hand to trace her jaw with one finger. "You are not teasing me."

"No," she whispered, her gaze pleading for understanding. For him to believe her. "I wouldn't tease about this."

James nodded slowly, his eyes glassy and unseeing as he grasped at the concept.

"I . . . I . . . You have actually managed to render me speechless. . . . I cannot remember the last time that happened." A small smile touched his lips. James continued to run a finger along her jaw and then cupped her cheek with his entire hand. All the while, looking intently into her eyes. Finally, with another noisy swallow, he continued.

"Truly, 2012, you say? Two hundred years? That's . . . astounding. . . . No, no, more like stunning, utterly astonishing," he finished with another tentative grin.

"Mind-blowing? A bombshell?" Emme offered. And then with a teasing smile and a cocked eyebrow, "Totally cray-cray?" That one earned her a gentle laugh.

She wrapped her fingers through his on her cheek and turned her head, pressing a kiss into his palm. Grasping his hand, Emme pulled it from her face and held it loosely in her lap, tucking her palm into his. James stared at her for a long moment, considering, thinking.

"What caused your memory to return?" he asked at last.

"It was the purse on your desk. The one you pulled out yesterday morning. It was my purse. I remember having it with me right before I . . . before I came through the portal, I guess. How did you come to have it?"

"I found it. In the wreckage of the oak tree, just lying on the ground."

Emme nodded in understanding. "Yes, well, that makes sense then."

He glanced down at the phone.

"Is that one of the items from the bag? May I see it?"

"Of course." Emme disconnected the earbuds, tucking them into her coat pocket and handed him the phone. She watched as he felt the weight of it in his hand, ran his fingers over its glossy surface.

"It's heavy. Heavier than it looks." James hefted it slightly. "I take it this is some oddity from the future? Is it made of glass?"

"The case is made of glass. It's called a telephone. A smart phone, actually. And it . . . well, it does a ridiculous number of amazing things."

"Really?" He looked at the phone and then back at her in disbelief. "I would have thought something from the future would look . . . more . . . future-ish. This seems decidedly anti-climactic. It's just a lump of glass."

Emme laughed. "Yes, I guess it could seem somewhat bland, but trust me, it's pretty awesome."

"Awesome?"

"Oh yeah." Emme winked at him and reached over and pushed the home button, bringing the phone's lockscreen to life. James inhaled sharply and started a little, glancing at her in surprise. She smiled lightly and slid closer to him, their arms touching.

"Without an internet connection, the phone is somewhat limited, but it seriously does just about everything."

Emme swiped her finger to unlock it, typing in her passcode. James eye's widened as the screen lit up with apps and folders.

"Good heavens," he murmured. "What is all this then?"

Emme laughed. "Welcome to the 21st century," she said, patting his arm.

Still smiling broadly, Emme proceeded to show him all the interesting features of a smart phone. Loving the way James gasped with delight over each new thing, crowing like a small child. His questions were never ending. They sat, shoulders touching, for several hours as Emme explained her life to him.

She showed him the maps of Herefordshire she had cached as part of her research. He found them endlessly fascinating, comparing what had changed and what was still the same.

She plugged the headphones back in and put them into his ears, showing him exactly why she hadn't heard him earlier. James jerked his head in surprise at her raucous rock-n-roll.

"Okay, that might be a little too advanced for you right now," Emme chuckled, stopping the track. "But trust me, you'll learn to love it." She flipped through her music until she found some Mozart. "Try this instead." James' eyes widen in wonder.

"It's incredible," he whispered, shaking his head in near awe. "I can't even comprehend being able to listen to such beauty whenever I would like. With such a device always with you, how can you manage to concentrate on anything else?"

"Careful!" Emme chuckled at length. "You might start to sound like my mother with lines like that. But yes, to answer your question, a smart phone can be an incredible time waster."

Digging into her photos, she showed him images of Marc, her mom, Jasmine, her apartment in Seattle, her cousin's wedding outside Nassau, her sabbatical research work .

"So, you are a professor of history?" James asked. "You hardly seem old enough."

"Now you're being too kind," Emme said, nudging his shoulder with her own. "I turn thirty this year, so I'm plenty old to have finished up a doctoral degree."

"Thirty? Truly? Heavens, that makes you only a year younger than myself! And here I thought you were closer to Georgiana's age."

James continued to ask question after question, wanting to know about cars, airplanes, computers, television, current politics. The list was endless.

"So you mother works as a . . . what did you call it?" James looked quizzical.

"A flight attendant. She cares for people when they fly in an airplane and generally manages the passengers."

James paused and then said, "Truthfully, I don't think I can get my head around that right now. Flying through the air like a bird. But these cars sound fascinating. Tell me more about them. Can anyone drive one?"

Laughing, Emme told him about the airport fiasco with the small car and then showed him images of the upgraded BMW. He was suitably appreciative of its sleek, glossy look. She also remembered she had some video of Marc's fight scenes. James watched the clips over and over, finding the martial art moves engrossing.

And he raised his eyebrows at the photo of her in tight jeans, moto jacket, knee-high boots and huge sunglasses.

"I think I could get used to seeing you dressed like this," he said with a teasing wiggle of his eyebrows.

Emme snorted. "Well, that's good, because I'm a little done wearing a dress all the time. It feels . . . a little too 19th century." James laughed in delight. "Here," Emme took the phone from him and scrambled to her feet. "I think I need a photo of you."

"Me?" James said in surprise. "It creates the images too?"

"Of course! Now stand up and look manly, please."

James laughed again and obligingly got to his feet. He leaned back into the tree, folding his arms, causing the muscles in his chest to bunch together. Hair windblown and disheveled. Eyes sparking with mischief. He lifted a knee and rested one booted foot against the trunk, his long overcoat rippling in the gentle wind.

He looked impossibly delectable.

Emme took several photos and then switched to video. "Say something," she said, watching him through her phone screen. "Something smooth in that urbane aristocratic accent of yours."

James stared at her with a penetrating smile on his face. Drinking her in.

"You are utterly irresistible," he said. "Just when I think it isn't possible to adore you more than I already do, you find a way."

Oh my.

Emme raised her head from her phone and locked eyes with him. Answered his smile with her own. She stopped the video and walked back to him, snuggling against his side as he wrapped an arm around her, tucking her close.

"Look," she said and showed him the video. He shook his head in amazement. Emme gave him a small smile, dropping the phone into her coat pocket.

James sighed and pulled her even closer, brushing a kiss against her forehead. "I can scarcely believe I am going to say this," he murmured into her hair, "but I think you have convinced me. You really are from the future." And then he paused, as if only suddenly realizing something. "But what about the locket? I don't understand how that factors in to all of this?"

Emme nestled into his shoulder, breathing him in. "I don't know either, actually. It is from your time period. I found it in an estate sale in Portland, Oregon years ago." She paused, the emotion of it finally overwhelming her. Choking against the sudden tightness in her throat.

He was here! The man that she had yearned to be with for so long, puzzled over, ached for. Here in her arms at last. All those feelings of connection and rightness utterly vindicated.

Drat Jasmine and her psychic abilities!

She buried her face in his neck, turning to twine her arms around his head, pressing her nose into that hollow between his ear and throat. As she had longed to do for more years than she cared to admit.

With a sigh, Emme whispered against his neck, "I found the locket and felt an intense connection to the man in it." She paused to rub a tear off her cheek. "Like a seriously intense connection. Profound and spiritual. Transcendent. But I knew nothing about the locket. About the sitter." She sniffed. "I was actually in Marfield to try to find out more about it. The portrait is the work of Giovanni Spunto, or at least my research indicated as much." Emme shook her head and pulled back, taking James' face in her hands.

His eyes were wide, searching hers.

"I still have no idea who the sitter is, James. But I strongly suspect he . . . he is actually you. There is no one else. There is . . . and has only ever been . . . you."

James responded in the only way a man could to such a statement.

He bent his head and kissed her.

Chapter 27

Auntie Gray's cottage
The next day
June 15, 1812

So you see, Auntie, the oak really does house a portal, a door into another time, as it were. We were hoping you might have more insight for us," James said quietly.

He and Emme sat in Auntie Gray's small cottage, Emme dressed again in Georgiana's riding habit. She had committed to behaving as a proper genteel lady. Running around broadcasting anachronistic clothing, behavior and speech patterns would not help their current situation.

They had also agreed, for the time being, to not tell anyone about her returned memory, not even Georgiana. Knowing Emme had regained her memory would necessitate far too many explanations.

James was still trying to wrap his head around her tale. He had been ready to accept any number of dastardly reasons for Emme to have been upon his lane that night, but he had never remotely considered the truth. Why would he have? True, Emme embodied adventure, but this twist had startled even him.

What they were to do about the situation they found themselves in, James didn't know.

After talking for hours and hours the day before, they had returned to Haldon Manor. Emme had brought her purse into his study, and he had spent hours exploring the fascinating objects within. James had found her wallet and passport particularly interesting, even if Emme had not appreciated him laughing at her driver's license photo. Though there were things he did not understand. Like how could a rigid card—a 'credit card' Emme had called it—be considered a form of currency?

And cinnamon gum? Who knew?

Then there was her tablet, the larger version of her phone. He struggled to comprehend what she meant by the word 'internet,' finding the entire concept utterly foreign.

But he had grasped Angry Birds easily enough. Emme had finally laughed in exasperation and left him to play late into the night until the tablet's battery expired. How could annihilating those pesky pigs be so addicting?

Today, they had called on Auntie Gray to see what more she knew about the portal. How specifically did it work? Could Emme return to her own time? Was she to remain here?

"Please, Auntie," Emme said. "Please tell us what you know."

Auntie looked calmly at Emme and then gave a quiet smile. "You seemed like a traveler to me, child." Her aged voice gentle and low. "I do not know much about the portal, only what my mother told me, which she learned from her mother and so on back through time. The gate does not operate indiscriminately. It is specific in whom it chooses to let through. One who would travel the portal must have a powerful reason to do so. Something that is more than mere want or curiosity."

"But I had no idea the portal even existed, that such a thing would be possible." Emme shook her head. "It seems so confusing. Why would it recognize me?"

"The portal knows the longing of the heart. Perhaps even better than you yourself."

Emme laughed, soft and wistful. "Yes, that much is true. I did know the longing of my heart. Just not that it could be fulfilled."

James thrilled at her soulful look, her hazel eyes adoring.

"Indeed," Auntie agreed. "In the end, the reason for traveling the portal must be vital. A pull beyond time. The destiny of one's soul."

James looked at Emme, feeling the weight of her gaze.

"Would any of us be able to pass through the portal?" James asked. Auntie Gray tilted her head, pondering the question.

"I cannot say, m'boy. To the portal, time is not a straight line, moving from one event to the next. Instead, all history—past and future—is fully present. Time is a vast ocean where all things occur at once. The lives of everyone exist together as rippling circles on its surface. And from time to time, the rings of one soul's expanding circle intertwine with those of another. At that point of contact, the portal provides a gate. A link that can be traversed."

James heard Emme draw in a sharp breath, as if Auntie's words had touched a chord, resonating within her.

"The portal is not indiscriminate," Auntie cautioned. "It is purposeful. If the path of one's life requires a trip through, then it will happen."

James reached out and took Emme's hand, gently squeezing it.

"I am glad you have come to us, child," Auntie Gray continued, her eyes sparkling. "You have been a delightful ray of sunshine here in Marfield. Please tell me you will stay for a cup of tea and a nice coze. I should love to hear something diverting about the future."

After leaving Auntie Gray, James unthinkingly steered their mounts toward the meadow and the ancient oak tree. He walked Luther into the meadow, dismounted and then turned to help Emme off her mare. His workmen were at the sawmill today, but he could see the beginnings of the foundation being cut. The house would probably be framed and roofed before the first snowfall.

James took Emme's hand but instantly hated the gloves that separated them. Catching her eyes, he removed his gloves from his hands. And then, bringing her knuckles to his lips, he gently kissed them. Lightly, he pulled the gloves from her hands, stripping them off one finger at a time, and tucked them into his coat pocket. She cocked an eyebrow at him and with a smile reached for his hand, lacing her warm fingers through his.

Hand in hand, they walked up to the remains of the enormous stump. It had been cut down significantly, but the empty center still gaped, dark and yawning. There was heaviness in the air, the tingle of something powerful. James clutched Emme's hand tightly. She sucked in a deep breath.

He turned and gazed at her. "What are you thinking?"

"I don't know," she whispered, giving her head a plaintive shake.

"Would you stay here with me?"

"Giving up my family, my life, my world? It seems impossible. But then, having finally found you, I can't imagine relinquishing you. That also seems like an impossibility."

"Would there be work for a man like me in the 21st century?"

Emme turned her head sharply toward him. "You can't possibly be serious, James! What about Haldon Manor? Your family? Your tenants?"

James shrugged, pulling her closer to his side. "I've been contemplating leaving for a long while. It really is a pity I can't just turn everything over to Arthur. That it is entailed on me. But if I am for all intents and purposes dead—or at least dead to this time period—well, that changes everything. Arthur would inherit." He gave a teasing look. "I am not afraid of going into trade. I am not too proud." He wagged his eyebrows at her.

Emme looked at him appraisingly, a smile touching her lips. "Oh, heaven forbid you find yourself in trade. I'm sure you could find work in any number of things. Though to be honest, you are a wealthy man right now and have time on your side. Two hundred years of it. That is plenty of time to have something grow."

James tilted his head at her, confused. "You might have to explain what you mean."

"I don't know if there is much of a stock market right now, but if you put something into a trust, like . . . an old master painting or something else of antiquity, then you could sell it in the 21st century and have plenty of money to live on. I don't know that you would necessarily need to work. You could remain a kept man of leisure." Her eyes glinted teasingly.

"We could just take it with us through the portal?"

"Possibly, but when it comes to things of antiquity, provenance is almost as important as the object itself. Modern science has ways to determine the age of something. So it would need to be genuinely old. And held in trust somehow, somewhere. So people knew it existed. If you could find a way to ensure that the items reached the 21st century intact, well, they could be worth a large sum."

"Interesting." He shook his head. That most certainly did give him a few ideas. "So much to contemplate."

Emme stilled, as if considering. "Could you really do it? Leave Haldon Manor and everything you have ever known?"

James turned and looked out over the meadow, the piles of stone waiting to be placed for the foundation, pondering, thinking.

"I have always felt out of place here," he finally said. "Like I don't belong. Like I was meant for a different life. Only Georgiana holds me here."

"Georgiana," Emme murmured, nodding as if something had just occurred to her. "She is truly dying. Of tuberculosis. Though I guess you don't call the disease tuberculosis yet."

James paused, the word unfamiliar to him. "She has consumption and, yes, it is generally fatal. Though some people have been known to recover. I am still determined to find something to save her."

Emme gave his hand a tight squeeze, her hand warm and soft in his. "She would live, you know. In the 21st century, TB is rarely fatal, particularly in someone like Georgiana where her infection most likely isn't drug resistant. She would take medicine for a couple weeks and would be completely whole. Cured."

James gasped. He hadn't considered the possibility.

Georgiana would live!

Painfully wonderful, the thought tore through him. To see his sister whole. To give her back her future. It was everything he had spent the last year working for. He blinked and swallowed, trying to rein in his emotions, taking a deep, measured breath before speaking.

"That would be . . ." He stopped as his voice cracked. Paused. And then tried again. "To see Georgiana restored to health would be miraculous. She has been so dear to me for so long. To not have to part with her so soon . . ."

His voice trailed off. James closed his eyes, struggling to bring his emotions under control. Emme wrapped her arms around his waist, burrowing her head against his neck, holding him tight for long moments. Clutching her in return, James finally found his voice.

"I would give up everything if it meant Georgiana's life." He pulled back to look into Emme's eyes, touched her cheek. "I would."

She nodded, blinking back tears. "I would do the same," she whispered and then repeated. "I would do the same."

James pulled Emme close again. Buried his face in her hair. Breathed in the scent of her . . . lavender and fresh summer air.

"What if the portal doesn't work?" she murmured against his shoulder. "What if Georgie doesn't want to come? The 21st century can be a confusing place."

Excellent questions to which he had no answer.

"I don't know. What is this medicine they would give Georgiana?"

"Antibiotics."

James frowned slightly. "Another thing I'm not familiar with."

"Yes, well, you are over a century away from their discovery. The simplest explanation is that they are like a kind of mold that targets the infection."

"Mold?" James pulled back to look in her eyes. "Truly?"

Emme nodded her head.

"Well, who knew it was so simple."

She laughed. "I don't know that antibiotics are that simple, though they certainly save lives. But there is still time. Georgiana is ill but hardly at death's door, and from what I remember, tuberculosis takes a good while to kill a person. It is not a fast disease."

Silent for a moment, Emme rested her head against his shoulder, holding him, her body melting trustingly into his. She shifted slightly in his arms.

"What if the portal doesn't work?" she asked quietly, her voice muffled against his coat. "What if I never see my family again?"

James pondered it for a moment, running his hand soothingly up her back.

Finally, he said, "I've always thought that life is a pattern of opposites. In any relationship, there is a line. A point where you cross over, and you can no longer extricate your life from another's without pain." James paused, hugging her more tightly and then continued. "For example, I only feel the terror of Georgiana's death because I love her so well. The desperation of losing her is directly tied to the joy of having her in my life."

He stilled for a moment, trying to gather his thoughts. Realizing what he needed to say, James gently pulled her away from his shoulder and took her face in his hands.

"I love you, Emry Wilde. You have my heart. And I cannot . . . no . . . I will not live my life without you. Not as long as you are willing to accept me."

The rightness of his words pounded through him. He watched as Emme's eyes drank him in, suddenly brimming with tears.

"I love you too, James Knight," she whispered.

She hiccupped and closed her eyes, catching her quivering bottom lip in her teeth. After a second, she rubbed her cheek against his hand and opened her lovely hazel eyes, bright gold and green and fathomless.

"I have loved you for so long," she whispered. "So incredibly long. Yearned for you. Sought you. And now to have you here. With me. . ."

Her words faltered. Emotions skittered across her face.

"It's more than just a dream. It's a fantasy. You are the most amazing . . . the most unimaginable gift."

Emme paused, glancing down for a moment before raising her eyes and continuing. "But what if it is not enough? What if the portal doesn't work? What if I'm stuck here, in 1812?"

James raised an eyebrow.

"I mean, I would struggle if I had to stay here permanently. Not only would I miss my family and friends, but I would feel so helpless watching those I love suffer from easily treatable diseases. There is just so much that I would miss. . . ."

James let his hands drop from her face, taking her hands in his and holding them tightly.

Emme continued, "Or worse, what if you came forward with me and hated it? At least I know what I'm getting into here, but all you have is my word that the future is a decent place. I've barely scratched the surface on all the problems of the 21st century. And trust me, there are a lot of them; it's not just all sleek electronics and Angry Birds and—"

"Emme, there will be difficulties no matter what—"

"Just listen, James. I worry that one of us might come to resent the other, to resent the life we have chosen." She bit her lip, fighting against emotion. "I would hate for something to slowly eat away at us. At our love."

James sighed and nodded slowly. Thinking again.

"My love, there are no guarantees. No promises I can make that will ensure everything will be fine ten years from now or next year or even next month."

He lifted her hand and brushed a kiss across her knuckles.

"But, Emme, I do know this. We have crossed that line. Utterly and thoroughly. It is foolishness to think that life's greatest joys don't also come with some of life's greatest pain. If we wish to be together, one of us will have to give up our current world. Our family. Our friends. Everything. And the other will have to watch it happen—"

"But James—"

"No, now it's my turn to talk." He placed a finger over her lips. "I often think it's harder to watch someone I love in pain than to be the one in pain. Georgiana's suffering consumes me. But for you and I, darling Emme, there *will* be sorrow and loss. As of right now, that is part of the contract. The price of our being together. Any decision we make will involve some pain. The only decision I cannot make would be to part from you. That, my love, is the one thing I could not bear. The one pain that would be too terrible to endure."

Emme wrapped her arms around his neck, burying her head into his throat again.

"Why do you have to be so perfect?" she muttered into his neckcloth.

James chuckled and held her for a few long moments. At last, she pulled back and gazed at him, leaning against his arms twined around her waist.

"Fortunately, I think we do have some time to work through this decision," she said. "Georgiana's health seems stable and Duir Cottage needs to be built, the portal secured. And, well, there is the locket to consider."

She touched the locket where it lay around her neck. Since realizing that James actually was the man in the locket, she had begun wearing it more.

James tilted his head, trying to make sense of how the locket continued to be an issue. Emme smiled at his puzzled look.

"I have seen enough movies to know not to mess with the space-time continuum." Her voice sounded a little prim.

James laughed. "Space-time continuum? I think you are making up words now, my dear."

Her answering laugh was light and silvery.

"Oh, James, it's a real thing. Let me try to explain. The locket is where it all began. If the locket isn't created, then I don't find it in Portland in 2008. And, if I never find the locket, then I never obsess on you, never come to Marfield, never stay in Duir Cottage. In effect, I never find you. So creating the locket is the most important task to complete before we can even attempt to pass through the portal. Until that is done, all this wondering is actually a moot point."

James nodded his head. He thought he understood. Maybe.

"So how did the locket get from here to Portland, Oregon?"

Emme shrugged. "I have no idea. I found it in the bottom of an antique traveling trunk. But it can't end up there if it never existed here in the first place."

"True, very true," James nodded. "I suppose that makes sense. I'll have to check with Arthur, but I do believe Spunto is scheduled to arrive this week to take our portraits. Yours included. If you get a locket of me, then I most certainly get a locket of you."

She smiled at him, wry and amused, her eyes sparkling in the afternoon light.

He kissed her nose, because really at that moment she looked too adorable not to kiss.

She took a deep breath. "Okay, so we are agreed. We make sure the locket is painted, created and done."

"Exactly," James nodded. "And then we move on to settling my affairs so I can travel through the portal, assuming that we can. Or arrange our lives here, if we cannot."

James watched Emme suddenly blink back tears, her lips trembling. "Agreed. But the decision seems so final," she whispered. "I could spend the rest of my life here or you could find yourself stuck for forever in 2012."

"But that's just it, my love," James murmured in reply. "Regardless of where we are, I want us to be together forever. I want your forevers. All of them. Past, present and future."

HALDON MANOR
THE DRAWING ROOM
TWO DAYS LATER
JUNE 17, 1812

Giovanni Spunto had arrived to paint the portraits James had commissioned. He was exactly as Emme had imagined: small, wiry and bouncing with an artist's energy. He surveyed them all and then announced his intention to begin with James.

Emme watched quietly from the drawing room doorway as Spunto positioned James into the three-fourths position of the locket. James had donned the new coat he had received from his tailor. The exact blue-green coat in the locket.

Glancing surreptitiously over Spunto's shoulder as he worked, Emme watched the image in her locket come to life. Saw the small strokes that created her original obsession, as the artist sketched the portrait.

She lifted her head and caught James' eye. Held and stared. Feeling the wonder of him hum through her.

Later that evening, after Georgiana and Arthur had retired, Emme followed James into his study.

"You must keep this jacket," she murmured, tucking her hands around his lapels. "I have loved you in it for far too long."

James laughed softly and bent down to capture a sweet, lingering kiss.

"That reminds me," he whispered against her lips and then, with one final peck, he released her and walked over to his desk.

Puzzled, Emme followed and watched as he pulled out a pair of scissors. Turning back to her, James reached up and touched the one stray curl over her ear that always managed to escape. "I think I'm going to need this." Reaching out, he gently kissed the curl and then snipped it off.

Emme smiled as he walked back to his desk and placed the locket of hair on a piece of paper.

"Not so fast," she said. She came to his side and removed the scissors from his hand. "Two can play at this game."

Kissing his cheek, she ran her fingers leisurely through his hair, studying for a moment before snipping. She laid his blond lock next to her dark one on the paper. He carefully folded the paper, trapping its contents.

"You will need this too." She looped the locket off of her neck. "Let me trace the design off the back. It will need to be on the locket and carved into the stone in the basement of Duir Cottage."

Emme sat at his desk and carefully copied the intertwined initials, James watching quietly. When she finished, he took the traced design and wrapped it around the locks of hair.

"Now, we just have to wait for Mr. Spunto to finish the portrait. He said it should only take a couple weeks."

Emme nodded in agreement.

Leaning against his desk, he gazed at her. "Miss Wilde, what strange things are you going to unfold to me tonight? What 21st century wonders await?"

Emme pondered for a moment, tapping her lips. With a mysterious chuckle, she pulled out her phone and pink earbuds. She stepped close to him and placed one earphone into his ear and put the other into her own. Scrolling through her music until she found the right song, she pushed play and then slipped her phone back into her stays.

"Mr. Knight, I think it's about time you learned something other than a waltz."

James raised an eyebrow as she assumed a closed dance position with him.

And then he smiled more broadly as Emme proceeded to teach him how to tango.

Chapter 28

Have I mentioned that you are enchantingly radiant this evening, my love?" James murmured in her ear. Emme stood at the edge of the ballroom, her arm nestled into his elbow, watching the dancers move through a quadrille.

"Let me think." She cocked her head as if trying to remember. "Only about six times. I wouldn't mind hearing it at least once more."

"Please permit me to say you look captivatingly incandescent, milady." Smile hovering, James raised her gloved knuckles to his lips.

"Thank you, good sir. And have I mentioned that you are a ridiculously hot piece of eye candy?" She dropped her upper-crust accent for the last part, making it sound decidedly American.

Emme patted his arm as James chuckled. But really, he did look swoon-worthy in a black coat and blue waistcoat which perfectly matched his eyes. It really was almost too much.

Emme caught a glimpse of her own reflection in the mirrored walls of Sir Henry's ballroom. Her satin wine-red ball gown gleamed in the candlelight. She had even put on a little blush and light mascara, clean and natural looking. Her dark hair curled around her face, threaded through with pearls.

She felt like Cinderella at the ball with Prince Charming. Only with fewer anthropomorphic mice, musical fairy godmothers and frighteningly hazardous glass slippers. Not to mention that Georgiana would never be an ugly step-sister.

Okay, so maybe the analogy didn't work all that well when she thought about it. Except that James was her prince. And she transformed whenever she was with him.

Tightening her hold on his arm, Emme watched the assembled dancers moving through the country dance figures. The entire scene seemed like something from a movie set: elegant ladies in glittering fabrics and men in dark cut coats and tight pantaloons. Lilting music weaving through it all.

The last few weeks had been the most idyllic of her life. That giddy, effervescence of new love deepening into something weightier. Something more. Laughing with James, understanding him as 21st century Emme. And James coming to know her as her whole self.

Emme had quickly realized that actually living in 1812 was remarkably useful when it came to doing historical research. James had helped her understand the nuances of the local economy. Additionally, she had taken to informally interviewing tenants as she and Georgiana visited them, making note of what she would be able to academically substantiate if and when she returned to 2012.

For his part, James seemed to be settling into the idea of 21st century life, were that to happen. He asked incessant questions and had instantly adopted her multi-tool as his own.

"It's like everything all at once," he kept saying, pulling the little scissors in and out. He was particularly fond of the toothpick.

And the MRE's? Well, he had found the whole process of heating them with the warmer utterly fascinating but had been less than impressed with the beef stew. The barbecue chicken he had declared passable.

And then there were her electronic devices. He was constantly hunched over a lit screen (when no one else was around). He continually asked her things. Some of which she knew the answer to (calculator, note-pad) and others she did not. (*I don't know why Siri keeps talking to you; I think she has personal space issues.*)

It didn't help that Marc had long ago developed the obnoxious habit of stealing her phone and putting something ridiculous on it for her to later discover. Which explained how James ended up loving Fat Booth. Pretty much everyone at Haldon Manor had unknowingly fallen victim. Arthur looked particularly ridiculous with an enormously enlarged head and three chin rolls. Fortunately, Emme had managed to delete Atomic Fart before James found it.

Was this what everyone meant when they said James didn't care much for propriety? That on a certain level, he was perpetually twelve-years-old?

In particular, James loved delving through the media on her devices: books, videos, photos and music. He was reading through her e-book library at a voracious pace. Though Emme hoped his taste in music improved over time. He absolutely loved (loved!) Donny Osmond. As in, Emme would catch him listening to *Puppy Love*, swaying with her pink head phones stuck in his ears. Marc really did have a sick sense of humor sometimes. And a decidedly questionable taste in music.

The music drew to a close and the swirl of dancers stilled. Watching guests bow as the set finished, Emme wondered if it wasn't time to introduce the concept of digital detox. James shifted next to her as the quadrille ended, and the orchestra struck up the bars of a waltz.

"I believe this is my dance," James said, taking her hand and leading her onto the floor. Emme had memorized all of the country dances and could now participate in them with more ease. But the waltz still remained her favorite.

Emme caught a glimpse of Linwood talking with Arthur and Mari-anne, who looked lovely in her lavender half-mourning. At the love-lorn couple's side, Sir Henry offered his arm to Georgiana to dance.

James slipped his hand around Emme's back and began twirling her through the lilting phrases. She fell into the rise and fall of the music, the spinning of mirror and candle and shimmering satin.

It was one of those perfect moments. Where your heart takes a picture and you store it away, so that when life becomes *less than*, you can pull out this one perfect memory and remember. At one point in time, life had been decidedly *more*.

Emme sighed. It was almost perfect enough to make her want to remain here. Stay in 1812 and just take what life gave. Did it really matter when she and James lived, as long as they were together?

She was still pondering the question as the music ended. James tucked her hand back into his elbow and escorted her toward Georgiana and Sir Henry. Emme curtsied to Sir Henry, noting that Georgiana looked particularly pretty tonight dressed in ivory silk with a gauzy overdress. She was all cream and gold and sparkling blue eyes. Her cough had been better, but her weight loss was still relentless. Her dress hung loosely on bony shoulders.

"I was just apologizing to Sir Henry for my lack of breath during the dance," Georgiana said, smiling faintly. "In fact, I was wondering if you wouldn't come with me to the ladies' retiring room, Emma. I feel the need to rest for a moment."

Emme nodded and took Georgiana's arm as they walked out of the ballroom. Not telling Georgiana about her restored memory had been difficult. But both Emme and James had worried how Georgiana would take the truth, both good and bad.

"Oh, Miss Knight. Georgiana!" Emme heard as they stepped into the darkened hallway. They both turned to see Marianne Linwood gesture for them to join her through a side door.

Exchanging a quick puzzled glance, Emme and Georgiana followed her into Sir Henry's library. To the right of the door, a fire flickered in the hearth bouncing light off walls of books and honey wooden paneling. Candles illuminated the space. Moonlight streamed through a large window opposite the fireplace.

Marianne half-closed the door behind them and glanced around, apparently assuring herself that no one else was in the room. She turned back to them.

"My dearest Georgiana, I must beg you for a favor." Marianne appeared anxious, which only increased Emme's curiosity. What was Marianne up to?

Oh, and please could it be just a little juicy?

"Am I to suppose that you would like me to do what I have done in the past?" Georgiana asked.

Marianne nodded mutely, suddenly blinking back tears.

Georgiana smiled and reached out to place a hand over Marianne's. "Please, don't fret, Marianne. Linwood will relent. He loves you too well to see you unhappy. And Arthur is nothing if not persistence personified. You must have faith. Here, wipe your tears." Georgiana dug out and handed her a handkerchief.

"I am so sorry, Georgiana, truly I am," Marianne said, dabbing daintily at her eyes. "But Timothy makes it nearly impossible for Arthur and I to have even two minutes private conversation. I do not wish to act with impropriety, but sometimes my brother can be difficult."

"You are of age, Marianne," Georgiana said with a shake of her head. "Free to make your own decisions. You know that Linwood can only control your happiness if you allow it."

Marianne bit her lip, nervous and indecisive. "Yes, I know, but Timothy has been such a kind and good brother to me over the years."

Emme's eyebrows raised in disbelief.

Marianne continued, "I cannot bear the thought of disappointing him and going against his wishes. I love him too well to hurt him so. You will do this then?"

"Of course, dearest friend. Your happiness, and Arthur's too, is my fondest wish. Would you like me to fetch him?"

"That will not be necessary. He knows if you leave the ballroom, he is to come searching for us." As if on cue, the door open behind them. "Oh, and here he is." Emme turned to see Arthur walk into the room, closing the door behind.

Marianne's face lit up upon seeing him, all longing and love. Arthur's returning gaze was equally love-struck.

Emme looked questioningly at Georgiana, cocking an eyebrow. Georgiana gave her a tiny grin and gestured for Emme to sit in one the chairs facing the fire. Arthur and Marianne walked to the opposite side of the room, talking in low, hushed whispers, silhouetted against the window.

"I take it we are to act as chaperones?" Emme murmured to Georgiana once they had seated themselves, their backs to the couple, giving them a degree of privacy.

Georgiana nodded. "They are both concerned about appearances and do not wish to misstep. But it is hard when you are young and in love. Not to mention that Linwood would put a bullet through Arthur if he caught him alone with Marianne."

Emme couldn't resist a glance over her shoulder and saw Arthur take Marianne's hand and bring it tenderly to his lips, lingering on her knuckles.

"I usually avert my eyes," Georgiana said with a small smile, gesturing for Emme to turn her attention back to the fire and away from the love scene being enacted.

They sat in silence for several moments. Emme wondered if it would be bad form to analyze the small noises she could hear behind her.

Was that rustling sound a tight embrace or just Marianne moving closer to the window? She listened a little more intently. . . . She didn't know what that sound was. Okay, but that last sound . . . that was definitely a kiss.

Emme and Georgiana jumped as the door suddenly opened.

"How dare you!"

Emme stood and turned to see Lord Linwood.

She sighed. Really, that had been a little too predictable.

Linwood strode angrily toward Arthur who had quickly released Marianne and was now backing away from the enraged viscount.

"Timothy!" Marianne exclaimed. Her look one of exasperation more than worry, she moved to intercept her brother.

"Please, Linwood, it was nothing untoward. We were chaperoned." Arthur held out his hands placatingly, gesturing toward Emme and Georgiana standing in front of the fire.

Linwood whirled around and took in the two ladies, his eyes narrowing dangerously. Emme resisted the urge to wave a hand in greeting and instead bobbed a small curtsy with Georgiana.

"Heavens, Linwood, calm down. Nothing has happened," James drawled as he came through the doorway, calmly closing it behind him. He stood next to Emme.

In the middle of the room, Linwood processed the scene, looking back and forth between his sister and Arthur. He clenched his jaw.

"I have had enough of this, Arthur," he said after a long moment. "Your association with my sister is at an end."

Marianne's loud gasp echoed through the room. Arthur stiffened. Linwood's face remained a haughty mask.

Silence. No one spoke or moved.

"Come, Marianne. We are leaving now. This evening has most definitely lost its appeal." Linwood held out his hand for his sister and half turned, not even looking to see if she followed.

But she did not move.

Instead, she stood still and shocked for a moment, as if warring within herself. And then something changed. Marianne's shoulders suddenly straightened, her eyes determined. With a jut of her chin, she reached out to Arthur and clasped his hand in hers.

"No, Timothy." Her voice may have wavered, but the firmness of her jaw made her resolution clear.

"Pardon me?" Linwood said icily, turning back to his sister.

"You heard me, Timothy. I said no. I am not leaving. I will remain the rest of the evening here . . . with Arthur." The last bit said more softly with an adoring glance at her not-betrothed.

Linwood's expression turned into a full on angry scowl. There was no other way to describe it. It was the most emotion Emme had ever seen him display. And he turned the full force of his anger on Arthur.

"You are responsible for this. How dare you turn her against me!" he hissed.

But Arthur's stunned expression clearly stated he found Marianne's behavior as surprising as Linwood.

"Oh please, Linwood. Arthur has done no such thing and you know it," James said quietly. "Though I must applaud Marianne for standing up for what she wants."

Marianne raised her chin a little more, buoyed by James' support.

"Indeed," she said in ringing tones. "I have obeyed your wishes long enough, Timothy. I love you dearly, but enough is enough. Arthur and I wish to marry. I would appreciate it if you gave us your blessing, but I will not ask for it." She took a deep breath. "I do not require it."

Linwood let out a snort. "I cannot believe that you are actually thinking of allying yourself with this . . . this family. It is not to be born," he said disdainfully gesturing toward James. "A man who blatantly keeps an unknown woman of most likely ill repute under his roof with his unwed sister."

Emme raised an eyebrow, but Georgiana let out a small indignant cry.

"How dare you imply such a thing, Lord Linwood!" Georgiana exclaimed. "Miss Emma has been all that is proper."

"Bah," Linwood scoffed. "What else explains her presence here? She has no connections. No one has come to claim her. The woman is a disgrace!"

Emme exchanged a glance with James, easily reading his thoughts. There was no helping it. They were going to have to tell them about her returned memory.

But the truth was just, well, too truthful. They wouldn't believe it. And in the end, the truth wasn't necessary. They just needed something that would allay Linwood's concerns.

"With all due respect, my lord," Emme began, taking a deep breath. "My memory has returned. And I can assure you that I am not what you have asserted me to be."

Emme heard Georgiana's shocked gasp next to her.

"I'm sorry, Georgiana. I should have told you sooner," Emme said pleadingly. "But the truth is somewhat complicated and . . . sensitive."

If she intended to lie, Emme figured she might as well make it a good one.

Georgiana looked at her with wide surprised eyes.

"Sensitive?" Arthur asked.

"Sensitive, indeed." Linwood sounded incredulous.

"Yes, my lord. I will have to swear you all to secrecy, however. It's a matter of national honor and security."

"Pray continue, Miss Emma. We are all eagerness to hear your story." Linwood said, his tone dry and sarcastic.

"Well, where should I begin?" Emme paused, trying to pull her story together. All eyes in the room stared at her, expectant and waiting. James looked decidedly amused. With a glance in his direction, she had a flash of inspiration.

"You see, first of all, my name is Emry Wilde, not Emma. I am an American." She dropped her British accent. "Well, my mother is American, my father British. My father's family has noble connections. My grandmother often mentioned how much she enjoyed visiting her Cavendish cousins on the Duke of Devonshire's estate. In any case, I grew up between both countries. . . ."

Emme paused as everyone continued to stare at her. She took a deep breath.

Simple. She needed to keep this simple.

"As you well know, the British are currently at war with the United States," she resumed and then winced slightly.

Okay, probably not good to remind them of that.

Moving on.

"My mother's family has been long involved in travel. . . ." Emme paused, briefly trying to gather her thoughts. "Perhaps more like merchant trade than travel, which of course is a sore point with my father's more illustrious relatives. . . . Therefore, I have spent most of my life abroad, moving amongst various peoples."

That was better.

"So, . . . while living in Nassau several years ago, I was privileged to make the acquaintance of . . . of her most royal Highness, Princess Pepsi of Toyota Camry . . . which is a small principality to the east of the Crimean, south of Russia proper."

That bit she said as an aside to Georgiana, as if that easily explained everything.

Linwood blinked. "Why would a royal princess from the middle of Russia be in the Bahamas?"

"Excellent point, my lord, I wondered the very same thing," Emme agreed. Paused. "Perhaps she found the weather pleasing. It is lovely and warm year round in Nassau, and Her Highness does suffer from arthritis."

Okay, so maybe not so simple.

But there was no going back now.

Time to work in some history.

"Her Highness was most concerned over the state of affairs in her small country, because at that time as you know, Russia was currently allied with Napoleon in the war against Britain. Her Highness desperately wished to sway Russia's alliance back to Britain. She encouraged me, along with his grace, Calvin Klein, the Grand Duke of Kleenex, to assist them in their cause."

Emme settled in. It was flowing better now.

"My brother, Mr. Marcus Wilde, currently runs our family affairs and I found myself accompanying him—acting as his hostess—but also relaying information whenever possible to assist the people of Toyota Camry in their plight. In early April of this year, I received intelligence which led me to believe the French would invade Russia as soon as mid-June, formally breaking their alliance and allowing Russia to ally itself with Britain. But the wicked French spy, Buick Chevrolet, was on my heels. I was captured and hit over the head and must have been left for dead here in Marfield. But for Mr. Knight's fortunate presence, I greatly fear the worst would have happened."

No one said a word after she finished.

So much for simplicity. This exemplified why lying was a bad idea in the first place.

Silence.

"That is remarkable," Georgiana looked awestruck. "I had never contemplated such possibilities, and I thought I had considered everything." She paused, a stunned grin spreading across her face. "Though it most certainly explains why certain things were familiar to you and others were not. Where do you think the wicked Buick Chevrolet is now? I fear for your safety."

"I do believe other British agents have caught up with him," James offered quietly. "At least my discrete inquiries have indicated as much. Our dear Miss Wilde should be safe."

Emme risked a sideways glance at James, willing herself not to smile.

"Indeed, it is quite the tale," Linwood intoned. "And if I were not privy to information that France did indeed begin an invasion of Russia only ten days ago, I would find it hard to believe. You really expect me to believe that you are a spy, Miss Wilde?"

"Yes, my lord, I do. My brother, Mr. Marc Wilde, has been well-trained in the secret Oriental arts of the ninja, assassins in the service of Japanese samurai. Training that he passed on to me, as well. I have found it to be most useful."

Linwood merely cocked a decidedly wary eyebrow at her.

"Indeed," he repeated.

Emme grabbed and held his gaze. "Indeed, my lord. I have found my skills to be particularly useful in defending myself against ill-mannered, boorish men."

Linwood clenched his jaw, sucking in a breath at her not-so-subtle jab.

"And zombies," James deadpanned. "Her ninja skills are also useful against zombies."

And, really, that did it.

Any part of Emme that had not been in love with James thoroughly collapsed in that instant. She was his. Utterly and completely.

The moment was beyond perfect. The most perfect of all her perfect memories.

"And would you also care to explain how this account of your history renders you respectable, Miss Wilde? It sounds as if your family is in trade." Linwood's tone remained skeptical.

"Heavens, Linwood," James exclaimed. "Our Miss Wilde is something of a national hero, aiding our country in her time of need. And you did catch the part about Miss Wilde being a cousin to the Duke of Devonshire?" James asked pointedly, as if that explained everything. "Such an illustrious connection cannot be overlooked."

Linwood nodded his head slowly.

James did not wait for Linwood's response but continued, "Miss Wilde is hardly what you think her to be. And I do believe we were discussing Arthur and Marianne's future, which really is not tied to Miss Wilde's past."

Linwood sighed and stood stiffly, looking back at his sister and Arthur, still standing hand in hand. Marianne's chin determined and firm.

James took a step closer to Linwood. "What say you, Timothy?" he asked quietly. "Look at them. They are so in love. Why not let at least this little corner of the world experience some happiness? Between you and I, we will ensure that they will want for nothing. And Arthur will always treat her with love and respect. You of all people should know that."

Linwood stood still for a few moments. And then Emme noticed a small sag in his shoulders. A weary sign of acceptance.

He let out a long breath.

"Please call on me tomorrow at Kinningsley, Arthur, to discuss your future with my sister."

"Oh, Timothy!" Marianne cried and launched herself into her brother's arms. "Thank you so!"

Linwood grimaced at her display of affection, but he did wrap his arms around her and return her embrace.

Chapter 29

On a country road outside Marfield
Five days later
July 11, 1812

D oes that cloud look green to you?" Georgiana asked.

A bilious thundercloud loomed ominously over them.

The skies had been clear earlier when Emme and Georgiana had left Haldon Manor to take a basket of goodies to Auntie Gray. All day, the air had been heavy with summer. Hot and sticky.

But now, as Emme drove the gig the last few miles to Haldon Manor, the weather had shifted. Wind whipped through the trees and the clouds had turned the most alarming shade.

James had been gone for three days and Emme felt the painful ache of his absence. Spunto had delivered the finished portrait, lovely and bright on its thin ivory board. Now the panel needed to be set into a locket. Given the complexity of the design, James had decided to deliver it personally to a jeweler in London.

Their last conversation still lingered, playing over and over in Emme's mind.

"I wish I could go with you. London would be fascinating," she had said, sitting on the settee in his study.

James merely nodded, coming to sit beside her, nestling her hand into his.

"I wish you could come as well, my love. But Georgiana's health will not permit her to come, and you and I cannot travel together unchaperoned. With Arthur's betrothal to Marianne officially announced, I feel responsible to preserve some sense of propriety until their wedding in autumn. Though they have not yet decided, I do not think that they will marry before the year of mourning for Marianne's mother is through." James leaned in and brushed his lips across her cheek.

"Besides I promise to return within a fortnight. No longer."

"A fortnight? Oh dear, so long?"

James laughed. "This is not the 21st century. I can only travel as quickly as my horse. Things take longer, my dear. Patience. I will need to see my London solicitors in regard to some estate business as well."

"And what will we do when you return?"

"Well, the locket will take time to create. I will merely be delivering the painted panel and ordering the case when I go to London. From there, I will most likely need to return to retrieve it when it is finished. Duir Cottage should be completed by autumn. My thoughts had been to address our possible leaving sometime after that."

Emme nodded in agreement. "I was also thinking about the locket. Perhaps we should give it to Auntie Gray? Who knows how it came to be in Portland, Oregon, but I would trust Auntie to understand how and when to send it on its way."

"Brilliant, my love," James grinned in agreement. "Auntie is the perfect choice. Now come, no more glum looks. You may save them all for when I am gone and you pine for me. Even take some photos of yourself at your saddest to torment me with when I return." He laughed as Emme swatted his shoulder. "Promise me you will miss me terribly?" He pressed his forehead against hers, eyes teasing.

"You know I will," she murmured against his mouth. "Every possible second." And then he kissed her, long and sweet.

Emme smiled at the memory.

Wind suddenly buffeted the gig, and Emme clicked at their horse. James was still at least ten long days from returning. She sighed, feeling the twinge of him not being at her side. Emme had taken to wearing the locket obsessively in his absence. Its comforting weight helped to banish some of her loneliness.

A strong burst of wind brought her back fully to the present. With alarm, Emme looked at the blackening sky. Dark clouds roiled over the trees of the surrounding forest, limbs bending and flailing.

"Truly, Emme. Look at it. Have you ever seen a green sky before?" Georgiana repeated, this time more urgently.

Emme assessed the clouds again. Yes, they were most definitely a terrifying shade of green. The kind of green that she remembered from her childhood in Denver. The kind that usually warned of a tornado.

Tornado.

Seriously? Wasn't that a bit much?

Besides, she was wearing the locket, so nothing could happen. James' portrait would keep her safe as it always had. Right?

A gust of wind hit them again, causing the horse to dance slightly in his harness. She tasted rain in the air and realized they would not make it back to Haldon Manor before the storm hit. Tightening her grip on the reins, Emme anxiously scanned the surrounding forest for some shelter, wanting to get Georgiana under cover. Spotting a woodcutter's shed through the trees, she turned the gig off the main road and made for the structure.

Within just seconds, the wind picked up, whipping twigs and leaves around them. Georgiana let out a cry of alarm, covering her head with her arms to shield herself. Frustrated, Emme realized the forest would hide a tornado from them until the last possible second.

Stopping in front of the shed, Emme pulled the horse under the cantilevered roof. Quickly climbing down, she turned to help Georgiana.

Emme wrenched the door open and pulled Georgiana inside, just as rain began to pelt heavily, drumming the roof, the sky opening in a torrent of water and wind. The walls shuddered.

Eyes adjusting to the dim light inside, Emme closed and latched the door. The shed was small but more or less waterproof, which was all that mattered at the moment. Emme could feel Georgiana trembling at her side. The temperature had dropped significantly, all the humidity turning into a bone-dampening chill. Georgiana doubled over in a deep hacking cough, digging a handkerchief out of a pocket.

"It's alright, Georgiana," Emme said in what she hoped was a soothing tone, wrapping an arm around her shoulders and holding her until the coughing fit calmed. Glancing around at the stacked wood and listening to the weather rage outside, Emme guided Georgiana to sit on a larger log wedged in one of the corners. The shack quaked as a rough burst of wind hit it.

"Heavens, what a storm!" Georgiana said with a game little smile, coughing yet again. Emme noticed the pink tinged mucous on her handkerchief.

"Sorry," Georgiana muttered. "Wind always seems to aggravate my cough. At least we managed to stay dry."

Emme nodded. And then she heard something on the wind.

The sound she had been dreading.

Like a freight train. Just as it was always described.

"What is that terrible noise?" Georgiana asked, her eyes widening with alarm.

"Get down! Protect your head!" Emme called, pushing Georgiana to the ground, throwing her own body on top, covering her.

Emme heard the roar. Her ears popped painfully, as air was sucked from her lungs. The shed groaned and shrieked.

The hut exploded around them, the powerful fury of the tornado raking her skin. The wind whipped her around, wrenching Georgiana away. Pelting rain instantly soaked her. Emme felt wind born debris stinging her skin. Something clubbed her in the chest, knocking the breath out of her and throwing her to the ground. She instantly curled into a ball, instinctively covering her head.

The whole event took just seconds and then the tempest receded, traveling away from them. Gasping for breath, Emme pushed herself up. She seemed okay. Looking at her arms, she could see small cuts from flying debris, but a quick flex of muscles and bones convinced her that she had, amazingly, suffered no real harm.

But where was Georgiana?

Rain poured from the sky, making it hard to see.

"Georgiana!" she called, lurching to her feet.

Brushing water out of her eyes, Emme spotted Georgiana's crumpled form a short distance away. Stumbling over debris, Emme reached Georgiana's side. Breathed a sigh of relief to see her move, to hear her moan.

"Georgiana? Can you hear me?" Crouching next to her, Emme quickly tried to assess the damage, feeling through Georgiana's sodden clothing. There were no obvious cuts or wounds. Georgiana opened her eyes, staring into Emme's.

"Good heavens!" Her voice was hoarse and weak. A terrible cough cut through her and she shivered uncontrollably. Emme wrapped an arm around her.

"W-what ha-p-pened?" Georgiana chattered through clenched teeth.

"It was a tornado. You're freezing. We need to get you back to Haldon Manor before you catch your death. How do you feel?"

"C-c-c-cold."

"I don't see any wounds." Emme placed an arm around Georgiana's shoulders and helped her stand. However, as soon as Georgiana put weight on her right foot, she cried out in agony and sagged against Emme.

"M-my ankle," she said in anguish.

Gently helping Georgiana to sit down, Emme pushed back Georgiana's skirts to inspect her ankle encased in a tight half boot. Emme immediately realized the boot probably provided some much needed support and stability. So instead of removing it, she gently pressed along the outside. No response. However, Georgiana moaned in pain when Emme took her ankle and rotated it in the boot. The ankle was definitely sprained, if not broken.

Sighing, she acknowledged that Georgiana could not walk back to Haldon Manor. Emme looked around, trying to see what had become of their horse and gig, but the driving rain was nearly blinding. Georgiana curled herself into a ball on the ground, coughs wracking her body.

"Come, let's get you out of this rain," Emme said, kneeling back beside Georgiana.

Later, Emme wouldn't remember exactly how she managed to half carry Georgiana to the shelter of some trees that were still standing. Georgiana's shivering became even more pronounced, and Emme held her close, hoping that the warmth of her own body would help. Georgiana coughed until Emme feared she couldn't breathe, her inhalations sounding heavy and labored.

The rain let up somewhat, changing into a steady drizzle. Emme considered leaving Georgiana and going for help. But she was hopelessly turned around. The road had vanished under a layer of debris. She worried she would not be able to locate Haldon Manor and then find Georgiana again.

How long before someone came looking for them?

Georgiana's shivering abated slightly, which Emme initially thought to be a good thing. But Georgiana became lethargic and sleepy. Terrified, Emme realized that she was actually slipping deeper into hypothermia. If she fell asleep, she might not wake up.

Hugging her closer, Emme said, "Don't you dare fall asleep on me, Georgiana! You must stay awake. Sleep could mean death."

"I'm so sleepy," Georgiana whispered. "So tired."

"Fight, Georgiana. Don't give up!"

"Why? Death will claim me soon enough. Why continue to fight the inevitable? I am so tired, Emme. So very tired."

A chill coursed through Emme. She had to do something. Anything.

Scrambling for something to keep her attention, Emme said, "I lied last week. At Sir Henry's ball. I'm not a spy."

She felt Georgiana's surprise. Though not quite the way she wanted to tell Georgiana, it most certainly served its purpose. Georgiana was instantly more alert.

Georgiana paused for a moment. "Does James know?"

"Yes, James knows. We . . . we lied because the truth is more complicated."

"More complicated than assisting Princess Pepsi of Toyota Camry while being hunted by the French spy Buick Chevrolet?" Georgiana's voice communicated her disbelief.

Emme laughed. She couldn't help it.

"Yes, Georgie, it truly is. Even worse than being a spy. You probably won't believe me, but it is a tale you will relish—full of mystery and even a touch of the supernatural."

Georgiana's eyes widened, though Emme couldn't tell if it was from shock or excitement. "Tell me," she whispered after a moment. "Tell me the truth."

And so Emme did. She told her about airplanes and cars and television. About jeans and lip gloss and penicillin.

To Emme's relief, Georgiana stayed awake through it all, asking eager questions. Particularly about antibiotics and the very real chance that if she traveled the portal with them, she could be cured.

"So you see, you must fight to live because there truly is hope," Emme said when Georgiana drooped with weariness. "You have everything to live for."

"To live," Georgiana coughed. And then coughed again. "To have my future back. That would be so wonderful. Would it hurt? This 21st century medicine?"

"No . . . well, it might hurt a tiny bit as they would probably need to give you an IV, but it would feel like a pin prick."

"Is that all? So little?"

"Well, the needle is somewhat large, so it would be a large pin prick, but, yes, that is all. Though you would most likely be treated at a hospital, not in your own home. And the hospitals can be somewhat cold. Lots of white."

Georgiana smiled wearily. "I would be okay with that."

After hours of sitting huddled on the ground, Emme heard shouts. Releasing Georgiana, Emme climbed stiffly to her feet, yelling back. She almost wept with relief when she saw Arthur and several other men coming through the torn and battered trees toward them.

"Praise be to God!" Arthur exclaimed. "We had almost despaired of finding you alive!" In a matter of seconds, Georgiana was wrapped in blankets and carried to a waiting horse.

Arthur turned to Emme, unfolding a blanket to wrap around her shoulders too. And then he paused, looking at her upper chest in surprise.

Emme glanced down and for the first time noticed that something had hit her there, ripping through her pelisse and the walking dress underneath. Gingerly brushing her fingers over her sternum, she realized there was no wound in her skin. Instead, her hand came away with James' locket.

Mangled. Shattered.

Something sharp had penetrated it, destroying the outer case and its inscription. Splintering the portrait on the ivory panel. Stopping at last at the cracked back case, fracturing the intertwined initials, but not penetrating them.

Saving Emme.

Shaking for the first time since the tornado hit, Emme covered her mouth, refusing to allow her sob to escape. Grateful for Arthur's considerate arm around her shoulders.

Chapter 30

HALDON MANOR
GEORGIANA'S BEDROOM
TWO DAYS LATER
JULY 13, 1812

S he still breathes?"
Emme looked up as Arthur entered. It was more of a question than a statement.

Late afternoon sunlight slanted through the window, its warmth mocking the chilled clamminess of Georgiana's pale skin.

Emme nodded her head. "But for how long, I wonder. Her condition is serious."

They still hadn't heard from James. Arthur had sent multiple messages to him in London, but too little time had passed. It was still several days before he could reasonably be expected to return home, even if he rode all night.

And the locket. Emme had held it tightly in her hand after returning to Haldon Manor. Seeing such an old friend mangled and maimed had been painful.

Its shattering troubled her. Was the destruction of the locket a symbol of something more? Though she pushed negative thoughts from her mind, they kept returning. Whispering treacherous things. Would she ever see James again?

And then there was Georgiana. For two days, she had lain wracked by fever, slowly weakening. Fading before Emme's eyes.

The doctor had come and gone. Georgiana's ankle was badly sprained but not broken. However, the cold and wet had deeply affected her lungs, leaving her cough rasping. Georgiana struggled to suck in each breath, air wheezing. The doctor recommended bleeding as a cure but had backed down in the face of Emme's fury.

Instead, Emme had been carefully giving Georgiana ibuprofen from her first aid kit when no one was looking. The pain killer seemed to lessen the swelling in her lungs and definitely helped abate the fever. But it was not enough. It just eased Georgiana's symptoms. There was nothing in Emme's purse that could help the underlying cause.

After two sleepless nights, Emme realized Georgiana was dying. Her friend lay so still under the covers, her breathing labored. Something wet rattled in her chest, her weakened body not strong enough to fight off the infection that now raged.

Helplessly, Emme sat and watched her friend struggle to breathe.

"Perhaps she will pull through." Arthur ran a hand through his hair, so reminiscent of his brother.

Emme's lungs tightened.

She shook her head. They both knew that was not likely.

Georgiana lay unconscious as she had been for the last day, so thin and frail. Her skin a terrifying shade of grey-white, breathing shallow and harsh. Suddenly she convulsed, coughing raspy and deep, curling into a ball. Emme held a handkerchief to her mouth, noting the blood on it. How much longer could Georgiana hold on?

Arthur stared stonily throughout the incident. At a loss.

Emme swallowed, turning back to him, and took a deep breath. Faced her options.

There really was only one answer at this point.

She made a decision. The decision that James would make if he were in her situation.

"Arthur," she said firmly, raising her eyes to his and holding them. "I lied to you last week in Sir Henry's library. I am not a spy. But I can save Georgiana. However, I will need your help to do so."

In the end, it was fairly easy to convince Arthur. After the initial shock and outrage, Emme pulled out her purse. It took less than five minutes with her phone and tablet to make Arthur believe her. Surprisingly easy, all things considered.

He apologized for thinking the worst of her. Emme merely gave a quiet, sad laugh and forgave him. She then proceeded to explain about antibiotics and the near-surety of Georgiana's cure if they were able to travel the portal. Arthur's eyes bulged from his head as he dashed from the room, racing to find a stretcher to transport his sister.

While Arthur had a wagon prepared to move Georgiana, Emme slipped into James' study and sat at his desk. She paused for a moment, thinking. Then, she pulled out a sheet of paper and wrote:

My dearest James,

I don't know where or when I will be when you receive this letter. Georgiana is dying; there is no longer hope for her here. Death is such a final thing. More final than any trip through a portal. And I can't in good conscience watch her die knowing that there is something . . . anything I can do to prevent it. This is the decision you would make were you here. You would want Georgiana to live.

You have saved me in so many ways. Forgive me as I try to save something for you.

This isn't exactly what we had planned, but I pray you will be able to follow us through the portal once your affairs are settled. In the meantime, I am sorry that I did not have one more kiss from you. One more chance to hear your laugh in my ear.

Do not worry, my love. I will wait for you on the other side. Please take care of your darling self.

You are my heart. Now and forever. I love you.

Emme

She folded the letter and wrapped it around the remains of the broken locket. She packed everything into her purse and gently left it on his desk, her note nestled inside. She only retained her phone, stuffed into her stays.

Arthur drove them quietly through the fading light to the meadow, tense and silent by her side. Georgiana's arduous breathing came from the wagon bed behind.

"You really think this will work?" he asked quietly.

"Yes. It truly is our last hope."

"And why can't I come too?"

Emme sighed. This was at least the tenth time he had asked this question.

"What would you do there, Arthur? How would your presence help?"

"I could protect my sister. Ensure that she receives the proper attention."

"That will happen regardless. Besides you have Marianne and your life here. Even if you were able to come with us, there is no guarantee you could come back. I don't think that you would much like life in the 21st century."

He merely grunted.

"What if the portal doesn't work?" he said again after a few more moments.

He really was persistent.

"As I said, that is a real possibility. If it doesn't work, at least we tried. I could not sit and watch Georgiana die and not do something. I couldn't forgive myself. I couldn't expect James to forgive me."

Arthur nodded his head in agreement.

"But our need is great," she continued. "And our lives intertwined, so perhaps it will work."

"What if you never see James again?"

Emme choked back a sob. Thinking of him. Her premonition over the shattered locket.

"I trust he will find a way," she whispered. And then more emphatically, "We will find a way."

Arriving in the meadow, she helped Arthur lift the still unconscious Georgiana from the bed of the wagon and followed as he carried his sister the last few steps to the portal. The meadow was quiet and still.

Waiting. Expectant.

Arthur stood before the sawn off trunk, its dark interior still yawning. Emme felt the same heaviness she had experienced in the past. The same tingling along her arms.

"Thank you, Arthur Knight," she said, looking him in the eye. "If I never see you again, thank you for all that you have done. Tell James that I love him. And make sure he gets the note I left."

Arthur nodded. "I will. I promise. And for your part, please take care of my Georgiana. Keep her safe. I give her to your care." He kissed his sister's cheek. "Adieu."

"Here," Emme whispered, "stand her up against me. I can support her."

Arthur slowly lowered Georgiana, resting her feet against the ground. Georgiana groaned. Emme sagged slightly as Georgiana's full weight hit her, but wrapping an arm around her waist, Emme was able to keep them both upright.

Taking a deep breath, Emme stepped forward and placed a foot into the wide space cut into the trunk. The electrical tingling became stronger, the tug more insistent. The hair on her arms stood on end as the hum of some invisible current coursed through her.

Suddenly, something pulled her forward. Insistent. Almost greedy.

Vertigo and blackness took her.

Emme blinked in the darkness and sank to the ground, using all her strength to lower Georgiana gently. She could hear the low rumble of a voice. Could see a sliver of light above her head that must be from the trap door. Georgiana moaned, her breath rasping.

"Help!" Emme called. It seemed the easiest way to get attention. "Help me!"

She heard a thump of movement and the scramble of steps. She didn't know who was up there, but she figured after everything that had happened, she could probably deal with it.

Emme fumbled in the dark, trying to free her phone from her stays. But it was difficult with Georgiana half lying on her.

After a few seconds, she heard the trapdoor moving and light poured down the steep stairs, illuminating her and Georgiana.

A head gazed down at her, blocking some of the light.

An extremely familiar head with dark curling hair and a stunned look of surprise.

There she was, sprawled on the dirt floor, clad in a high-waisted Empire dress, covered in a pelisse. A straw chip bonnet on her head. A blond woman wrapped in a dressing gown and blanket, half dead and gasping across her chest.

"What the hell?"

Emme would know his shocked voice anywhere.

"What are you doing down here? Where have you been?" Marc scrambled down the steps to kneel beside her, shaking his head as he looked her over.

"Were you captured by Jane Austen bandits and held captive for the last two months?" he continued. "I swear, Emme, you will be the death of me! Even by your disaster standards, this is truly impressive."

"Marc!" Emme cried, relief pouring through her. "Oh, Marc!" She hiccupped, fighting back sobs, grabbing his arm. "Please call an ambulance! We have so little time and Georgiana is dying!"

Chapter 31

DUIR COTTAGE
NEARLY TWO MONTHS LATER
SEPTEMBER 15, 2012

Will it ever get any easier?" Georgiana said softly from the passenger seat. "This not knowing is unbearable."

Emme sighed as she pulled into the driveway, turning off the BMW. Duir Cottage still looked charming. Perhaps even more so with autumn beginning to creep in.

Grimacing, Emme looked over at Georgiana.

"I honestly don't know." Emme sucked in a deep, weary breath, reaching out to lay a comforting hand on Georgiana's arm.

Georgiana had been released from the hospital nearly three weeks earlier. They had just returned from the doctor who had given her a clean bill of health. She would need to maintain her antibiotic regimen for the next six months to guard against a relapse, but she was no longer quarantined.

Georgiana was lucky. She had received treatment just in time, the doctors said. Even another day and she would have been beyond help. But her tuberculosis had responded well to the antibiotics, surprising everyone.

Emme had tested positive for latent tuberculosis, but as the bacteria wasn't active in her system, she had only needed to take antibiotics for a of couple weeks. Grateful to not be quarantined. Again.

"Let's go see what Marc has made us for dinner, shall we? He knows how much you love chow mein." Emme grabbed her phone and purse and then paused as Georgiana made no immediate move to get out of the car. Instead, she sat frozen, furiously blinking back tears.

"What if he doesn't come?" Georgiana whispered, turning her watery blue eyes to Emme—eyes so like her brother's. Emme's heart constricted painfully.

"He will. We just have to have faith—"

"But that entry we found—" Georgiana hiccupped and covered her mouth, trying to shove all her worry back.

Emme exhaled haltingly and moved her hand to Georgiana's shoulder, rubbing it gently. How many times had they had this conversation over the past month?

Once Georgiana had recovered enough to be coherent, she had insisted they search out what had happened to Arthur and James. Emme had quickly found record of Arthur and Marianne's wedding in the Marfield parish registry and then subsequent information indicating that Arthur had inherited Haldon Manor.

But finding anything about James had proved challenging. There had only been a snippet inserted between baptism records in the parish registry.

The honorable James Knight, 31, late of Haldon Manor, deceased in a carriage accident.

Emme's heart still clenched. The words emblazoned in her mind, seared permanently. Dancing before her eyes almost every second of every day. Taunting her. Challenging her to believe them.

There had been no date associated with the entry, though the baptisms before and after it were from July 1812. Had James been killed while rushing back to Georgiana's bedside?

Emme swallowed, forcing her emotions away. She refused to give up hope.

"He'll come. He will," Emme repeated firmly. "Remember, the entry was squeezed between the registry lines and written in a different hand. The vicar still isn't sure if it's contemporary to July 1812 or added later. And even if it is legitimate, the carriage accident could just be a cover for James to come forward in time. We must have faith, Georgie."

Georgiana shook her head and turned away, swiping at her tears. "Have faith," she murmured. "Do you say that to convince me? Or yourself?"

Emme drew in a stuttering breath. How many times would they say these words to each other?

Trying to lighten the mood, Emme said, "Remember, tomorrow we're going to the Jane Austen Festival in Bath. We will dress up like proper Regency ladies, take tea in the pump room and stroll through town as if the last two hundred years had never happened. It's magical. You'll see."

Georgiana turned and give her a brave wistful smile, her eyes still red. Even through her tears, Georgiana glowed with a health and vitality that Emme had not seen in her before.

Emme still wasn't used to seeing her friend in 21st century clothing. For her part, Emme had happily shed her long Regency dresses for tight jeans and soft t-shirts. And showers. Steamy, lengthy, finger-wrinkling showers.

Georgiana, however, could not feel comfortable in pants and instead chose to wear long maxi skirts. Today she looked particularly beautiful in a floor-length, cream-and-lace confection Emme had found in a local boutique. Her teal silk blouse shimmered in the dwindling sunlight. Emme had at least convinced Georgiana to wear her hair down. It now hung, golden and loosely curled, down her back.

That said, Georgiana had eagerly taken to wearing some make-up. She loved mascara and could not seem to buy enough lipstick, always finding a new shade to try. And between local pizza take-out and Marc's cooking, she had put on some much needed weight.

But there was a deep worry in her too. A sense of loss and uncertainty.

Emme found herself fighting the same feelings. A heaviness. A dullness that would not pass.

Was James truly all right, just making final arrangements in 1812? Or was the carriage accident real? Would he come through the portal?

He will come. Have faith.

Sometimes Emme found herself repeating the words over and over. A haunting talisman. That if said enough—if believed enough—would come true.

Emme often sat in the basement, staring at the stone slab with the carved initials, hoping by some miracle to conjure him. They had taken to leaving the trapdoor and closet door open. Just in case.

Once Georgiana had been released from the hospital, she had been determined to try the portal. Georgiana had to know. They had packed a healthy supply of antibiotics and snuck down to the basement. But no matter how they touched the portal and thought desperate thoughts of James, nothing happened.

For now, there was no return. For either of them.

And James still did not come.

What if he never came?

They would need to figure out how to move on—without James. Dealing with all the pesky problems of modern life, like money and jobs and passports.

They only had a week left in Duir Cottage and then their lease would be up. Emme hadn't figured out what to do next. Leaving Marfield—abandoning the promise of the portal—felt impossible, but she had her life and job back in Seattle to consider too.

And Georgiana. She was slowly trying to adapt to modern life, but it seemed to be a love-hate relationship for her. She obviously appreciated being alive and loved modern conveniences like toilets and showers and television. But she struggled with the whirlwind pace of the 21st century—the constant, frenetic bombardment of sound and ideas.

Not to mention the fact she had no identity, at least none the modern world would recognize. Marc said he knew people who could help and

Georgiana was indeed a British citizen. Just not a modern one. But until they managed to get her an ID and a passport, she wasn't going anywhere.

Marc had been a godsend. Both she and Georgiana had explained multiple times what had happened to her. Marc acted like he believed them—and Georgiana's presence was certainly compelling—but Emme wondered if it wasn't just a polite front. He had even tried to go through the portal himself, standing in the basement vigorously rubbing the engraved stone.

"Is this how you do it?" he had asked, somewhat teasingly.

"It's not a magic lamp, Marc," Emme had said in her most exasperated voice. "And you need to have a strong desire to go through the portal. Your life needs to be intertwined with someone's from the past. Do you have that?"

Marc had just shrugged and winked at her in amusement.

At least he found the images on her phone impressive. Though he had made more than one teasing comment about how dashing 'Fabio' looked in his pretty boy clothes.

"His name is James, Marc," Emme had said in frustration.

"Whatever. I've said it before and I will say it again, he will always be Fabio to me."

Emme had just rolled her eyes.

She missed James. Viscerally at times. She found herself constantly pulling out perfect memories, running them through her mind. Matching his teasing banter. Waltzing in his arms.

Emme obsessively watched the videos she had taken. Over and over. Not wanting to forget the mellow sound of his voice telling her that she was 'utterly irresistible.' Memorizing every nuance in his face, in his body.

But seeing James, hearing his voice, only made his loss worse somehow. Made her remember acutely that he was no longer with her.

Jasmine had been more helpful. More hopeful.

"I'm telling you, he is still your destiny," she said every time Emme talked to her. "He will find you."

And so Emme nodded her head and went through the motions each day. She finished her sabbatical research and made tentative plans for herself and Georgiana, all the while ignoring the dullness and lethargy in her heart. The ache of having found that one missing part of her, only to give it up again.

Too many problems. Not enough answers.

Emme had saved Georgiana's life, but at what cost to them all?

The next day, Emme and Georgiana descended the stairs of Duir Cottage in full Regency clothing: muslin walking dresses covered with pelisses and straw bonnets upon their heads (which Georgiana assured her were the first stare of 1812 fashion). Emme smiled at Marc's look of appreciation as they strolled into the great room. He was busy hooking up his laptop to the flatscreen TV by the fireplace.

"Are you still sure you won't come with us, Marc?" she asked.

"Oh yes," Georgiana sighed. "It would be vastly diverting to have you along."

Marc merely raised his eyebrows and laughed.

"As much fun as it sounds to stuff myself into tight pantaloons and fight my way through crowds all day, I think I'm going to enjoy the Bronco's game that I have DVR-ed back home and relax." He winked teasingly at Emme.

Emme sighed. She had spent the better part of last night begging Marc to come along with them. But he was adamant. And given everything else he had done for them over the last two months, she felt ungrateful continuing to push the issue.

"If you change your mind, we have reservations for high tea at four o'clock. The clothes I brought for you are upstairs in my closet. And I do appreciate you dropping us at the train station," Emme said. "The traffic into Bath is so bad during the festival."

"I just can't believe you two are seriously taking the train dressed like that!"

"We won't be the only ones," she answered with a laugh.

Chapter 32

Emme stood in the Grand Pump Room overlooking the Roman Baths below. The sunlight, gold and slanting, washed over Bath Abbey which loomed beyond the ancient baths.

After finishing their tea, Georgiana had stepped around the corner to visit the ladies' washroom; Emme had chosen to remain for a few moments longer.

Emme had always loved the historic Pump Room, with tall, paned windows down each side—one side looking out to the streets of Bath, the other overlooking the Roman Baths—bookended by enormous arched alcoves. Finished in 1799, the building had changed little over the intervening years, the interior all classical white columns and fluted pediments.

The room behind her slowly emptied of diners; tea service was through but dinner had not yet begun. Most everyone was still dressed in Regency era clothing, giving the room an almost discordant air. Ladies in their gowns and gentleman in their top hats strolling amongst tourists in jeans and windbreakers.

As if trapped between modern and Napoleonic England. A feeling Emme knew all too well.

The day had been lovely. Georgiana glowed, enjoying being a proper lady once again, nodding regally to passersby as they strolled through Bath. She had seemed more at ease with herself than she had in weeks. Even Emme had admitted to enjoying wearing a corset and clinging skirts again.

But the afternoon had also emphasized what she was missing.

James.

Emme had spent most of the day trying to not think about him.

At least to not think about him every other second. And she had been mildly successful—for about two minutes somewhere between Newport and Bristol on the train when she thought about his horse, Luther.

The pain of his absence was not ebbing. If anything, it grew worse over time. She kept expecting to hear his voice. To feel his warm hand on her back.

Her obsession with the locket had been bad enough. But that was before she actually knew the real man himself.

Now she knew him. Knew the sound of his laughter. Knew the generosity of his heart. She wondered if the ache of his loss would ever abate.

And being in Bath, on this of all days, had been particularly difficult. The city teemed with men in traditional Regency dress. Every other moment, she would see a blond man in a blue coat—or brown or green or black—and her heart would seize until he moved and she would note that he was too short or too old or too whatever to be James. How could there be so many blond men in Britain? And why were they all here in Bath?

It had been a keen sort of torture. Like constantly pressing against a sore, feeling its sharp pain over and over. And how could such a wound, continually tormented, ever heal? How could she even want to heal, to move on from him?

Why didn't he come?

Emme sucked in a stuttering breath and stared at the Roman Baths outside the window, at the jade green water, at the lingering people moving among the columned ruins.

Clenching her hands slightly, she looked up and shifted her gaze from the scene outside and focused on the glass of the window. Shadowy shapes of people strolled through the room behind her. Blurry ladies in long skirts moved around two gentleman who had recently arrived through the door in breeches and boots. One gentleman doffed his hat to them in greeting.

Mirrored ghosts of the past. Would this be how she would keep James? In memory, fleeting and fuzzy. A nearly tangible shadow always just out of reach.

Emme looked away, her throat thick with emotion. She closed her eyes, swallowing, trying to still the aching pain.

Letting out a long breath, she opened her eyes. Lifted her head and looked back at the window.

And then blinked.

She shook her head slightly, trying to breathe through the sudden tightness in her chest. A figure advanced toward her in the reflection.

Blond, blue-eyed, chiseled with his mouth hinting at shared laughter. Blue-green, high collared jacket, crisp white shirt and neckcloth.

Golden hair finger-combed and deliciously disheveled.

She choked back a sob and raised her hand to her mouth. Held his eyes in the reflection. Drank every little detail of him. Tasted her tears.

He stopped at her shoulder, sliding his hands slowly around her waist. His touch hot and searing. Emme hiccupped and her body went boneless, melting back against his.

She felt him press his mouth to the backside of her ear, felt the warmth of his breath as he inhaled, the nuzzle of his nose against her neck.

"I warned you," he whispered, low and rumbly in his divine aristocratic accent. "You are the one and only thing I cannot live without. I would follow you to the ends of eternity, my love."

His lips brushed her throat. Lightly. Gently.

"So when you think about it, giving up only two hundred years is a bit of a bargain," he continued softly.

Emme sobbed and turned into his arms. Wrapped her own arms around his neck. Buried her face in his cravat.

And breathed him in, that lusciously familiar scent of leather and sandalwood and him. The heat of his arms wrapped possessively around her.

And then his lips were on her forehead. Her cheek. Her mouth.

Hungry and greedy. Aching. Longing. Drugging her nearly senseless.

Emme clung to him. Finding that she was unable to hold him close enough.

"Oh, my love, how I missed you!" James half moaned against her mouth. "It has been a lifetime without you."

He pulled back slightly. "Well, several of them, in fact."

And then he kissed her again.

And again. And again.

Someone cleared their throat behind them.

"You know, I'm pretty sure that kissing a lady witless in public is not part of a gentleman's code of conduct," Marc drawled. "And people are starting to stare."

Emme gave a stuttering laugh and pulled away from James. But he didn't let her get too far, keeping her trapped in his arms as they turned to face her brother.

"I think there's someone else who would like to greet you, James." Marc gestured toward Georgiana standing beside him, looking at James with wondrous tears in her eyes—healthy and whole and rapt with gladness.

The air whooshed from James as he took two steps and swept his sister into a tight hug, picking her up and spinning her around, laughing in disbelieving delight.

He set Georgiana down and then took her face in his hands, staring at her with such joy and wonder.

"Georgie!" he barely whispered. "Oh, Georgie. . . ." At a complete loss for words, James merely hugged her again, clasping her tightly, wiping at his cheeks.

Happiness flooded through Emme. Crystalline and effervescent.

This was the most perfect of all perfect moments.

She walked to Marc and wrapped her arm around his waist, watching as James talked privately with Georgiana, his eyes drinking her in.

"Thank you, Marc," she murmured relaxing her face against his chest. "Thank you for bringing him to me. Really and truly."

DUIR COTTAGE
FOUR HOURS EARLIER
SEPTEMBER 16, 2012

James stood swaying in the darkness for a moment. The vertigo had been almost overwhelming. Taking a deep breath, he could see stairs and light coming from a doorway above. He could hear a muted noise, like a thousand trees rustling, and someone yelling loudly, if indistinctly.

Puzzled, he climbed up the stairs and quietly stepped into the hallway. The noise appeared to be coming from the back of the house. Taking the few short steps down the hallway, James stopped in the doorway to the great room. His eyes roamed over marble and steel and wood.

The house had certainly changed. This part of it now seemed to be a kitchen of sorts with a large, rough-hewn table. Farther down was an over-sized fireplace that probably lost a ridiculous amount of heat in the winter. In front of the fireplace was a large sofa, facing away from him.

A dark haired man sat on the sofa, his back to James, yelling at whatever was happening on the illuminated screen next to the fireplace.

A television. James was proud of himself for deducing that detail.

Fascinated, he walked quietly over to stand behind the couch, watching the screen. It was some sort of game, similar to the mob football men from the village would play on festival days. Only more organized and with all sorts of padding. As if they were afraid of a few bruises.

James snorted.

And the man on the couch jumped around with blinding speed at the noise. Yelping in startled terror. Stumbling over a footrest in front of the sofa, nearly tumbling to the floor in surprise.

James couldn't resist a small laugh. What would Emme say?

Oh yes . . .

That was totally awesome.

With a look of stunned surprise, the dark haired man righted himself and reached over and muted the sound on the television. They faced each other for a few moments. Assessing. Taking each other's measure.

The man slowly straightened and then nodded his head in greeting.

"James," he said, assessingly.

"Marc," James replied, a larger smile breaking across his face. He walked around the sofa and held out his hand, grasping Marc's in a firm grip. "It is a pleasure to finally meet you."

He had instantly recognized Emme's brother from the photos she had shown him. But even without the photos, he would have marked the resemblance. They had the same dark curly hair. The same wide-set eyes and welcoming smile.

"Sorry I jumped," Marc said good naturedly. "Your arrival was somewhat unexpected."

James chuckled. "I'm sorry to have alarmed you. Though, I must admit, it was remarkably funny. Does Emme know you scream like a girl when startled?"

Marc threw back his head and laughed.

"Emme forgot to tell me how much I would like you. I guess I can't call you Fabio anymore, can I?"

"Fabio?" James shook his head in confusion. That made no sense.

"Forget about it. It's nothing," Marc said with a grin.

"Where are Emme and Georgiana?" James asked, looking around. "Are they here?"

"No, not exactly."

James felt a momentary stab of terror.

"Are they . . ."

"Oh, they're good. Emme is fine and Georgiana is well. Completely recovered and not quarantined anymore."

Relief poured through James. Cleansing and incandescent. Georgie was alive. She would live!

"That is such wonderful news," James said with a relieved sigh. "She is really well?"

"Yeah, amazingly so. And she's been putting weight back on. You'll be stunned when you see her. They'll be ecstatic to see you too, actually."

"So, where are they exactly?"

"They're off to the Jane Austen Festival for the day."

James blinked and then remembered Emme telling him about the festival. How everyone dressed up and pretended to be characters from a Jane Austen novel.

"Why are you here?" James asked. "I assume the ladies would have needed someone to chaperone them. Did someone take over that duty for you?"

Marc eyed him warily for a moment. James raised an eyebrow.

"Did you allow them to go alone, Marc?"

Marc shrugged. "This is the 21st century, you know. Women don't need a man at their side all the time. They'll be just fine."

"Perhaps." James frowned slightly, feeling the annoyance build in his chest. "But *when* I'm from, there is a code of conduct that a gentleman follows."

He held up a gloved hand and ticked off his fingers. "You don't cheat at cards, your word is your bond and you always ensure any unmarried woman in your household is protected and honored."

Marc cocked an eyebrow, obviously wanting to disagree with him but didn't. Instead, Marc looked James up and down.

"Nice jacket," he said, gesturing to the blue-green coat James wore. "That the one from the locket?"

James nodded.

Marc grimaced slightly and then sighed.

"I knew Emme would find a way to make me go to the festival in the end. Well, if I'm doing this, I'm doing it right."

Puzzled, James watched as Marc walked around him and out of the room, gesturing for him to follow.

"C'mon, James. You're going to have to play valet. I have no clue how to tie a cravat."

An hour later, James sat in the passenger seat of the BMW. He felt he had done an excellent job helping Marc dress in breeches, waistcoat and boots. He had even managed to tie Marc's neckcloth into a perfect mathematical.

This BMW was utterly fascinating, however. Emme had never really described or shown him photos of the inside of a car. It smelled a lot like the inside of one of his carriages, all leather and wood, but that's where the similarities ended.

"What's this?" James asked pointing to the odd nobs and buttons and screens on the dash between him and Marc.

"It's the stereo, navigation and stuff," Marc said casually.

"Really? How interesting!"

In delight, James pushed one of the buttons and jumped when music suddenly blared around him. Smiling, he pushed another button. And then another. Loving how the music changed each time.

He was reaching for another button when Marc's outstretched hand stopped him.

"Enough," Marc said with a shake of his head. "I know my sister loves you, but seriously, man, you touch my stereo one more time and I may have to hurt you."

James cocked his head toward Marc in puzzlement.

"You might have your code of conduct and all, but *when* I'm from, there are a couple rules guys follow. You drink your beer cold, you wear pants around the hips not your ribcage, and you don't mess with a man's woman or his stereo. Got it?"

James laughed and then crowed with delight as Marc punched the accelerator and the car raced down the road, the sudden force pushing him against his seat.

"How can I acquire one of these myself?" he asked appreciatively.

Marc chuckled. "Well, we're going to have to figure out a lot of things before you can get a driver's license. But we might be able to swing a few impromptu lessons between now and then." The last part he said with a wink.

"So how will we know where to find the ladies in Bath?" James asked.

"Emme had reservations at four o-clock for tea in the Pump Room. So we'll look for them there. And if all else fails, I'll just text her. She still took her phone with her. She's not going that period on me."

"Excellent," James said, feeling satisfaction. "Also, I have a small favor to ask. Could we make a stop on our way through Marfield?"

Bath
Parade Gardens
Later on September 16, 2012

Emme and James found themselves strolling through Parade Gardens after leaving the Pump Room. Marc and Georgiana had gone to find Marc something to eat. However, they all knew it was just an excuse to give Emme and James time together.

The park was still full of people lounging on chairs and children laughing despite the fading light. Bath Abbey was a dark silhouette against the setting sun.

Emme's hand was nestled into the crook of James' elbow as they strolled along. It felt so frightfully right to have him here, with her.

Hugging his arm closer, she said, "We thought you might have died in a carriage accident. I can't express how worried we were."

"A carriage accident?" James looked puzzled for just a second and then realization dawned. "Oh, my darling, I am so sorry. I never thought you would find out about such a thing. Goodness, it's such a story."

"Tell me then!" Emme pressed her cheek against his shoulder. "Oh, James, I'm just so relieved that you're finally here."

James' smooth laugh heated her through.

"Where to begin? As you may already know, Arthur and Marianne were married last week. Well, last week in 1812. Marianne was radiant. Arthur sends his regards. Linwood gave the bride away. I think he may have actually smiled, but it was hard to tell. Linwood can be difficult to read at the best of times."

Emme gave a knowing grin. "How wonderful. I am so happy for them. Did our sudden disappearance cause you too much trouble? Did you have to resurrect the dastardly Buick Chevrolet to explain our absence?"

James chuckled appreciatively. "No, unfortunately. Though that would have been a nice twist to the whole tale," he conceded with a nod. "With the tornado tearing up half the county, the severity of Georgiana's illness went generally unnoticed. I put it about that you had accompanied her north to Liverpool, seeking treatment from Dr. Carson for her consumption."

Emme nodded. "And your own disappearance? Please tell me it was a carriage accident."

He grinned and pulled her closer. "Well, for the time being I have merely joined you and Georgiana in Liverpool. But Arthur will tell of *our* untimely death in a tragic carriage accident should we not return. And given that my death has already been announced, that seems to be the case."

Emme paused. "So you don't think to return?" she asked quietly.

James was silent for a moment.

"You left your tablet with me, you know, in 1812."

Emme nodded her head in agreement. "Yes. I didn't have the heart to deprive you of Angry Birds. Not to mention *Pride and Prejudice and Zombies.* I know how much you wanted to finish it."

She smiled faintly at his bark of laughter.

"I did finish the book. Delightful, by the way. Who knew that Lady Catherine de Bourgh kept ninjas? But I also found other things in your research notes that gave me ideas."

Emme cocked an eyebrow at him in question.

"I remembered what you said about provenance and needing to make sure that things came forward in a respectable manner."

Something was nagging at the back of Emme's brain. Some little piece of a puzzle that she couldn't quite put together. She frowned, thinking for a moment. Trying to drag it forward.

And then it clicked.

"Sir Henry's coin collection! Your father's coin collection!" she gasped.

James chuckled. "Exactly! I placed the collection in trust with my solicitors, Hartington, Chatham and Ware. Sir Henry, bless his soul, acted as advocate for the collection and ensured that it was properly protected."

"But the collection was just sold at Sotheby's. I heard it on the news. It went for some astronomical sum, over £100 million pounds!" Emme paused as another thought hit her. "I had that article on my tablet, about the sale of the coins. You recognized them?"

"I did indeed. It seemed fate had already provided me with a solution. I just needed to put it into action. . . . And I also understand it is bad form to mess with the space-time continuum." That last bit said with a sardonic lift of his eyebrows.

"I'm going to make you watch *Back to the Future*. Then you'll see what I'm talking about." Emme wagged a knowing finger at him, her voice mock-serious.

"Well, it all worked. Marc was kind enough to stop by my solicitor's office on the way down here. I assume Arthur will inherit. . . . No, I guess that is not quite right. . . . Arthur *inherited* Haldon Manor as my heir. In any case, it took some time—nearly two months of it obviously—but I managed to amend the entail before I left. After my supposed death, Arthur could move Duir Cottage into a separate trust for me to be held by our solicitors. It seemed vitally important to protect the portal. So in addition to the proceeds from the sale of the coins, I also own a beautiful cottage in the Herefordshire countryside that has a time portal in the basement. All in all, I thought I might explore the 21st century for a while." He winked at her.

Emme laughed, stopped and threw her arms around his neck, holding him tightly.

"I think that to be a perfectly brilliant idea!"

James chuckled and guided them off the path to stand under a tree somewhat sheltered from the rest of the park.

"Which brings me to another question. I have always wanted to see the West Indies, as you well know." His smile was warm and buttery, melting Emme's heart into a heavenly puddle. "And I understand it is possible to be married on a beach there. Under palm trees. At sunset."

Emme's heart jumped into her throat. Tears sprung in her eyes. "Oh, James," she whispered.

He also seemed to be struggling with his emotions. He reached a hand up and brushed her hair, trailing his hand down her neck.

Feather light and scalding.

"Emme," he murmured. "I love you, my darling. I have missed you so. . . ."

His voice broke and James took a deep, steadying breath, his blue eyes liquid and naked, drowning in hers.

He continued brokenly.

"I have missed you so very much. The brightness of your smile. The quickness of your mind. The delight of your wit. I said I would go through forever and back to find you. But I would really prefer not to wait so long to have you as my own."

Emme drank him in, loving every sound of his voice, every flicker of expression.

"Oh, darling," she breathed, "there is nothing . . . nothing now . . . nothing then . . . nothing in any time that I love so well as you."

She leaned forward and slid her fingers possessively into his hair. And then kissed him. Soft and slow. Lingeringly sweet.

James let out a small groan and then pulled back slightly.

"I promised myself I would do this properly," he murmured against her lips.

With a deep breath, he took a step back and went down on one knee. Emme's eyes widened, tears instantly threatening again. Really, hadn't she already cried enough for one afternoon?

"Oh, James, kneeling and everything?" she asked.

James laughed. "No breaking my concentration, love. I may not care about propriety, but certain things are too important to not get just right."

Taking her hand, he smiled into her eyes. "Dearest, darlingest Emme, will you make me the happiest of men and agree to be my wife? For now and forever?"

Emme nodded her head vigorously. "Yes!" she choked.

With a delighted chuckle, James surged to his feet and Emme drowned herself in his kiss again.

After a minute, James pulled back, much to Emme's frustration. She tried to force his mouth back to hers, but he merely laughed softly and pecked her lips.

"I thought I would give this to you as a wedding gift, but I find I cannot wait." He brought out a thin box from his jacket pocket and handed it to her, eyes expectant as he wrapped an arm tightly around her waist.

Puzzled, Emme slowly opened the box. Inside there was something oval and thin. Emme could feel the heft of it in her hand. Giving James a quizzical look, she handed him the box and then carefully unwrapped the object.

A golden locket emerged in her hand. Bright and polished, filigree covering its gilt frame.

Emme gasped, blinking through her sudden tears. The back of the locket was partially covered in transparent crystal. Under the crystal, two locks of hair were braided into an intricate pattern—one bright and fair, the other a dark chocolate brown.

Gilded on top of the crystal, two initials were nestled together in a stylized gold symbol. Emme sucked in a breath.

She traced the letters—E and F. Familiar. Like a sense of home.

And then she quietly opened the locket. And let out a small sob.

She had expected to see the portrait of James, staring enigmatically out at her.

But instead, she saw two faces.

His broad and crinkly smile, blue eyes dancing and kind.

And then there . . . next to him.

Her own face. Serene, happy, incandescent. Gazing out as if she held the world in her hands.

Both of them. Together.

All painted with Spunto's careful detail. Each minute feature delicately rendered.

Emme glanced to the left of the locket case. She read the inscription.

To E,
throughout all time,
heart of my soul,
your F

Puzzled, Emme looked up.

"Still with the F?" she asked.

"Oh yes," he replied softly and raised a hand to stroke her cheek in wonder. "That was the most important detail of all."

"Really? The most important?"

James nodded. Leaned forward. Rested his forehead against hers.

"Indeed. Because I am truly your . . ."

He paused and smiled.

Then whispered one word.

There are moments in life that sear into the soul. Brief witnesses of something larger.

When so many threads collapse into one. Coalesce into a single beautiful truth.

This was one of those moments.

Emme gasped and let out a muffled sob and pulled him fiercely to her and kissed him.

Kissed him until people cat-called and whistled. Kissed him until shadows stretched and purpled. Kissed him knowing she would never, ever let him go.

Kissed him as that one perfect whispered word echoed in her soul.

Forever.

Epilogue

Happily-ever-after began on March 20, 2013 around 7:12 pm.
Though Emry Knight *née* Wilde generally considered it more of a continuation of her already blissful happiness rather than any real beginning.

Of course, her brother Marc, her mother and new sister, Georgiana, completely agreed.

Emme's best friend, Jasmine, had merely smirked knowingly, stating she had always believed in this divinely mystical union of predestined souls. Emme's new husband—dreamy in full Regency gentleman's dress in colors of cream and tan—asserted that 'mystical' was far too tame a word to describe the depth of his love for her.

It all happened one beautiful evening on a secluded beach outside Nassau in the Bahamas.

Marc had walked her along the sand toward James, all broad smiles, his eyes full of wonder and promise. Georgiana as her maid of honor at his side, healthy and glowing. Emme had worn an ivory high-waisted Empire dress of flowing chiffon with a wildflower wreath in her hair. The new locket glinted around her neck.

Drawing near James, Marc had placed her hand in his, smiling as he pecked Emme's cheek, telling James to care for her. James, for his part, had merely nodded, his eyes too full of emotion to speak.

They had said their vows over the lap of waves and the rustle of palm fronds, the sun skimming the horizon and bathing them all in golden haze. Promising to have and hold and honor, though Emme secretly added the words live and love and laugh, as well. Afterward, Jasmine—still dabbing at her eyes—had hinted at little Knights in their future.

It had been another perfectly perfect moment. But with James around, Emme had sort of given up counting perfect moments. There were too many of them.

Emme had thought nothing could be more delicious than James in full Regency dress. But then, that first week after coming through the portal, he had walked out in a pair of Marc's designer jeans, a tight t-shirt and sunglasses.

Emme had melted into a little puddle on the spot. It was the closest Emme had ever come to a full-on swoon.

Life with James had most certainly not been boring. They spent nearly all their time in a constant whirlwind of travel. Moving almost nonstop from one new place to another. James' curiosity seemed insatiable at times. He loved different people and different places, loved exploring the nuance of culture.

Marc had secured documentation for James and Georgiana. Emme had chosen not to ask him for too many details. His only comment had been that money could buy just about anything and that he had acquired everything legally. Sort of. Again, Emme wisely chose not to ask questions.

To Emme's dismay, she still experienced the occasional traveling disaster. But somehow they were never as bad with James. He always found the unexpected to be thrilling, forcing her to see the fun in the situation (*Look, Emme, grubs! Who knew they could be so tasty?*).

Marc had also been teaching marital art forms to James. While James, for his part, had helped Marc add 'fencing master' to his resume.

Emme was still trying to figure out what to do with her last name. She had always intended to just hyphenate when she got married, but Marc had been the first to realize that would make her Emry Wilde-Knight. Which was not exactly the professional vibe she was going for in a last name. And Marc, being Marc, couldn't just let it slip by. The jokes were still on-going, many of which had made even James blush.

This balmy October day found them outside Escalante, Utah, exploring the red rock canyons of the southwestern United States.

"Wow, this is really high . . . not looking down . . . tell me I can do this."

"You can do this."

"Okay, now say it in your sexiest I-was-born-a-nineteenth-century-aristocrat voice . . . with extra gravitas."

James chuckled.

"Emme, my dearest love, you are the bravest woman I know. You can do this, darling."

Silence.

"Oh . . . wow . . . it's sooooo high. . . ."

Emme swallowed and forced herself not to look down. Marc snapped the rope below, causing it to jump slightly in her hand.

"Marcus David Wilde!" she shrieked.

"I think you're going to have to throw her over," Marc called up to James.

"That doesn't seem particularly sporting," James yelled down to him. "Though how long before the harness starts to chafe?"

Marc shook his head. "C'mon, Ems. Just do it," he called up. "I would hate to show James the video. You know the one I'm talking about. When you were twelve and still liked My Little Pony but also had a crush on Jason Hawks and you pretended to kiss . . ."

That did it.

Marc stopped talking as Emme walked backward over the edge, rappelling smoothly down the red sandstone cliff, Marc's laugh following her all the way.

"Works every time," he said with a chuckle as she landed at his feet. "You really should've destroyed that video when you had the chance."

Emme just glared mock-daggers at him.

"Marc, what is My Little Pony?" James called down. "And why would Emme want to crush this Jason Hawks?"

Marc laughed even harder. Emme shook her head and then smiled ruefully, watching as James clipped in and slid easily down the rope to join them.

The narrow slot canyon glowed burnished orange, washed and sculpted from eons of water and wind. Sunlight filtered slowly down its steep walls, nearly fifty feet high but only two feet wide.

James slipped an arm around her as Marc coiled rope behind them.

"What was that you asked me earlier? If I had claustra . . .?" James trailed off, trying to remember.

"Claustrophobia," Emme helpfully prompted. "It's a fear of enclosed spaces."

James paused, considering the idea for a moment. And then shook his head.

"No, I can't say this place makes me feel anything other than awestruck."

He looked around at the narrow undulating canyon walls. Nature scrubbed of life. Raw and elemental. Just rock and sand and wind, twisting, bending, coiling around each other. The reddish walls blushed with vibrant color.

"You were right. This is breathtakingly unique. Who could have imagined that such a place existed?"

Emme nodded. "I can think of few places that are as opposite Duir Cottage in lush green England than the slot canyons of the American desert southwest."

"Yes, though I am glad that Georgiana enjoys life in Herefordshire. Her last message indicated that she is doing well. I wish she could really love 21st century life."

"Not everyone is as adaptable as you," she said, giving him a small hug.

"True," James let out a wondrous sigh. "I never knew such content-ment was possible. It's as if the entire universe has finally righted itself for me. I have never felt so complete, so much myself."

Emme laughed and kissed his cheek fondly.

"Come now, something must have surprised you."

"Well, of course a great number of things have surprised me. And I still may never forgive you for not telling me about football."

"Seriously, Emme!" Marc said, coming to stand next to them, rope coiled over his shoulder. "You really have a shocking tendency to ignore the important things in life. By the way, Bronco kick-off on ESPN is in less than three hours. So we should really keep going. I think there is an arch just around the next bend, and I want to savor every inch of this canyon. It's too amazing to do otherwise."

This pretty much summed up how Emme felt. As she turned down the narrow canyon, she vowed to treasure every moment of life together with James.

Author's Notes

When writing a story where most of the action occurs in the past, I have incorporated some aspects of historical truth and then taken literary liberties. Allow me to sort through some of it for you.

Let's start with historical facts. Tuberculosis was (and quite frankly, still is) a terrible disease. By some estimates, TB caused up to 25% of all deaths in the early 19th century. Though deadly, the disease was not a fast killer. It can sit latent in the body for decades before becoming active. Once active, victims succumbed over a period of months and sometimes years. But once the disease set in, death was generally inevitable. Only a small fraction managed to fight off the infection. Dr. James Carson, who I mention in passing, was an early researcher working in Liverpool in the early 19th century. Though many treatments were posited and tried over the centuries, it wasn't until the advent of antibiotics in the 1940s that TB stopped being such a widespread killer.

On a happier topic, gooseberry clubs and competitions were an actual craze in early 19th century Britain. Sir Henry's obsession was rooted in very real historical fact. (You can't make this stuff up, people.) Curry was widely eaten and *The Jane Austen Cookbook* (by Maggie Black and Deirdre Le Faye) contains a recipe for curry from Austen's own household. Speaking of Jane Austen, I must apologize for pushing the publication date of *Pride and Prejudice* earlier to accommodate my plot. The book wasn't actually published until January 1813.

Other interesting historical facts. The little story about Baron Berwick marrying a popular London courtesan is absolutely true. Thomas Hill, Baron Berwick, did marry Sophia Dubochet on February 8th, 1812 (though I may have taken liberties when explaining why he did). And Napoleon did indeed begin his ill-advised invasion of Russia in late June 1812.

Emme's traveling disasters are actually also reality. All of Emme's 21st century disasters have happened to my parents. They were held up by pirates on the Cozumel ferry, stranded in Hungary when the Iceland volcano erupted, stuck without luggage in Guatemala during terrible floods, quarantined when the swine flu hit Mexico, interrogated by the TSA for being terrorists, and so many others that I didn't list. They are the original traveling disasters.

Things I completely made up: the town of Marfield, all the estates listed in the book and Giovanni Spunto. My apologies if you went looking for them. I also recognize that Emme's amnesia and recovery is a stretch of medical possibility. I prefer to think of it as something that fate decreed for her.

As with all books, this one couldn't have been written without help and support from those around me.

For starters, I would like to thank all of my fellow photography friends and fans. Over the years, you have given me friendship, support and a much needed artistic outlet. I still love everything about photography—that exhilarating creation of breathtaking, show-stopping images. But thank you for giving me the confidence to branch out into a different artistic field, expressing many of the same dramatic concepts in writing.

To my beta readers—Jefra Linn, Lyndsie Campbell, Kelly Crawford, Kristin Villano, Monica Winder, Solomon Campbell and Annette Evans— thank you for your helpful ideas and support. Thank you especially for sending me messages of encouragement when the doubt-demons hit. Also, an extra large thank you to Norma Melzer for her fantastic copy editing skills.

I owe a huge shout-out to Lois Brown, author extraordinaire, for lending your valuable experience and expertise to the manuscript. Your editing wisdom and overall brilliance were greatly appreciated.

Most importantly, I need to give a wet, sloppy kiss to Erin Rodabough. Without you, my dearest friend, this book would have never happened— best. writing. buddy. ever! Thank you for your encouragement, brilliant insights, clever editing and just all-around awesomeness. As I have said over and over, a book is only as good as its editor is insightful. And you, my friend, have that amazing ability to hone in and provide solutions to all sorts of writing problems. Not to mention that you are just all-around fun to hang with. Thirty years later and we're still trading manuscripts. Love that what began as two little girls writing stories in your gabled bedroom has morphed into this.

Thank you to Andrew, Austenne and Kian for your patience and lend-ing your mother to this project. Though you didn't mind eating all that take-out pizza and cold cereal for dinner as much as you should.

And finally, no words can express my love and appreciation for Dave. I would say you are the wind beneath my wings (but then, let's face it, I would have to listen to you make wind-whistling sounds every time I walked by), so let me just say thank you for your support. For always looking me in the eye and saying 'I know you can do it,' no matter how hare-brained the idea. I consider myself beyond blessed to travel through life with you at my side.

Reading Group Questions

Oh yes, this book has reading group questions.

Why?

Well, the English professor in me couldn't let this book go to press without making it vaguely educational. And obviously your reading group would show excellent taste by selecting this book—reading groups don't always have to be about the classics and Oprah's Book Club. Sometimes you just need a shameless don't-judge-me read. And any book that has reading group questions has to have redeeming literary qualities, right? So you're totally justified in assigning it.

You're welcome.

1. "You are eternal in both directions. If you look far enough into the past, you'll find the future there." This is my paraphrase of a quote by Paul Tillich that I used as a philosophical basis for the book. Thoughts? Have you ever felt this way about your own life?

2. As a writer, I feel that the look of words on the page can communicate meaning as well. Therefore, I deliberately used line breaks, non-traditional punctuation and visual cues to help convey tone and cadence. Did you find this helped as a reader, making your reading flow more easily? Why or why not?

3. When writing historical fiction, as a writer you face a conundrum. Do you stay completely true to the language of the period, knowing that it will feel stilted and perhaps boring to many readers? Or do you relax the language and allow it to be more modern, therefore making it more engaging to present-day readers (but not entirely historically accurate)? How well do you feel this book deals with the differences between modern and early 19th-century English?

4. Considering Albert Einstein's Theory of Relativity (Yes, I really just went there.), one could argue that time is merely a construct of our limited understanding of the universe. Based on this, did you like the visual metaphor of all events being present, occurring simultaneously on a vast cosmic ocean? Could all things be present?

5. Alright, let's cast the movie of the book. (Cause hey, we can dream big, right?) Who plays Emme? James? Etc. In the movie version, what aspects of the book should be thrown out, condensed or altered? Also, what should the theme love song be?

6. Are we having fun yet?

7. What came first, the locket's creation or Emme finding the locket? How do you feel about these 'chicken or the egg' situations that often occur in time travel novels?

8. As an author, I do have plans (as of this writing) to redeem Linwood in the last book of this series. Can this be done? Could he actually change enough to become the hero in his own novel and get the girl? Is he truly a bad person or just a product of his environment? Please feel free to email any good ideas you come up with!

9. I chose to self-publish this book and never considered seeking a publisher for it (long story why . . . you can email me for that explanation too). How do you feel about the indie self-pub book market? Are you more or less likely to read a book that has been self-published? Do you even notice/care if a book is self-published?

Upcoming Books

I plan for there to be four books in this series and probably a prequel novella, showing how the locket is sent on its way to the US. The other books will follow Georgiana, Marc and Linwood.

As of this writing, the books in the series are/will be:

Intertwine (James and Emme)
Divine (Georgiana and Sebastian)
Clandestine (Marc and Kit—coming Spring 2015)
Refine (Linwood and, yes, Jasmine—coming Summer 2015)

Please turn the page for a small teaser from the next book in this series—Georgiana's.

Divine

HOUSE OF OAK, BOOK 2

The letter arrived on a Tuesday.

Brittle, yellowed, moth-eaten with age.

Georgiana Knight immediately read it, letting the thrill of the words pour through her, absorbing their implications.

The letter seemed innocuous enough at first glance. The direction was clearly inscribed in a looping calligraphic hand on the outside.

Haldon Manor
Herefordshire

Neat and plain. Just as any letter written in 1813 should be addressed.

Georgiana instantly recognized the handwriting—knew it as well as her own, because indeed it was.

Her own.

Which really summed up the problem entirely. As Georgiana was most decidedly not in 1813. Never had been. And she had not written this letter.

At least, not yet.

With her health restored, she had spent the last year adjusting to the twenty-first century: mastering the terror of motorway driving, resisting the time-sucking vortex of Facebook, earning a green belt in taekwondo and reconciling to wearing tight jeans.

And now this letter arrived, written in her own hand.

Visit www.NicholeVan.com to buy your copy of
Intertwine today and continue the story.

About the Author

Nichole Van is an artist who feels life is too short to only have one obsession. In former lives, she has been a contemporary dancer, pianist, art historian, choreographer, culinary artist and English professor. Though Nichole still prefers the label 'adaptable' more than 'ADD.'

Most notably, however, Nichole is an acclaimed photographer, winning over thirty international accolades for her work, including Portrait of the Year from WPPI in 2007. (Think Oscars for wedding and portrait photographers.) Her unique photography style has been featured in many magazines, including *Rangefinder* and *Professional Photographer*. She is also the creative mind behind the popular websites Flourish Emporium and {life as art} Workshops, which provide resources for photographers.

All that said, Nichole has always been a writer at heart. With an MA in English, she taught technical writing at Brigham Young University for ten years and has written more technical manuals than she can quickly count.

She decided in late 2013 to start writing fiction and has loved exploring a new creative process.

Nichole currently lives in Utah with her husband and three crazy children. Though continuing in her career as a photographer, Nichole is also now writing historical romance on the side. She is known as NicholeVan all over the web: Facebook, Instagram, Pinterest, etc. Visit http://www.NicholeVan.com to sign up for her author newsletter and be notified of new book releases. You can see her work at http://photography.nicholeV.com and http://www.nicholeV.com.

If you enjoyed this book, please leave a review on www.amazon.com. Wonderful reviews are the elixir of life for authors. Even better than dark chocolate.

Printed in Great Britain
by Amazon

77987818R00173